She's EVERYTHING

By
Sable Hunter

The
Cowboy Craze
Series

This is a work of fiction. Names, characters, places and incidents are either the product of the author's imagination or used fictitiously, and any resemblance to actual persons, living or dead, business establishments, events or locales is entirely coincidental.

She's Everything
All rights reserved.
Copyright 2017 © Sable Hunter

Cover by JRA Stevens
For Down Write Nuts

Cowboy Craze is a Hell Yeah! spinoff series introducing the Blackhawk brothers – Daniel, Easy, Sam, and Benjen. These men are the ultimate catch – handsome, kind, and sexy as hell. While making new friends, the reader will be able to catch up with old ones – the McCoys and their entourage will be as real in this world as they are in their own. Welcome to the hill country of Texas – where you can satisfy your craving for cowboys – and have a hot time doing it!

Daniel Blackhawk never believed in love at first sight until he falls for Sarah Riley like a ton of bricks. From the moment he sees her rush out into a busy highway to save the life of a little child, he knows she is the woman for him.

Daniel isn't the only one who's captivated. Like a bolt from the blue, Sara is struck by the handsome cowboy who insists they are meant to be.

He's hard to resist, especially when he sets his mind on proving to her how good they can be together.

There's only one problem, Sara isn't free.

She's been hurt, tricked, and abandoned by someone she trusted, so making herself vulnerable again is a difficult choice.

Laying his heart on the line, Daniel sets out to show Sara he is exactly who she's been waiting for all her life. He wants to be her champion, her dragon-slayer, and her knight in shining armor – all rolled into one.

With exquisite attention to her every need, Daniel begins to woo her – making her happy, keeping her safe, proving that there is nothing he won't do for her. Their chemistry is off the charts, the heat between them is irresistible.

Sara is Daniel's everything.

Their happy-ever-after seems assured…until the unthinkable happens.

When their world falls apart, only the power of love can save them.

Contents

Sable Hunter

CHAPTER ONE

"Hey, Easy, I'm stopping at Mike's to pick up lunch and I ordered you something to go. Are you going to be at home in about a half an hour?" Daniel Blackhawk held his phone to his ear, speaking to his brother as he pulled his white pickup and gooseneck trailer into the parking lot of Rev. Mike's Dam Pub.

"I'm home now and hungry as hell. Did you get me a burger all the way and onion rings?"

"Yep."

"Good, you read my mind."

"Are Benjen and Sam back from Austin?"

"No, they won't be home until later. They got tied up in the lawyer's office. Zane thinks he's worked out a deal for the land near Comanche."

"Great news! I want to drive up and take another look at the property." Expanding their holdings was a wise idea, especially since they'd decided to split the acreage so each brother could have land of their own. Daniel was fighting mixed feelings about the decision, Blackhawks had lived on the ranch near Packsaddle Mountain since before Texas became a state. As the oldest, the others figured he'd be the one to claim the old rock house, but no one knew better than he did how his brothers felt about Packsaddle. No, if one of them moved off the original home place, it would be him.

7

Putting his family first was just the way Daniel did things. "What else is going on?"

"I bet you'll never guess who stopped by to see you this morning."

"Who?" Daniel unbuckled his seat belt and picked up the tan Stetson from the passenger seat and placed it square on his head. "Did Perry come over to borrow the tractor again?"

"No, not Perry." Ezekiel chuckled softly. "Fiona was here. Bold as brass and asking for you."

Daniel grimaced, rubbing his eyes. This rising before the crack of dawn every day to bale hay was catching up with him. "Oh, really? How'd she look?"

Ezekiel whistled. "Hot, as usual. She said to tell you she was back in town and would be expecting your call."

"Really? She must be in the mood for some slumming."

"Don't say that."

Daniel could hear the hurt in Easy's voice. "I'm sorry, buddy. I didn't mean it." Ezekiel wanted to pretend nothing bad had ever happened to them. He wanted to think people didn't remember. Easy wanted to live in a world where prejudice and racism didn't exist.

Well, Daniel did too. But such a world didn't exist.

Nevertheless, for his brother's sake, he could pretend. "Hey, I'm a Blackhawk. Fiona can't help that she has the hots for me. Can she?"

"No. She seemed pretty determined to hook up with you."

"Well, we'll see. Maybe, an evening with Fiona is just what I need." As Daniel opened the truck door to climb out, he heard a commotion behind him by the road. People were screaming and shouting to the tops of their lungs. Whirling around, he saw a tiny boy standing in the middle of the highway with an eighteen-wheeler bearing down on him with brakes screaming heinously. His feet started to move, but before he could cover the distance, a young woman darted out into the street and grasped the child, jumping out of the way just before the massive diesel truck came barreling down on top of them. "Oh, my God." The horror of what almost happened made him weak. He could see the mother sink to her knees in front of the toddler, grasping him to her breast. Various customers and waitresses from the pub were all gathered around, each as blown away and disturbed as he felt. Daniel was about to raise the cell phone to his ear again when his gaze focused on the angel who'd flown to the little boy's rescue. "Holy Merciful Hell…" he breathed reverently.

He felt as if he'd been struck by a bolt of lightning from the blue.

"Daniel? What's all that noise? Is there a bar fight going on at this hour?"

He brought the phone closer to his ear and spoke as if mesmerized. "We've had some excitement. A youngster wandered out into the road and this lady ran out and rescued him just before he was hit by a big truck." As he watched the woman stand up from where she'd been kneeling by the child, she brushed off her jeans, pushed her hair over her shoulder and smiled. The grateful mother gave her a hug and various folks stepped forward to shake her hand or pat her arm. Daniel's heart sped up, his cock turned to stone, and thoughts of any other woman fled his mind as if they'd never existed. "Well…I don't think I'll be seeing Fiona, not after this."

He moved away from his truck slowly, his eyes never leaving the beauty. She was perfect. Fuckin' perfect. Daniel forgot to breathe as she picked up an empty tray from the ground and began to walk toward a food truck parked beneath a big spreading oak. Dressed in tight jeans and a red plaid shirt, which was tied in an intriguing knot at her waist, he could see she was slender, yet with exquisite curves in all the right places. And her hair! God, her hair was right out of his fantasies – thick, dark, wavy, and long enough to brush the delectable cheeks of her ass.

"Why won't you be seeing Fiona? What's going on, Daniel?" Ezekiel's voice sounded impatient and curious.

He answered his inquisitive brother as he gravitated toward the woman, like the tide being pulled to the shore. "Nothing's wrong, everything is suddenly very right." A smile creased his face. "If you'll excuse me, I need to go and introduce myself to the future Mrs. Daniel Blackhawk."

"What? Your future what?" Ezekiel's voice was cut off as Daniel abruptly ended the call. He might be jumping the gun about the wife part, but he sure intended for the two of them to get better acquainted. By the time he moved through the lot, there was a dozen people standing around the silver food truck with a sign on the side that read Sweet Treats. "She sure is that and I have a weakness for sugar," he whispered under his breath. Seeing the crowd surrounding the object of his desire, he knew he wouldn't get within speaking distance anytime soon. With reluctance, Daniel headed into the pub to claim his to-go order. However, one thing was for sure…he had no intention of leaving without dessert.

Over at the food truck, Sara gave each customer

her undivided attention. The adrenaline rushing through her veins was dissipating and now she felt lightheaded and weak. Still, she was super aware of the handsome cowboy as he sauntered toward the pub. She could feel his eyes on her – warm and interested and she found it hard to get sufficient air in her lungs.

When he disappeared from view, she exhaled sharply and continued to fill orders as people requested slices of the pies she'd made the night before. No use to get all excited, she'd given up on romance. Sara was down on love. This wasn't the time to be vulnerable, this was the time to get tough.

"Peach, please," a little girl piped up, reaching high to put her money on the counter.

"Coming right up," Sara promised. "This was made with fresh peaches, I picked them myself."

"Yum," another lady remarked. "Did they come from nearby Fredericksburg?"

"Close, I found them at an orchard in Stonewall," Sara answered as she made sure the small girl held her carry-out container securely.

"You sure were brave, young lady. You saved that little boy's life." A pleasant looking elderly woman adjusted her glasses as she peered over the counter at Sara.

"Oh, I wasn't brave. I was scared to death," Sara confessed sincerely.

"Well, you were the only one with the presence of mind to react in time." An older gentleman added, stepping up next to the bespectacled lady that Sara presumed was his wife. "Is that blackberry?" He pointed to one of her pies.

"Dewberry," Sara informed him. "I prefer their tart flavor."

"Oh, I do too." The woman elbowed her husband

and rubbed her tummy. "Give us four slices. One each for now and two for later."

"Sure thing. Coming right up."

During the next ten minutes, she fended off more compliments for her actions and filled a dozen more orders, until there were only two customers left. A skinny man who looked to be in his forties and the hunky cowboy.

"Hey, you're new around here," the first man said, leaning a little too far over the counter. "I'm Oscar Robinson."

"Hello. Yes, I am. What can I get you?"

"A hunk of that chocolate meringue and a date tonight. I bet we could have a hot ole time, Miss Sweetie-pie."

"Well..." Sara began, feeling uneasy. "Actually..."

"Actually, she already has a date. With me."

Sara swallowed, but didn't contradict her self-appointed rescuer.

The thin guy wheeled to see who was challenging him. When his eyes fell on the powerful man behind him, he immediately calmed. "Well, Daniel Blackhawk, I should've known you'd already have your sticky red hand in the cookie jar."

"Don't talk that way about the lady, Oscar," Daniel good-naturedly admonished the fellow, ignoring the joking racial slur. Instead, he kept his eye on the woman who'd captured his complete and utter attention.

"I didn't mean no harm. I wasn't trying to insult her." The local hayseed snickered. "I was trying to insult you."

"Better luck next time, old man." After seeing he wasn't making any headway getting a rise out of

Daniel, Mr. Robinson paid for his pie and moved on.

Sara folded her hands on the counter and licked her lips nervously. "Thank you, I appreciate what you did."

"No problem. You're welcome. The lady was right, how you saved that child was amazing." He pretended to study the menu, but Daniel already knew exactly what he wanted.

He wanted her.

"Thanks, anybody would've done the same thing." Sara avoided looking at him straight in the face for as long as she could. The sun was right behind him and the rays were hitting her right in the eye, but the main reason she avoided his gaze was because he was so magnetic and intense. Just being near him made her heart rate accelerate and chill bumps rise on her arms and chest.

"Yea, but nobody else did, did they? I was too far away, but there were others nearer than you who didn't put their life on the line."

"Right place. Right time." She shrugged. When she did hazard a glance at him, Sara had to admit he was an incredibly hot man. Tall. Broad. What she could see of his hair on either side of his cowboy hat was dark and a little on the shaggy side. His face was masculine perfection with vibrant amber eyes and thick dark lashes, some would say far too lush to be wasted on a man – but they weren't wasted on him – far from it. All in all, the cowboy was rugged and tempting, with a sexy five o'clock shadow and a flirty smirk on his kissable lips. "See anything you like?" she asked, breathlessly.

Daniel chuckled. "Now, that's a leading question if I've ever heard one."

"I didn't mean it to be." Sara flushed. "I meant

pie."

"You've got some great looking pies here." He took a whiff. She smelled good too, fresh and sweet, like a summer rain. "I don't think I can choose. What do you recommend?"

"What's your favorite flavor?"

"Anything I could taste on your lips." Daniel knew he was being forward, but once you find what you've been looking for, waiting to stake a claim seemed foolhardy.

"You're a tease."

When she looked up at him and smiled, her face went from pretty to heart-stopping and Daniel almost went to his knees. Her big eyes were an amazing sapphire blue and even though there was a mischievous tilt to her soft pink mouth, he could sense a sadness in her gaze. "Well, Sara… Is that your name?"

"Yes. Sara. Sara…Riley." She refused to call herself anything else.

"Sara." He repeated. "I love it, it feels good on my lips." She was even more beautiful up close, where he could see the emotions flit across her face and her eyes twinkle at him as she spoke. When she offered her hand, Daniel lifted his to take it. The moment expanded, seeming to grow beyond the bounds of time and space. And when his fingers closed over hers, he felt a rush of energy flowing between them – electric, heated, sensual. "I'm Daniel Blackhawk and I love…" He gave her a dazzling smile. "Coconut."

"Coconut." She repeated inanely, hesitant to reclaim her hand. "I have an Almond Joy pie I bet you'd enjoy." With his lips curled into a smile, he transformed from a knight in cowboy boots to an angel, one of the fallen variety who spent their time being naughty because they'd turned their back on Heaven for the privilege. She blushed at her own thoughts, knowing she was staring, almost hypnotized by his presence. Tingles of guilt began to make their way up her spine. If he knew her better, he wouldn't want her. "Would you like to try it?"

"Yes, I would and give me a piece of that lemon for my brother." He thought better. "In fact, give me the whole pie, if you can spare it." If he took a piece to Easy, he'd better take plenty for Ben and Sam.

Sara busied herself while Daniel watched her like a hawk. When he saw another customer approaching, he knew he couldn't wait any longer. "About the date, I was serious. I'd love to take you out. I think you're as beautiful as you are brave. I really want to spend some time with you, get to know you better."

Sara's hand shook. "Thank you. I'm very flattered." She wanted to accept, there was no doubt about it – but she couldn't, not until she figured out how to solve the mess she'd made of her life. "I'm afraid I can't, I already have plans."

"Another date?" The question slipped out of Daniel's mouth before he could call it back. Jealousy needled his soul. "Break it."

"No, not a date." She shook her head. "I'll be busy most nights. I have to bake, this is the way I make my living." The code she'd been living by was to do her best, never rest, and she'd go far – or at least lift herself from the miry clay she'd been stuck in for so long.

Daniel was disappointed, but he refused to give up. "I bet I'd make a good baker's assistant, if you'd give me a chance."

Sara chewed on her lower lip, presenting him with the pie. "Take this, try them, on the house." She wanted to give him something and this was all she was free to give. Hiding her scars was all she knew how to do.

Daniel accepted them, but he put a ten and a twenty in the tip jar labeled Children's Miracle Network. "In your honor." He held up the to-go box. "I'll relish every bite and I'll see you tomorrow. I'm almost certain my…hankering for pie is not going to be satisfied anytime soon."

He kept his eyes locked to hers until she broke the spell, turning to wait on another customer.

Daniel moved to his truck, then watched her from a distance as he set the pies on the passenger seat next to the bags of carry-out. She was gorgeous, pure poetry in motion. He grinned, amused at his sentimentality – so unlike him. Yea, he was smitten, he had it bad. And one little rejection wasn't about to dissuade him – hell no.

His heart was set on getting to know Sara Riley a whole lot better.

* * *

Daniel made his way west from the Dam Pub, named such by cool Reverend Mike because of its proximity to Lake Buchanan Dam. He'd hauled a trailer full of round bales to the McCoy's Highland Ranch, then stopped to get some lunch on the way back. And to think, he'd almost opted for a bologna sandwich at home. He didn't get over this way very often and the idea that he would've missed meeting Sara was unthinkable.

As he drove, Daniel kept an eye on the traffic, but he wasn't aware of much more. Instead, he remembered how Sara rushed to the tiny child's aid, while his mother was frozen on the side of the road in abject disbelief. What courage it had taken for her to risk her life to save another. She hadn't hesitated for even a second. While grown men stood by, she'd acted with no thought to her own safety. What an amazing person she must be.

When it came time to turn south toward Kingsland, his thoughts gravitated to how attracted to her he found himself to be. Just one look, that was all it took, as the old song used to say. Normally, his mind would be on the chores awaiting him, but not today. Daniel found himself wondering what she might think of him. What if she didn't feel the same pull toward him that he felt for her? Had he imagined their connection? Thinking back to her smile, the blush of rose on her cheeks, and the quickening of her breath as they'd spoken, Daniel dismissed that concern. No, she'd felt the same drawing, the same longing, the excitement at the prospect of what they could share together. He smiled with relief. She was probably just shy. Needed to get to know him better. Yes, that was it. He'd see her again and this time Daniel would convince her to spend time with him.

At least for a little while – or until she heard the talk.

As he drew nearer home, Daniel slowed down a bit. He was about to pass his favorite place in the whole world and he never grew tired of the view. He and his brothers were lucky enough to own a prime piece of Hill Country real estate. Their ranch was nestled in the shadow of Packsaddle Mountain on the banks of the Llano River, just before it flowed into LBJ Lake. This portion of the ranch road passed over the river and on either side, huge slabs of natural pink granite had pushed their way up from the earth. The river flowed over the granite, creating a wonder the locals called 'the Slab', a waterway shallow enough to wade in places, deep enough to tube in others. The Blackhawk boys had spent many idyllic days floating down the river in this very spot.

When he passed beneath the arched gate of Blackhawk Ranch, Daniel was anxious to get his day's work completed. He might just head back to Rev. Mike's for supper if there was nothing pressing to be done at home. Pulling to a stop in front of the old farmhouse, he saw Easy waiting for him on the porch.

"About time you got here, I'm starving." He stood and opened the screen door so Daniel could go in ahead of him.

Every time he stepped through this door, Daniel expected to hear his mother's voice. She'd been gone for eight years, yet it still seemed like yesterday that they'd come home to smells of her home cooking and a welcome hug. "Man, we need to take a day and give this place a good cleaning. Mom would be walloping us with her broom if she saw her house in this condition." The pine floors were clutter free, but they deserved a good mopping. There was a layer of dust on the end tables and the comfortable couch and recliners needed recovering. As they moved into the kitchen, Daniel could see the sink was full of dishes and the counters were piled high with items that begged to be put away.

Ezekiel grabbed a couple of sodas from the fridge and joined his brother at the round oak table where they'd shared many a meal with their folks. "Well, when you bring home the future Mrs. Blackhawk you met today, I expect she'll straighten all of this right up."

The mention of Sara made him smile. "If I'm lucky enough to get Sara through this door, housekeeping won't be my first priority." He unpacked the bags, setting out burgers, fries, onion rings, and the pies. "You can have a slice of the lemon – the coconut is mine."

Tearing into their burgers, the brothers began to eat. Once Ezekiel had appeased his initial hunger, he eyed his older brother. "So, what's she like and when are we going to meet her?"

Daniel wiped his mouth with a paper napkin, stopping to take a sip of cola before answering. "She's gorgeous. Long, dark hair. Blue eyes. Sweet." He shook his head. "I told you how she saved the little kid, just ran out in front of that eighteen-wheeler and snatched him from the jaws of death."

Unable to resist trying the pie, Ezekiel took a big bite. "Oh, Lord. Pretty and talented. Damn, this is good. When's the wedding?"

Daniel shifted in his chair. "Well, there's a hitch in my get-a-long." He looked at his brother sheepishly. "She turned me down."

"You really proposed?" Ezekiel hit the table with a fist as he laughed.

"No, Easy, I didn't propose. I asked her out on a date."

"And she turned you down?" He continued to chuckle. "What's the world coming to? The Casanova Cowboy is cut off at the knees."

"I'm not a Casanova," Daniel protested. "I haven't dated that many women." Not lately, anyway. Most of his romantic encounters couldn't be considered dates, liaisons maybe. There were plenty of women who enjoyed having a Blackhawk for their dirty little secret.

"Only about half of the ones chasing after you, I'll grant you that. You attract women like clover attracts bees." Ezekiel finished his pie and reached for

Daniel's

"Don't touch my pie." He snatched it out of harm's way. "Right now, I'm only interested in attracting one particular bee.

"I don't think I've ever seen you like this. You're usually the love 'em and leave 'em type of guy." Ezekiel watched Daniel savor every bite of the chocolate covered coconut pie. "Good?"

"Amazing." Daniel sighed. "I've just got to figure out how to make Sara want to go out with me."

Ezekiel sobered. "You're serious."

Daniel frowned. "Hell, yes, I'm serious." He gathered up their trash. With a faraway look in his eye, he spoke softly. "I've never felt like this. Ever. I took one look at her and it was like I'd never seen a woman before. There was just something about her, Easy." Daniel met his brother's gaze. "It was like I'd known her before and I was just waiting to find her again."

"Wow." This time Ezekiel didn't laugh. "I wish I could find someone who made me feel that way."

"Well, let's wait and see if it works out. She might break my heart, you never know." Daniel's tone made his pronouncement seem like a joke, but he was dead serious. What he'd said was true, this feeling was new to him. He'd been attracted to women before – obviously. But he'd never felt this overwhelming, desperate need – not for sex, necessarily, but for a person. One single, solitary individual that seemed to be his other half. His soulmate. "Whoa." He shook his head. "I'm heading out to the barn and work off some of this energy. The stalls need mucking and I'll check on Elsie and see how near she is to calving."

"Just as soon as Ben and Sam get here, Ben and I are going to ride the north fence line. Our next-door neighbor corralled one of our horses and I don't think it jumped out, I'm afraid there's a gap in the fence somewhere."

"What about Samuel? How's he feeling?" Daniel held the empty carry-out container that had held the pie in his hand, reluctant to throw it away. After staring at it for a good thirty seconds, he placed it on the counter next to the refrigerator.

Ezekiel had the presence of mind not to tease his brother. In fact, he was a bit jealous. "Sam's healing up fine. I hope this near-miss cures his penchant for bull riding, but somehow, I doubt it. He's supposed to go over the ranch books tonight and make a call on whether we can afford to buy that breed bull from Jaxson McCoy. Did you happen to spot it when you delivered the hay?"

"Nope. Hopefully we can swing it. See ya." Daniel picked up his hat and let himself out the back door and made a beeline for the barn. The faster he moved, the sooner he could head back to town. The summer sweet scent of fresh mown hay hit him like a welcome wave as he let himself into the dim interior of the barn. Sounds of nickering horses, lowing cows, and even the plaintive mew of a cat made him feel right at home. Finding a pitchfork, he went to work, his thoughts centered on one blue-eyed beauty and what he'd say to her the next time they met.

* * *

Sara stopped to lift her hair from her neck. Even at this late hour, the heat was almost overwhelming. She rested for a few seconds, gauging how much further she had to go, before picking up the handle of the small wagon and setting out once more. "I shouldn't have bought so much flour." The supplies needed to make her pies just didn't last long enough. Thank goodness.

Sara didn't know what she would've done if Rev. Mike hadn't suggested she take over his food truck. She'd wondered why he didn't just serve the pies exclusively in the pub, but he'd explained that a lot of the residents and people passing by might hesitate to come into a biker bar, but the sight of the gaily painted food truck welcomed all with a sweet tooth. It had been over a month since she'd walked up to the Dam Pub and asked for a job, any kind of job. The old biker had felt sorry for her and let her wait tables that night. Her quick smile and natural rapport with almost anyone who came through the door prompted the reverend to offer Sara a full-time position. And when she'd filled in for one of the cooks during an emergency, her talent for baking had not gone unnoticed or unrewarded. In the short time she'd been here, Sara already had garnered quite a loyal following.

Besides the opportunity to run the food truck, she had another, more important reason to be grateful to Rev. Mike. With no home of her own and only the money she made from the pies to live on, Sara literally had no roof over her head. Until she could save up, he allowed her to sleep in the storeroom of the pub on a narrow camp cot.

As she tugged the unwieldy cart over a rough patch, Sara lost her focus and thoughts of Daniel Blackhawk slipped into her mind. She couldn't stop the smile from blooming on her lips. He seemed so nice and he'd liked her, she could tell. "Stop it, you've no right to think those thoughts." When the realization of her circumstances settled on her anew, Sara vowed to get to the bottom of her predicament – one way or the other. She hadn't heard from Doug in months, she'd given up on him coming home a long time ago.

…Meanwhile, back at the Dam Pub, Daniel stood by the food truck, glaring at the Closed sign. He'd stormed in to ask Mike where Sara lived, but the answer he'd received was a very unsatisfying 'none of your damn business, Blackhawk'. Who knew Mike had a fatherly bone in his old biker body?

Stomping to his truck, he didn't even try to hide his disappointment. Grabbing the door handle, he took one last look around the parking lot. Expecting the food truck to be open this late was just wishful thinking. Having lost his appetite, he pulled out into the road with no particular destination in mind. He'd just drive for a bit and try to imagine where the lovely young woman called home. He could picture her in a white gingerbread cottage with a picket fence or in a neat craftsman style house with window boxes and a rocker on the porch. As he pulled out onto the highway, Daniel absently rubbed his chin, he hadn't even taken time to shave. He'd been so all-fired anxious to see Sara, he'd just rushed off half-cocked. Daniel chuckled and adjusted his package in his jeans. No, half-cocked wasn't accurate, his manhood was fully engaged and ready for action.

Blowing out a sigh, he flipped on the radio, finding a country western station. Brad Paisley's *She's Everything* was playing and Daniel found himself humming along. "Everything I wanted, everything I need." As he sang, his eyes roved until they collided with a sight that made him slam on the brakes and pull over to the side of the road. Sara was walking next to a rustic pasture fence, sunflowers peeking through the strands of wire, pulling a wooden cart filled with groceries behind her. "What in Sam Hill?"

Sara put one foot ahead of the other, it wouldn't be long now. Surely. She'd made this trek before, one would think it'd get easier. So far, that wasn't the case.

"Need some help?"

The male voice coming out of nowhere made her jump. She jerked, turning to see if her mind was playing a trick on her. "Daniel? Where did you come from? I didn't hear you drive up." God, here she was in a plain checkered dress, her hair a mess. Sara placed a hand over heart, afraid it might beat right out of her chest.

"What are you doing, girl? It's too hot for you to be exerting yourself like this. Why didn't you drive to the store?"

His questions were coming fast and furious, but he was even faster, coming to her and taking the handle of the wagon from her hand.

Even in the sultry temperatures of an August evening, she was aware of the heat this man generated. A heat that would burn her in an entirely different way than the sun. "There's no need, Mr. Blackhawk. I'm almost back to the pub."

"There's every need. And it's Mr. Blackhawk, now, is it?" Daniel picked up the cart and placed it on the bed of his truck, pushing it inside, and raising the tailgate. "A moment ago, it was Daniel."

"Daniel, please…" Sara laid a hand on his arm and they both froze at the touch. Sara looked up into his face and was amazed at what she saw there. Tenderness. Hunger. Need.

"I just want to help you," he said softly. "Let me do this for you. Do you think I could drive away and leave you here?"

The tone of his voice made her chest ache. "All right." He moved to open the passenger door for her and she climbed in, with him hovering right behind her, a steadying hand on her arm. "Thank you."

When he came around and crawled in beside her, she rubbed her palms on the skirt of her dress, wincing as she did so.

"What's wrong?"

"Blisters." Sara glanced at him as he picked up her hand in his, cradling it gently.

"Dammit, baby."

He released her hand, but bent over, his big body curving to reach beneath the seat. His shoulder and head were almost in her lap and she could feel the strength in his upper body. Her breath caught in her throat. "What are you doing?"

"First-aid kit." Daniel's hand shook as he tended to her, cleaning the raw spots with great care, then placing a small bandage over them. He'd never been more aware of a woman in his life. Her hand quivered in his like a small bird preparing to take flight. "I can't believe you hurt yourself like this. Why didn't you tell me today that you needed help with your groceries?"

His gruff, almost chastising words struck a chord within her, he almost sounded as if he were in pain himself. "I don't like asking and it didn't seem right to assume…" Her voice trailed off when he lifted her hand to bring it to his lips. She was hypnotized by the sight of him placing his lips to her palm. The moment she felt his touch, Sara gasped, the heat and energy traveling from his lips to her skin was so powerful, she couldn't catch her breath. "Daniel…"

Slowly, he released her. Unwillingly, he released her. "That's right, call me Daniel. There is no room for formality between us."

She sat still as he started the engine and drove her the remaining short distance to the food truck. "Are you sure you want to go here? Is it because it's more convenient for you to cook here than cart the pies from your house in the morning?"

Sara didn't want him to know her circumstances. She was ashamed. "Yea, it's more convenient."

Once he parked on the side nearest the door, he placed a hand on her knee. "Sit still."

She obeyed, not sure what he intended. When he came around to help her down from the high seat, she went into his arms as naturally as water flowing downhill.

He was reluctant to let her go so soon, holding her felt too right. He gave himself a good ten seconds of joy, his body becoming acquainted with hers. The closer he drew her, the more aware he became of her fragility. Seeing her selfless act of valor and knowing how heavy was the burden she'd tackled in the fully loaded wagon; these things gave the illusion of great strength. Instead, she was small and soft, only her spirit was of great dimensions. "Sara," he whispered, loving how her breasts pressed to his chest like they belonged and how the top of her head fit so perfectly under his chin.

"I should go," she muttered, needing to push away, yet wanting to remain where she stood. "I have much to do."

Her sweet voice was so captivating, he would've agreed to most anything – except leaving her. When she looked up, she sucker-punched him with the eloquence of those big blue eyes. An almost imperceptible shiver racked her slight frame. "I'll help you," Daniel offered, because he could conceive of nothing else. "I told you I'd make a great assistant, you just give me a task and I'll do it to the best of my ability."

This wasn't right, she shouldn't agree to it. Yet, Sara found herself nodding, then standing back while he removed the wagon from the back of his truck.

"Hey, Blackhawk! Come have a drink!" a man's voice called and Daniel whirled around, quite surprised to find there were people milling in and out of the pub just a few dozen yards away. He'd forgotten where they were, this thing between them felt so big that it blocked out the whole world.

"No, thanks! Some other time!" He waved, noting the crowd of people, mostly men, lounging around on their bikes, many with drinks in hand. "You know, this isn't the safest place for you to be this time of night."

Sara unlocked the door of the silver food truck and climbed in first. "Just hand the things to me and I'll see to them." She'd rather do this on her own, having this beautiful man so close to her was almost more than she could bear.

As he passed her sacks of flour and sugar, gallons of milk, and cartons of eggs, he covertly studied the gentle sway of her walk and the delicate lines of her face, completely devoid of makeup. And Lord knew, she needed no artifice to be exquisitely beautiful. His pulse quickened as he observed the thrust and jiggle of her breasts, the elegant line of her neck and back. His desire for her was growing like a wild thing with a will of its own.

"That's all of it," he announced as he placed a tin of chocolate and a bag of flaked coconut in her hand. "I think I see the makings of another Almond Joy pie here, don't I?"

"Possibly." She gave him a shy smile. "Thanks for the help, it would've been much more difficult without you."

"I'm more than glad to do it." Daniel stepped up inside the food truck with her. "Now, I'm ready to help. How many pies do you need to make tonight?"

Sara knew the best thing would be to turn him away, but she was too weak. The truth was, she wanted him here. With her. Near to her. She felt energized when he was by her side. Not so alone. "A dozen, if there's time."

"Well, let's get to it."

His smile was contagious and she gave one back to him. "You'll have to follow my lead."

Daniel didn't argue. "I think I'd follow you anywhere, Miss Riley."

For the next three hours, they worked side by side. Sara made the pie crusts, while Daniel sliced peaches and apples. She made cream fillings, chocolate and coconut, while he dusted blackberries and blueberries with sugar. Soon the air was filled with marvelous smells. And while they worked, they talked. Not about anything serious, more of a sharing, an introduction, a familiarizing. "So, you have three brothers?"

"Yea, three. I'm the oldest, then Benjamin, next comes Easy, and last Samuel."

"Easy?" She laughed.

He brushed a speck of flour from her nose. "Ezekiel, Easy is just a nickname. We shortened the other two to Benjen and plain Sam. Sometimes I'm called Danny, but Ezekiel never liked to be called Zeke."

"So, he became Easy. I like it."

"Is Sara short for anything, like Sara Lee?" Daniel teased as she removed four pies from the oven and put four more in.

His nonsensical suggestion made her laugh. "No. Sara, plain Sara."

Daniel caught her hand, causing her to go motionless by him. "There's nothing plain about you, Sara. You're gorgeous."

Sara shivered and pulled away. "Tell me about where you live."

He allowed her to move unimpeded. "Our ranch was a great place to grow up. We have several thousand acres, a beautiful view, and river frontage. The four of us have split the land and split the profits. We'll never be rich, but we're happy and comfortable."

"There's more important things in life than money." She stated what she thought was obvious, her musings straying away from pie and conversation to linger on the vain imaginings of how his work-roughened hands would feel petting and stroking her body. Exploring her. Learning her. Sara quivered, knowing her fantasies were just that. Her only experience with sex had been a disaster, one she wasn't anxious to repeat. She had no desire to see disappointment in another man's eyes.

"Where did you grow up?"

Daniel's question shook her from her reverie. "North of Llano. My father owned a small quarry. He drowned in the lake after losing control of a loader he was driving, it was a terrible accident."

"Oh, I'm sorry."

His sympathy did little to erase the memory of the mistakes she made in the aftermath of her father's death. She was the one who was sorry. "Don't be, I survived. I'm here." Who she was, was so much more than she liked to talk about.

A wave of relief swept over him. "Yes, you're here." Surrounded by the sweet treats she'd made, he wanted to celebrate the good fortune that had brought her to him. "And I couldn't be happier."

"Daniel." Sara hung her head. "I appreciate what you did so much, all the help – but we can't…I can't."

He had her insides sizzling, her nipples were tenting her bodice, and her femininity was flexing and pulsing, aching for something she didn't even fully understand.

"Oh, yes, we can." He reached for her and brushed his lips over hers. Softly. "Oh, you're so sweet, baby. So hot." She wasn't pushing him away. "God, I've been dying to do that from the moment I laid eyes on you." He joined their mouths again and nibbled her lower lip.

"Oh, Daniel, I'm not worth the trouble."

"I beg to differ." He lifted his hand and traced her lips with the pad of his thumb. His imagination was running away with him. He could picture this pretty mouth stretched around his cock, her tongue swirling sweetly around the crown. "I think you're worth anything a man possessed." Daniel tried to control himself. He wanted her so much.

"Really?" Her eyes locked with his, her tongue darting out to lick the corner of her mouth, glancing against his thumb. "Fuck, baby." His dick jerked in his jeans. "I have to have a kiss. Just a taste. Don't turn me away. Please," he begged. When she didn't move, he cupped the back of her head and crashed his mouth to hers. The very second she parted hers, he claimed the kiss, devouring her mouth as if there was no tomorrow. Her delicate hands crept around his neck, her fingers kneading his flesh, and the kiss escalated, taking them both by surprise.

"Stop. Stop."

She turned her head to one side breaking the kiss, but she didn't move out of his arms and he held onto that – holding on to her. "Why? Don't you feel what I feel? This is different than anything I've ever known before. More. This is meant to be." Daniel knew he was behaving out of character, waxing eloquent, saying things he never thought to say to a woman. "I want to see you again and again. I want to kiss you over and over." He pressed his mouth to her neck, loving the beating of her heart beneath his lips. "I want you so much."

Sara tore from his arms and turned her back to him. "I can't, Daniel. I can't."

"Why?" He could think of no conceivable reason. Unless…

"Is it because of who I am? What I am?"

"No! Of course not!"

"Why, then, why?" he asked, his voice hoarse with emotion.

"I'm not free, Daniel," she said with anguish. "I'm not free."

CHAPTER TWO

Daniel froze, every muscle taut with dread. "You're not free?" He glared at the woman who'd wrapped him around her little finger from the first moment they met. For her to say she wasn't free was the same as if she'd stuck a knife in his chest. "What do you mean?"

Sara hated what she was about to say. Daniel would never know how she wished her situation was different. She realized this thing between them wasn't real, it couldn't be. All her life, she'd dreamed of a happy ending of her own, but longing for one was a waste of time. She'd already made her bed of thorns and she was going to have to lie in it. "I'm sorry, Daniel." Sara hung her head. "I'm married."

"Married?" Daniel bent forward, grasping onto the door frame. He couldn't breathe. Closing his eyes, he let the waves of pain wash over him. Fuck! How did he let himself get so wound up in this woman so fast? He grabbed her hand. "You wear no man's ring." Looking at her accusingly, he yelled, "Why in the hell didn't you tell me? Why did you let me make a fool out of myself?"

Tears began to well in her eyes. He was upset, she could see that. She gazed at his handsome, stricken face. Big, beautiful Daniel Blackhawk was hurting – for her. Sara wanted to scream at the unfairness of it all. The last batch of pies they'd put into the oven were burning – but she didn't care. "I didn't mean to. And you aren't the fool, Daniel. I am."

He acted like he didn't hear her speaking. Giving her one last long look, he flung the door open and disappeared into the darkness.

Sara sank down to the floor and cried.

…Later, Daniel would wonder how he even made it home. Good thing his old truck knew the way. With every turn of the wheel, he cursed his own tendency to jump headfirst into anything. Usually, his hard-headed decisiveness worked in his favor – not this time. How could he have been so wrong? Did he imagine the heat between them? And what kind of woman did this make Sara? Her deception stunned him? How easily he'd been misled.

When he arrived at the old rock house, Daniel did something unusual. He snuck in the back, unwilling to face his brothers tonight. All he wanted to do was take a scalding hot shower and put this night behind him. Tomorrow, he'd work on forgetting that Sara Riley ever existed.

* * *

The next morning, Daniel worked alongside his brothers, manhandling a gas-powered post hole digger. Not only did it get the job done faster, it made enough noise so he didn't have to attempt a conversation with his inquisitive siblings. Their efforts today would complete an eight-foot high fence that would enclose several hundred acres, specifically designed to house exotic deer. The Blackhawk boys planned on breeding the game for a few years before they introduced a hunting program, but this was something many ranches in the area were doing, not only for profit, but also for ecological and preservation purposes for the wild game.

Eventually, the time came that Daniel had to lay down the equipment and take a break. Sure enough, they were just awaiting the opportunity to broach the one subject he wanted to avoid.

"So, Easy tells us you've met a woman." Benjen asked with a smirk on his face, "What's her name?"

"Doesn't matter." Daniel shook his head as he filled a cup with water out of the cooler. "The whole thing was a mistake."

"What do you mean?" Sam asked as he hopped onto the tailgate, favoring his injured leg. "What went wrong?"

Daniel drained his cup and threw the empty into the bed of the truck. He glanced at his brothers, seeing concern on their faces. Anyone who saw them, wouldn't doubt they were related, they were all cut from the same mold – from their build, to their height, to their facial features. The only difference was that Easy's eyes were blue while everyone else's was some shade of brown from amber to chocolate.

"She was perfect for me. I fell for her like a ton of bricks." He stood with one hand on his hip, the other pulling at the head of a nearby sunflower. "God, she's beautiful." Daniel took time to recount the way she'd saved the small boy. "You should've seen her, like the old saying goes, she rushed in where angels feared to tread. That little boy will live to be a man because of her."

"So far, I don't hear a problem," Easy remarked as he gazed down the newly built fence, gauging how straight they'd kept the line.

Daniel raked a big hand through his hair, mussing the dark mane into a tangle. "We seemed to hit it off like gangbusters. Too bad she neglected to mention that she was married."

"Married? Damn," Benjen whispered. "Sorry, bud. That sucks."

"Where's her husband?" Sam asked.

"Hell, if I know, she wasn't wearing a ring," Daniel muttered. "When I went to see her last night, I found her pulling some damn cart from the grocery store. She doesn't even have a car. What kind of husband leaves his wife in that kind of a fix? She's baking pies at a biker bar!" Daniel didn't say it, but he kept thinking that if she belonged to him, he'd take better care of her.

"Doesn't sound right to me." Easy wiped the sweat off his face with a red bandanna. "If I were you I'd ask some questions before I just gave up on her."

Benjen nodded. "Yea, me too. She might be in trouble."

"Yea," Sam agreed. "If you like her as much as you say you do, find out more about this husband of hers. Any man worth his salt would take better care of his woman."

Daniel gritted his teeth, he didn't like to think of Sara as anyone's woman but his. "Maybe."

Easy clapped Daniel on his shoulder. "If you're as blown away by this woman as you say you are, I think I'd investigate a little more before I walked away from her."

…At Rev. Mike's Dam Pub, Sara wasn't moving very fast. She hadn't been able to sleep, so she'd stayed up half the night making more pies to replace the ones she'd burned. Thoughts of Daniel weighed heavily on her heart. She couldn't forget how it felt to be held against him. How wonderful it felt to be kissed by him. Shame made her cheeks burn. He'd been right, she should've been honest with him from the beginning. The only excuse she could claim was the fact that she didn't feel married. After all, she'd hadn't seen the groom since the day after the wedding. Once he'd gotten what he wanted from her, he'd disappeared.

For Sara, the day passed in a daze. She'd gone through the motions, speaking to people, serving them pie, taking platters into the pub as they were needed. Anyone observing her, saw nothing amiss. Inside, she was aching with the knowledge of what Daniel must think of her now.

During a lull in business, she took the opportunity to wash up a few dishes. Most of the pies were gone, all she had left was a chocolate silk, a peach-blueberry, and a pear tart.

"Excuse me."

The sudden voice startled Sara and she dropped a glass bowl in the sink, sending soapy water all over the floor.

"Oh, I'm sorry!"

Sara grabbed a towel and turned to find a pretty woman, flanked by two very handsome men – one blond and one who reminded her very much of Daniel. "No worries, I was wool-gathering, my head wasn't in the game." Grabbing a towel, she dried her hands. "Can I help you?"

"Hey, I'm Ryder Duke and…" she lowered her voice, "these are my husbands, Samson and Gideon." The men tipped their hats.

Sara tried not to react. Wow, she thought, this woman has two great men and she had…nothing. "So glad to meet you, I'm Sara."

Ryder shook Sara's hand in greeting. "We live just up the road, everyone knows us in these parts, so we don't try to hide."

Gideon pushed her hair over her shoulder and Samson rubbed Ryder's back. Sara could see how much they cared for her, she didn't blame the woman for wanting to show them off. "Sounds good to me. How can I help you?"

Ryder leaned over the counter to peer into the truck. "I'm having an impromptu family gathering and I was wondering what you might have left. Anything?"

"Sure." Sara moved the three pies to the front so Ryder could see. "Peach-blueberry, pear, and chocolate."

"Yum, chocolate." Gideon licked his lips.

"We'll take all three." Samson pulled out his wallet. "How much?"

She told them the price and they paid. As the men carried the pies to their truck, Ryder studied her face. "Do you live nearby?"

Sara was a little embarrassed. "I'm bunking in the back of the pub until I can afford better."

Ryder didn't blink an eye. No judgment. "Since we're neighbors, I'd love to have you over for coffee one day."

"How nice. Thank you." Sara couldn't help but smile. She'd needed this distraction. "I don't have a lot of time off. We're closed on Sundays, though."

"Perfect. Here's my number." Ryder gave her a card, then an extra for Sara to write her own number down.

"I look forward to hearing from you." She pocketed the card, grateful for the offer of friendship.

"Great!" Ryder gave her a wave. "You'll be hearing from me soon. I'll introduce you to my sister, Pepper. I'm sure we'll be great friends."

Once she was alone, Sara finished cleaning up the

food truck. She'd lowered the window, with nothing to sell, there was no use to draw customers. When she was finished, the interior of the truck seemed too small. She knew this restlessness was a reaction to the heartbreak of the night before. Even though she had no appetite, Sara knew she needed to eat something or she'd get a headache.

Locking up, she set out on the short trek to the pub's entrance. About the time she got halfway, a dozen Harleys roared in, surrounding her completely. Before she could beat a path to the pub door and the relative safety of a crowd, Sara found herself enveloped in a throng of slightly inebriated bikers. "Excuse me." She tried to push past a burly man who grasped her around the waist.

"Look what I found!"

Sara tried to stay calm. She knew most of these motorcycle clubs were made up of weekend bikers – doctors and lawyers, professional people who enjoyed an opportunity to cut loose and let their hair down. "I'm just on my way in for a bite to eat. I think the special tonight is pulled pork."

"I think I'd prefer you, you seem to be pretty special, little lady," another man said as he caught her after being slung between the men like a doll.

"Please, don't," Sara managed to mutter before two others joined in. When one of them grabbed her ass, she yelped, "Hey, knock it off!"

"Oh, come on, sweetheart. We just want to be friendly with the locals."

Sara struggled as a tall, bearded man tried to kiss her neck. "No! Stop!"

"Stop? We're just getting started. We just want you to be friendly, sweetheart. We won't hurt you."

"The lady said stop!"

A familiar voice broke through the confusion.

Daniel.

Before Sara could stop her head from spinning, the big cowboy waded into the fray throwing punches. He would've been severely outnumbered had a few locals not joined in, coming to his aid. Sara backed up, getting out of the way, her heart racing, her gaze never leaving the man who'd walked away from her in anger the night before. What was he doing here? Not for her, surely.

Before the fight could get out of hand, Rev. Mike came out with a bull horn, a baseball bat, and what looked to be a gun of some kind. Yelling at the sparring throng, he gave strict orders. "Cease and desist or I'll call the sheriff to haul away the lot of you!" He punctuated his demand with a flare gun, shooting a blazing starburst into the evening sky.

Quicker than Sara thought possible, the crowd dispersed.

Leaving her alone with Daniel.

"Are you all right?" he asked without touching her, hovering near her – big and powerful.

"Yes, thank you so much." She wanted to touch him so badly she quaked with the need.

"Where's your husband?" The question was a harsh demand.

"I don't know." Sara turned to head to the back of the pub, there was no use continuing the conversation.

Daniel caught her arm. "What do you mean, you don't know? Isn't he coming to pick you up?"

"No, he's not." She didn't want to discuss the painful subject with the one man who'd touched her heart as no one ever had before.

"Why not?"

Sara didn't answer, she just kept walking.

"Are you through for the day?"

"Yes."

"Come on. I'll take you home, I think we should talk."

Talk. Oh, no. "I don't think so. We don't have anything else to say." Sara was moving forward and then she wasn't. Daniel snagged her wrist and pulled her against his big body. "Daniel, what are you doing?"

"Giving you a ride. I want to hear about this husband who leaves you unprotected to fend for yourself."

Sara tried to resist. She had nowhere to go. "Daniel, I live here."

Her admission brought his own steps to a halt. "What did you say?"

Hanging her head, she pointed. "I sleep in the storage room at the back of the pub."

"Christ Almighty!" Daniel couldn't believe it. "Show me."

Sara didn't want to. What was the use? "There's not much to see."

"I didn't expect there was." He planted a big hand on the small of her back and pushed her gently forward. "At least it'll be private." As soon as he said the words, he questioned them. "You do have a damn lock on the door, don't you?"

"Yes, there's a lock." She was beginning to get frustrated. "I just don't understand why you care."

Daniel felt like she'd punched him in the gut. "Hell, if I know." He just did.

With his lips pressed together and his jaw aching from a well-placed blow, he trudged next to Sara Riley as she walked to the back of the slightly run-down building. Every nerve cell in his body was hyper aware of the woman at his side. God, she turned him inside out! Even knowing she had a husband, he had to steel himself not to gather her close and never let her go.

"In here." She pulled open the back entrance. Sounds from the kitchen were evident, the clanging of pans and the yell of an 'order up'! Strains from the juke box could be clearly heard and several men stood in the hall near the restroom. She stopped before she got that far and opened a door, leading into a room no bigger than a broom closet. A utilitarian cot sat to one side and a rolling rack stood behind it with a few pieces of clothing hanging from the bar. There was one straight back chair and that was where she indicated he should sit. "Sorry, I don't have anything to offer you."

He blinked and bowed his head, wishing to high heaven that she was wrong. Nothing to offer? Ye, gods. He would've taken any crumb she wanted to throw to him. "You sit." He pointed to the narrow cot. Daniel needed distance between them. "Now, talk. What kind of husband lets his wife go without a car or a roof over her head?"

Sara sank down on the thin mattress. "A sorry one, I suppose."

Very slowly, Daniel was getting the picture. "You really don't know where your husband is, do you?"

Sara hesitated to say. She raised her head and met his eyes and to her surprise the coldness was gone and they were kind. "I'm so ashamed," she began.

"Ah, hell." Daniel rose and joined her on the cot, which creaked beneath his weight.

Sara giggled. "We're going to end up on the floor."

Daniel stroked her hair. "I'll catch you if you fall. Now…talk to me."

"His name is Doug Wright. He worked for my

father." She trembled at the memory. "He was nice to me, but Dad watched me like a hawk. My mom…" Her voice broke.

Daniel continued to play with her hair, weaving his fingers through the strands. "Go ahead, honey."

"My mom left when I was a kid, it was just me and Dad. He owned a small granite quarry and Doug hauled the rock to vendors. One day, my dad had an accident, he drove his track-loader off the cliff into the lake. Doug got him out, but he couldn't revive him." She paused for a long moment. "After that, my life was pretty much a blur. I didn't have anyone. My mom's folks had disowned her when she married my dad and when she left us, she never came back. Her folks don't know where she is either and they have no desire to know anything about me. I was alone. Doug stepped in and handled everything and I…let him."

"Did you love him?"

Sara shrugged. "I don't think so. I was so innocent and scared. He brought me some papers he said I needed to sign, then he told me we needed to get married so he could run the quarry and take care of me."

Daniel growled, but said nothing.

"After the funeral, I went with him to the JP's office." She blushed furiously. "The next day, after the…" Her voice dropped off. She couldn't say the word 'honeymoon'. There'd been nothing sweet or romantic about what they shared as man and wife. "He took our truck, cleaned out the bank accounts, and left me with nothing but a ring that turned my finger green. I found out quickly enough that the bank held a note on our house and the business, a note that was three months past due. I'm sure he wasn't counting on that disappointment. After he left, I kept expecting him to send for me or call, but he never did."

The silence in the room grew to overwhelming proportions.

"I lost the house and the business. When I tried to call him, the phone number didn't work." Sara refused to tell him the worst part, she couldn't even begin to voice the sadness.

"Son-of-a-bitch," Daniel whispered under his breath. "He just left you?" He couldn't believe it. A girl like Sara? Was the man crazy? "He stole from you and left you to the mercy of the world?"

The way Daniel put it, she sounded like a pitiful case. "I'm probably better off."

"Why did you stay married to him? Was the marriage even real?"

"I guess so. He had a license and everything." Sara sighed and twisted the hem of her shirt between her fingers. "I visited a free legal clinic to see about a divorce, but they told me papers had to be served and I didn't know how to find him."

"So, you were married for one day." Daniel was still processing this crazy news.

"Shouldn't be enough to count, I know." Sara felt so self-conscious. "So, that's my stupid story." She stood. "I'm saving up money for an apartment, but it's slow. I didn't have any work experience and the jobs I've been able to get don't pay much." For a while she hadn't been able to work, but Daniel didn't need those details. "So, if you'll excuse me, I'm a little hungry."

"So, you're going to brave the pub and those bikers?"

"I'll just go to the kitchen and get something."

"If you can get past the thugs in the hall." Daniel stood. "Get your stuff."

"What? Why?"

"You're coming with me. I'm not leaving you here."

His edict surprised her. "I can't. I need to make pies."

He knew how late they'd worked the night before and the thought of her repeating the process night after night, right by herself, tore at his heart. "Look, we need someone at the ranch. The work won't be hard, we all pitch in, but we need a woman's touch." He needed a woman's touch.

"You're offering me a job?"

Daniel knew she didn't realize it, but he was willing to offer her a lot more. "And a place to stay. There's what mom used to call a mother-in-law suite attached, a relatively new edition compared to the rest of the house. It even has a private entrance." She hesitated and Daniel cleared his throat. "Please? I don't think I'll be able to rest worrying about you down here by yourself."

"It's not right," she began in a whisper.

"We'll make sure it's proper and we'll also talk to our family lawyer about how to proceed with your…" Daniel almost choked on the word, "marriage." He'd beat the first person who had something ugly to say about her or their situation to a bloody pulp.

"Proper isn't what I meant when I said it wasn't right, it isn't fair for you to take on my troubles."

"I always enjoyed a little trouble."

"What will your brothers think?" Sara couldn't believe she was considering his proposition.

Daniel gave her a reassuring smile. "If you'll make a few pies, I can guarantee they'll be grateful to have you around." He knew he sure as hell would. "You take care of us while I take care of you and we'll figure this thing out."

In a few minutes, she'd packed her small duffle. "I really should tell Rev. Mike, he's been good to me."

"Does anything in the food truck belong to you?" Daniel asked as he took her bag from her hand.

"No. Everything was there from before, only the sign was new and he paid for it." She stepped out into the hall, then stalled when she saw one of the men who'd harassed her in the parking lot loitering by the bathroom door.

"It's okay." Daniel took her hand and led her past the paunchy, middle-aged man, who didn't appear nearly as brave as he did when flanked by his comrades. "We'll go through the pub to speak to Mike. While we're in there, I'll get you something to eat. You did say you were hungry. What do you want?"

"Grilled chicken sandwich?" Her voice was hesitant.

"You got it, baby."

Sara marveled at how nice it was for him to care whether she ate or not. "They owe me a meal, so don't let them make you pay."

To say Rev. Mike was less than pleased was putting it mildly. "I'm sorry," she told him, "and I'm very grateful for the opportunity."

"You're leaving me in the lurch, Sara," he told her as he wiped down the counter. He had to speak loudly over Willie Nelson's *Angel Flying Too Close To The Ground* and the roar of the bar's patrons. "The customers really liked your pies. I'm going to get complaints."

"She's not safe here." Daniel felt like he didn't have to explain. "She was attacked in the parking lot a few minutes ago."

Mike frowned. "Well, I can't be responsible for what goes on outside my door."

"Well, actually, you can. You should. This is your property, your problem."

Taking Sara by the hand, he escorted her through the throng. She noticed the crowd parted for Daniel like the Red Sea parting for Moses. All eyes were on him – the men viewing him with respect and the women with lust. He didn't seem to notice them, focused only on exiting the building and protecting the woman who'd placed herself in his care.

Sara wasn't sure how she felt about being his task, his responsibility. It wasn't until they arrived at his truck and he helped her into the seat and proceeded to fasten her seat belt as if she were a small child, that she had the presence of mind to ask him a question she should've asked long before. "Daniel, why did you come tonight?"

Because he couldn't stay away.

But Daniel didn't say that. He didn't answer until he walked around the truck and climbed behind the steering wheel, yanking the truck door shut with a heavy thunk. The truck was old enough that it required a key to start the engine. Daniel pulled the gear shift into reverse and backed out of the parking lot and pulled onto the road before he answered, "I got to thinking. Eat your sandwich."

She pushed her hair over her shoulder and chewed on her bottom lip as she unwrapped the grilled chicken. The dashboard instrumentation gave off just enough light for her to see his masculine profile. Daniel was such a big man, he filled up his side of the truck and made her feel small. She wasn't afraid of him though, his strength was protective, not intimidating. "Thinking?" About her? "That can be dangerous." She took a bite and sighed at how good it was. She'd been hungrier than she realized.

Daniel snorted. "Yea, maybe." He cut his eyes toward her and she met his gaze. "After you told me you were married, it knocked me for a loop."

"Why?" She felt the same way, but she wanted to make sure she understood.

Daniel exhaled loudly, as if he questioned the wisdom of what he was about to say. "Hell, I don't know. From the moment I saw you rescue that kid, I couldn't see anything else but you. No matter if I was here or at home, awake or asleep, I haven't been able to think about anyone but you." With one hand hung over the top of the steering wheel, he pushed his hat back on his head with the other. "This type of thing doesn't happen to me."

"This stuff doesn't happen to me either." People usually left her and they didn't come back.

"Yet, you kept a vital piece of information from me, don't you think?" Daniel was still searching for meaning in all of this. He liked for things to make sense and this didn't.

Sara closed her eyes, then turned her head to look out the window. She was tired of feeling guilty for her mistakes. Big and small. Present and past. "I'm sorry. I've tried so hard to put Doug and that painful part of my life out of my head. Sometimes, I'm just living, going about my business. The other day was one of those times – and bam! There you were. Nothing was planned, my reaction to you wasn't calculated."

Daniel rubbed his palm across his chest, a strange ache was lodged there, like something he'd swallowed hadn't gone all the way down. "I understand. There are things in my life that I try to suppress too." Big things.

"Are you sure my going to your house is a good idea?"

Her question clarified his thoughts like a drop of

bleach in colored water. "Absolutely. You need me and I…" He hit the steering wheel with the palm of his hand. "I need you to need me. Does that make sense?"

"No." A small laugh escaped her lips. "My life is a mess." She touched her mouth. "The kiss you gave me is the only thing that's made sense in a long, long time. And I know that's wrong. Right?"

Daniel rubbed his chest again. The ache was back. He hadn't been able to forget that kiss either. "No, it's not wrong." He pushed aside an urgent need to pull the truck over to the side of the road to kiss her again. This wasn't the time. "We'll sort all of this out."

"Really?" she asked, feeling a sense of hope for the first time in a long time.

"For sure and certain." And when they did sort things out…neither hell nor high water would stop him from taking her into his arms and claiming the promise he could see in her eyes.

Finishing the sandwich, she folded the paper and put it back in the bag. "Okay." Sara hugged herself and stared out into the passing shadows. "How far to your ranch?"

"Not much farther, I think it's fifteen miles from my house to Rev. Mike's. We're just west of Kingsland. You can see Packsaddle Mountain from our kitchen window."

"You live with your brothers?" She hoped her questions weren't intrusive.

Daniel chuckled. "Don't get the wrong idea. We're all responsible grown men. Think of us like the Cartwright brothers on the old west show *Ponderosa*. Actually, we're thinking of building our own homes. If we ever have families, we'll need our own space. We're even looking at some more land we might buy."

"Oh, I wasn't judging. I think it's nice for a family

to be together." She knew exactly how lonely life could be on her own. "I met a new friend today."

"You did?" He automatically assumed male and a wave of jealousy swamped him. "Tell me about him."

"Her."

Daniel let out an inaudible breath as he turned off the main road and headed out into the more rural setting of Blackhawk land. The headlights pierced the darkness, illuminating a rabbit crossing the road. "What's her name?"

"Ryder Duke and she has two husbands."

He didn't sense any judgment in her voice at all. In fact, he picked up a hint of awe. "Jealous?" Daniel didn't question how anyone else wanted to live, but he didn't like to think of Sara wanting someone besides him...or in addition to him. In light of their circumstances, he knew his chain of thought was completely irrational.

Sara laughed sadly. "No, not jealous. I can't deal with the wayward one I have now." She shifted in her seat. "They just seemed so happy."

He nodded. "From what I've heard, they are. I don't know if she told you, but Ryder Duke is Ryder McCoy Duke and her husbands are the power behind OuterLimits, the company that's launching rockets into space and planning to send a manned mission to Mars."

"Wow. And I was selling slices of pie on the side of the road," she whispered disparagingly. "I wonder why she bothered with me?" Hugging herself tightly, she also wondered why Daniel was bothering with her.

Her comment didn't set well with Daniel. "Don't sell yourself short, there's a light within you, a pure energy that draws people." He cleared his throat, not mentioning the obvious attraction he had for her.

"I don't know about that," she muttered, uncomfortable talking about herself. "Anyway, it was nice. She said she'd call." Who knows if she would or not. "Enough about me. What do you raise on the ranch. Cows?"

As he turned onto Blackhawk lane, he smiled at her innate innocence. "The ranch is basically a cow/calf operation. The cattle numbers depend on available water. We run a mixed herd and when conditions are good, we expand with stocker cattle."

"Anything besides cattle?"

"Yea, we also have a Quarter horse operation at the ranch and soon, you'll find Grevy's Zebras, Nubian Asses, and Scimitar Oryx, to name a few of the beautiful exotics we're planning on bringing in. Some of these breeds are currently endangered in the wild."

"I'm impressed!" Sara couldn't help saying. "And to think, I just assumed you were some run of the mill cowpoke," she teased. "You're J. R. Ewing."

"Hardly. Ryder's brothers, the McCoy's, they're more akin to the Ewing's than the Blackhawk's are. In the old pairing of cowboys vs. Indians, I'll give you a hint…" He leaned over to speak softly. "We weren't the cowboys."

Sara laughed with delight. "I wondered. You have this sexy, exotic thing going on, but I have a hard time pinning people's backgrounds down. I never knew where the Riley's originated, as far as I know we're mutts."

Daniel grinned as he pulled into his normal parking place next to the barn. She thought he was sexy! "As far as I can tell, you ought to get down on your knees and thank heaven, because you've got some damn good genetics, baby."

"Thanks," Sara muttered, not knowing what else

to say.

He held up his hand for her to wait where she was and she did. When he came around to help her to the ground, she wasn't surprised. Daniel Blackhawk was a gentleman. Her hands lingered on his shoulders and the surrealism of the moment wasn't lost to her. In twenty-four hours, this man had turned her life upside down. Something deep down inside told Sara nothing would ever be the same again.

"You're welcome, Pet."

She noticed the nickname and she liked it. A warm feeling flooded her as he reached in the back for her bag. She let her eyes wander across the yard and the pastures beyond. A few well-placed security lamps illuminated the area and she could see a big house, multiple out-buildings, and land that seemed to stretch on forever. "Wow, this is nice."

"Thanks. We take a lot of pride in our home. Tomorrow, I'll tell you a little history of the place. Our dad taught us to be good stewards of the land, it's been in our family for over a hundred years."

As they moved toward the house, Sara could hear cattle making soft mooing and lowing sounds. "Are they greeting you?"

"Yea, the beggars, they're always wanting a handout."

"What breed of cattle do you raise?"

"Brangus and Angus crossbreds, with a few Longhorn mixed in. Benjen is implementing a non-hormone treated program, which allows the ranch to qualify our cattle for export. There's a lot more strategic planning in all of this than you'd realize."

"I'm sure there is." She took his offered arm when the path became too dark for her to discern the terrain. "Sounds complicated."

"The hardest part of the ranching business is Mother Nature," Daniel confided as they began to mount the steps to the house. "She's either working with you or against you, and she seems to work against you more often than not. Finding employees who are willing to work as hard as we do is a problem. One guy complained that we're the best bosses he's ever had, that we only make him work half days and we don't care which twelve hours of the day he works."

Sara laughed. "I can relate to a degree. The pies wouldn't make themselves and I had to start over every day. I'm sure you have to love ranching, it seems to be a lot of hard work."

"Yea, my dad always said that ranching is a business and needs to be treated as a business...but it's more than that, it's our way of life. We've implemented a lot of new things, like embryo transfer, but we live in a part of the world that's very rich in ranching heritage here in the heart of Texas. We still work our cattle on horseback."

"I can't wait to see you on the job." She lowered her voice when they walked through the door. "Oh, this is amazing," she whispered, captivated by the rich wood on the floor and the stone on the wall. "It's like your brought the outdoors inside. I expect to see a creek meandering through." Sara could see the place needed a woman's touch, but with four men living here, it didn't look too bad. "Yea, I'll enjoy taking care of your house."

"Wait until you see the kitchen, it was my mom's pride and joy. We've updated it a little, but she was ahead of her time." He smiled, remembering. "Mom was a wonderful cook, one of her greatest joys was taking care of us. She dished out as much wisdom and love in this kitchen as she did food."

Sara followed Daniel into a huge kitchen with oak floors and cabinets, granite tops, commercial appliances, and a dining table long enough to seat a dozen or more. "The double oven is a dream."

He watched her run a hand lovingly over the surface by the cooktop. "Watch this." He pressed a button and the venting mechanism rose up from a hidden pocket as if by magic. When she giggled with delight, he couldn't hold back his own laugh. God, she was pretty. He wished things were different and they were about to go to bed together. Speaking of… "I guess it's late, let me show you to your room." He didn't know where his brothers were hiding, but he'd love to get her safely ensconced away before they showed up and began their teasing routine.

"All right." As she followed him out of the kitchen and down a hall, Sara touched his arm. "Daniel, thank you for this. I've been scared…in the storage closet. Nothing's ever happened, but it wasn't a good place to be. I'll work hard for you, I promise. You won't be sorry."

Daniel couldn't take anymore. He opened the door, allowing her to step inside, then took her into his arms. "Stop it, there's no need to thank me. I'm being immensely selfish." He framed her face, gently kissing her lips. "I want you here. I want you here with me more than you'll ever know."

CHAPTER THREE

Daniel eased the bedroom door shut, resting his forehead on the wood for a heartbeat of two. Knowing Sara was on the other side made it hard to walk away.

Fuck! The woman was turning him inside out!

A noise from the front set his feet to moving. His brothers were home and he wanted to catch them before they started making too much racket.

On the other side of the door, Sara sat down on the edge of the tall bed, running her hand over the slightly worn quilt. There was no doubt in her mind that Daniel's mother made the quilt, she let her fingers touch the tiny stitches, reading the fine handwork like braille. The message she received from the raised threads was love. She hated to be envious, she'd had a great father, but growing up without a mother's love made her sad.

"What am I doing here?" she asked, gazing around the room. Sara pressed her feet into the floor and bounced a bit on the mattress. Sleeping in this soft bed would be heaven. A distant noise caused her to raise her eyes. Daniel was speaking to someone, most likely his brothers. She shivered and hugged herself, wondering at the twists and turns her life had taken. One thing was for sure, she'd never met anyone like Daniel Blackhawk. She had a sneaky suspicion he was the type of man who couldn't walk away from someone in trouble, particularly a woman. A wistful smile played on her lips as she remembered how he'd waded into the midst of those drunken bikers and saved her from their clutches.

The man was a hero.

In her darkest days, after Doug left her homeless and pregnant, she'd dreamed of being rescued. She'd lain in a series of narrow beds, in various shelters, and fantasized about someone striding with confidence into the communal room and announcing he was there to take her away.

At last, it had happened. She'd held out for a hero and he'd finally arrived. Pity, she didn't believe in fairy tales any longer.

Down the hall, Daniel entered the living room and found Easy and Sam standing around Benjen, who was carrying something in his arms like a baby. "What you got there?"

"A dog," Benjen answered tersely. "I could kill the person responsible for this in a heartbeat. Stupid-ass-fuckin-son-of-a-bitch. We found her on the side of the road, barely alive. She's been stabbed several times and her mouth was taped shut with fucking duct tape. Almost starved to death."

"We've been to the vet," Easy explained as he, Daniel, and Sam shared a look. They all knew how Benjen felt about animals. He couldn't stand the thought of one being abused. "She's going to be all right."

Daniel knelt down by Benjen. "Poor girl. With you in her corner, she'll be great in no time. What are you going to call her?" He took one finger to stroke the small terrier's paw.

"Hope." Benjen placed her gently on the rug in

front of the fireplace. "The doctor gave her pain pills, she's going to be out of it for a while. Did you bring the food in Easy?"

"I did." He set down a bag on the coffee table. "And her medicine."

"Let me get an old quilt to make her a bed." Sam turned to leave the room and Daniel grabbed his arm.

"Don't go in the spare room, it's occupied."

Sam froze and the other two men jerked their heads up to stare at Daniel.

"You didn't." Easy smiled. "You brought Sara home, didn't you?"

"Yea, y'all were right. Her husband's AWOL and she was sleeping on a damn cot in Mike's storeroom. When I found her tonight, she was fighting off a whole motorcycle club. She's not safe there. I offered her a job, we've been needing some help around here." He said his piece fast, then looked from one of his brothers to the other. "Anyone have a problem with that?"

Benjen stared at the small dog. "Not me."

Sam and Easy both answered simultaneously, "Fine with me," before Sam took off after a quilt and linens to make a dog bed.

Daniel expected nothing less from his family, he knew how they felt about standing up for those who couldn't stand up for themselves.

It was a family tradition.

* * *

After spending a restless night with Sara haunting his every thought, Daniel was up before the chickens. As he showered and dressed, he found himself stopping and staring into space every few seconds. Even his skin felt odd, like it was alive with static electricity. Finally, he realized he was nervous. With a huff of disgust at himself, he made his way out of his room and over to the room where Sara was sleeping. Lightly, he tapped on the door. He thought they'd have coffee together and sort out plans for the day. When she didn't answer, he eased the door open, expecting to find her in the bed. His imagination had given him a preview of her snuggled down in the covers, partially exposed from where the blanket had meandered to one side as she shifted in her dreams. He'd been hoping for a glimpse of creamy skin and lush curves.

No such luck. The bed was empty. She was already up.

Or, she'd left during the night.

With quick steps, he headed to the front room. He'd only gone a few feet when a heavenly scent assailed him. Cinnamon buns and coffee. Without looking to the right or to the left, he turned to the kitchen and found the old Mr. Coffee full to the brim and a pan of luscious pastries waiting on the counter. "Sara?" Strange. She wasn't here either.

Retracing his steps, he made for the living room, only to find Benjen standing in front of the fireplace. "How's Hope?" Daniel asked before he drew near enough to see for himself.

"Sleeping soundly," his brother answered. "They both are."

Daniel approached to find Sara spooning the little dog, it's head on her arm, both sound asleep. The sight squeezed his heart and he felt an overwhelming sense of rightness. "Well, I'll be damned."

Benjen looked up and caught Daniel's eye. "If you don't keep her, I will."

"Oh, she's already claimed." He gave his brother a straight look.

"Yea, the missing husband, I forgot."

That wasn't what Daniel meant at all, but he let the comment rest. Sara was stirring, her limbs shifting. "She's waking up."

Sara opened one eye. "Oh, gosh. I fell asleep. I'm sorry." She eased her arm from beneath the small dog's sleeping head, careful not to disturb her. "She was whimpering. I just wanted her to know she wasn't alone." Embarrassed, she tugged on her top and rose to her feet.

Daniel was aware that Benjen was staring at Sara with near awe in his eyes. Obviously, he'd found a fellow tender heart when it came to animals. "I'm sure she appreciated the company and I'm grateful you cared enough to pay her some attention."

"Sara, this is Benjamin, my brother. Benjen, this is Sara Riley." As he made the introductions, he remembered that Sara said her husband's last name was Wright and it heartened him to realize she didn't use it. Extracting her from this relationship was job one as far as he was concerned.

"I'm honored." To Daniel's dismay, Benjen took Sara's hand and kissed it. He barely restrained himself from pushing his brother back a few feet.

"Hey, what's going on?"

Sara looked up to see another of Daniel's brothers approaching, rubbing his eyes as he padded barefoot into the room. Another brother followed closely behind him, bracing one hand on the wall for support.

"Why don't you use your cane?" Daniel asked as he eyed Sam.

Samuel nodded toward Sara. "I could smell perfume. I wanted to appear manly."

"Fat chance." Daniel gestured to their guest. "Sara, this is Samuel and Ezekiel. Guys, this is Sara Riley."

"Hello." She shook their hands. "Sam, nice to meet you." She giggled when he hugged her neck. "Hello, Easy."

"Ah," Easy said with a laugh as he bowed from the waist, "I see my reputation precedes me."

"Hey, I didn't get a hug," Benjen complained as he gave Hope one last pet and rose from a kneeling position to get in line.

A growling noise emitted from Daniel's chest as he stepped closer to ward off any further displays of affection. "Watch it." He didn't like it that they'd gotten a morning hug and he'd been left in the cold.

The amused trio watched on as their big brother provided a human shield between them and the attractive brunette who appeared to be slightly confused as to what was happening. "Is anyone ready for breakfast?" she asked as she dodged around Daniel's large form to make for the kitchen. "I have cinnamon rolls ready and I see you have plenty of eggs and bacon."

"Cinnamon rolls?" Sam followed right behind her. "I love cinnamon rolls."

Daniel had no choice but to hang back as his siblings crowded ahead of him. He was beginning to wonder if this was such a good idea.

Over the next half hour, Sara prepared bacon, eggs, and toast for four strapping men. As she cooked the eggs to their specifications, they consumed the platter of sticky buns. The sweet pastries went fast and Daniel expressed his dismay that he hadn't received seconds. Sara just opened the oven and took out a fresh batch that had been keeping warm.

In the short period of time since they'd convened around the table, Sara had learned a lot. She kept everyone talking as she worked. "So, what's everyone's favorite food?"

Her question brought quite a response, everything from "lasagna," to "chicken and dumplings," to "pork roast and sweet potatoes," to "beef pot pie."

"Great." I'll check my ingredients and since I saw some chicken breasts in the freezer, tonight we'll have dumplings." She winked at Daniel, as the dish had been his choice.

He grinned with a sense of superiority. "Good choice."

"When is everyone's birthday?"

Again, she was met by a chorus of answers and she committed each to memory, noticing that Daniel's would be there before they knew it. "How do you usually handle lunch?"

After some discussion, she realized the situation varied every day. "I can just make a one-pot meal and keep it warm for whoever might show up. How does that sound?"

Daniel was beginning to realize this was going to be a bigger job for Sara than he realized. "Sandwiches would do just fine most days."

"Sure, sometimes," Sara agreed. "While you all finish up, I'll check on Hope and try to get her to eat something before I start cleaning house. Benjen, is it time for her antibiotic?"

Benjamin wiped his mouth and took off after Sara. "Yea, let's try to get some water down her. I have an eye dropper we can use."

Once they were alone, Easy raised his coffee cup to Daniel. "I have to say, you sure know how to pick 'em. This one's the complete package."

Daniel frowned. "I'm afraid I've made a mistake bringing Sara here."

Sara who was just about to return to the kitchen heard Daniel voice his concern. She didn't wait to hear more. Backing up rapidly, she excused herself to Benjen. "I have to go to my room for a moment."

"What do you mean?" Sam asked as he sopped the last of his soft eggs from the plate with a piece of toast. "I think she's great."

"I know she's safer with us, but I'm afraid she's going to end up working harder here than she did in the food truck," Daniel mused.

Benjen cleared his throat. "You need to work on your timing, big brother. Sara was coming to the kitchen for a spoon to dish up Hope's food and all she heard was that you think you made a mistake where she's concerned."

"Aw, hell." Daniel threw down his napkin. "Easy, you check on Elsie, she's gonna give birth today, if she didn't last night." He stood and pointed at Sam. "You take the Jeep and check on the water level in Honey Creek. We need to make sure it's still flowing free during this dry spell we're having."

"I'll take that last load of hay to the McCoys for you."

"Thanks, Benjen, that's what I was planning on doing." He gestured toward the hall. "I'm afraid I have more pressing matters at the moment."

"I think so. Tell her that she's welcome and we're glad to have her and those were the best cinnamon…"

Daniel was out of earshot before his brother could finish speaking. By the time he came to the door of the room where Sara had slept the night before, she was coming out with her small bag in hand. He didn't let her get a step further, he moved forward through the doorway and she had no choice but to retreat. "Where do you think you're going?"

"Away." She realized her mistake, she'd come on too strong. Assumed too much. She should've asked Daniel what he expected from her and left it at that. "Like you said, this was a mistake. Can I call a cab?"

He took her by the shoulders and backed her up against the wall. "Before we go any further, let me ask you one question. Just to make things crystal clear." He thought a second. "Well, two questions."

Sara's heart was hurting. She needed to leave. "Just make it quick. I need to go."

"No. You don't." He framed her face. "Question one. Do you intend to rid yourself of Doug Whatshisface?"

"Yes." She pushed against his broad chest and it was like trying to move a mountain. He was so close. So warm. So big. This was torture. He had no idea what he was doing to her. "I told you I intended to do that when I could figure out how. Lawyers cost money and I don't really know how to go about finding him." She huffed the words out, very near tears.

"Leave that to me. Question two."

His abrupt, take charge, minimalist style conversation was confusing. "I don't know what you want from me."

"Answer this question first." He passed his thumbs over her cheeks, looking deeply into her eyes. Daniel knew she had to be aware of what was happening to him. His body was pressing hers to the wall and his cock was getting harder and thicker by the second. "How do you feel…about me?"

Loaded question. Sara stared into his face. "What do you want me to say?"

"The truth." He gritted the words out between his teeth.

"Gratitude."

Wrong answer. "Is that all?"

His tone sounded a bit anguished.

"No." She looked down, unsure of what to say or how to say it. "I feel more."

He moved one hand to tilt up her chin. "Look at me."

She didn't want to, he could see too much in her eyes.

"Do you want me?"

A tremor of need flashed through her and she melted against him, pressing her face into his throat.

"I take that as a yes." He swept her up in his arms and stepped back to the bed, sitting down and holding her cradled to him. "For my peace of mind, before I kiss a married woman again, tell me I'm not out of line."

Sara soothed her palm over one side of his face, tracing the dimple at the corner of his mouth. "You're not out of line. Maybe I am, but I don't care. I've done without for so long."

"Done without what?"

"Anyone in my life." Affection. Love. Sex.

"Well, that's about to change." Daniel was mesmerized. He loved looking at her this close. There were flecks of silver in her eyes. Her mouth was so soft and sexy, with a natural bow shape. Her nose was straight, slightly tilted on the end, with a smattering of freckles dancing across it. "You're so beautiful," he whispered in a husky voice.

"Don't. I'm not."

Her voice was so soft he could barely hear it. "You are, you're the most beautiful thing I've ever seen in my life." His eyes went dark and he ran his hand up under that wealth of gorgeous hair. "Come here." Daniel pulled her face to his and covered her lips with his wide, firm mouth. He teased her closed lips with the tip of his tongue until she opened to him. His arms tightened around her, coaxing her as near to him as existing in two separate bodies would allow. The kiss he gave her was tender, slow, and incredibly thorough.

If he hadn't been holding her, Sara would've swooned. She loved the way he kissed her. No one had ever made her feel like this. It was perfect, it was right, it was like touching the stars after she'd spent a lifetime in a veil of shadow. She whimpered, moaning softly, helplessly, giving herself completely to him.

Daniel gave a gruff moan of his own, his mouth never leaving hers. He had to steel himself to not take it farther, his hands itched to cup her breasts, to learn how her nipples felt grazing his palm. He ached to run his fingers into the soft folds of her femininity to discover how wet she could get for him.

But he wouldn't, not yet.

He would bide his time and do this right. Crushing her mouth with his, he loved how her hands moved over his shoulders and chest as if she were hungry for what he only could give her. For long moments, Daniel rocked her in his arms, kissing her with breathless tenderness. Her taste was so sweet, every time he slid his tongue over hers, the exquisite friction felt like little explosions of delight. Unable to stop, he kissed her again and again – long, deep, and achingly gentle...until they pulled away, spent. He pressed her head to his chest and told her what was in his heart. "I don't want you to leave. I want you to stay. I don't know what the future holds, but I feel a connection with you and I need to learn everything about you I can."

Sara rubbed her face on his shirt, lifting her head

high enough that she could press a kiss on the warm, hair-roughened skin exposed by the two undone top buttons of his shirt. "There's not much to know. I'm almost twenty."

Daniel let out a groan mixed with a chuckle. "God, you're just a baby." But his baby, dammit. He used his teeth to graze a gentle nip on the tender flesh below her ear. "I want to know if you slide down the hall in your socks. Do you leave a trail of clothes behind you when you undress? Do you like bubble baths and can I give you one?"

Sara moaned, trembling in his arms.

"I mean, when you're free, can I kneel by the tub and touch you while you bathe?"

"Yes." All she could manage was the one word.

"Yes." He smiled. "To which question?"

She blushed hotly. "To all of them."

"God, baby, give me your mouth."

She lifted her face and he claimed her lips, kissing her until he was vibrating with need.

"We've got to stop," he groaned, "or I won't be able to."

She eased from his lap and he let her go. "What did you mean, in the kitchen, when you said this was a mistake?"

He stood up and ran his hands up her arms. "I just don't want you working harder here than you did in the food truck, that's all."

"Are you sure I'm not in the way?" She stared at his face, needing to believe him. Doug had told her what he thought she wanted to hear and none of it had been real.

"No, no, absolutely not." He traced a finger around her pretty lips. "After that breakfast, if you left now, my brothers would riot."

"Okay."

He kissed her on the forehead. "I'm going to head out and do some chores. After lunch, I'll show you around. Does that sound good?"

"Yea, perfect." A little dazed, Sara let him lead her out of the bedroom.

"Make yourself at home."

He froze in his tracks. "Hold on."

"What?"

He pulled his wallet from his back pocket. Sara noticed it was leather and attached to a side belt loop by a chain. No one would be pickpocketing Daniel Blackhawk. He pulled several bills out and handed them to her. "Here is money for your first month and here is more to buy whatever you need."

Sara's eyes widened. "This is too much." She tried to give some of the money back.

"No." He enclosed her small fist in his. "Keep it. You take stock of what we have in the pantry and the freezer and let me know if you need more." She didn't get a chance to argue, before he walked to his desk and extracted a key fob, then searched in the drawer until he found two keys. "I'm giving you a house key and a key to the Jeep. Use it when you want to. Okay?"

"You don't know me, Daniel. How can you trust me with this? I might rob you blind."

He didn't tell her that she'd already stolen his heart. "When I saw you risk your life for that child, I learned all I needed to know about you."

With a wink and a wave, he let himself out the door and Sara stood there, dumbfounded, watching him go.

…Three hours later, Sara sat down on the floor next to Hope. The little dog was sitting up and hassling happily. "You're doing so much better!" As she stroked the small head and looked into grateful brown eyes, it hit her that she was much the same as Hope. She'd been rescued. Most likely, the Blackhawk brothers regularly took in strays and she was one of them. "No." Sara shook her head, remembering what Daniel had said to her. She needed to believe him, she needed to believe in someone. "We're lucky, but we'll show them, won't we? You'll be the best guard dog in the world and I'll…I'll OD them on pies." Her heart was wide open, she was ready to be loved. Yes, she'd lost a few times in the game of life, but a person would only lose until they won. Right?

Letting out a satisfied breath, she mentally assessed everything she'd accomplished. Breakfast dishes were cleaned and put away. Lunch, a big pot of hearty beef stew, was ready in the slow cooker. The dumplings were rolled out and ready for supper and the chicken was simmering in a delicious broth. She'd also dusted the furniture and mopped the floors. To top off her morning's work, she'd baked two pies – a tart cherry for lunch and a pecan for supper. Glancing at the clock on the wall, then at the door, she let out a nervous breath. "Now, all we need is for someone to come have lunch with us, Hope." The dog's ears perked up as she watched the door. "You hear something, don't you?"

Sara barely got up off the floor before she heard boots stomping on the porch as the Blackhawk brothers knocked the extra dirt and dust off their feet. "Sara! We're home!" Sam announced their arrival – as if they could sneak up on anyone.

"Wow, something smells fantastic," Easy exclaimed as he hung his hat on a hook by the door.

"Hey!" Benjen greeted her, then his eyes fell to the floor. "You're up! And you're smiling!" He went to his knees next to the terrier. "I'm so glad to see you!"

Sara smiled as she saw the small dog's tail wag so hard, she almost fell over.

A touch on her arm caused her to jerk around...and there he stood. "Daniel. Are you hungry?"

He studied her face, then stared at her mouth. "Starving."

"Well...let's eat." She let him steer her to the kitchen and to her surprise, he sat Sara down and served her.

"This looks delicious," Daniel said as he filled her bowl, then his, with the fragrant stew.

Sara didn't know what to think. "This is my job."

"Looking around at the place, I think you've done enough for one day." Daniel hooked his foot around the leg of a chair and pulled it out so he could sit next to her. "Here, eat up. When we finish, I'm taking you for a ride on horseback."

"I need to work." Her response was weaker this time, for four men were giving her a steady, serious look that spoke volumes. One of those faces was fast becoming very dear to her. Telling him no, about anything, would probably be impossible. "I don't ride very well. I haven't had much practice."

"A Texas girl who doesn't ride?" Benjen asked the question as he snuck a piece of stew meat under the table for Hope.

"I admit my talents are few." Sara saw no use pretending. "I stayed at home and took care of my dad. I've never traveled. I didn't go to college." She pushed her hair over her shoulder. She'd also never had an orgasm, but that wasn't something to announce at the dinner table.

"You're young, your life's just beginning. There's time to do it all."

There was such optimism on Daniel's face and in his voice that Sara couldn't help but believe him. During the next half hour, she laughed more than she ever had before. The Blackhawk brothers loved to banter and joke, telling tales on one another. Anything, it seemed, to make Sara smile.

"You should've seen Sam, Sara." Easy laughed, pointing at his brother. "He always said he couldn't swallow a pill. Even when he had to take an Aspirin, Mom always melted it in water and fed it to him in a spoon."

Sam just shook his head, he'd been the brunt of this joke before.

"So, when he went into the hospital after the bull stomped him, he was refusing to take a pill. Told this nurse that he couldn't swallow it."

When Easy dissolved into another fit of laughter, Benjen took up the tale. By now, he was holding Hope in his lap and feeding her right off his plate. "He picked the wrong nurse to mess with, Sara. She wasn't a little lady, she was a big red-headed woman, reminded me of that female knight on Game of Thrones. I think her name was Bertha."

"Her name wasn't Bertha," Sam said calmly, "it was Maude."

"Ah, yes, Maude." Benjen drained his tea glass and Sara rose to fill it, making sure everyone had plenty. "When Sam asked Maude to melt his pill in water, you could actually see steam coming out of her ears. She told Sam that he'd either swallow that pill on his own or she'd climb up in the bed to straddle him and make him swallow it."

Sara giggled helplessly. "Most men would enjoy

a woman climbing into bed with them, wouldn't they?"

"Benjen is an ass man, for sure. But I think Maude was a wee bit wide in the stern." Easy stood to refill his bowl and Sara jumped to aid him. Daniel caught her arm, shaking his head.

"Let him wait on himself."

Sara frowned. She was almost about to say that it was her job – again. The rest of the men seemed not to notice.

"Daniel's not an ass man, are you Daniel?" Sam asked, trying to get a rise out of his big brother.

Daniel didn't blink, nor did he answer.

Sam patted his chest. "Our big brother likes big…"

"That's enough." Daniel raised his hand, effectively stopping the conversation.

Sara wanted nothing more than to cross her arms over her less than spectacular chest. Instead, she bowed her head while red roses bloomed on her cheeks.

"I think it's time you hooligans went back to work. I need to go out and check on the windmill to make sure the new gearbox I installed is working properly. I'm taking Sara with me to show her around the ranch." He could see they'd embarrassed her. He wouldn't say so, it would only make things worse, but he found every feature on Sara's body to be to his liking. From her spectacular ass to the breasts that he suspected would just fit his hands. She was lovely – from the tip of her upturned nose, to the tips of the dainty toes that he'd just glimpsed this morning when she'd been lying on the floor next to the injured dog. "Supper might be a little late."

"Oh, I have it almost ready to go. All I'll need to

do is thicken the broth and drop in the dumplings."

"See." Daniel picked his Stetson up from where he'd laid it in the spare chair. "We have time to play."

"You two have fun," Benjen said as he carried Hope back to her bed.

"Yea, make sure he takes you to the Slab. You'll love it there," Easy inserted his opinion as he picked up the empty bowls from the table and deposited them in the sink.

"I plan on it." Daniel wished he didn't get quite so much coaching from his family. "Make sure y'all check on Elsie, if she hasn't done anything by supper time, we might have to call the vet."

"Will do." Sam walked slowly to the door, picking up the twisted, highly varnished cane he didn't really like to use.

"What's wrong with Elsie? And who is Elsie?" Sara couldn't help but inquire as she put away the remainder of the stew, just enough for someone to have a late-night snack.

"Elsie's our milk-cow, she's a little Jersey, and she's due to have a calf just any minute."

Daniel grinned as Sara's eyes widened in wonder. "Can I play with the calf when it comes?"

"Yes."

"Can I pet it?"

"Yes."

"Can I name it?"

"Yes." He hooked his arm around her neck. "You can do everything but sleep with it, how's that?"

She looked a bit disappointed. "I bet the straw would be comfortable."

"We'll see," Daniel said, guiding them to the door. Since he planned on installing her in his bed, as soon as she was legally separated from her idiot husband, he didn't want her getting comfortable elsewhere – even in a pile of hay with a baby calf.

He held her hand as they made their way to the barn, explaining and sharing things as they walked. "We share the chores. I guess I play boss, being the oldest."

"How old are you?"

He felt a pang of doubt. "Older than you, I'm thirty. I'll be thirty-one in a few days."

"You're a man, not a youth," Sara mused. "I find that comforting."

"Comforting." Daniel wasn't sure that was the response he wanted to draw from her.

Not realizing that she'd made him doubt, she unknowingly eased his uncertainty. Looking up at him, she chewed on her lower lip. "Yea, you're all man. How big are you, anyway?"

Daniel chuckled. "My mom fed us well. We're all on the larger end of the scale. I'm six-foot five and weigh two-hundred fifty pounds."

"You're over two of me," Sara whispered with a bit of awe. Before she thought, her hand slipped to test the hardness of his bicep.

"I can promise my strength will always be used for you, never against you." He leaned in to speak into her ear. "And I'll be careful not to crush you, I'll be gentle when I love you."

Sara quaked with anticipation. "You sound so sure."

"I am." He'd never felt surer of anything. "The only thing that could keep me from wanting you, would be if you decided you didn't want me."

His admission thrilled her. She couldn't imagine a woman who wouldn't want him, but she was too shy to say so.

Inside the barn, he saddled up two horses and helped her mount. "Let's head toward the hills, we can get a good view of the whole ranch from there."

Sara clutched the reins tightly, her knees buried into the mare's side. "What's her name?"

Daniel could see she was nervous. "Apple." At Sara's surprised look, he explained. "She loves apples. We almost lost her to colic when she was a colt, because she ate too many green ones." Reaching across to stroke Sara's arm, he assured her that all would be well. "She's as gentle as a lamb and I'll be right next to you the whole time. Nothing will happen to you, I promise."

Sara relaxed a little. She trusted Daniel and the horse more than she trusted her own clumsiness. "I'll probably fall off like a sack of potatoes."

"Hold up." He had a better idea. Dismounting from his big stallion, he held up his arms for Sara. Daniel couldn't help but smile as she came to him like a dream, fully trusting he would care for her.

"We aren't going?"

"Oh, yea, we're going. We're just going to let Blackjack carry us both."

"Are you sure I won't overload him?" This horse was much bigger than Apple, but she didn't want to hurt him. "Where would I sit? Behind you?"

"He's part draft horse, so no." Daniel took care of Apple, then returned to her side. "Let me mount first and you'll sit in front of me." He climbed into the saddle and held out his hand.

She took it, but could see no way to maneuver into position. "I think this is harder than it looks."

"Nah, not hard at all." Daniel leaned over, clasped her around the waist and swung her up and into his lap. "Now, swing your leg over and just settle into me."

"Oh, good gravy," she muttered as her body nestled into his. She was firmly wedged between the saddle horn and…him.

"I'm gonna like this," Daniel admitted with a laugh as he wrapped his arms around her. "See, there's no safer place in the world for you than right here." He kissed the top of her head and relished the feel of her body leaning into his.

"I feel safe," she admitted. He would hold her tight, she wouldn't tumble out of the saddle. Of course, she was still in danger of falling – for him.

"Good." He headed the horse out the back of the barn and across the pasture. In the distance, she could see rocky hills and peaks. "This is really scenic, looks like the setting for a wild west movie." They were surrounded by brushy oaks, juniper cedars and mesquite. Large boulders peppered the landscape. The closer Sara came to the rocks, the more fascinated she became. "The stones look like they're encrusted with jewels."

"They are, they're quartz and granite." Daniel buried his nose in her hair and breathed deeply. "You smell so good."

Sara giggled. "Lemon dishwashing soap. I forgot to get my shampoo from the pub bathroom and I didn't want to use the last of yours, so I raided the kitchen."

Daniel rubbed his lips in her hair and kissed her head. "I feel like I've won the jackpot, like a kid who's been given the toy he always wanted. I can't keep my hands off you."

A thrill shot through Sara and her heart skipped a beat. "You say the wildest things to me. I don't know what to think about you."

"I know." Daniel tugged on the reins to carry them closer to the large stone-covered hill in the distance.

"I'll behave. For now."

As they rode, he pointed out Packsaddle Mountain, the Llano River, a cave many thought might have once contained silver, and a windmill. "We still use this to bring water up from the river to this part of the pasture, that way we can fence off sections for different breeds, or a few head we're separating for sale or a visit to the veterinarian."

When they came near to the tall rustic structure, Sara wiggled in his arms. "I would love to climb up to the top and see everything!"

"Not a chance, sugar. Too dangerous." He slung a leg over and hopped down, smiling when she slipped into his waiting arms without being beckoned. "I could get used to this." Daniel held her a moment before setting her aright. "We can look, but you can't climb. I'm not taking any risks with you."

"Do you climb it?" Sara walked to the windmill and stared up at its slowly turning blades. Things like this had always fascinated her.

He ground tied his horse and came to where she was standing. The sky was a beautiful blue, not one cloud blemished the expanse. "Yes, but I'm careful."

"You'd better be." She shivered at the thought of anything happening to him.

"So, you care?" he smirked as he asked, but her answer mattered to him.

"Of course, I care." While he checked the gearbox, Sara gazed toward Packsaddle. "Will you take me up on the mountain sometime?"

"We'll pack a picnic lunch one day, if you'd like." He wanted to do anything for her she asked. "This looks good, all it needs is a tiny adjustment." Taking a wrench from his back pocket, he adjusted a few bolts holding the gear shaft.

"I'd like that." She stepped a few feet away from him, seeing something glinting on the ground. "Look, Daniel."

When she raised up, she held out a tiny arrowhead for him to see, only about an inch and a half long. "I can't believe how small it is. And it sparkles, it's made from the same stone as those rocks we saw."

Finishing up, he moved to join her, taking the ancient piece of rock from her and holding it up between his fingers. "It probably belonged to some little boy, maybe for his first bow. He probably hunted pheasant with it."

Sara could imagine Daniel as a young boy, carrying a bow and arrow. "I'm glad you're here with me, that you're living now instead of a hundred years ago."

"I am too." He took her hand and they walked nearer the water reservoir. "Let me check the water level here. We have to keep a close watch, this has been a dry summer." They stood out in the open, watching the sun glint off the water. "Looks good, everything's working fine." Clearing his throat, Daniel broached a subject he'd been wanting to bring up. "Tomorrow, I want to call our lawyer and explain your situation to him. If I make an appointment, would you go talk to him?"

"Yes," she said a bit hesitantly, "on one condition."

Daniel didn't like the way she sounded. "What do you mean?"

"You take the money you would pay me for working and use it to pay the lawyer."

His heart clenched. "Why don't we negotiate the terms of our agreement later?" He brought her close. "I'd much rather you pay in kisses."

"Pay the lawyer with kisses?" she asked teasingly, knowing full well what he meant.

"No. I'll pay the lawyer and you give me the kisses." He bent close enough to layer his mouth to hers, rubbing his lips across hers tenderly. "I think I'll start collecting payment now."

Sara was just about to kiss him back, when she felt the hair on her head begin to raise. The sensation was so strange and scary that she tensed, a memory from years ago storming her mind. In the millisecond it took for her to mentally connect the dots, she panicked and grabbed Daniel's hand. "Run! Run! Run!"

Daniel didn't understand, he wanted to look around to see what the danger could be, but Sara's insistent demand and the terror in her voice, sent him moving along beside her. "What's wrong?" he asked as they sprinted across the ground in a dead heat, reminding him of the hundred-yard dashes he'd run in high school.

His question was answered one heartbeat later when a bolt of lightning came blasting from the blue and struck the very spot where they'd been standing only moments before. "God, help," Daniel breathed in awe, seeing the scorched circle of earth and imagining what it would've been like if they hadn't moved. "How did you do that?" He was panting with exertion and shock.

"A long time ago, when I was a little girl, I was playing with my dolls out near the quarry." She bowed her head and leaned it against his arm. "Suddenly, my skin started tingling and my hair lifted up. I didn't know what was happening, so I grabbed my dolls and ran. The next thing I knew, lightning struck the bench I'd been sitting on, blowing it to tiny bits."

Daniel wrapped his arms around her. "What is it

about you? You saved my life, just like you did the little boy." He kissed her once, hard, then squeezed her again. "A bolt from the blue. You know the same thing happened to me in another way when I saw you for the first time."

Sara was limp with relief that they were safe and his sense of humor was still intact. "Can we go home now?"

They looked around, but the horse was nowhere to be seen. "I guess he took off for the barn when the bolt hit."

"I hope he's okay." When Daniel put his arm around her, she clung to him.

"I'm sure he's fine." He kissed her forehead. "I'm just thankful we are. You're amazing, did you know that? You're my lucky charm."

Sara wasn't so certain. She didn't know if she was good luck or a lightning rod for trouble.

CHAPTER FOUR

As they made their way toward the ranch, Sara gradually began to feel better. She still glanced up into the clear sky, periodically, hoping another lightning strike wouldn't shatter the stillness. "That was close, huh?"

Daniel shook his head, still stunned. "When you started yelling for us to run, I didn't know what was going on. My first instinct was to stand my ground and fight whatever was threatening you. It all happened so fast, I saw your hair move, but I guess I thought there was a breeze I wasn't feeling." He removed his hat and raked a big hand through his own shaggy mane. "Only your frantic insistence kept me from being killed."

Sara smoothed her hand down the back of her head, making sure her hair was still lying flat. "If I hadn't experienced it before, I couldn't have known either, and probably wouldn't have panicked. When I was little, running toward home was my first instinct when something happened I didn't understand and that action saved my life. I never forgot how it felt and later, when I was older, I did some research. The lightning we experienced is called a 'positive giant' and can originate in a storm and travel fifty miles from its source before it strikes."

"So, this has happened to you twice." There was

still wonder and disbelief in his voice.

"Yea, maybe you shouldn't walk too close to me."

Daniel wrapped an arm around her shoulders and tugged her closer to him. "I would've come to check the windmill today, whether you were with me or not. So, maybe you were just in the right place at the right time to save me."

"Maybe." She tilted her head to look up at him. "If that's true, I'm glad I was here."

Over the next ridge, they found Blackjack. Daniel eased up to him, knowing the big animal had been spooked badly. "Good boy." He rubbed the horse's neck, soothing him. Once he was sure the horse was ready, he helped Sara mount, then climbed up behind her. "At least we can ride back to the house."

"I'm feeling better now, if you want to continue on with our plans, I'm game."

"You're game?" he teased. "You're cute, that's what you are." He pulled her hair off her neck so he could give her a kiss. "I'm fast becoming addicted to you, pet." Daniel noted the worn place in the knee of her jeans, the tiny gold cross around her neck, the slightly run-down running shoes she wore on her feet. Everything about her fascinated him.

At her suggestion, he headed Blackjack toward Packsaddle. "As promised, you'll get a good view of the area from up there."

As the horse started uphill, Sara clasped her arms over Daniel's as he held her tightly around the waist. "This is steep. Why do they call it Packsaddle?"

"Because of its shape, although I've never really seen the resemblance, to tell you the truth. My ancestors lived on this land long before my grandfather on my mother's side purchased it in the early 1900's."

"You mean your Indian ancestors? Or do you prefer to be called Native American?"

Daniel shrugged. "I'm not picky. Being called an Indian doesn't bother me. In fact, I sort of like it." They rode to a plateau about midway up what the locals called a mountain, even though it was less than seventeen hundred feet in height. "Look out there. This is all Blackhawk land." He jumped down, then helped her to the ground. "Right here in this spot, in 1872, the last skirmish between the Calvary and the local Indian tribe took place."

"Was anyone hurt? Why were they fighting?"

His voice became emotionless and he repeated the facts as a tour guide would. "According to the historic record, there were twenty-one Indians camped out, some sleeping. Eight armed ranchers came upon them. The look-out for the Indians happened to be asleep, exhausted maybe. After the battle, one of the white men lay wounded and most of the Indians were killed. The band of settlers said they were tracking the Indians after one of their cattle had shown up with an arrow in its side. The wording on the marker down on the highway reads that 'the brave men routed a band of Native Americans thrice their number'."

"I'm sorry." She could tell the event meant more to him than a footnote to history.

"No need to be sorry, it was a long time ago. My great-great grandfather was one of the ones killed, but I have no information other than what's been handed down to me. The conflict is well known, a whole nation was outnumbered and pushed out of their home by a people with superior weapons. Such things are the way of the world."

Sara came up to him and put her arms around his waist. She kissed him between his shoulder blades.

"Sometimes I wonder why things work out the way they do."

"Just this past March, some kids vandalized the historical marker I was quoting, or at least I think it was kids. They painted over the marker with black paint. 'White history celebrates genocide.'" He knelt and chunked a rock down the hillside.

Sara squatted next to him. She knew emotions ran high. Just a few weeks before, riots and demonstrations had broken out all over the south, protesting the removal of Confederate statues. "I think we're all a product of what we've been taught. Different perspectives. Nothing is ever as black or white as it seems."

"I agree," he told her, "no one alive today is responsible for anything that happened in the past, yet we all have to live with the consequences." He pointed toward the highway. "After the marker was defaced, the sheriff showed up at our ranch and questioned me and my brothers about the incident."

"Did they think you might know who did it?"

"No, they searched our property for black spray paint."

Sara was taken aback. "Why? You're grown, respectable, model-citizens. Land owners. Tax payers. How dare they!"

Daniel became amused at her defense of his family. "Yea, that's what I said!" He laughed. "My history with this particular sheriff is a little shaky."

She glanced at him with affection. "Did you raise a lot of hell when you were younger?"

"No." He shook his head. "Just the normal amount of hell."

"They didn't find any paint, though. Right?"

"No, but even if they'd found some, that wouldn't

have meant we vandalized the marker." Daniel didn't really know why he was telling Sara this, he sure wasn't ready to admit the shame of his past. The safest thing would be to change the subject. "Come on, let's head back. We'll save the Slab till it gets cooler tonight and I'll take you swimming. How does that sound?"

"Perfect." She grinned at him. "I love the fringe benefits that come with this job."

As he helped her astride the horse one last time, his hand grazed the curve of her hip. Daniel felt his cock respond to the slight touch. "If you think these little excursions are something, just wait until you learn the other perks I have in mind."

"Oh, really?" His lighthearted teasing made her happy. Once he was settled behind her, Sara relaxed in his arms. "I'm all about perks. There weren't many advantages to working at the Dam Pub, if you didn't count the free peanuts they kept on the bar."

He took her right hand in his and held it to his mouth, kissing the empty ring finger. "This is better than peanuts, I promise. In fact, I can't wait to explain to you all the opportunities for advancement."

She wasn't immune to the promise in his words, but instead of feeling confident in the future, she felt uneasy. Sara had learned from harsh experience that things seldom worked out the way you hoped.

* * *

Putting aside her worries, Sara let herself enjoy the ride. Daniel urged Blackjack to a trot and the wind in her hair felt good.

"Look, I think you've got company."

"Me?" Sara held her hand over her eyes to shade them from the sun. "That's Ryder! I can't believe she found me."

"News travels fast." He pulled the horse to a stop between the house and the barn. "Does it bother you for people to know you're here with me?"

"Not at all." Sara held her arms out for him to take her even before he was in position. "I just can't imagine why she's here."

"To enjoy the pleasure of your company, why else?" He clasped her close, grinning as she gave herself into his care so naturally. As far as he was concerned, they were making headway. When she would've slipped away, he held her fast for a fast moment. "Hold on, don't send me off without a kiss." She clasped her arms around his neck and gave him what he needed. "I'll be back in a few hours. Have a good time."

"I will." I hope. She glanced down at her casual attire, wishing she didn't look so unkempt. "Hi!" Sara raised her hand in greeting as she walked toward the elegant woman leaning next to her sports car.

"Hey, yourself! Hope you don't mind that I dropped by for a visit. I stopped at the pub and Mike told me you were here." Ryder glanced over to watch Daniel ride off across the field. "I can't say I blame you, this looks like a much nicer place to hang out." She gave Sara a friendly grin. "Better clientele."

"Daniel offered me a job. I have my own room and everything." She blushed, unsure how to explain something she didn't really understand herself.

"Hey, no judgment here. Remember, I'm the one in the polygamous relationship."

"One can't argue with happiness, I don't think." Sara showed Ryder in. "I'm so glad you're here, I look forward to getting to know you."

"Thanks. I came here with a purpose, I'm not stalking you, I promise."

The very idea made Sara giggle. "I didn't think that at all, I'm thrilled to make a friend." She was also glad she'd cleaned the place this morning. "There's still a lot to do here. Four men living together can leave things a bit…cluttered."

Ryder scoffed good-naturedly. "Don't I know it? Believe me, Pepper and I have been cleaning up after our four brothers for years."

"Come to the kitchen, I'll fix some coffee. There's pie too, if you'd like some."

Ryder ran her hand over the smooth wood of the sturdy dining table. "Coffee's great, I think I'll pass on the pie. I consumed enough calories last night sampling all three of your pies, I need to hit the gym instead of eating more."

"I understand. I don't eat many of my own wares. If I did, I'd be big as a house." She put on a pot of coffee to brew. "So, you live near the pub?"

Ryder shook her head, her long golden brown hair tumbling down her back. "I live a few miles away, up on the east side of the lake. My family runs Canyon Eagle resort and our ranch adjoins that property. I married our next door neighbors, so I didn't move far."

Sara picked up a dish towel and pleated it. Ryder had said nothing amiss, but the chasm separating them as far as wealth and position was concerned seemed vast to her. "I don't suppose you work, do you?" As soon as she voiced the question, she blushed. "I didn't mean that in a bad way, everyone works at something."

With a laugh, Ryder touched Sara's hand. "I know what you mean. I wear a couple of hats, actually. I'm involved in running my brother's businesses and I do some volunteer work at the hospital. My brother, Jaxson, really picked up that banner since he was injured." She tapped the table with one long, elegant fingernail. "He talked to Samuel Blackhawk when he came in for rehab the other day." Seeing Sara's perplexed expression, Ryder explained, "I know Sam was injured in a fall he took at the rodeo during a bull ride. My brother, Jaxson, suffered a similar injury, then he'd barely recovered from that accident when he reinjured the leg in an incident at or ranch." She let out a long breath. "He ended up losing the leg."

Sara expressed her concern. "Oh, no. I'm sorry."

"Well, you know how things work, silver linings and all. He's really done some great work in a rehab/support group he sponsors at the hospital. It deals with everything from amputations, to PTSD, to head trauma, and brain injuries."

"I didn't know Sam…needed therapy."

"Oh, I think his visit was just routine." Ryder waved her comment away. "I'm not saying anything about that, the subject I'm…awkwardly trying to broach is a fundraiser I want to propose." She cleared her throat and shifted in her seat. "After tasting your magnificent pies, I was wondering if you would help me put on an auction. We could have a get-together at Highlands Ranch and serve BBQ, invite all the movers, shakers, and wheeler-dealers I know and get them to bid exorbitant amounts for your pies as donations to the hospital."

"Oh, wow." Sara smiled, feeling flattered. "Of course, I'll help. I'd be honored. Just tell me what you need and when you need it."

"Great!" Ryder clapped her hands together. "I'm so pleased!"

Sara rose to pour their coffee. "Me too. I've been wanting to do something extra, to sort of fit in to the community. Working at the Dam Pub was great, but I never really had time to do anything but bake."

"And here I am asking you to bake more."

"No, no." Sara set Ryder's coffee in front of her, then moved containers of sugar and creamer nearby. "This will be different and I can contribute something worthwhile to a good cause."

"Oh, I think you've done a lot of good. A reporter was asking about you at the pub when I was there, wanting to interview you for a human-interest piece about saving the little boy."

Sara blushed. "I'm glad I wasn't there."

"I understand. I avoid publicity myself." Ryder raised her eyebrows. "My husbands are famous in their field, but we try to keep our private life private."

"I'm sure you do. People can be cruel. Some live to judge people for their differences." She thought about what Daniel had shared with her about the battle when his great grandfather had been killed and how his family's guilt had been assumed in the vandalism.

"Samson and Gideon's family are from Hawaii. Their mother is descended from Polynesian royalty and the practice of having two husbands is tradition. She, herself, has two adoring men in her life. I…" she laughed and blushed, holding her hands to her cheeks, "I was just lucky enough to catch the eye of the Duke brothers and I couldn't imagine my life any other way." She took a sip of coffee. "Although, I will tell you that my conservative, cowboy brothers definitely had a problem with my decision, until my future husbands proved their worth in my family's eyes by risking everything they owned to protect me."

"Wow, sounds like a romance novel."

Ryder swirled her coffee in her cup and gave Sara a wink. "Your situation here has definite possibilities. Is romance in the air at Blackhawk Ranch?"

Sara chewed on her lower lip. "Well...my situation is complicated." She dipped her head and covered her eyes. "I can't deny that I feel something for Daniel, but we're not in a position to do anything about it...yet."

"I won't pry." Ryder held up her hand. "Just know that I want to be your friend. My sister will be back home in a few days. She's touring with her husband." At Sara's inquisitive look, Ryder provided the answer. "Pepper's married to Judah James."

"Oh, wow."

"Yea, they had a tumultuous courtship, but they love one another madly. Anyway, once she's home, we can get together and plan the auction."

"Sounds perfect. I can't wait."

Ryder drained her cup. "Well, I need to go. I'm expected at home soon. My husbands like for us to have dinner together every night possible."

"I'm sure you love that." Sara couldn't even imagine their interactions.

"Oh, I do," Ryder assured her. "I definitely do."

Sara was a bit surprised when the other woman impulsively hugged her. "Thanks for coming to see me."

"Thanks for volunteering to help with the fundraiser!" She picked up her purse and started for the door. "After tasting your pie and remembering your friendly face, I just had to come up with an excuse for us to do something together. Fate, you know. Sometimes you just have to go with it. Things happen for a reason."

As Sara walked Ryder out, she contemplated her words. A flood of change had come upon her, a hero had come charging into her life, plucked her from an unfortunate situation, and delivered her into the safety of his keeping. Whether or not this was fate, she did not know. But…if Daniel Blackhawk was her destiny, she would welcome her future with open arms.

* * *

As evening fell, the Blackhawk brothers began making their way to the homestead. She was all ready for them, having prepared the chicken and dumplings, green beans with bacon, and corn on the cob. All of this would go well with the pie she'd made earlier. So much had happened since the sun rose, Sara felt as if a week had passed.

Hope alerted her when Benjen arrived, hobbling to the door and whining a greeting. She knew the cute little mutt wasn't hungry, she'd had her fill when Sara deboned the chicken earlier. "Hey, girl!" The big man bent to scratch his canine admirer behind the ears. "You're looking better."

"Yes, she is, I think. I gave her the medicine and changed her bandages already," Sara announced as she set the table with pottery plates and bowls. "Are you hungry, Benjen?"

"I am, indeed. Have you had a good day, Sara?" He came striding into the kitchen with the dog in his arms.

"I have." She nodded. "A busy one."

Easy came in from the hall, drying his hands on a small towel. "Busy isn't the word for our Sara's day. I see she's cooked up a storm and if my eyes weren't deceiving me, she entertained one of the Highland McCoys no less."

"Wow." Samuel joined them, taking off his boots at the door. "The McCoy's! If we're receiving visits from those society folk, we're definitely coming up in the world."

Sara was very aware when Daniel came into the room. She could feel frissons of excitement break out across her skin. To stop from staring or reacting, she busied herself by filling glasses with sweet iced tea.

"I just called the vet, Elsie's going to need a little help. I'm afraid the bull we bred her to has produced a bigger calf than she can handle alone. A couple of us should be here to help him."

"I'll do it," Benjen offered.

"Me too," Sam chimed in.

"Good." Daniel took a seat, then patted the one next to him. "Sit here, Pet."

At the term of endearment, three pairs of eyes settled on them. Sara cursed her tendency to blush as she sank down into the chair.

Daniel didn't give them any time to conjecture. As he held her bowl to the tureen and filled it, then did the same for his, he let them know what was on his mind. "After we eat, I'm taking Sara to the Slab. She's earned a reward."

Easy closed his eyes and sighed over his first bite of the savory chicken stew. "I'd say a reward is well earned. These are the best dumplings I've ever tasted."

"True enough, but the deed of which I speak is of far greater import than the miracles this lady has performed in the kitchen." The spoons carrying food to his brother's mouths froze mid-journey. When he saw that he had their attention, he went on with his story. His voice softened. "Sara saved my life today."

"No, I didn't. It was mere luck," she protested softly.

"What happened?" Benjen asked with concern.

Daniel looked from one brother to another. "I took her out for a ride and we stopped at the windmill so I could check the output after I installed the new gear box. When I was through, we stepped away to look at an arrowhead she found." He paused for effect.

"What was it? A rattlesnake?" Sam asked, mesmerized.

"A cougar?" Easy's eyes were wide with curiosity.

"One of the sheriff's cronies take a potshot at you?"

This last suggestion from Benjen troubled Sara. "What do you mean, a potshot?"

"None of those things." Daniel held up his hand. "Somehow, Sara became aware of energy in the air. Her hair stood up, like this." He picked up a strand of dark silk and held it high up beside her head. "I was too spellbound by her beauty to notice, but she grabbed my hand and yanked me to safety. In the next breath, a huge, jagged bolt of lightning cracked the sky open and plunged into the very ground where we'd been standing only moments before."

"Jesus," Benjen breathed. "Lucky she was with you."

"That's what I told her," Daniel covered her hand with his. "She tried to brush it off as nothing, but I am thankful she was standing next to me when the bolt from the blue came and I'm thankful she's here with me tonight."

The brothers echoed Daniel's gratitude and by the time the meal was finished, Sara was ready to escape center stage. She jumped up to do the dishes, but Easy wouldn't stand for it. "While Ben and Sam go meet the vet, I'll clean the kitchen." He nodded toward the door. "Daniel, you take our heroine for a cool dip in the river."

Daniel clapped him on the shoulder. "Thanks, bud." Meeting Sara's eyes, he gave a head nod to indicate that she should go. "Change into your swimsuit, then slip on a dress or a cover-up of some kind. I'll grab some towels and a bottle of wine. We'll take the Jeep and go around by the road. You won't have to ride a horse tonight."

Sara nodded and took off, but she didn't get so for that she didn't couldn't hear Easy joshing Daniel. "Save a horse, ride a cowboy, huh?"

A few minutes passed before the teasing made sense to Sara. When it did, she fell on the bed and covered her head with a pillow. She wasn't a virgin, but she was so near, she might as well have been. She wasn't completely ignorant, her brief tenure as the unwanted wife of Doug Wright, didn't mean she was unaware of the whispered ways and rewards of the sensual act. Sara understood that Daniel wanted her…or he thought he did. He didn't realize that she wasn't good at sex, she was more than likely frigid.

Save a horse, ride a cowboy?

She wouldn't even know how to start.

Once she regained her composure, Sara changed clothes, putting on a modest bathing suit, then pulled a wrap-around sundress over it and donned a pair of sandals. She grabbed a tube of sun cream that she'd used to protect herself when she'd make her walks to the store for groceries in the heat of the day.

Taking time for one peek in the mirror, she put on a dab of cherry lip gloss, a swipe or two of waterproof mascara, and went to meet Daniel. The outing set her a bit on edge, but in an enjoyable way. She longed for a bit of fun and there was no one's company she enjoyed more than the handsome cowboy whose days seemed to be intertwined with hers in some indiscernible way.

Daniel was waiting, albeit impatiently. He wasn't

so much restless about waiting as he was anxious for Sara's company. He'd thought about her all afternoon, how she'd acted in time to save them both, how fuckin incredible it felt to hold her as they'd ridden together on the horse. The only thing holding him back was those damn vows she'd taken and when morning came – he'd set out to see what could be done to aid her in undoing them. Until such time, he'd keep his hands to himself.

Well…mostly. Daniel knew he wouldn't be able to resist her completely.

"Ready?" she asked from the doorway.

He stood, wearing a pair of jeans and a tank top. The sun would be far enough down in the west to still give them light, but not be so bright as to be painful. Beneath his jeans, he wore a pair of swimming trucks and he, too, wore a pair of sandals on his feet.

"Oh, yea, I'm ready." She looked as fresh as a damn daisy. He could picture her running through a field of wildflowers, her hair bouncing in a high ponytail, a smile on her face bright enough to put the stars to shame. "I've been ready a helluva long time." For you.

"Sorry, I hurried."

"No worries." He herded her out to the Jeep, lifting her into the seat.

"This is becoming a habit," she murmured. "I'm not helpless, you know."

"Tis a habit I have no wish to break. Each time I'm privileged to touch you is a cause for celebration."

His heated declaration sent tingles between Sara's thighs and she bowed her head, unable to meet his eyes without giving away how confused and aroused he made her feel. "I can't wait to see the Slab, isn't that what you call it? I keep thinking about the ice cream place, makes me hungry for a cheesecake cone."

"When we go into Austin to meet with Saucier, I'll buy you an ice cream cone." With that edict, he started the engine, put the vehicle in gear and they started off. The vehicle was open air, so she wound her hair around her fist to keep it from flying about.

"Okay?" Daniel asked, observing her expression when he went off road and he saw she was clinging to the overhead roll bar.

She nodded, giving him a faint smile. He slowed down for her, placing a steadying hand beneath her breasts. The contact burned in the most delicious way, making her nipples swell and ache. "I'm in so much trouble, so much," she whispered to herself.

The distance to be covered from the rock house to the Slab wasn't far, but to Daniel it seemed like forever. He didn't know why this felt so momentous, sentimentality wasn't usually his forte. He'd been on his share of first dates in his life, but this felt like his last first date – and that was damn special. Daniel let his knee nudge the canvas bag holding the wine, glasses, and cheese he'd brought along. Yea, plastic would've been a smarter choice than his mother's crystal, but he wasn't thinking too clearly these days.

Sara was so busy sneaking glances at Daniel – god, the guy was sexy – the natural wonder they parked beside took her by surprise. To be told about it was one thing, to see the Slab was another. "Oh, how beautiful!" She'd always loved this part of the world, tubing had been a treat for her when she was allowed to go. For Sara, swimming in the quarry had been forbidden, her father said it was too dangerous. Many local kids crept onto their property and took a dip, but she never disobeyed her dad. They'd gone through too much together and she always tried to be his good girl.

"We're in luck, I think we're going to have the place to ourselves." He gathered their towels and the bag, finding a place in the shade to spread a blanket.

"The colors are amazing." Sara was enthralled by sight of the blue water cascading over the pink and orange granite. "Are the rocks sharp or can you walk on them?"

"No, they aren't sharp. Eons of water flowing over the rocks have worn them smooth."

Daniel stripped off his shirt and Sara forgot all about the rocks. Her breath hitched in her throat and her heart skipped a beat. She knew he was sinfully handsome and solid as an oak – what she hadn't known was that his body would be so magnetically beautiful. "Oh, I see…" And see, she did. She couldn't help but stare at the perfection of the planes and angles of his chest – the rippling muscles, the chiseled abs – bronzed and inviting her touch. Sara pressed her lips together so her mouth wouldn't drop open.

"Sara, are you ready?" Poised to help her down the rocky path, he glanced up. When Daniel looked at her face, he became aware of her inner turmoil. The heat in her eyes reflected the heat in his own. "Give me your hand." He offered his and held her gaze until she took it, placing her palm directly over his. At the contact of skin on skin, Daniel shuddered, the pleasure radiating all over his body. She might as well have been stroking his dick, for it jerked and swelled in his trunks.

When he aided her steps to come even with him, he could tell her breathing was as uneven as his own. "Allow me." He helped her to the blanket. "Let's take off your cover-up, you'll be cooler." Daniel's teeth clamped down on his tongue, not only to provide some alternative sensation to the rise of passion in his blood

– but also to prevent him from saying what was on his mind. He was dying to see more of her body. If his imagination was even halfway close to reality, the sight would bring him to his knees.

"You brought wine?" Fortifying her courage seemed like a good idea. She held onto the ties of her dress, thinking it provided a shield, an illusion that what lay beneath might be as perfect as the man standing before her.

"Yea, want some?" He could wait. He could wait. Not for the wine – for her. Dropping to his knees, he uncorked the bottle and poured them both a glass, holding one out to her.

With a shaking hand, she took it, bringing it to her lips with such haste that she splashed a drop or two high on her collarbone. "I'm so clumsy," she said in apology.

Daniel rested his glass on the flat surface of a stone. "Allow me." He took her glass, sat it next to his, then moved closer. He wasn't thinking – he was reacting to a need greater than any he'd ever known.

For Sara, the moment crystallized, like the flying seeds from a dandelion flower being captured in amber forever. Even though she made no move, every fiber of her being reached out to him. She held perfectly still as his head bent, the first touch she felt was his breath on her skin.

And then his lips brushed her flesh and she gasped, fire flaring through her body when his tongue soothed and claimed the droplets.

"Daniel…" she whispered, her whole body electrically alive in response to his touch.

He could feel her sweet surrender. All he had to do was reach out and take what had already been given into his care.

"Hey! Let's go!"

A childish voice broke the spell. They were no longer alone.

A harsh sigh of regret exploded from his lips. "We have company." He observed a shadow of regret pass over Sara's face. He shared that disappointment. "The locals pay no attention to boundaries and we choose not to enforce them at this point."

She nodded. "Cutting off access to a place so enchanting would seem criminal."

Daniel nodded. He felt he same way about that damn dress she was wearing that shielded her body from his hungry gaze. "Do you want your wine?"

She took the glass he held out to her, bringing it to her lips. To hide her nervousness at his proximity, she took more than a mere sip. "Is the water cool?"

Daniel sipped his own wine, willing his cock to be patient. "It's refreshing. We'll take a dip in a bit. I didn't bring tubes, but we can wade." He winked at her. "Gives me an excuse to hold your hand."

Sara swallowed more wine, it was really tasty. "I didn't think you needed an excuse." She licked her lips.

Daniel found it hard to respond, he was hypnotized by her pink tongue peeking out to capture the vestiges of the wine. "I don't." He couldn't be plainer than that.

She took another sip and then another. "You know what's funny?" At his quizzical expressions, she went on, "I lived in a pub and this is my first taste of alcohol." Sara gave him a tiny, mischievous smile. "I think I like it."

Daniel chuckled, taking her near empty goblet from her. "One glass of wine and you're tipsy?" And cute as hell.

"I guess." She threw her head back and the sensual line of her throat made Daniel groan. "Makes me feel all warm and…" When she brought her head back into position there was a very recognizable heat in her eyes. "…hungry."

Daniel knew the feeling. He noticed the kids had floated on down the river. They were alone once more. Against his better judgment, he gave into temptation. She didn't protest when he pulled at the strings holding the sundress in place.

Sara found herself tongue-tied. A moment ago, she'd been ready for more and now she felt vulnerable. In her wine-fogged state, she'd forgotten that he'd wanted to see her. She stiffened, closing her eyes, not wanting to witness his reaction. She knew he was aware of her general shape, she was willowy…coltish. Not lushly feminine. "I'm not much…"

Daniel was torn between listening to Sara speak and appreciating the wonder he was unveiling. She was exquisite. Imminently feminine. Soft. Sweet. The white one-piece she wore showcased every golden inch of her delectable form. While it covered everything, it revealed a shape so perfect, he could barely speak. "You're so beautiful." He swallowed, then moistened his lips. "Seeing you like this, having you so near, knowing I can't have you…" He closed his eyes and fought for self-control.

"I'm not his."

Her soft declaration stunned Daniel. She was giving him permission to do something he was dying to do. "I want you so much," he muttered in a coarse whisper, "what I feel is so much bigger. My soul demands that I treat you with honor, with respect."

Sara swayed toward him. *He thought she was beautiful. He wanted her.* Yet, he was being gallant. A gentleman. The paradox was intoxicating. "Just a taste…please?"

A taste? He wanted to make a glutton of himself with her. "You don't have to beg me, everything I have to give is yours." He glanced around again – they were still alone. "I just want to protect you."

She went to her knees before him, seeking his warmth. "I just want to be close to you. I've been so lonely."

Daniel's eyes danced over her face, seeking a connection, craving her kiss. "God, what you do to me, Sara." He covered her mouth with his, drinking from the sweetness he found there. With lips and tongue, he proved his need, feeding her with the very sustenance he was starving for.

More. More.

With ragged breath, he devoured her, running his hands over her back, up to her shoulders, and down to cup her breasts. He moaned at the feel of her in his palms, the firm globes, the berry-hard nipples. The thin cloth between his hand and her flesh was little barrier to his quest.

Sara strained against him, pushing her breasts into his grasp, feasting on his mouth as if she couldn't exist without his kiss. She'd never known such desire was possible. Giving herself to him – if he wanted her – seemed paramount. With fevered strokes, she caressed his shoulders and back, letting her nails score the hot, hard muscles she couldn't seem to touch enough.

The whimpers coming from her throat fueled his desire and Daniel reached the limits of his restraint. "I have to…I can't stop." Shielding her with his big body, he pulled down the top of her bathing suit, freeing the mounds of her breasts. With a moan of wonder, he let his eyes feast on the twin globes. Full, round, and firm, the nipples tilted upward seeking his mouth. He framed them, his hands so hungry they shook with ardor. "So perfect," he breathed as he touched them, absorbing their beauty, the silky skin, the pillows of womanly flesh, the succulent, distended nipples that he had to draw into his mouth – lest he die. "Sara…" he whispered reverently as he brought one to his mouth and began to suckle.

Sara clasped his head, her mouth open, her head tilted back. The feel of his lips on her breast was the most perfect sensation she could ever imagine. Every tug made the place between her legs draw in on itself. She pressed him to her, wanting this never to end. "Oh, Daniel…Daniel…"

He swirled his tongue, he sucked hard, drawing pleasure with every draw. When his mouth on one wasn't enough, he began to knead her other breast, finding the nipple with his fingers and rubbing it between them. The sounds coming from Sara's lips gave him permission to partake of this most sumptuous bounty to his heart's content. He'd never received so much pleasure from a woman's breast and he found he couldn't get enough. If he could spend hours licking, kissing and playing, he would. When she bid him with a nudge to see to the needs of the jealous twin, he switched from left to right and set out to please her, and thus himself, with renewed zeal.

Sara was ablaze with rapture. She couldn't be still, her hips moving, her hands clutching. "Daniel, I can't stop…." Burying her face in his hair, she began to shake, a mad rush of fiery bliss consuming her.

When Daniel felt Sara shiver against him, he felt like a fuckin' conqueror. This beautiful woman was flying apart in his arms, paying him the highest compliment. As she trembled, he continued to nuzzle and suck, one hand sliding down to cup the quivering mound of her femininity. When his hand grazed the heated pad, she jerked, crying out. Mercy! She was coming for him, coming hard. Just from his kiss, his touch.

Sara pressed down on his hand, riding it, gasps of wonder erupting from her lips. "Oh, Daniel, Daniel," she cried, her body singing with a joy she'd never known. "I never knew," her voice broke in a whisper.

"I know…I know." He soothed her with his touch, tightening his embrace. This might be new to her, but Daniel had enough experience to recognize he held heaven in his arms.

CHAPTER FIVE

Sara stared at the pillow opposite hers. "If someone finds you in my bed, we're both going to be in trouble, I'm afraid." The big brown eyes looking back at her blinked once, but not a word of response was forthcoming.

"Okay, five more minutes." She placed a hand on the small dog and closed her eyes, but sleep continued to be elusive. A smile teased her lips. She couldn't stop thinking about the time she'd shared with Daniel. "Oh, my goodness," she whispered, remembering how he'd made her feel – what they'd done, how he'd whispered to her, telling her this was their first date of many. After he'd brought her such pleasure, they'd romped in the water like children, splashing and laughing. They'd stayed out until the moon was high in the sky and when they arrived here, to Daniel's home, he'd kissed her at the bedroom door and told her how one day soon, he wouldn't have to say goodnight.

"Oh, Hope, I'm falling for Daniel. So hard. So fast." As she stared out the window toward Packsaddle Mountain, she knew there was no use to continue lying about in the bed. "Come on, lazy bones, time to get up." Sitting up, she lifted the small dog to the floor. "Are you hungry?" This question got her a yip of an answer. "I thought so."

Sara yawned as she washed and dressed quickly, putting on the best she had to wear. She hoped it was good enough. Today, Daniel would be accompanying her to Austin to meet with a lawyer. She looked forward to the meeting and dreaded it at the same time. "Come on, we'd better get busy." Their absence from the ranch didn't mean the others should go hungry.

The smell of bacon frying brought Daniel's eyes wide open. One second later, he was smiling. He had the best reason in the world to wake up and start his day. There was a woman waiting for him, one who'd managed to wrap his whole soul and body around her little finger in a short amount of time. As he showered, he caressed his cock, recalling how she'd shuddered against him with the orgasm he'd given her. The first of many, if he had anything to do with it. He didn't take time to jack-off, he fully intended to be buried deep within Sara Riley the next time he came.

Once he was dressed, he made his way to the kitchen, to find his three brothers fighting their faces and staring at his woman with absolute adoration in their eyes. He couldn't fault them for it, he felt the same way. "What's this? Did you save me anything?"

"Not much." Easy waved his hand over the table laden with biscuits, gravy, sausage, bacon, eggs, and fried apple pies. "You'd better hurry and grab your share or you'll be stopping at a drive-through on your way south."

"You're spoiling these no-counts, Sara." Daniel set himself down and began to fill his plate.

She gave him a serene smile, but kept to herself the knowledge that she was doing her best to spoil him. "I don't know what time we'll be back, but there's a roast and vegetables in the crock-pot. For lunch, I found some smoked ham in the freezer, it'll be thawed out in time to make sandwiches."

"Thanks, Sara." Benjen ladled more gravy on his biscuits. "I got up for a drink of water in the middle of the night and found Hope's bed empty. You wouldn't know where the minx slept last night, would you?" he asked her with a twinkle in his eye.

"Haven't a clue." Sara put her lips together to whistle an innocent tune.

Daniel smirked, then sat up straight. "I forgot to ask, how's Elsie?"

"We've got a fine little heifer," Sam informed them. He bent over to adjust the cast on his foot. "I have to go into the hospital in Burnet to get this thing removed today. On the way in, I'll stop and pay the vet for last night's emergency visit."

"Good deal. I'll go check on them before Sara and I take off for Austin."

Sara, while listening to their exchange, sat down between Daniel and Easy to eat a piece of bacon wrapped in a biscuit. "Sam, Ryder told me about Jaxson's work at the hospital. Does he have a good program there?"

Sam looked at her inquisitively, but answered, "Yea, I think so. He's helped a lot of people, especially hard-headed men who hate to admit they need help. McCoy's able to talk about his own past problems in such a way that folks can see themselves in his story."

Nodding, Sara smiled. "Great. His sister asked me to help plan a fundraiser." She glanced at Daniel. "Ryder's got it in her head that she can auction off some of my pies to rich people for a pretty penny."

"She'll raise a fortune with your pies," Benjen said with near reverence in his voice.

"When will this be?" Daniel asked as he munched the last of his bacon.

Sara fingered the buttons on the front of her dress. "I'm not sure, the plan isn't firm yet."

"Just let me know what you need and when you need it. I don't want you trying to cart around a ton of staples if you need to restock the larder."

Daniel's offer didn't surprise Sara, she was fast coming to realize what a good man he was. Still, she did not wish to take advantage. "So, you don't mind?"

"Why would I mind? Sounds like a good cause and Ryder made a wise choice of a pastry chef." He stood and took his hat from the rack. "While you finish up, I'll check on Elsie's newborn. When you're ready, meet me out front. Zane's expecting us before noon."

…On the road to Austin, Daniel and Sara learned a lot about one another.

"I can listen to country music," Sara mused as she tapped her toe to the rowdy rhythm coming from the radio, "but I prefer rap."

"Rap!" Daniel spat the word like it burned his lips. "You listen to rap?"

"Ha!" Sara smirked. "I don't just listen, I can rap with the best of them."

"Seriously?" he asked with a grin. "Do it. Rap for me."

She thought a minute, then set a beat by snapping her fingers.

You could find me at the pub, cooking lots of pies.
Better than on the street, telling lots of lies.
Thought I was doomed to spend my days alone.
Till long came a cowboy and offered me a home.
His face is like an angel, his kisses taste like wine.
I try not to let it show, but damn the man is fine.

Slowing down, Daniel stared at her hard and for a moment, Sara was afraid she'd offended him. Before she knew what was happening, he whipped off the road and parked under a tree. "Come here, you sexy thing, you." After unsnapping her seat belt, he hauled her across the console with one powerful move.

She squealed with joy, then wrapped her arms around his neck and kissed him until she was dizzy with longing. "Did you like my song?"

"Oh, hell yeah, I like your song." He nipped her cheek. "Even more, I like you."

She cupped his cheek, loving the warmth and affection in his eyes. "If I had to choose between living a long life or having this time with you, I'd choose you, Daniel Blackhawk."

"Life's not the number of breaths you take, it's the moments that take your breath away, my Sara." Daniel swallowed, floored by her words. "And I plan on taking your breath away…over and over."

He leaned his head to hers. "As much as I'd love to continue holding you, we need to travel on. I told Zane a little bit about your case when I first contacted him, so he should have something to tell us today. The sooner we rid you of your husband, the sooner I can make you mine."

* * *

Daniel sat by, tense as a trap wire, while Sara told Zane her story. "I married Doug Wright a few days after my eighteenth birthday. He arranged everything and we eloped. A justice of the peace performed the ceremony."

"Do you have a copy of the license with you?"

She shook her head. "It's registered at the Llano County courthouse, I checked."

"Yes." Zane nodded. "When's the last time you saw your husband?"

Daniel's hand formed into a fist at the questioning

proceeded.

"He informed me the day after we were married that Dad's business was in trouble and he had to leave town to get a job." She blushed with shame at her naivety. "He told me he'd send for me when he got settled and found a place."

"And how long has that been?"

"Eighteen months."

Daniel watched Zane's face and wondered how he could be so calm. He guessed the lawyer heard things like this all the time, but his own blood pressure was spiking.

"And you've had no contact with him during this time?"

Sara shook her head in the negative. "I never talked to him again. The phone number he gave me didn't work." She shrugged. "I guess he lost my number."

Zane cleared his throat, but made no judgment. "Did he take anything of yours or your father's when he left?"

Sara nodded. "He took Dad's truck and all the money in the bank, both accounts." He'd left her penniless.

"How did he get the money? Did you give it to him?"

Sara coughed, then cleared her throat. "My mouth's dry."

Daniel jumped up to get her some water from a pitcher sitting on Zane's credenza. He poured a glass and brought it to Sara, wishing he could take care of all this mess for her.

Taking a sip of water, she looked down at the floor. "After my dad was killed, I was so distraught, I didn't know what to do. Doug stepped in and took care

of everything. He made the funeral arrangements…"
Her voice broke. "In the days leading up to the funeral
he was so good to me. He told me he loved me and that
he would take care of me. I didn't know what to do.
When he said he wanted to marry me, it seemed like
the answer. During those days before the funeral…and
even before he left on the job, he brought me papers to
sign." She began to cry. "I signed them. I trusted him."

Daniel wanted to stop this and talk to her, but
Zane held up his hand. "Not too much longer. I just
need a little history. Tell me how this all started?"

Sara forced herself to speak. "Doug worked for
my father for a few months, ingratiating himself into
my dad's life, making himself seen indispensable. He
was a great mechanic, he could fix any of the heavy
machinery. My father was not as young as he used to
be and Doug took a load off him. He didn't really court
me," she laughed wryly, "he courted my dad."

Daniel turned his head, looking out at the window,
listening, trying not to react.

"My father was always careful. He never drove
the loader or the dozer too near the lake. His policy
was to drag the stones to a flat area where they could
be handled easily." She looked down at her hands,
twisting her fingers together. "Something happened, I
guess he forgot. He drove too close, the loader turned
over and tumbled into the quarry. Doug jumped in
after him, pulled him out…but it was too late. He'd
drowned."

"Enough!" Daniel could see she couldn't take
anymore. Not now.

"I'm sorry, Sara. Daniel. I know that is painful."
Zane stood and poured himself some water. "I just
need some background."

"I understand." She picked up her purse. "Do you

have what you need?"

Zane stopped her with an indulgent chuckle. "Not so fast, you've done all the talking, now it's my turn."

Sara looked confused. "Sorry."

"Don't be, it's my job to solve your problem. Right, Daniel?"

"I hope so," Daniel answered, his attention on the woman beside him. She looked sad and defeated. He wanted the chance to change those things for her.

Gesturing toward Daniel, Zane Saucier returned to his seat, taking a folder from the right side of his desk. He opened it and spread out a couple of papers. "When Daniel called me, he gave me the name of your husband."

Sara flinched at the word.

"One of my staff checked the registrar's office in both Burnet and Llano Counties and we discovered the filed document. We also checked your father's tax record's, specifically concerning his employees." He tapped his pen on the desk. "What we discovered is that Doug Wright's name and social security number belonged to a man who died several years ago. Do you have a photograph of the man you married?"

"No, I don't. I don't have the same phone as I did then, and that's where any photos I'd taken were stored." Sara was stunned. "He used a false name? Why?"

"Could be many reasons. A criminal record. Another wife. Something to hide, apparently."

"Oh, my God," Sara said with shocked disbelief. She glanced at Daniel, expecting to see a disgusted look on his face. When she didn't, Sara was relieved, but still so humiliated she could cry. "What am I going to do?"

"Well, leave that to me. Excuse me a moment."

Zane pressed a button and smiled. "Presley, could you come in a moment?"

Sara moistened her lips and sought Daniel's hand. He freely gave it, squeezing her fingers gently and with reassurance.

"My wife." Zane gestured toward the door.

Sara looked up to see a pretty woman arrive with a soft drink in hand. She was dressed casually, wearing a Texas Longhorns T-shirt over a pair of faded jeans. "I'm not dressed for clients, Zane." She nodded at Sara and Daniel. "Forgive my appearance. Today is my day off and I've promised our munchkin a trip to the zoo."

At the mention of a child, Zane seemed to dissolve into a puddle of domestic tranquility. "Do you want to see a picture?"

Sara immediately agreed. "Please." She took a framed photo from the lawyer's hands and admired the little girl, who looked to be just out of diapers. "She's gorgeous! What's her name?"

"Lisa Marie." He grinned at Presley. "What else? We must carry on the tradition. I'm just glad she wasn't a boy or we'd be showing you a photo of Elvis."

Sara laughed, her eyes meeting Daniel's. "You must be so proud."

"Oh, we are," Presley assured her. Glancing between Sara and her husband, she asked, "Now, what can I do for you?"

"You're the expert in these matters, give Sara a rundown of how we're going to go about ridding her of this unwanted spouse." Zane sat back to watch his wife in action, a look of pride on his face.

Presley pulled up a chair to sit next to Sara. "First thing we'll do is attempt to find a photograph of the man if you don't have one."

"She doesn't," Zane affirmed.

"Can you think of anyone who might?" Presley asked.

Sara wracked her brain. "There was another employee of my father's, a man who retired not too long after…Doug…came to work there. I think there was a small get-together. He might have made photographs." She gave Presley the name. "Ned Sprague. He lives nearby in a small community called Bluffton."

Presley nodded. "I'll contact him and see what we can find. In the meantime, we're going to start publishing an announcement using the name Doug gave you, to proclaim your intention for the dissolution of the marriage."

"Isn't this fraud? How can the marriage be legal?" Daniel exclaimed, wanting Zane to just wave a magic wand and make this whole thing disappear.

"The legalities of fraud and the bonds of matrimony are uneasy bedfellows, Daniel," Zane said with a flourish of his arm, rising to place his child's picture back in place on the corner of his desk. "We plan to cover all the bases while uncovering the truth and making sure Sara is freed from all encumbrances."

"How will we go about this?" Sara asked, impatient and concerned.

"Well, do you have any idea where he is? Where he was going when he left you?" Presley studied Sara's face. "Did he speak of his plans at all?"

"Not much," Sara confessed, she tried to think back through the cloud of pain separating the past from the present. "I was in such a daze of shock and grief at the time." She stared into space, her mind racing. "I seem to remember him mentioning West Texas."

"Ah, do you think he went to work in the oil field,

perhaps?" Zane asked, cutting a glance toward Daniel. "A good mechanic would find work easily there."

"Sounds reasonable," Daniel agreed.

"All right, here's what we'll do." Presley stood and began to pace. She looked at each person in turn – Daniel in dress jeans and a pressed shirt, her husband in a gray suit and tie, and to Sara, sitting primly in the navy-blue sheath she wore to her father's funeral. "I'll publish a notice of your intentions in every major and local paper in the area, from Dallas to Austin, from Houston to Odessa-Midland, and all points in between. The small ad will run for a week. If there is no response, we can either continue with the process of divorce on grounds of abandonment or...seek an annulment in the case of fraud."

Daniel set up with interest. "Can she do that?" He stared at Zane. "The bastard was fraudulent."

"Absolutely, an annulment will be the quickest way to make Sara a free woman..." He turned his attention to Sara. "I can't help but think we might find something of interest were we to pursue the true identity of this man and his motivations."

"Motivations other than stealing and lying?" Sara asked, stunned at what her life had become.

Zane placed his hands on the desk and leaned closer to his clients. "I understand your frustration. Insuring the dissolution of this union will be our highest priority. But...if there are other crimes, I think we owe it to society to bring a criminal to justice." He stood and smiled at the group around his desk. "Give us a week, Sara. Presley will put our best investigators on the trail. This Doug Wright will find it hard to hide from my wife once she gets on his scent."

Daniel thanked his friend and led Sara out to his truck. Once he had her settled, he stood next to her in the open door. "What are you thinking?" He wanted to see the same happy face she'd worn when rapping out her impromptu tune.

Sara took a deep breath, trying to calm her nerves. "I'm overwhelmed. I feel as if everything I thought to be true in my life is a lie."

He ran a finger down her cheek. "What's between me and you is damn real enough."

A sense of peace enveloped Sara. "I know." She placed a hand on his chest, comforted by the steady beat of his strong heart. "It's just so much to take in. I feel overwhelmed, I don't know what will happen." Frowning, Sara sighed. "What the lawyer suggested, all the ads, the time – this will cost a fortune. Maybe, I shouldn't…"

"Stop." He couldn't stand to see Sara upset and discouraged. "You have no need to worry." Daniel took each of her hands in his and placed them high on his chest. "These broad shoulders will carry your burden." His eyes captured hers and compelled them to hold his gaze. "No matter what happens, I will not let you down. I will stand by you. When you need to cry, I will dry your eyes. I will hold you tight and when the time comes, I will fight for you. I don't intend to let you fall, but if you do, I'll be here to catch you."

Sara felt an immense sense of relief. She didn't have to face any of this alone, she had Daniel at her side. How this amazing thing came to be, she couldn't fathom. "Okay." Sara slid her hands up to play in the long hair at his neck. "Just don't let me take advantage of you."

Daniel chuckled, his chest rumbling and vibrating against her. "Oh, baby, I can't wait for you to take advantage of me."

* * *

"Oh, this is good." She licked the small cone. "I can't believe you remembered the ice cream."

"There's no way I could forget anything you say to me." He gave her a wink. "Just save room for food, we're stopping in Kingsland for a supper date before we go home."

"Another date?" She brightened considerably. "I'm dressed like a nun." Sara soothed her hand down the front of the plain dark dress. "This is a nice material, but it's hardly sexy." Her admission colored her cheeks. "Not that I need to be."

"Shhhh, hush your worrying. I'm enchanted anew every time I look at you."

His assurances pacified her. "You say the nicest things." So many compliments. She decided to return the favor as she admired the man who seemed to take joy in doing things to make her happy. "Do you know how much I love to look at you?"

Daniel's hand jerked and his front tire veered off the road. He got the vehicle under control quickly, but he kept spearing her with frequent glances. "You do?"

"Yea." She could see the fascination on his face. "I love how you look and I love how good you are. You're pure, in this wild, manly way."

"Pure?" This pleased Daniel, but confused him a bit. "I don't think anyone could say I'm pure, I've been pretty well corrupted over the years."

"I don't believe it, you're a man of honor. Your word is your bond. If you ever make a promise to me, I know I could stake my life on it."

Her confidence left him shaken. "I meant what I said earlier, I'm here for you. You have a champion, Sara."

She finished her cone, considering his promise,

hiding the words away in her heart to cherish at another time.

As his truck ate up the miles, Daniel considered how quickly things were progressing between him and Sara. This time last week, he hadn't been aware of her existence. Now, she was everything to him. One of his favorite country western songs came to mind and he couldn't help but smile.

The smile faded as he wondered how long it would be before she was free of the past that haunted her.

…When Daniel told her where they were eating, Sara hadn't known what to expect. "I feel we've stepped back in time," she told him as she took his arm and he led her up the steps of the Antlers Hotel.

"I thought you might like to see this Victorian showplace before we go to the restaurant. The Antlers was constructed by the Austin and Northwestern Railroad in the early 1900's, when a bridge was constructed across the Colorado at the point where it meets our Llano River. Built as a resort, it brought such VIP's as President McKinley, who stayed here just before his assassination."

"You sounded like a tour guide there for a minute," Sara teased him and he blushed.

"I was just trying to pass on my vast knowledge of local color."

"I know. I like this kind of thing." She nudged him. "In fact, I've always been fascinated by these old homes. My fam…"

Abruptly, she stopped speaking and Daniel couldn't read her expression. "Your what?"

Sara shook her head. "Nothing. My favorite joke is about a railroad track. Want to hear it?"

"So, when you're not rapping, you're a stand-up

comedienne?" At her smug look, he said, "Let's hear it."

"Okay. Here goes. Two drunks were walking down the railroad track." She moved in front of him and took two or three long steps. "One drunk said, these stairs are killing me!" Then she bent over, finger trailing on the ground, still taking extra-long steps. "The other drunk said, I know, but it's not the stairs that's killing me, it's this low handrail." With that, she stood up and did a ta-dah movement and curtsied.

Daniel laughed aloud. "That's the worst joke I've ever heard. Don't quit your day job, Pet."

"I won't. Who would take care of you?"

Her quipped answer left him speechless. Who indeed? He couldn't think of anyone else even remotely qualified.

When they stepped inside the hotel, Sara could clearly see the significance of the name, for some of the walls were covered in deer antlers. "Do you like to hunt?" If he did, she wouldn't express her discomfort at the sight.

He rubbed her back as they stood next to one of the richly paneled walls, observing people coming and going. "You mean with my bow and arrow?" She pinched him right above his belt and he jerked and chuckled. "No, not really. Benjen hates it so much that the rest of us just found something else to do."

"Like pursuing beautiful women?"

He gave her a wicked grin. "Maybe, except Benjen, he's shy." Pointing out the window, he turned her attention to several train cars sitting on sections of tracks. "They've converted some old cabooses into guest accommodations."

"Sounds fun." She stared at one caboose painted bright red and all she could imagine was a big bed inside that she could share with Daniel. The thought made her feel all tingly and warm. Since he'd given her an orgasm and she realized what all the fuss was about, Sara could scarcely think of anything else.

"What are you thinking about?" he asked slyly, reading her like a book.

"Nothing!" She blushed even hotter. "Can we get something to eat now?"

"Yes, ma'am. I forgot to tell you I have special Native American psychic mind-reading power. I know you were thinking about me and you sharing one of those cozy rooms."

"Your ego is very large," she told him as he led her across the way to another Victorian home on the same grounds.

"Everything I have is large and proportionately appropriate to my overall size." He leaned in to whisper in her ear, "Especially my manly parts."

"How big is it?" she asked as they started up the steps to the restaurant.

Daniel missed a step. "Will you quit shocking my shorts off!"

Now, Sara laughed. "Isn't that the idea?"

Once they were inside the Grand Central Cafe, a hostess seated them at a quaint table and a smiling waiter brought them a basket of bread. Daniel picked up a yeast breadstick, about nine inches long and six inches in circumference and waved it at her. "About this big."

Sara, who was studying the menu looked up at him with a puzzled expression. "What?"

"It's about this big."

She looked from his face to the breadstick and back before it hit her what he was talking about. "Oh!"

He was enjoying her discomfiture until she

reached for the breadstick, brought it to her mouth and bit the end off, chewing it thoughtfully as she went back to the menu.

Daniel laughed uproariously. "I love you. Did you know that? What did I do before you came along?"

Sara almost choked. He loved her? She knew he was kidding, but still…

"Daniel Blackhawk, fancy meeting you here."

The distinctly female voice caused Sara's head to jerk around. When she saw the tall, blonde, busty beauty, she almost wished she hadn't looked.

"Fiona."

"I've been expecting your call." She glanced at Sara. "What have we here?"

"Fiona Meadows meet my date, Sara Riley," Daniel said evenly, watching Fiona's less-than-happy face carefully.

"Hello." Sara nodded, taking note of the tightening of Daniel's jaw. He used to date this woman, she knew it without being told.

Fiona placed one well-manicured hand on her hip. "Daniel, are you playing with this child? Clearly, she's not your type."

Sara wanted to draw up into a knot and crawl under the table. If one were to compare her physical attributes to the bombshell standing close enough to Daniel for one of her generous breasts to be rubbing his shoulder – Sara was clearly lacking. In several areas.

Daniel didn't like Fiona's catty comments. At all. "Fiona, such classlessness is beneath you. My taste in women has evolved over time, like my taste in bed linens. I used to sleep on rough, cheap sheets and now I prefer satin and silk."

Sara pressed her lips together to keep from

giggling as her heart sped up at Daniel's defense. The look of vitriol on the other woman's face was startling. "Don't bother calling me, Blackhawk. I won't answer the phone."

"Wasn't planning on it."

About the time Fiona huffed off, the waiter came to take their order. Daniel deferred to her. Sara was so jittery from their visitor that she went right for what she needed the most. "Chocolate cake and a strawberry walnut salad with salmon, cake first."

Daniel started to protest, then he wondered why he'd want to change a thing about her. "I'll take a T-Bone, medium rare, baked potato all the way. Bleu cheese on my salad."

The waiter nodded and when they were alone, he reached for her hand. "Don't let Fiona worry you, she's nothing but a distant memory to me. We went out a few times, but it was never anything serious."

Sara shifted to sit on her foot, moving ever slightly closer to Daniel. "I don't think she would agree with you."

He looked around the restaurant as if he expected something to jump out at them.

"What's wrong?" she asked.

"Well…" he began, a mischievous look on his face, "if something weird was going to happen, this would be the place." He leaned closer to her, loving how her eyes grew wide. "I know you think this is just a pretty old house with a green roof, but it's not."

"What are you talking about?" She grabbed his forearm with both hands and his blood pressure shot through the roof. He wouldn't trade her for a barrel of gold monkeys.

"This house was where the movie *Texas Chainsaw Massacre* was filmed."

"No!" she exclaimed, glancing around.

Daniel halfway expected her to jump into his arms. "Yea, this house was moved from the La Frontera area in Round Rock to Kingsland a few years ago." He pointed to the staircase. "They used to keep a life-like dummy of Leatherface up there to stare down at everybody while they ate." He waited for her response, ready to give her all the hugs and comfort she needed.

"Do you mean..." she started speaking slowly, then sped up with a grin, "that Matthew McConnaughey was here in this very house?!"

"Oh, Lordy, Lordy." He hung his head. "I'll never understand women as long as I live. But...no. This was the location of the first movie, the one with Matthew came later and it was filmed in a farmhouse east of Pflugerville. Same area. Different house."

She pooched out her lips. "Shoot." Her pout turned to a smile when the waiter brought her cake. They were quiet for a few minutes, concentrating on their food until Sara spoke up, "Thank you for today. This wasn't your responsibility and I appreciate you so much."

Daniel laid his fork down. "You don't get it, do you?"

She studied his face. "Get what?"

He took her hand and turned it up so he could trace her lifeline with his finger. "I know we haven't known one another long, but you're holding my heart in the palm of this delicate hand."

"Daniel." She didn't move her hand, but let him hold it. "I..."

"Well...who do we have here?"

Another interruption took Sara by surprise. Did everyone know everybody in this small town?

This wasn't an ex-girlfriend. This time a man interrupted their meal, a man in a khaki uniform with a metal badge on his chest. He didn't look friendly.

"John. How can I help you?"

"Blackhawk." The lawman glanced around the homey restaurant. "I thought this place had higher standards. I guess they'll let just about anyone in, if their door is open for redskin scum like you."

The insult was so wrong and so politically incorrect that Sara thought the man must be joking. But when Daniel's face hardened, instead of breaking out into a smile, she knew the jerk in uniform was serious.

Fury flashed over Sara like wildfire. She jumped up and shook her finger in his face. "Hey! You've got no right to speak to this good man that way. Just who do you think you are?"

John Mansfield moved one step closer to Sara, his hands forming clenched fists.

Daniel moved quicker than light, placing himself between Sara and one of Mac Briscoe's deputies. "Back up, Mansfield. Strike out at my lady and you'll draw back a nub."

Sara didn't understand what was going on. "We can go, Daniel."

"Yea, Daniel, I think that's a good idea. Decent people patronize this establishment, they don't need an ex-convict littering up the place." The man's sneer looked evil.

"Let's get out of here." Daniel held up his hand for the check, then indicated he'd meet the waiter at the front. Sara shot the man named John a look that could kill and hurried after Daniel. She had no idea what the lawman was talking about, but she knew where her loyalties lay.

Daniel felt like he'd been punched in the gut. He was beyond embarrassed. He was humiliated. It wasn't the fact that people had seen John Mansfield giving him a hard time – it was that Sara had heard the truth about him from someone else.

Fuck!

Why hadn't he told her himself? What had he been waiting for? His history to rewrite itself?

He pasted a smile on his face and gave the checkout clerk his credit card. The woman wouldn't meet his eyes and he could feel other people staring at him.

When a small, soft hand touched his arm, he jerked.

Sara.

He stood stock still until his credit card was returned and he'd jotted his signature across the dotted line.

Without saying a word, he started for the door, not knowing if she'd follow or not.

She did.

"Daniel, wait."

He stopped. He wouldn't go off and leave her. Ever. Yet, facing her would be the hardest thing he'd ever do. "I meant to tell you." Daniel helped her into the truck, then took his time getting behind the wheel.

Sara didn't know what to say. The whole thing had happened so fast. "You can tell me anything, you know."

Her soft assertion paralyzed him. What he needed to confess wasn't about guilt, it was about vulnerability – and he hated to appear weak. Helpless. Judged.

Placing his hands on the steering wheel, he stared out into the darkness. "I spent time in prison for rape." He wouldn't insist on his innocence, he just said the words, then waited for her response. Would it be a slamming door as she ran away from him? Would it be an exclamation of disgust?

No. Sara's reaction was something else entirely.

"Why did they send you to prison for something you didn't do?"

Her faith in him washed over Daniel like a refreshing spring rain.

CHAPTER SIX

Why would they send you to prison for something you didn't do?

Daniel let out a long breath as the tension eased from his body.

"Why are you assuming I didn't commit the crime they convicted me for?"

Sara had never heard Daniel speak with the tone he was using now – so carefully. Cautious. Yet, a faint hint of hope pervaded his words. "Because I know you. You are a protector, not a threat."

"Thank you." Daniel bowed his head as a rush of relief shot through him. "I didn't do it."

"You don't have to tell me anything if you don't want to, Daniel."

"I want to."

When he started the truck and began to drive from the parking lot to head toward the ranch, Sara thought their conversation was over. But as they put distance between themselves and the restaurant, he began to speak. "This was some years ago."

He cleared his throat and coughed. Sara remained silent. Supportive. Listening.

"I was coming home one evening from a cattle sale. I was by myself, driving on the main road through town, very near the river. The weather was cool and my window was down. As I passed a small roadside park with a couple of picnic tables, I heard a scream."

Sara gasped and Daniel paused, but he kept his eyes focused on the road ahead of him.

"I slowed down and pulled off the road and when I did, I heard another scream. I stopped the truck and got out to look around. At first, I didn't see them, but when my eyes adjusted to the shadows, I saw a woman lying on the ground with a man on top of her. I ran to help, pulling him off. The guy jumped me. I didn't recognize him, but I landed a few punches. When a siren sounded, the guy took off into the woods."

The cadence of his speech was measured and void of emotion. Sara couldn't stop herself from reaching out to place her hand on his arm. He didn't flinch at her touch, but he didn't respond either.

"I went to the girl. She was crying and straightening her clothes. I recognized her, it was Priscilla Briscoe, the sheriff's daughter."

A pang of dread shot through Sara. Even though the events he described weren't recent, she could feel an inevitable fog bank of disaster approaching.

"My memory of what happened next is a blur, everything went crazy." He swallowed and slowed the vehicle, aware that he was approaching the turn-off to the ranch. "Two cop cars pulled up, her father was in one. They raced over, gauging the situation. I tried to tell them how I'd found her and about the man I'd saved her from."

"Oh, no, Daniel. Oh, no."

Sara's dismay echoed his own. "Briscoe came to his daughter and asked her what happened."

There was a long silence. Sara could hear nothing but the truck engine. Inside the cab, the lack of any other noise was deafening.

"He asked her if she'd been raped and she yes. When he asked his daughter the name of the man who'd raped her...she said it was me."

Sara began to cry. "I'm sorry. I'm so sorry."

Daniel cleared his throat. Twice. Seeming to gather strength.

"They arrested me. I called my brothers. I was interrogated. I denied the charges, I told and retold my story a thousand times. No one believed me. All they could see was a lying Indian who attacked white women. There was a trial, but the whole thing was handled locally, I was set-up."

"How long?"

"I was tried and convicted to twenty years in prison."

"But..."

"Nine months later Priscilla had a baby, it wasn't mine. She'd been afraid to tell her father she was sleeping with a guy from Austin. Even after they quarreled or..." he paused and sighed heavily, "...or whatever game they were playing that night, she kept seeing him. When the child was born, she confessed to her father that I'd never touched her, that there had been no rape. I'd just come along in time to break up a lover's quarrel."

Sara wiped tears from her eyes. "How tragic for you."

Daniel barked a laugh. "Yea...tragic. I spent seven months in prison for something I didn't do. And when I was released, when I came home, I found that some people still treated me as if I was guilty. When they looked at me, they didn't see an upstanding, innocent man, they saw a man with Apache blood who'd never be good enough to escape the stigma of the color of his skin."

Sara waited until he parked in front of the old rock house, then she was out of her seat and in his lap before he'd known she moved. "Oh, Daniel, you are so wonderful."

Daniel didn't understand her declaration, all he knew was that he had an armful of soft, sweet-smelling woman who was raining kisses on his face and throat. "Wonderful?"

"Yes." She gasped and buried her face in his neck. "Despite what you've endured, you are still so resilient, so determined to take care of your family. You rescued me, stood up for me, you're ready to slay my dragons. Those men didn't break you. You passed through the fire and emerged stronger."

Daniel tightened his arms around her, absorbing her faith and trust into his body like the warmth of a fire on a cold night. "Thank you, Sara, for understanding."

"What I understand is that you have done nothing wrong." She wove her fingers through his hair and kissed him with utmost tenderness. "I am so proud of you."

Daniel kissed her twice more, drawing comfort and solace from her touch. "Ready to go in?"

"Yea, I'm glad to get back home," she sighed, holding onto him as he opened the door and climbed from the truck. "Aren't you?"

"Very." He carried her into the house and shut the door, leaving the rest of the world and its troubles behind them.

* * *

For the next few days, Sara fell into an easy rhythm, living among the Blackhawk family. She kept herself busy so she wouldn't worry about what was going on in the quest to end her faux marriage. Daniel and his brothers worked long hours on the ranch, tending cattle and storing hay. She worked around the house until it gleamed, polishing floors, washing curtains, and performing a million mundane tasks that hadn't been done in a while, probably not since their mother passed. During her down time, Sara spent time in the barn, playing with the new spotted heifer, which she named – unoriginally – Spot. All in all, she made herself at home.

When provisions ran low, Sara borrowed their Jeep, not telling Daniel her driving skills were less than spectacular. She also paid a visit to the clinic to get a prescription for birth control. This made her so nervous, she backed into a dumpster. So, when she returned from town with more scratches on the Jeep than she'd left with, Sara dreaded showing him what she'd done.

Since the night he'd confessed the travesty he'd endured at the hands of the local sheriff, Daniel had been a bit distant. This worried her. She didn't know if he'd changed his mind about them, or if he was experiencing regret over confiding so much of his past. Sara knew Daniel was a man of great pride and she longed to show him in some tangible way how much she admired him. After all, he wasn't the only one who'd kept a secret.

Sara still harbored one as well.

She had every intention of telling him...if the right time ever came. At the moment, however, the more pressing matter was the dent in the fender of Daniel's Jeep.

To butter him up and distract him from the bad news, Sara whipped up two Almond Joy pies to go along with the big meal she'd prepared for the family.

Now, all she had to do was wait.

Standing at the kitchen window while she gave his mother's crystal a rinse, Sara kept watch on the barn, waiting for him to come riding home.

…Holding the gate open for his brother, Daniel waited for Easy to ride through, before leading Blackjack between the posts, fastening the latch, and sliding the cross plank into place.

"What's been festering in your craw lately, Danny Boy?"

"Nothing." Daniel kept his path straight as he made for the barn door. "Just work."

"If that's true, I got a wheelbarrow full of cow shit for sale and I swear each turd has a gold nugget center."

Daniel grimaced. "No, thanks. I've just got something on my mind."

"What is it?" Easy asked, a more sympathetic look on his face. "Is it Sara? Did you get bad news from Zane?"

"No, Zane did call, but just to say Fraser accepted our offer for the land north of Llano. As far as Sara's concerned, Saucier's still waiting on the investigator's report." Daniel pulled the saddle off his horse and placed it on the rack, then took a curry comb and began brushing Blackjack's dark coat.

"So…have you changed your mind about her? Is that what this is about?" Easy poured some grain into the horse troughs. "She's done a good job here, Daniel, but that doesn't mean you owe her anything more."

Daniel looked at Easy as if he was crazy. "Don't make assumptions, Easy. Sara is not the problem. I'm battling my own demons."

"I'm your brother, Daniel, just point me in the direction of those horny bastards and I'll kick their forked tails!"

Daniel shook his head at his brother's tom-foolery. "I took her to the Antlers on the way home from Austin and we ran into John Mansfield."

"Was the old ass up to his usual stunts?"

"He called into question my suitability to be served food in the same restaurant as the local white folk, considering my prison record and inferior heritage."

Easy growled, "Stupid fucker."

Daniel chuckled. "Yes, true that." Just retelling the sorry incident eased the hurt of it somewhat.

"Was Sara shocked?"

"She stood up to him and told the sorry bastard off, but that was before she learned the rest of the story."

"What did she say then?"

Daniel patted Blackjack on his flank. "She proclaimed my innocence before I explained myself. Never a doubt in her mind. As far as our Apache blood is concerned…" He gave Easy a big grin. "I think she finds it sexy."

Easy roared with laughter. "Lucky you."

"Daniel?"

Sara's voice sounding from outside the barn caused Daniel's feet to move. "What's wrong, Pet?" He found her waiting for him next to the Jeep, something akin to dread in her eyes. "Are you all right?"

She met his gaze with her heart in her eyes. "I'm so sorry, Daniel. I've done something terrible."

Daniel's mind didn't know which way to go. The most terrible thing he could think of was if her interest had turned toward another man.

Yet, since he trusted her implicitly, something

else must be awry. "Just tell me, Sara. Whatever it is, I'll fix it."

She pointed to the Jeep. "I backed into the dumpster at the grocery store." Kneeling next to the ancient vehicle, she carefully touched the battered bumper and scratched fender.

Daniel let out a harsh breath – of relief. Shutting one eye, he carefully considered the slight, yet fresh blemish. "Sara! How could you!" He clutched his chest and rocked back on one foot.

Sara's mouth trembled and she covered her eyes. "I'm sorry. I'll pay to get it repaired." She turned on her heels to run, but she didn't get far. Two strong arms surrounded her and lifted her up. Two firm lips covered hers and the kiss they gave her was tantalizing and without reservation. Clinging to him, Sara succumbed to his passion. If this was the price required for recompense, she'd pay it a thousand times over.

Once he set her aright, Sara clung to his shoulders, searching his face for absolution. What she saw wasn't forgiveness – it was amusement. "Daniel?"

He picked her up with a happy shout and swung her around. "Ah, sweet Sara, there are so many dents and scratches on that Jeep, any new ones just blend with the old."

When the weight of her guilt lifted, Sara just sank against him, resting her head on Daniel's chest. "I'm so sorry."

"Shhh, no biggie." He put an arm around her. "When we get through with supper, I want you to go see a piece of land with me. Will you do that?"

"Sure, yes," she agreed, anxious to be alone with him again. "Has there been any word from Zane or Presley?"

"No, not about your situation. The only word we

received from their offices concerned this piece of land I just mentioned. We're purchasing it to expand our holdings. I'm thinking about building a house on the property and I'd love to hear your opinion."

"Oh, all right, I'm not sure what I can contribute, but I look forward to seeing it."

Knowing they were soon to go off on what she considered to be an adventure, Sara didn't waste a moment getting dinner on the table for the hungry brood of Blackhawks. Hope, who was practically well, bounced around at her feet, begging for a hand-out. To appease Daniel after her tangle with the dumpster, she'd gone all out with an Italian feast. Lasagna. Spaghetti. Garlic bread. Roasted root vegetables and pie for dessert. Watching the four big men eat did her heart good.

"Sara, I swear, I've never tasted better food." Samuel shoveled lasagna into his mouth like he was feeding a steam engine.

"I agree." Easy raised his glass of tea to Sara. "Every meal you make tops the last."

"Thank you." She dipped her head, their compliments making her uneasy. To occupy herself, she made sure everyone was taken care of, always keeping one eye on Daniel to see to his needs.

The extra care and attention she gave to Daniel did not go unnoticed or unappreciated. She tried to foresee his every whim and she did an admirable job – except for the unquenchable, aching need barely contained behind the zipper of his Wranglers.

"Hey, Daniel, I heard about the property at Baby Head, congratulations." Benjen offered as he cut himself a piece of the chocolate-topped, coconut pie.

Sara blinked at hearing the odd name. She'd heard Baby Head mentioned a couple times before over the years and wondered about it, but she'd never been there.

"Thanks, Ben, I'm pleased the deal is going through."

Benjen nodded, holding a spoonful near his mouth for a bite. "Why don't I ride with you to look at the property when we finish here?"

Sara held her breath. She wouldn't interfere, Daniel would do what he needed to do.

"Maybe another time, Brother." He winked at Sara. "I've already asked Sara to go with me."

"Ah, okay." Benjen held up his hands in surrender. "I can't argue with that plan, you all have fun." He nodded to the dog at his feet. "I have a girl of my own to take for a walk."

"Awww, you do that." Sara squatted on the floor to give Hope a hug. "She's my new bed buddy, aren't you, girl?"

"Not for..." Daniel began, then bit his tongue. He'd almost said, 'not for much longer'. Easy gave him a knowing smile, then hid his amusement when Sara glanced at him by taking a sip of tea.

"Not for...what?" she prompted Daniel.

He cleared his throat to give himself time to think. "I was going to say, not for me. I don't think...a dog would be my choice of a bedmate." By the time he got the sentence out, he was chuckling and so were his brothers.

Sara rose and cleared the table, choosing to ignore their guy banter.

"Hey, we need to go before it gets any darker. Would one of you clean up the dinner dishes?" Daniel asked as he stood and pushed his chair under the table. "Come on, Pet, let's take a drive."

Benjen came and dipped his hands into the

dishwater next to Sara's, slowly pushing her out of the way until she relented and grabbed the towel to wipe her hands. "Leave them. I'll finish when I get home."

"Not a chance, fancy pants." Daniel hooked his fingers in her back pocket and tugged. "Let's go."

Sara followed, not unwillingly.

…In the truck, they drove with the windows down and Daniel found himself entranced with the way Sara's long hair flowed behind her and the contented smile on her face as she enjoyed the moment. "Happy?" he had to ask.

She glanced at him as she caught a strand or two of hair that whipped over her mouth when she changed the angle of her body to face him. "Yes. I am. I feel hopeful and content." *With you*, she could have added. "Are you happy?" She found herself staring at him, captivated by the chiseled cut of muscle across his cheeks, defining the handsome lines of his face. "You've been distant toward me."

A wave of disquiet made Daniel's chest ache. "I didn't mean to be." He kept his head facing forward, his eye on the endless yellow stripe dividing the highway that led north from Kingsland. "I guess I was embarrassed by what you witnessed. I figured once you thought about my being in prison, you might see me differently."

"I guess I do, in a way." She saw him stiffen at her statement. "I admire you more."

"Why?"

"Despite the injustice that was done to you, you've remained the best of men. Look how good you are to me."

"You're easy to be good to." He cocked an eyebrow and surveyed her with amusement. "You do realize I have less than pure thoughts about you. As

134

soon as it's proper, I plan on coming onto you like a house on fire."

Dipping her head, she confessed, "I thought you'd changed your mind. I mean…you've kept me at arm's length."

A rumbling growl rose from deep in Daniel's chest. "And you'll never know what it's cost me."

Sara wanted to know more, but flashing lights in the road ahead of them drew their attention and Daniel had to slow down due to a wreck. By the time they'd crept by the damaged vehicles and the attending police, their turn loomed ahead of them and the moment had passed. There was only an hour or two of light remaining in the long summer day, but there was enough for her to see that the surrounding land seemed rocky and uninhabited. "Are we close?"

"Not far. There's a gate up ahead. I've been wanting to explore it a little farther, see what the creek looks like after this many days without rain."

"It's been a dry summer." She remembered the lightning from the clear sky that almost claimed their lives. "Are there springs about?"

"Yea, we'll check them first." He drove the rest of a way down a short lane and pulled up to a gate.

"Let me." Sara hopped out to tend to the opening and shutting of the gate while Daniel drove through.

He appreciated her help, this woman could prove to be a true partner. As Daniel eased onto the property he'd just agreed to buy, he kept an eye on Sara in the mirrors. Watching her move was pure pleasure. She was graceful, gorgeous, and sexy beyond words. He shifted in his seat, tugging at his damn tight jeans.

"Okay, ready," she announced as she climbed back into the truck.

"Thanks." Easing off the brake, Daniel set off on

the aforementioned path. "You mentioned your mother left when you were a child, who taught you how to bake?"

Sara smiled, remembering. "A neighbor, Mrs. Hammock. I stayed with her after school most days until my dad finished work. She let me help in the kitchen."

"Mrs. Hammock did an excellent job," he observed, keeping their pace slow on the rough ground.

"You've mentioned your mother several times, Daniel, but not your father."

Her comment wasn't a question, but her curiosity was implied. "He died before I went to prison, thank goodness. My incarceration would've killed him." Shrugging, he summed things up. "He was the best man I ever knew."

"I'm sure he was, all of you seem to have been raised well."

Daniel nodded. "My brothers are fine men too, none of them have a shameful secret like me."

Sara wanted to tell him he wasn't the only one carrying a secret, and she would have, if he hadn't stopped the truck and motioned for her to get out. "Let's take a walk."

"Okay." She managed to get the door open just before Daniel came around to help her to the ground. "Thanks, you're always so considerate."

"My pleasure." He took her hand in his.

Sara enjoyed the tactile pleasure of their palms pressed together, their fingers entwined. She held on tightly as they moved over uneven ground. Ahead of them stood a good size hill, not as big as Packsaddle, but large enough to dominate the landscape. "So, this is Baby Head?"

"Yea, it is." He waved his hand in a sweeping gesture. "Plenty of trees for shade, the grass is high in nutrients, and there's plenty of natural water – I hope."

"I've heard people mention this odd sounding place. There's a Baby Head Mountain, a Baby Head community, even a Baby Head cemetery. Do you know the story behind the name?"

"Unfortunately." Daniel tucked her hand in the crook of his arm. "It's a dark piece of history." He paused, halfway hoping she'd pick a new topic. "Not pleasant in the telling or the hearing."

Now, he'd just intrigued her. "Tell me, Daniel."

"Well…" He slowed his steps. "As the story goes, in 1855 a little girl was kidnapped by Indians, thought to be Comanche. A band of settlers from north of Llano, pursued the raiding tribe. Accounts of the past affirm that Native Americans sometimes took white children, raising them as part of their tribe. Some fared well, some not so well. Nevertheless, the men hurried, hoping to rescue the child. Continuing the wild chase, the Indians, some on horseback, some on foot, were failing to travel as fast as they needed to escape. They climbed this hill," he pointed at Baby Head, "and according to the tales told, they made a horrible choice. They killed the little girl and put her head on a pike stuck into the ground for the pursuing settlers to find."

"No!" Sara was horrified.

"Well, that's the common story, but there is another, a more specific one told by a ninety-year old man just before he died. According to him, the date was right after the Civil War, and the killers weren't Indian at all, but wealthy local ranchers. Their plan was to murder a family to get the attention of the Calvary, in order to force their hand in ridding the area of Indians. They also hoped to scare any homesteaders who might want to lay claim to the common ranching land."

"So, the child was killed for money and power, basically?"

"To no avail, no troops were sent and the settlers kept coming."

"And her death was blamed on someone other than the culprit." Sara understood the parallel between the tragic story and Daniels own experience. "How sad."

"Yes, sad," he agreed softly. Jerking himself to the matter at hand, Daniel surveyed the landscape. "So, what do you think? What do you see here?"

Sara let her gaze wander the countryside. "Well, apart from the eerie history, the land is spectacular." She knew there probably wasn't a square foot of land upon this earth where someone had not met their demise, so she wasn't put off by the strange account. In fact, she felt inclined to offer comfort to whatever small spirit might still linger. Narrowing her eyes, she tried to picture the place as a homestead. "Daniel, look at that small rise, the one framed by the oak grove. I could see a house there, one with a view of the mountain and the spring fed creek."

"What kind of house do you envision?"

Sara smiled. "I think you'd want to continue the tradition of a rock house, maybe one that combines native stone with logs. A wide wrap-around porch with a swing would be gorgeous."

Daniel let his imagination flow until he could see what she described – only he saw more. "Sounds perfect."

They stood side by side, each lost in their own fantasy. He pictured Sara opening the front door and standing on the porch, awaiting his return. Sara could see herself sitting in the swing, next to Daniel, as they held hands.

In the midst of their reverie, the wind picked up. Chill bumps ran over Sara's arms and she chafed them, cocking her head to listen. What was she hearing? The sun was going down and the moon was on the rise when a noise floated to them on the breeze. "Is that a baby crying?"

Daniel tilted his head, listening. "I don't hear anything but the wind."

"I guess that's what I'm hearing." The plaintive noise made her heart ache, causing her to remember something she never wanted to forget. Tears began to rise in her eyes and before she could stop, Sara dissolved into heart-wrenching sobs.

Daniel whirled, catching her to him. "Hey, hey, sweetie. What's wrong?"

Sara's arms rose to encircle his neck and she cried against him, her shoulders shaking with grief.

"Talk to me, love." He rubbed her back, not knowing what to do. "What happened? Are you afraid? Don't be. I'm here. I've got you."

Daniel's whispers gave her comfort. She'd known she needed to tell him her secret, but she hadn't expected to be so suddenly swamped with sorrow. "I lost a baby."

The four simple words lanced through his gut. "You had a child?"

"I…" She tried to speak, but her voice broke. Sara clutched his shirt, her tears straining his chest. "She only lived three days. She was premature. I named her Faith."

"Oh, sweetheart." Daniel was shell-shocked. "I didn't know." He would've never guessed. He stroked her hair, wondering at the still waters that ran so deep in her life.

"Yes, he left me with nothing…but a baby." She rubbed her face on the soft cotton of his shirt. "I didn't want Doug, but I wanted my baby. After she died, I was afraid I'd been punished for hating her father."

"I don't think the world works that way, Pet." He kissed her temple. "Or at least I hope it doesn't."

"I would've taken care of her, somehow."

"Of course, you would've. A mother's love is the strongest thing in the world."

She let him hold her for long moment, until the shadows fell thick around them and the wind had settled down. "I don't hear it anymore," she whispered, feeling a sense of peace wash over her as she rested against him.

"Good." He squeezed her tightly, before bringing her under his arm. "Time to go home. I think we found what we were looking for."

* * *

When they arrived at the ranch, there was no one to welcome them but Hope. "Where are your brothers?"

Daniel found a note on the counter, reading it quickly. "They drove into town for a beer, this says they'll be back soon."

"So, we're alone?"

Her question made him aware they were thinking along the same lines, albeit for different reasons. "Don't worry, your honor is safe with me."

"I know." Dang-it, she bit back a smile. "Pity," she whispered, as she checked in the kitchen to make sure everything was put away and Hope had plenty of water.

"What did you say?"

"Nothing." She didn't want to ask for something he wasn't ready to give. The truth was – their earlier conversation haunted her. Sara had no desire to be alone.

"I'll remind you that my desire to be a gentleman is only rivaled by my desire for you."

The soft-spoken conviction gave Sara pause. "I love how you treat me and I respect the boundaries you set, I just need to be held," she confessed quietly. "I read somewhere that sleeping with someone, just sleeping, could be more intimate than sex. Do you think that could be true?"

Daniel's heart began to thump like a bass drum in his chest. "I don't know, I guess we could test the theory out." He moved to the old-fashioned hutch that held his mother's china and crystal. A metal tray sat on top with a few bottles of whiskey and scotch. He took a glass and poured himself a shot of Jack Daniels. "May I pour you one?" He held up another glass.

Great. How heartening to know the man needed to liquor up in order to face lying in the same bed with her. Shaking her head, she knew she was over-reacting. He'd stated his position and after learning how he'd been treated by a woman he'd only endeavored to help, she could understand his self-imposed rules. "No, thank you. I'm good." She picked up Hope and started for the room she'd been allocated. "Don't worry about my request, I shouldn't have asked. I'll see you tomorrow."

"Sara."

The way he said her name stopped Sara in her tracks. She didn't turn around, she just waited to hear what he had to say.

"Wait on me."

Even though his voice pulled her like a magnet,

Sara didn't move. "No need, Daniel, I'm okay now. I just felt lost for a little while."

She could hear his footfalls moving across the floor. He moved so near she could feel the heat from his body branding her skin.

"You're not going to offer a drink to a man starving for water, then dash the life-giving droplets to the ground, are you?"

His eloquent, descriptive sentiment accomplished just what it was supposed to. Breathless, she braced herself against the wall.

"Go get ready for bed, I'll join you in a few moments." He tugged a strand of her hair. "I can do intimacy better than any man you'll ever meet. You'll see."

Sara lost no time getting ready for bed. Even though they wouldn't be consummating their relationship, if Daniel was going to be in her bed, she wanted to be as perfect for him as possible. Despite showering in record time, Sara made sure she was smooth and sweet smelling. The only quandary she faced was a sexy sleeping garment...she didn't own one. Staring into her underwear drawer, she frowned. No matter how hard she looked, there was nothing even remotely seductive to be found. Finally, she chose a pink sleep shirt and a matching pair of boy shorts. Pulling the soft garments onto her body, she paced the floor nervously.

After showering and changing into a T-shirt and a pair of lounge pants, Daniel went to the kitchen for a little help in coping. Going to the freezer, he filled a plastic bag with a few ice-cubes, then slipped them into his shorts. "Jeepers Fuckin' Creepers!" he hissed, doubling over with the shock. "That's right, down-boy, down-boy. I'm going in there and hold Sara until she goes to sleep and I will not be dictated to by my errant cock!"

He withstood the freezing ache for as long as he could, then jerked the bag out and tossed it into the trash. "Now, you've got honest to God blue balls, numb nuts."

When he was as steady as he was going to get, Daniel set off for Sara's room. He'd pledged himself to do and be exactly what Sara needed – and he'd do it – even if it killed him

A tapping on her door almost sent Sara diving beneath the covers, but she clutched the top of the quilt and held on. "Come in," she called and in the heartbeat between her invitation and the door opening, Sara attempted to arrange herself in some semblance of a seductive pose, lying back on the pillow and leaning on one arm. But just as the door opened, she abandoned her sultry guise and just sat up straight in the bed, leaning against the headboard. Being something other than what she was would be foolish.

Daniel stepped in, his eyes finding her waiting for him, sweet and wide-eyed, looking so beautiful, he found it hard to take air into his lungs. "Hey, got room for one more in that bed?"

She nodded, scooting over so close to the edge, he feared she might tumble to the floor. He flipped off the big light and turned on the small lamp. With a slightly shaking hand, Daniel yanked back the covers and climbed in next to her.

"Are you sure this isn't an imposition?" she asked, suddenly overwhelmed by his sheer size and proximity. Lying next to him was like being in the protective shadow of a high and mighty rock, safe from the heat of the day or the pounding of a storm.

"Stop." He pulled her into his arms, tugging her

to his body. "I'm right where I want to be." When he tucked her close, a sense of complete rightness enveloped him. "Let's just use this time to get to know one another. Okay?" He held up his hand and she fit hers to it. He caressed her hand, rubbing their palms together, weaving their fingers to mate with one another, interlocking and sliding side by side.

"Okay. I'm not afraid anymore." She trembled with delight at the heaven of being in his arms. "No matter what happens I have enjoyed being close to you…very much."

"Oh, me too. Me too." He looked into her eyes. "I love having you in my life." Holding her felt so good, feeling the soft press of her body to his. Holing her small hand in the eager clasp of his own, his every breath filled with her subtle, feminine perfume. Having Sara near him like this was pure luxury. A feast for his senses after a long drought of solitude.

"I love taking care of you and your brothers." She brought his hand to her lips and kissed it. "And remember, the money I would've earned goes to pay the lawyer. I still have what you gave me, I haven't spent any of it."

Daniel pulled her close and laid his lips on hers, kissing her gently. "I would do this for you, regardless. But since I will be the one who benefits most from ridding you of your husband, I am honored to fund the effort." He saw her wince when he called the scoundrel by the title he didn't deserve. "And once we know the outcome is imminent, you won't be able to keep me out of your bed…" He kissed her again, softly. "Unless you don't want me."

"I want you," she whispered, no future tense implied. "You've been through so much, to involve yourself in my problems is a lot to ask."

"You didn't ask," he reminded her. "I offered. Even more, I insisted." He kissed each eyelid closed. "Remember?"

"Why?" she asked, needing to understand. "I've made one mistake after another. I saw Fiona and I've looked in the mirror. You could have any woman you desire."

"Good to know." He joined their lips again, inhaling her breath as his own. "Since I desire only you."

They kissed and kissed, making out like teenagers in the back of a car. He played with fire, caressing her body, fueling an arousal of his own that he had no intention of quenching.

Not tonight.

Tonight, was all about Sara. "I love this, baby," he whispered. "We can make forever feel this way." He worshiped her with his lips and mouth, giving her what she needed, holding her until the sad memories drawn forth by the evening's events were once more relegated to the quiet place of simple regret.

Before she fell asleep, Sara cuddled closer to his chest and whispered, "It's a good thing we're waiting."

Daniel, who'd endured the sweetest torture, was almost beyond comprehending. "What are you saying, sweet?"

Sighing happily, she closed her eyes. "I'll have time to practice being good in bed."

"God, help me," Daniel groaned, his cock springing back to life with a vengeance. If he didn't have her soon, he would die.

CHAPTER SEVEN

From the moment Sara woke with Daniel in her bed, she knew things would be different. How things would change, she wasn't sure. Like a Hallmark card saved in an old pasteboard box, she knew she would take this memory out to examine again and again. But as good as the recollecting would be, the reality was billions of times better.

As her eyes opened, she was aware of feeling warm and secure. The reason for her comfort was the two strong arms cradling her close. Her head was nestled on a broad chest, her face cushioned on layers of muscle. Beneath her cheek, the steady beat of his heart and rhythmic intake of his breath was the most reassuring thing she'd ever experienced.

Knowing she needed to begin her day, she extricated herself from his embrace with great care, leaving him to sleep until she finished preparing breakfast for the family. Before she left the room, her gaze lingered on him, loving the way he looked in her bed.

Big. Masculine. Powerful. Sara smiled. And cuddly. He looked all kinds of cuddly.

By the time Daniel arrived in the kitchen, Sara was busy flipping pancakes and his brothers were in the middle of regaling her with stories of their high school football-playing days and the titles they'd won. "I didn't realize I was in the company of such athletes," she murmured, placing the syrup and butter on the table.

"You're in the company of a group of has-beens who are reliving their glory days," Daniel announced as he plopped down in a chair and gave Sara a wink. "How'd you sleep, Miss Sara?"

"Good," she stated without looking at him. "Haven't slept as well since I used to share a bed with my Teddy Bear."

Daniel choked on his coffee and Easy slapped him on the back. "Go down the wrong way, Bud?"

"I'm fine." He waved his hand, staring at the back of Sara's pretty head.

"Hope slept with me last night," Benjen mentioned, off-handedly, as he spread butter on his pancakes.

"At last, a woman in your bed." Sam smirked. "Thought it would never happen."

"Hey, I'm saving myself."

"What for, Benjen?" Easy asked. "Posterity?"

By this time Sara, was placing the last of the pancakes on the platter, listening to their exchange. She watched Daniel's brothers with interest, knowing she'd learn more about him by understanding them.

"I'm saving myself for the right girl." Benjen slid a forkful of the fluffy sweet bread into his mouth.

"Well, don't save yourself too long." Easy waggled his eyebrows. "Haven't you ever heard the old saying, if you don't use it, you lose it?"

Daniel held up his hand. "That's enough. Let's try to keep a little decorum at the table, shall we?"

His brothers settled down and soon they'd divided the chores for the day, Sam and Easy were moving the cattle from one section of pasture to another, while Daniel and Benjen were set to take some horses to a sale.

"So, only two for lunch. Will everyone be here for supper?"

She was thinking of what to cook when Daniel spoke up, "Just lay out some steaks and I'll cook on the grill tonight."

Sara nodded. "Okay, if you're sure. I'll wash the windows or something to pass the time."

"No." Daniel stood, plate in hand, heading to the sink, where he rinsed the dish off and placed it in the dishwasher. "Everyone follow my lead, clean up after yourself. Today is Sara's day off. She's going to do something fun."

"I haven't been here long enough to get a day off," Sara argued, not sure how she felt about this new development. Was he trying to tell her something?

"Most people get two days off in a week and you've worked six days straight," Easy agreed, following Daniel's line of thinking.

"Fun? What will I do?" she asked as the men started for the door.

Daniel tapped her on the end of the nose. "Whatever it is, just don't tire yourself out too much. You and I can take a long walk when I come home." He gave her a wicked wink. "If you hadn't noticed it, Pet, I'm courting you, good and proper."

With that flirtatious announcement, he was gone. Sara stood at the window after the door closed behind them, watching Daniel and his brothers saunter off to begin their day. Her eyes were hungry, memorizing the purposeful way he moved, the way the muscles rippled beneath the fitted western shirt he wore so well. "Courting, huh?" she muttered to herself. "Well,

I could get used to this."

With a wistful sigh, she turned and set to work putting the kitchen to right, wiping down the counters and placing a pork roast in the slow-cooker, just in case. If they didn't need it tonight, she could serve it for lunch tomorrow.

Yes, she was feeling at home on Blackhawk Ranch. There were moments, like now, when she dissected all that had transpired, every word he'd uttered, and the emotions he drew forth from her. Was this real? The man, with his courtly, gallant ways had swept Sara off her feet. She'd let him carry her into the sunset, and now she was awaiting freedom from one relationship so…she could begin a new one. He might call it courting, but whatever it was, his plan was working. She was already way over her head in a relationship with Daniel Blackhawk.

The thought made her blush, her lips unable to resist a smile.

No matter. The simple truth was that she trusted him.

With no idea what to do for fun, Sara just worked around the house. She didn't wash the windows, but she did the laundry, took Hope for a walk, and came back to press a dozen shirts and a half-dozen pairs of jeans. Still not able to tell what clothes belonged to who, she hung them in the wash room to be claimed by their rightful owner.

After completing that less than enjoyable task, Sara was about to reorganize the pantry when she heard her phone ring. At first the tone confused her, for she rarely received calls, unless it a random robo spiel trying to sell her a sewer system. Running to her purse, she pulled out the cell and answered, "Hello?"

"Sara? This is Ryder. I was wondering if you're

free for coffee."

…Until she headed the Jeep across the cattleguard and onto the main road, Sara hadn't realized Daniel was right, she did need a day off. The anticipation of spending a few hours in the company of other women was exhilarating.

As she drove, she imagined what it would be like when the lawyer proclaimed her to be a free woman again. For so long, Sara had lived with the mistake she'd made, knowing she'd earned whatever hardships had arisen for being such a trusting fool. Doug Wright, or whatever his real name could be, had seen Sara for what she was – an easy mark.

But she'd learned her lesson, hadn't she?

Daniel was different. He gave, he didn't take. Besides, he couldn't want anything from her, she had nothing anyone would want, nothing more to give.

"No," she assured herself, "Daniel is just what he appears to be."

A hero.

When she arrived at the junction to Ranch Road 2341, Sara turned left and headed toward the shores of Lake Buchanan. The scenery was breathtaking. Rolling hills, limestone cliffs, and crystal blue water. From talking to Daniel and Ryder, she knew the McCoy's resort, Eagle Canyon, lay at the end of the road. Before that, one would pass Highlands Ranch and the Duke estate, which was her destination today. Sara had been to none of these places, she'd only heard tell of them in passing conversations. Wealth wasn't something she was accustomed to, her father had worked hard, but any profit he earned was plowed back into his business. Her mother's side of the family was a different story, but that door had been closed in her face years ago.

As her thoughts wandered, Sara found herself at Ryder's home, Falconhead, sooner than she expected. There was no way she could miss it, the imposing home stood high on a hill, with all the splendor of an ancient fortress. "Oh, my goodness," she breathed the words in awe, "This place is otherworldly."

Feeling unsure, she parked the Jeep beneath a tree and strolled by a meticulously manicured garden of lush flowers. There was a circular drive and a valet attendant, who studied her progress with interest. "I would've parked your car for you, ma'am." He hurried to help her up the steps.

"That's quite all right, I enjoyed the walk."

"Allow me." He'd no sooner opened the imposing front door, that she was met by a stately English-looking butler who bowed at the waist. "Greetings. Madam Ryder and Madam Pepper will see you now. They are presently in the kitchen…creating. This way." He took off at a sedate pace and Sara followed meekly in his footsteps, uncertain of what she was getting herself into.

As she trailed the gentleman through the huge home, Sara stared at incredible rooms, furnished in only the best. There was no doubt in her mind that the art on the walls was real. The surface she was walking on was marble and everywhere she looked there were signs of vast wealth and no expense spared to create a palace-like atmosphere. The farther they ventured, the more she could discern the faint sound meeting her ears. Did she hear…giggling?

In keeping with her surroundings, Sara expected to find the sisters seated around an elegantly appointed table having tea. Instead, she and the butler walked into a gorgeous gourmet kitchen to find Ryder, and the woman Sara assumed to be Pepper, rolling out cookies and anointing them with sprinkles. Their hair was mussed and their faces and clothing was dusted with flour.

"Excuse me, Madam Ryder, may I present…"

"Sara!" Ryder didn't wait for a proper presentation, she ran over to give Sara a hug. The old butler let out a sigh of frustration and left the way he came.

"I think you hurt his feelings," Sara pointed out, returning the hug and gazing over Ryder's shoulder at the other woman in the room. She was enchanted. Pepper McCoy James was beautiful, with golden spiral curls hanging well down her back, and the most serene smile she'd ever seen.

"Oh, he'll get over it. Samson and Gideon let him have his way, but they are as down-to-earth as I am." She tugged Sara's hand. "Come meet Pepper. Pepper, this is Sara Riley. Sara, this is Pepper James, my baby sister."

"So nice to meet you." Sara offered her hand, but Pepper grabbed her for a hug.

"We don't stand on ceremony around here. Ryder has been telling me all about you. After reading that article on the local news website, I couldn't wait to meet you."

As Sara moved out of the other girl's embrace, she frowned. "What article?"

"You didn't see it?" Ryder exclaimed. "They interviewed the mother of the little boy who ran out into the highway and she sung your praises to high heavens. And who could blame her? You saved her child's life."

Sara shook her head, thinking about Daniel and the lightning strike. "I just reacted, there was no heroics involved."

"Your actions were ordained." Pepper touched her arm. "I believe in things like that."

"Pepper sees a fairytale everywhere she looks." Ryder teased her sister. "And why not? She's married to a man who writes sonnets for her and dedicates them to her onstage in front of stadiums full of people."

"How romantic." Sara could only imagine how amazing such an action would be. "I do love your husband's music, he's very talented."

"He is," Pepper agreed. "I'm a very lucky woman."

"Hey, we're all lucky." Ryder placed the cookies in the oven. "Are you and that handsome Daniel Blackhawk an item yet?"

Sara joined Pepper at the kitchen table and sorted through the K-Cup tree set in front of her. She chose a caramel coffee and handed it to Pepper, who popped it into the top of the Keurig. "Well, I'm not sure how to answer that…" She pushed her hair over her shoulder. "He's been very good to me and he seems interested, but he's a total gentleman." When they stared at her for a further explanation, she sighed. "I'm still married to someone else."

"Married?" Pepper exclaimed. "To who?"

"Pepper, maybe we shouldn't push Sara." Ryder filled her own cup and took a place at the table.

"It's okay, I'm embarrassed by it all, but none of it is a secret." She rubbed her thumb on the side of the cup, enjoying the warmth. "My husband's name is Doug Wright, he worked for my father, and…persuaded me to marry him when I was vulnerable. To make a long story short, he abandoned me after stealing everything I owned." She didn't mention the baby, Sara's feelings for her lost child were the exact opposite of what she felt for the man who betrayed her.

"I'm so sorry." Pepper touched Sara's hair. "You're not going to remain married to him, are you?"

Sara licked a bit of coffee from her lip. "Daniel is helping me obtain a divorce. I'm not sure how much longer it will take. I'm waiting to see."

"Ah, he's being a gentleman and biding his time." Ryder nodded, understanding the situation more clearly.

"Yes, well," she gave the other women a shy smile, "I'm not sure what will happen. We're sorting out our relationship."

"And it's none of our business," Pepper admitted, "but know we're here to help if you need anything."

Wishing to get the conversation back on stable ground, Sara glanced around the beautiful kitchen. "You have an incredible home. Cooking in this kitchen must be a joy."

"Oh, I love to try, I'm not sure how good I am," Ryder said, jumping up. "See, I've almost let the cookies burn." She grabbed a towel and pulled them from the hot oven. "I think they're okay. What do you say, Pepper?"

"Give me one, let me try." She reached for a cookie and grabbed another for Sara. "Join me."

Sara accepted the sugar cookie and took a small bite. "So, what's the word on the fund-raiser. Is it still on?"

"The fundraiser was our excuse for inviting you here, but we certainly do intend to go forth with our plans." She pulled a tablet close and turned it on. "How does this date sound?" She showed Sara a calendar and pointed, indicating the last Saturday in the month.

"A little over a month from now, sounds perfect." This would give her time to prepare and make the crusts ahead of time.

"Good, we'll have it at Highlands, like I said and..." Ryder tapped Pepper on the shoulder. "Judah might sing, if you ask him nicely."

"Oh, I'm sure he will. I'll check his schedule and make sure he's available." She touched her abdomen, giving them a mysterious smile. "He's staying pretty close to home since we found out I'm pregnant."

"Congratulations!" Sara's heart leapt in her chest. In the next breath, she remembered what she'd lost. Her baby. "You must be thrilled."

"Oh, I am. I can't believe I'm actually getting ahead of Ryder."

Ryder bit into her second cookie. "You just think you're ahead. When I do get pregnant, I'll probably have twins and I'll be one up on you."

Sara couldn't be sad in the face of their teasing of one another. Her baby was gone, but one day she might be blessed enough to have another. She let the image of a little boy come to mind, the mirror image of Daniel.

"Anyway, if this date is good for you, Sara, we'll start inviting people to the event." Ryder's eyes narrowed as she studied Sara's face. "I'm not asking too much of you, am I? We'll need about three or four dozen pies."

Sara rose and looked around the kitchen. "Getting them ready to bake is no problem, but I will need to farm them out to several kitchens to ensure their all freshly baked for the auction."

"We can use this kitchen, the one at Highlands, and the commercial facilities at Eagle Canyon. Will that be enough?"

Ryder's suggestion sounded perfect. "Yes, I think we can do it."

"Great!" Pepper bounced up from her chair. "I hate to eat and run, but Judah's waiting for me up at Highland's. We're meeting his friend and bandmate Zion for dinner in Austin."

"Your life is one big party these days, sister." Ryder gave Pepper a hug. "Tell Judah I said to take care of you."

"Oh, he will." Pepper's face showed no doubt at the truth of her statement. Turning to Sara, she held out her hand. "I know this is the beginning of a great friendship. The next time we get together, let's bring Judah, Daniel, and the dynamic duo."

Ryder laughed. "Dynamic is right. My husbands told me last night that they're thinking of riding one of their own rocket ships into outer space."

Sara rose too, knowing it was time to go home. "Could they do that? Without astronaut training?"

"Maybe." Ryder thought about it, then shook her head. "I vetoed the suggestion before they decided we three try to colonize Mars."

Pepper laughed. "I can see it now, Ryder and her two husbands, the new Martians."

Sara picked up her purse and gave her new friends a heartfelt hug. "You two make me dizzy with your rock stars and space men. I think I need to head back to the ranch to my uncomplicated cowboy."

* * *

Sara finished the last bite of her steak. "Grilled to perfection, Daniel. I enjoyed my meal, thank you."

"I just cooked the meat." He gestured toward the bar. "You conjured up everything else."

"Oh, it was nothing." She gave him a wink, glad she'd thought to have everything ready when the men arrived home. "Baked potatoes, corn on the cob, and a salad – that was nothing, they practically prepared themselves."

"I love these s'mores." Sam held up the gooey cookie sandwich, made with marshmallow, a small chocolate bar, and two graham crackers.

"Me too." Benjen fed Hope another bite of steak. "Easy, how about a game of chess? I might let you beat me this time."

"Fat chance, Brother." Easy pushed back from the table. "You're on."

"I play the winner." Sam held up his glass of tea.

"You all have fun." Daniel stood and cleared the table. They'd eaten outside and used paper plates, so clean-up was easy. "Sara and I are going for a walk."

"You and Sara are always sneaking off somewhere," Benjen said with a twinkle in his eye. "If I didn't know better, I'd think something was going on between you two."

"What you know wouldn't fill a thimble." Daniel whacked his brother over the head with a thin stack of paper plates. "Leave the porch light on, we'll be back."

"A walk sounds good, I ate too much." Sara rose to join him. "Where are we headed?"

"We've got enough light to get to the river and back. It doesn't really matter where we go, I just wanted to be alone with you. Having three other people around complicates matters."

"I don't care where we go, either. I just asked." She sought out his hand with her own.

Daniel was pleased by her boldness. He wanted her to feel confident. "I enjoyed sleeping with you, even if all we did was sleep."

"Yea, me too." They fell into step next to one another, enjoying the hint of a breeze that rose to caress Sara's hair. "I loved kissing you. You make me feel so much."

Daniel chuckled. "I was feeling too much, for certain. Before I came to bed, I iced my private parts so I wouldn't scare you with my monster hard-on."

Sara blushed. Even though she'd been married and had a baby, her sexual experience was almost nil. "I'm sure that was uncomfortable. I'm sorry."

"Don't be, it was worth it. I wouldn't have traded sleeping with you in my arms for anything." Anything but making her his, but he kept that to himself.

He sounded so sure, Sara didn't argue. "Have you had a lot of girlfriends?"

Her question took him aback for a moment, but he answered, "Yes and no."

Sara giggled. "That's no answer."

"Before the rape accusation, I had more than I could say grace over. Nothing serious, but I had a reputation. Fiona was one of those women." He let out a harsh breath, his eyes surveying the rocky horizon. "When I got out of prison, I became much more...selective. Careful. I realized how quickly things can slip out of control." Daniel glanced at her, gauging her emotional reaction to his revelation. "I dated a couple of women in Austin, no one local. Again, nothing serious." He squeezed her hand. "I never considered anything permanent until I looked up and saw you."

His beautiful words stole Sara's voice. She sought composure by noting a flock of birds take flight at their approach. The sun's rays were dancing off the top of Packsaddle Mountain, turning the rocks to brilliant shades of orange and pink. "You say the most beautiful things," she whispered. "I don't have much experience at all, despite..." Her voice faded to a whisper.

"Stop worrying, I'll take care of you." He moved

ahead of her to aid her down a steep incline toward the river. "What did you do today, anything interesting?"

"Yes, I had coffee with Ryder Duke and her sister, Pepper James. We discussed the fundraiser." She told him the date. "Still a way off, but I can start planning. They're going to help me with the baking, since I'll need access to several ovens."

"When the time comes, we'll help, you won't have to do this alone." She wouldn't have to do anything else alone, if he had any choice in the matter. Steadying her, they edged closer to the bank. "I want to show you something."

"What?" Sara stared at the rush of water over the rocks. "It's beautiful here."

"This is intriguing." A few feet away, Daniel pointed to the ground. "Look there."

Sara stared and it took her a few moments to realize what she was supposed to be seeing. "Footprints."

"Yes, dinosaur footprints, thirteen of them."

Holding onto Daniel, Sara traipsed by the footprints with delight, getting a feel for the large size of the creature who walked there so long ago. "This is amazing!"

"I think so, that's why I wanted to share it with you." He felt proud to make her smile. "Based on the shape of the prints, with their three toes, scientists think they were made by a carnivore called Acrocanthosaurus."

Sara stopped and stared at the footprints, molded into solid rock over thousands of years. "They're gone, but they left their mark. Most people who live and die do nothing to leave a mark in this world."

"True." Daniel led her over to a large boulder and sat down, pulling Sara to his lap. "Most people just go through the motions of living day to day, never thinking about doing anything that would make a lasting difference to anyone."

"Leaving a legacy, you mean?"

"Yes. Your actions when you saved…"

"Stop." She put her fingers over his lips. "I don't want to keep rehashing that day." The article in the news made her feel funny.

"But it's true," Daniel said, persisting, "that little boy might grow up to cure cancer, or make some amazing discovery that will save the world one day."

"I hope he's happy, that's all." She took Daniel's hand in between both of hers, not really aware of what she was doing. "I want another child someday, that's the only legacy I'm interested in leaving behind."

"And you will have one," he promised solemnly. He might not be able to give her everything money could buy, but he would gladly give her a child. "Or two. Or three."

Sara giggled and he hugged her tight, relieved he could make her laugh. "Come on, let's head home and see who won the chess match."

* * *

Over the next three days, the residents of Blackhawk Ranch seemed to live at a hectic pace. Their work kept them busy and when they weren't working, Daniel tried to fill every spare minute with some type of activity.

One night, they drove into Marble Falls and ate blackened catfish at a riverside restaurant. He treated her with such care, like a lady. Daniel made Sara feel special enough that she grew bold. "Will you take me dancing?"

"Dancing?" He tugged her chair closer to his. "I

have two left feet on the dance floor, Pet. I'm afraid my talents lie elsewhere and soon I'll show you first hand."

Sara blushed as he smirked at her and she knew well what he was referring to. She almost said he couldn't prove it by her, but she didn't. His courtship rules were fast turning into foreplay. When, not if, they ever came together, Sara was sure the fireworks would light up the sky.

"How about a movie?" Daniel suggested. "There's one just down the street. We could sit in the back, hold hands, and neck."

He gave what she knew was his version of a lecherous leer. Sara thought he looked cute as hell. "Okay, it's a date."

"Damn straight."

He paid the bill and they left the restaurant to find a large theater, with a colorful lobby. The floor was covered with marble and the walls featured posters of movies billed as 'coming soon'. The smell of popcorn would've been tempting if she hadn't just eaten her fill.

"Want anything, love? Something to drink?"

"Well, we didn't have dessert. Could I have some chocolate covered raisins?"

He grinned at her indulgently, then led her to the counter where he bought her raisins and a large drink to share. While he finished the transaction, she studied the movies playing and when he turned to her, she had a suggestion ready if he asked.

Surprisingly, he didn't. He just turned to her with these big puppy dog eyes and muttered, "IT?"

Since she was a Stephen King fan, the remake of the classic horror film was her first choice too. "IT, it is."

With only a few minutes to spare before the movie started, they quickly made their way to one of the many auditoriums, this one in the rear of the large building, sporting reclining seats. Sara followed in the dark, up the stairs and to the back row, where he found two seats away from any other movie goers. "This okay?"

"Perfect." She snuggled down into a seat and he joined her, lifting the armrest between them. "This is going to be fun."

Daniel enjoyed the movie, not only for the familiar story – the tale of the creepy clown who knew exactly what everyone was afraid of – but also because every time something scary happened, Sara buried her face in his chest. During the slow spots, and some not so slow, Daniel stole kisses, long deep ones, her tongue sweet and restless in his mouth. At one point, they abandoned all pretense of watching the show and when she would've tried to turn his attention back to it, he let her know how he felt. "Let me. We know how it ends, the good guys win." When he slipped his hand up her shirt, Sara relented, thinking she'd let this good guy win one too.

The next day and the next, the courtship continued. At some point in the day they'd slip away for some alone time. Daniel took her everywhere, from Enchanted Rock, to a night at Isaac McCoy's biker bar in Kerrville. On Saturday, they escaped to Longhorn Caverns, and he had a blast showing her around. Lucky enough to have a friend from high school as a guide, they were able to go off on their own. "I love this place," he told her. "We used to come up here and take the tour, slip away from the guide, and play in the tiered room." He gazed around at the naturally sculpted amphitheater. "It's hard to believe that a tropical sea used to cover most of Texas. This cave has been used as a hide-out for the Indians, the Confederacy, and as a speak-easy during prohibition. More recently, one of my favorite bands, Redneck Jedi, recorded here."

He escorted Sara around, showing her the different formations: The Hall of Diamonds, the Chandelier Room, the Eagles Wings, and the Viking Prow. Sara admired them all, especially the one shaped faintly like Hope, called The Queen's Watchdog. "This is just as beautiful as I remember," Sara whispered. "I love the calcite crystals on the walls."

"You've been here before?" Daniel didn't know why he should be surprised, but he was. So many things they'd done together had been firsts for her. Sometimes, he'd forget he wouldn't be her first in bed, she was such an innocent in so many ways.

"Yes." She hugged herself, stepping a bit deeper into the shadows. "This was one of the last places my mother brought me before she disappeared." Her voice softened. "She packed a picnic and we ate outside on the rocks."

"Sounds nice." He wanted to comfort her, but he didn't know how. "Tell me about your mother." Moving behind her, he pulled her close, so she could rest her head on his shoulder. "If you want to, I mean."

Sara's heart ached with the remembering. "She was a pretty lady."

"Well, she'd have to be, look at you." He kissed the side of her face tenderly.

"Her family had money, she angered them when she chose to marry my father." Her voice became monotone, flat. "She did it anyway, rebellion more of an incentive than love, I think. Because she didn't stay, even for me. My father thought she might've returned to her family in Mason, that's where they were from." She lowered her head and he pulled her hair back, cupping his big body around Sara, supporting her. "I can remember going with him to see, driving up to that big, stone, Victorian house that looked like something out of a movie. Three stories with gables, turrets, and balconies. The only home I'd ever known was a trailer house."

"Wait," Daniel said, curious, drawing her over to a seating area and tugging her down next to him. "There's only one house I know of in Mason that meets your description. Is your mother a Callum?"

"Yes, a Callum." Sara wasn't surprised he'd heard of the family. They weren't well known for their money, whatever wealth they once possessed was a thing of the past. Their claim to fame was the rare jewel once found only on their land, a blue topaz adapted by a long-time ago Texas legislature as the state gemstone. Unfortunately, the supply was limited and finding one now was more like finding the proverbial needle in a haystack.

"I've seen the house and I know about the family stone." People still came from all over the world to dig on the ranch for the minute chance of finding one of the rare gems. For jewelry, the topaz was always carved with a Texas star in the center. "The Callum gems are one of the iconic symbols of the entire state." He might've been impressed, if he didn't realize how badly she was hurting.

"And yet, I don't own one." Sara shrugged. "But if I possessed a ton of the stupid rocks, I still wouldn't have traded them for my mother."

"I'm so sorry."

Sara took a deep breath. "Wanting someone who

doesn't want you is foolish, I guess."

"Are you sure you understood what was going on?" He couldn't fathom turning your back on someone you love. "Maybe there was an underlying reason." Although, Daniel couldn't think of a good enough one to walk away from someone as precious as Sara.

"I was young, but she'd made how she felt pretty plain. She didn't love me anymore, if she ever did," Sara said the words quickly, as if they caused her pain. "Her parents said my mother wasn't welcome to come back to their home and we weren't welcome either." She sighed with sadness. "Looking back, they were old, I don't understand why they didn't want to mend fences with their daughter. Me, I can understand, they didn't know me, but she was their only child."

"Where did she go, did you ever find out?"

Sara glanced up at him, needing to see his expression. She found his face to be full of compassion. "Thailand." Trying to smile, she failed. "Could she get any farther from me?" Her mother had a new kind of family now, living in some type of cultish compound, but she couldn't find the words to relay that bit of information. "Like an abused child becomes an abuser, I don't think she knew how to treat other people in any other way than the way she'd been treated. Coldly."

"I'm so sorry you went through all of this, baby. I wish I could take all your pain away." He pulled her into his arms. "The only thing I can promise you, is that you'll never have to worry about me turning my back on you. I'd rather cut off my arm than hurt you."

Sara relaxed against him, letting him support both her slight weight and her burdens. "I know." She could feel it, Daniel would never hurt her.

"Come on, let's get out of here."

Standing, Sara took his arm and followed him out. "I'm ready for a quiet night, if that's okay with you." They made the trek out of the cavern and into the light of day. "We've been going and going. I love being with you, but I wouldn't mind sitting on the front porch and holding hands in the swing."

Daniel escorted her to the parking lot, finding his truck. "Sure, because this isn't working anyway."

"What do you mean?" she asked, a tinge of uncertainty coloring her tone.

Helping her into the seat, he claimed a kiss, dispelling the momentary doubts that had swarmed her mind. "I was trying to burn off my sexual energy, by doing everything with you, except the one thing I'm aching to do."

"Oh." His confession rocked her. He'd said as much before, but this time his eyes burned into her soul. The heat between them was incredible. Involuntarily, her hand came up to his chest. She wished she could unbutton his shirt and touch the warmth of his skin.

Daniel groaned and reached for her, just as his phone rang.

"Dammit." He started not to answer, but one glance told him it was Zane. Holding up one finger, he pressed 'accept'. "What's up?"

"Tell Sara to come in tomorrow and sign papers. We went through the publication process and got no response. My investigators did find where this same faux Doug Wright has married two other women, scamming them both. I took all this evidence to a judge friend of mine and got your friend an annulment. Except for the formality of signing on the dotted line, Sara's marriage is over."

"Thanks, man. That's the best news I've ever heard. We'll see you tomorrow."

When Daniel hung up, Sara was looking at him with excitement. She hadn't heard everything, but she'd heard enough. "Was that what I think it was?"

Daniel gathered her close. "Oh, hell yeah. You're a free woman, Sara."

Sara smiled, gazing up into his eyes. "It's over?"

"Yea, you don't have to worry about Doug Wright anymore."

"Well, in that case, let's go home." Framing his face, Sara kissed him on the lips. "If you're sure you want me, Daniel, I'm all yours."

CHAPTER EIGHT

The drive from Longhorn Cavern to Blackhawk Ranch wasn't long, only about six miles, cutting through some of the most magnificent scenery the Texas Hill Country had to offer. There are views along this road to confound the sensibilities; three of the Highland lakes, Buchanan, LBJ, and Inks, are visible from atop a very steep incline, known by the local cyclists as the Beast of Park Road 4. At this zenith, one can also see Packsaddle Mountain and an unexpected sight that stole Sara's breath. "What is that over there?"

A few seconds passed before Daniel comprehended her question, he was so intent on making it home before his cock exploded, that his ability to focus was severely handicapped. Following her line of vision, he saw what intrigued her. "That's Falkenstein Castle. An eccentric Texas couple, by the name of Young, had it built after being inspired by castles they visited while touring Bavaria."

"It reminds me of Ryder's home, only bigger." She was completely fascinated by the sight. "Look at all the turrets and spires. Undoubtedly, a princess must live there."

Daniel couldn't help but smile. "I think it's used for weddings, nowadays."

"Really?" she whispered. "I can't imagine having

such a fantasy wedding."

"You'd like that? To be married there?"

Sara laughed, shivering at the thought. "Oh, of course, who wouldn't?" She stared at the castle, even turning in her seat to look out the back window, drinking in the sight until it disappeared from view. "Sometimes it's fun to imagine the impossible, isn't it?"

"Hmmm, you never know." Daniel filed away the information for later. At the moment, he had something much more important on his mind. Picking up his cell, he called his brother. "Easy, I need for you to corral your brothers and head out. Tell them the drinks are on me, just don't come home until late and when you do, don't come knocking on my door."

"What's going on? Are you sick?"

Daniel rolled his eyes. "No, I'm not sick. We need some privacy."

Listening, Sara blushed to the roots of her hair. "Don't run your brothers off the place," she whispered. "We can be quiet."

Daniel grinned at her. "I hope not. I plan on making you scream."

On the other end of the line, Easy was laughing. "I get your drift. Consider the place to be all yours for the evening. However, if you plan on making this a regular event, you might consider insulating the walls."

"Nah, I'll just buy you all ear plugs." He hung up the phone, his attention split between keeping the truck between the ditches and watching the gorgeous woman next to him, who was wiggling in her seat like a cute worm on a hook. "Relax, baby, I'm going to make this the most amazing night of your life."

…Promises. He'd made promises. Daniel hoped

like hell he could deliver.

Fuck. He was excited.

Sara wanted time to freshen up and he was waiting, pacing like a damn caged tiger. Throwing himself to the floor, he did fifty push-ups, one after the other, straining and huffing, needing to release some of the pent-up sexual energy that had been building inside of him since Sara came into his life. And even before that, if the truth be told. If he didn't get a handle on his control, the self-imposed celibacy he'd endured would turn him into a rutting bull.

A cold shower, he needed a cold shower.

Across the house, in her room, Sara was nervous.

A moment she'd longed for had finally arrived. Standing in front of the mirror, she bounced in place, very unsure about her appearance. On a recent trip to town, she'd took a little bit of the money Daniel had given her and bought what she thought might be a sexy gown. It was white lace, practically see-through, and short, coming just to mid-thigh. "I don't think I achieved the look I was aiming for." Her shoulders slumped. "I need a boob job." Going to her closet, she swathed herself from head to toe in a white fluffy robe. Now, her outer look matched her inner look. "I think this might be a really bad idea."

The questionable gown was the only preparation she'd been able to make for her anticipated rendezvous. Her idea to do some cramming in proper bedroom tactics hadn't come to pass. Oh well, reading and studying a how-to book, most likely would be a poor substitute for…uh…hands-on experience.

For a heartbeat or two, Sara considered backing out. She didn't want to disappoint Daniel, but going through with this might disappoint him more.

Climbing from the shower, Daniel grabbed a

towel. He'd invited Sara to join him when she was ready, so when he stepped into his bedroom, he was hoping to find her waiting. The room was empty. He'd considered inviting her to shower with him, but he figured he might need to work up to things. All of this was basically new to her and he wanted to seduce her, not frighten her off.

The thought that she might've changed her mind hit him like a ton of bricks. "Not happening." Unable to wait any longer, he padded barefoot to her room.

"Hey. I've been waiting for you."

Even though his voice was gentle, hearing it sound unexpectedly behind her caused Sara jump. She whirled around to face him. "Oh, Daniel…" She couldn't say more – her voice box was paralyzed. The man wore nothing but a plush navy towel wrapped around his waist. Tantalizing droplets of water glistened on his broad chest. The man was absolutely breathtaking and Sara's heart pounded beneath her breasts. When their gazes locked, all the air was suddenly sucked from the room, leaving them in a vacuum of anticipation. His jaw flexed, as if keeping his distance from her was costing him everything.

"I was about to come, Daniel."

She saw one corner of his mouth lift and…if she wasn't mistaken…there was movement beneath his towel. Something was rising to attention. "Yes, you are. I'm going to make you come so hard your teeth rattle."

Sara gulped. "I think I would like that."

He moved a step or two closer. Slowly. "Aren't you a little over dressed for the occasion?"

"Maybe."

"I think so." He stalked nearer. One step. Two. Reaching out, Daniel snagged the belt on her robe, pulling it undone. "Let's see what you have on underneath this bedspread you're wearing."

She didn't resist. What woman could? "Just a gown."

As soon as the robe slid to her feet, her eyes gravitated to his. If she saw one iota of disappointment, she'd be out the door quicker than a wink. But, it wasn't disappointment she saw...it was hunger. Sara watched his eyes drop, taking in her small breasts, clearly visible through the thin fabric. They were swollen and achy, topped with nipples as hard as acorns.

When he said nothing, her arms rose to cross over her chest.

"Don't." His hand shot up to prevent the movement. "I want to see."

Her arms dropped, but Sara imagined she felt the caress of his gaze travel to her waist and down to the curve of her hips. Dampness gathered between her legs at the thought. Yet, he made no move to touch her.

"Sara...I...oh, hell." His voice was gruff, like he was in pain.

For a split second, it passed through Sara's mind that he was about to reject her. After seeing Fiona, she knew his taste in women ran to the more voluptuous. Maybe he'd seen enough to consider her not worth the trouble. After all, her husband left after the wedding night, telling her she needed to learn how to please a man. Be more aggressive. Well, she'd made no progress on the pleasing front, but perhaps she could make up for her lack of expertise by showing a bit of enthusiasm.

There was no doubt that she wanted him madly, even without knowing what the future held for them. Glancing up into his face, she tried to read the look she saw there. She couldn't. Oh well, some things were worth the risk. "My turn," she whispered.

"Sara."

"Hush." To prevent any protest, she placed one finger on his mouth, then she raised her other hand to the top of the towel at his waist and yanked it from his body. The absolute shock on his face was quite satisfying, especially when she held it up high in front of them, before dropping it at his feet.

A growl emanated from his throat, but he remained stock still while Sara discovered exactly what she'd uncovered. "Mercy me," she said with a small whimper. He was gloriously hard and thick. Remembering the incident at the restaurant, she whispered in awe. "You weren't joking, you are big."

"Thank you." He took her exclamation as the compliment it was meant to be.

Sara couldn't stop looking at him. Clothed, he was handsome. Unclothed, he was so beautiful, she couldn't breathe. When she looked up into his face, she saw his pupils were dilated, wild, and filled with raw desire.

"Since we met, I fantasize about you every night and wake up thinking about you every morning. My cock has been hard for you every minute of every day."

He was enchanting her with every word. "Show me your fantasy."

His eyes gleamed with fire and his mouth turned up into a mischievous grin. "Do you want to be my wet-dream, Pet?"

He prowled toward her, the sexy dimples on his cheeks making an encore appearance. The way he stared, eating her up with his eyes, made Sara want to shed even more of her inhibitions. "I've thought of little else." He'd been amazing to her. Kind. Supportive. Gentle. But the man before her now, was all-male, all hungry male. And she wanted him more than anything. "Can we?"

Her answer came in an unexpected manner.

The whole bed shook as Daniel fell on it with a bounce, pulling Sara along for the ride. She giggled as she landed on top of him. "In a hurry?"

"Hot damn, yes." He captured her face in both hands and brought her mouth down to his, kissing her with all the passion his heart could hold.

The first taste of her lips did little to soothe the frantic craving that held him in its grasp. Only his intense need to worship her as she deserved kept his baser instincts at bay. Acting as though they had all the time in the world, he kissed Sara, reacquainting himself with the beauty and sweetness of her mouth. Since learning the ties that bound her to that pretender were about to be severed, Daniel longed to make their first time together the first time she deserved. So, this was their first kiss, the only first kiss that mattered. Slowly, he offered her his tongue, waiting for her to accept it, stroking hers when she did. With the fire in his loins barely banked, he nibbled on her bottom lip, then soothed the spot with a kiss. When she whimpered and ate at his lips, he acquiesced to his need and kissed her deeply, losing himself in the luxury of her sweetness.

Daniel ended the kiss long before he was satisfied, knowing he'd never be satisfied. The only thing that pacified him was the fact this was their first time, their first time of many. He fully intended on loving her again and again.

She was lying atop him, her full weight resting on his body. "You feel so good lying on me." He smoothed his hands down her back, caressing her thighs, and edging her gown upward. "Let me see you." He was acutely conscious of the press of soft breasts to the planes of his chest.

Sara sat up at his urging, frissons of excited apprehension blooming on her skin. "Leaving it on might be better, I'm not made like Fiona."

He ignored her reluctance. "You'll never know how thankful I am that you're nothing like Fiona." With that declaration, he eased the garment up, coaxing her arms over her head until he could free her body of anything that could keep his eyes from indulging in her absolute perfection.

Daniel was speechless.

He let his hands speak when his mouth could not. With near reverence, he caressed her. Everywhere. Needing to touch her completely, Daniel slipped a hand around her back and eased her flat to the bed, so he could cover her. His skin craved hers. He held himself up just high enough that his body could slide against hers without crushing her delicate form. "Sara, my Sara," he whispered as he moved up and down, mimicking the erotic dance of sex, but indulging only in the miracle of feeling her beneath him. He was completely bewitched, on the verge of coming just from the rasp of her nipples against his chest.

"Sweet Jesus, baby." He sat up, breathing harshly. Sara lay there, looking up at him, her beautiful hair spread out on the pillow, her delectable body quivering for his touch. There was no lamp turned on in the room, but a slow moon was rising and the light of its rays caressed her skin. "You're so gorgeous."

"Am I?"

He could see the uncertainty in her eyes, the eagerness to please. "Are you kidding? Where would

I go to find a more beautiful sight? There's not a star in the sky more glorious than you. When I look at you, Sara, I've got a million-dollar view." He groaned, closing his eyes, "Hell, look at me. I'm about to go off like a Roman candle." His hand lowered to brush his strutted cock. A look of near agony flitted across his face. "I wouldn't be a man if I could resist a woman like you."

"Don't wait, take me," she urged.

Shaking his hand, he stiffened every muscle. "Too fast. I want to make this last. I've waited too long, wanted you too long to rush." Lowering himself to her side, he cupped one firm globe and brought his lips to the tender coral tip. Opening his mouth wide, he sucked lightly at first, then harder, increasing the heat and the pressure. Glancing up, he sought out her gaze, watching her eyes flutter closed in ecstasy. Her lips parted with tiny pants, their pink surface glistening from his kiss.

"More. More," she demanded, having never experienced anything so wonderful before. Sara clutched his shoulders as he suckled at her breast, his tongue swirling and licking, she almost fainted when he took the aching nubbin between his teeth and tugged. To her, this sharing was incomparable, the sensations unique and unfamiliar. A low moan of delight escaped her lips and she commanded her eyes to open. The sight of Daniel devouring her with his mouth was something she didn't want to miss. When he moved to her other breast and gave it the same exquisite attention, she was more than grateful.

"You have the most amazing pair of tits in the world," he said finally, when he kissed a path to the side of her breast and took a needed breath.

"Sometimes I can't believe the things that come

out of your mouth."

He moved his head back to her breasts, hungry for more. "I can do something else with my mouth you aren't going to believe."

"Oh, really?" Her voice was teasing, playful. Sara was having a good time.

With a sinful grin, he used his tongue to trace a path from her cleavage to her abdomen. "Open up, show me your pussy," he whispered, his tone changing from teasing to near desperate.

Sara obeyed, shyly.

"Spread your legs. Wider." Taking his hands, he showed her how wide.

A flash of heat seared Sara. Even before he touched her, she began to claw at the bed sheet. Never before had she felt so vulnerable. Locking her gaze on his face for strength, she saw him lick his lips, as if he was salivating. Her heart ramped up its beat, the sight of his need for her was the most erotic thing she'd ever beheld.

Moving lower in the bed, he used his thumbs to open her up. "God, you're exquisite." He leaned in and buried his face between her thighs and began to feast. Licking and kissing, he ravaged Sara, coaxing her to the brink of bliss. Having her pliant and trusting in his arms, giving herself to him eagerly was almost more than he could process. Daniel speared his tongue deep, tongue-fucking her until she was writhing beneath him. Anxious to give them both what they needed, he took her clit between his lips and sucked. The moan that burst from her mouth as she came was the most beautiful sound he'd ever heard.

A bolt of lightning, reminiscent of the one that had struck so close to them, shot pleasure through Sara. As the orgasm washed over her, she spiraled over the edge of forever and plunged into the endless expanse of eternity. She'd never felt anything so wonderful than his hot mouth on her body. He'd given her an unselfish gift, focusing solely on her. As he brought her down with gentle kisses, she eased up to drink in his powerful form bowing before her. His dark mane was tousled, the sleek, powerful muscles of his shoulders and arms rippled as he moved.

"Thank you," she said, overwhelmed by how he made her feel.

"You're welcome." He placed one more kiss on her throbbing clit, before crawling back up her body, his eyes hooded, his expression one of triumph. "I'm sure I enjoyed myself as much as you."

"I seriously doubt it." Her eyes never left him. As he stood to his feet at the edge of the bed, naked, Sara found herself responding. The craving in her body pulsed to life and she wanted more. Mesmerized, she watched him touch his cock, his hand gliding down the thick shaft. She sighed, indulging in the sight. Every inch of the man was beautiful, from the top of his head to the tip of his toes. And best of all, he was good and kind. Decent. Sara wanted him so much. To have a man such as he to call her own, forever? No woman could want anything more. "Love me, Daniel."

"Wild horses couldn't hold me back." He came to her, over her, taking her hands and threading their fingers together. Lifting their joined hands over her head, he covered her. Sara opened her legs wide again, inviting him to make her his. As she felt the broad head of his cock nestle into the tender folds of her sex, Sara's heart began to thrum. When he made no move to continue, just held himself up on his arms, searching her face, she forgot to breathe.

"Sara, my Sara," he whispered.

Lifting her face, she offered him her kiss. He smiled and brought his mouth close, their breaths mingling. "What are you waiting for," she asked softly.

He shook his head, kissing her once, sweetly. "Just enjoying the moment, drawing out the ecstasy. I want to live every second, feel every second, to never forget."

Sara was floating in a sea of joy. How different this was than anything she'd experienced or imagined before. Her soul and heart and body were completely attuned to Daniel's every move, every breath. When he gently began to push inside of her, his gaze was locked to hers, and the wonder she felt was mirrored in his eyes. "Oh, God, Daniel," she whispered. As he eased in, she felt her sheathe stretching to accept him, the feeling of fullness burned in the most delicious way.

Daniel eased his starving cock in and out twice more before sinking deeper. Rooted to the hilt, he stopped with a groan and held himself perfectly still. Closing his eyes, he reveled in the reality of being buried inside of Sara, enveloped in her silky warmth. Nothing, nothing had ever felt like this. Not even close. Being one with her felt so good, like nothing on earth. He didn't move a muscle, wanting the feeling to last and last.

Sara could see Daniel's reaction and she needed to convey what their union meant to her. "I love this," she whispered, her hands moving feverishly over his chest and shoulders. Wanting to be as close as possible, she wrapped her legs around his waist, and when she did, he slid deeper.

"Oh, fuck, baby," he moaned, throwing his head back, fighting for even an ounce of self-restraint. "Be still, I don't want to lose control."

The idea of Daniel letting go did something to Sara. She wanted to see him desperate for her. An overwhelming, hungry ache rose in her and she lifted her body, clinging to him, tightening her arms, her thighs, and her feminine walls around him. "Don't hold back, please. I want to feel you."

Daniel gave in to her gentle demands, moving his body, finding the exquisite rhythm that would bring them both pleasure. As he rocked into her, he found her lips and drank from their sweetness. Their bodies became slick with excitement as he glided over her, not crushing, but letting her feel the power of his love.

"Oh, God, Daniel, I love this," she whimpered, almost swooning with ecstasy as he moved his hips in a tight circle, undulating, filling her to the brim, his pelvis grinding against her clit. "Faster, baby, please."

Her ardent plea released something within him, something he'd hadn't realized he'd been holding back. With a growl, he began to pump his hips, thrusting into her body again and again until they were shaking with bliss. He pressed his face into her neck and pounded over and over, driving deeper and harder until there was nowhere for them to go but to the very gates of Heaven itself. Together.

"Look at me, Daniel," she whispered, not knowing if he would hear her request. To her relief, he raised his face, even as he hammered within her. Sara grasped him tighter, reading the signs that he was fast becoming undone. As they stared into one another's eyes, their worlds collided, the white-hot rapture of release cascading over them like liquid fire. "Oh, Daniel!"

Hearing his name on her lips, being called out with such emotion, freed something inside of him and he surrendered. Nothing would ever be the same. "Sara, I love you, I love you more than anything."

Sara held him, cherishing him. She'd always heard that you couldn't depend on words spoken in the heat of passion, but she chose to ignore that old supposition. "I love you too, Daniel. I'm crazy about you, cowboy." Cupping the back of his head, she held him to her. "I'm right where I want to be."

"Good." Daniel sealed their love with a kiss. "I'm glad, because I'll never need anything but you."

During the most wonderful night of Sara's life, she lost count of the orgasms Daniel gave her. When she finally fell asleep in his arms, her dreams were full of promise and hope. Her last thought, nestled close to his side, was how much she looked forward to waking up and beginning this new life with Daniel.

* * *

Her new life was not a disappointment. Sara's happiness knew no bounds. Everything was perfect, Daniel made sure of it. He didn't try to hide the way things were between them from his brothers. They'd known, to a certain degree, how he felt about her. Now, after the annulment, he made no bones about their relationship. Every moment they shared was a celebration.

And he couldn't keep his hands off her, he didn't even try. They made love morning, noon, and night. Daniel would take breaks, just to come in for a kiss. One kiss would become two, and two would become three. He fulfilled the fantasy of giving her a bath, kneeling at the side of the tub and washing her gently, before crawling in to join her. More water was on the floor than in the tub when they finished, but neither cared.

Seemingly by mutual agreement, Sam, Easy, and Benjen, found much to do away from the old rock house. Meal time and bedtime were the only times they sought out her and Daniel's company, otherwise, they gave them privacy.

One evening, Sara felt guilty when she realized what they were doing. "Hey, why don't we do something together tonight?" She offered the suggestion as she set a huge platter of fried chicken in the center of the dining table.

"Uh…man, this smells good." Benjen speared a thigh. "I've got plans," he stammered, "we've got plans, Sara." He caught Easy's gaze and bugged his eyes as if asking for help.

"Plans." Easy repeated his claim. "Big plans." He stared at Sam.

"Yea," Sam said, then delayed his comment by taking a big drink of iced tea, "plans to…uh…" He stared at the table, seeing bowls of mashed potatoes, green beans, and black-eyed peas. "Break up a garden patch! Yea!" He seemed so proud of himself. "Daniel wants you to have a garden."

Daniel smirked. "I do want Sara to have a garden." He took a big bite from a chicken leg. "You three can hang around tonight, though. You don't have to spend another night at the local bar." He winked at Sara. "Sara and I want your company. We have plenty of time to ourselves when we retire to our room."

Sara choked on her mashed potatoes, which was hard to do with mashed potatoes. She felt herself blushing and started giggling when Benjen fanned her with his napkin. "Stop, I'm fine." She busied herself by slipping bites of chicken underneath the table to Hope. "Why don't we watch a movie together or play monopoly or marbles or something?"

"A movie sounds good," Easy said, "we could watch the new Avengers, it just hit Netflix."

"Great." Daniel nodded, licking his fingers. "We'll have popcorn." His gaze caught Sara's and he winked at her. He could barely eat for smiling. He'd never been so happy in his life. "I think I'm going to hire a contractor to clear out a house place on the new property."

"Thinking about building?" Benjen looked between Sara and Daniel with interest.

"One of these days," Daniel admitted. "Never hurts to plan ahead."

Sara said nothing. She could feel all four of the brothers watching her carefully. Ever since the day her annulment was finalized, the tension in the house seemed to be building. There was an expectation in the air, like everyone was waiting for the other shoe to drop. Truly, she didn't know what to expect. She and Daniel were closer than ever, he never failed to shower her with attention, but he hadn't repeated the words he'd whispered to her after they'd made love. He hadn't told her he loved her again.

"I'll find the movie." Easy finished cleaning his plate, then rose to put it in the dishwasher. The others followed suit, over time, the brothers had set up a routine, helping take care of themselves so Sara's workload was more manageable.

"Okay, we'll be right in." Daniel placed his hand on Sara's "Hold on. I want to talk to you."

"Okay." She gave him a sweet smile. "What about?"

"Tomorrow. Don't plan on doing anything. We're spending the day together."

"Where are we going?"

He winked at her. "It's a surprise."

"I love surprises." She glanced around the kitchen. "I'll put on food tonight. There's laundry I was planning on doing…"

"Stop." He nodded his head toward the living room. "The guys can take care of themselves. You've been doing too much lately."

"No, I haven't." She didn't know what he was talking about. Of course, it was hard to think when he was touching her. His big hand was underneath her hair and he was massaging her neck.

"Are you kidding?" He let his fingers rove up into her hair, tangling in the long, dark strands. "You've come into our lives and taken over. You do everything around here except rope the cows."

She shrugged. "I'm just doing my job."

He bit his tongue, he didn't want to spoil his surprise. "You've done more than your job, baby. You've made yourself indispensable." He buzzed her cheek. "To me."

She shivered with delight. She hoped so. Sara had no desire to be anywhere else or with anyone else. She was sublimely happy with Daniel.

After picking up a few things, they popped some corn, poured some sodas, and joined the others in the den around the big TV. Sara was content to sit by Daniel on the couch as he hugged her close. The movie proved to be a little too hypnotizing for her, however. Soon, she couldn't keep her eyes open.

Daniel pulled Sara close and let her sleep. Although he craved her like a drug, holding her brought him joy and utter contentment. Once the movie was over, he whispered to his brothers that he was taking his angel to bed.

"We'll clean up here and lock up," Sam promised.

"I'll be out of pocket, tomorrow. Remember to

place an order for the grass seed we're going to need for this fall." He picked Sara up in his arms and started down the hall.

"I'll take care of it," Benjen promised as he bent to fasten Hope's leash to her collar, getting ready for the dog's last walk of the day. "You two just have a good time. I hope she gives you the answer you're hoping for."

Daniel cut his brother a warning glance.

"Big mouth." Easy punched his brother.

Despite their carrying on, Sara never opened her eyes and Daniel gave a sigh of relief. If everything went the way he wanted it to, this time tomorrow night, he'd be an engaged man.

* * *

Sara sighed in her sleep.

Such a good dream.

Wonderful.

Really wonderful.

"Oh, yes," she whispered, her body writhing with pleasure. Sweet heat flowed through her veins as she lifted her hips toward the rays of the sun. Rays that were somehow kissing her between her…

Her eyes sprung open as Daniel began licking her clit. Sara arched her back, weaving her fingers in his hair, chewing on her bottom lip. "God, this feels so good!" She bucked beneath him, his weight bracing her on the bed. "Daniel, oh, please," she keened as one of his hands slipped up her body to tug on her nipple.

"Come!" he demanded as he saw to it that she obeyed. Nuzzling her intimately, he used his tongue to part her folds as his mouth worked her over. Holding her thighs apart, he licked and speared into her wet channel, causing Sara to grasp the headboard with one hand and her own breast with the other.

"Daniel!" she sobbed as he concentrated on her clit, his fingers curling inside of her to find that one tender spot that would cause her to levitate from the mattress. She shook as the tension built and built, until she shattered, her pussy clamping down around Daniel's fingers. "What a way to wake up! You're better than a rooster crowing, Blackhawk." Sara panted and jerked as little aftershocks jolted through her.

"I'm not a rooster, Pet, but I do have a cock that's craving attention." He began to kiss his way up her body. "I can't wait to get inside you."

"I have something else in mind, something I've been dying to do."

Instantly, he knew what she meant. "Sara, no. You don't have to…"

"I want to." Sara sat up so abruptly, she almost dislodged Daniel from the bed. "I know I probably won't be good at it, but if you don't let me practice, I'll never be able to please you." She'd hinted at doing this before, but Daniel always seemed too anxious to be inside of her. When he resisted her nudge to ease him to his back, she cupped his face. "What's wrong, talk to me, why don't you want me to go down on you? Is it me?"

"No, no." God, what had he done? She was very near tears. "I just didn't want…hell." God, he never knew he had so many damn issues. He'd let a couple of silly women with prejudicial hang-ups color his life to such an extent, he was jeopardizing the feelings of the one woman he cared for more than life itself.

"You don't want what?" Sara asked, easing off the bed. "Me?"

"No, stop!" He snagged her hand and pulled her

back. How could he tell her about the women who'd wanted what he could do for them, but didn't want to dirty their mouth on him? "I didn't want you to have to do that for me, not if you didn't want to…"

Sara stared at Daniel as if he'd grown a second head. "I've been dying to…" Dammit! "No. It doesn't matter." She pushed away from him and sprang to her feet. "It's okay, I wouldn't have been any good at it anyway."

Hell. This was not the way he intended to begin the morning. He got up to follow her, then was stopped by the slamming of the bathroom door. Realizing he needed to correct this situation, he waited for her.

After taking care of business, Sara stood at the sink and dashed water on her face. She didn't really understand what had just happened. How could he want her so much, yet not want her to kiss him…there? As far as she knew, from popular culture, every man wanted a blow-job, sometimes even more than intercourse itself. True, Doug hadn't asked for it, but they hadn't spent enough time in bed together to know what the other wanted. She'd never been the attraction, Sara knew that now, he'd only wanted what he could take from her, not Sara herself.

"What's going on?" Sara whispered. Daniel wasn't like that, she knew he wasn't. He'd proved that over and over again. So, what was the deal? Taking deep breaths, she tried to remember what he'd just said. Sara knew when she was upset, sometimes she quit paying attention. *I didn't want you to have to do that for me, not if you didn't want to…*

I didn't want you to have to do that for me, not if you didn't want to…

By the time the thought repeated itself, Sara was thinking something entirely different. Daniel had suffered prejudice and racism. Not just the rape charge, but the willingness of people to believe the charges about him. The lawman's cruel jibe in the restaurant, and God only knew how many others that he'd never told her about. Could this be it?

Holding herself straight, Sara resolved to find out if she was right.

When she emerged from the bathroom, Daniel was waiting, propped up against the wall. "Sara, wait!" His arm shot out to halt her leaving.

"I'm not going anywhere." She didn't give him an opportunity to go anywhere either. Sinking to her knees, she hooked her fingers in the waistband of the lounge pants he wore and peeled them down his legs. For a moment, Daniel was too shocked to respond.

Sara took him in her hand and experimentally licked a circle around the head of his dick, then looked up into his eyes. "There is nothing about you that isn't perfect. And any woman who'd think otherwise is a fool." With that pronouncement, Sara took the head of his cock in her mouth and Daniel had no will to stop her.

"Sara, my Sara," he moaned, throwing his head back and letting it slam against the wall. The feel of her lips wrapped around his cock was indescribable. Chills raced up and down his body and his muscles went stiff as he rose on his toes.

Sara heard his breath catch in his throat as she took more of him into her mouth. Glancing up into Daniel's face, she saw the well-defined muscles in his beautiful face grow taut. Did he really want this? She chose to believe he did. She needed to make him feel wanted, the way he always did to her.

Taking a deep breath, she let her mouth slide down, taking him deep, then pulling her mouth slowly off so she could lick the underside and graze the thick length of him with her teeth. She might be without experience, but she'd read books, plus she possessed this great need in her heart to give him this gift. When she took the head between her lips and started to suck, she heard him groan and his big body shuddered. God, she hoped that meant she was doing this right. Going on faith, she took more of him in her mouth and began to suckle.

Ye gods, how could anything be so good! His greedy cock was pulsing with ecstasy and the more she sucked, the weaker his knees became. "Sweet, baby," he muttered, grasping her hair and twining it around his fist.

Sara wanted to do more for him, so she engaged her hands as well as her mouth, stroking his thigh with one hand and squeezing the base of his shaft with the other, squeeze-stroke, squeeze-stroke. Every touch and kiss she gave seemed to be welcomed by Daniel with wonder. Her own reaction surprised her, her nipples were swollen and achy, and she was wet and throbbing between her legs. Sara found herself so turned-on, she couldn't be still, her hips wanted to move and she kept clenching and unclenching her sex in response.

With his hand curved around the back of her head, Sara continued, surprised at how much she was enjoying herself. She loved the way he reacted, the sounds he made, the way his body tightened and shifted. Hollowing out her cheeks, she increased her rhythm and relished the way he gently pushed at her head, guiding her movements.

As she played with him, sucking and licking, marveling at the intimacy of the act they were sharing, her hand caressed his thigh and came up to cup his balls. This wasn't the first time she'd touched him, but her contact now was lingering instead of in passing. Letting her fingers play, she applied a little pressure and Daniel grunted and twitched. She didn't know if that was a good twitch or a bad twitch so she moved her hand and concentrated on what she was doing with her mouth.

Bobbing her head, she laved his hard, smooth flesh with her tongue, humming her excitement as she immersed herself in this new erotic task. There was no denying it, pleasing him like this felt good, better than almost anything.

"Sara," Daniel groaned thickly, rising to his toes again, every muscle tensing. He slapped the wall at his side, his body trembling. Glancing down, he watched his Sara on her knees at his feet, watched his cock sink into her beautiful mouth. Even without the heaven of her lips, he'd be able to get off on the sight of the woman he loved, loving him.

As her mouth worked ceaselessly, he shook as the pleasure built, his hands forming fists, his hips rocking to meet every down stroke of her head. Daniel was panting now, his body flushed with arousal, he wouldn't be able to hold on much longer. "Sara, honey, I'm fixing to come," he choked out the words, his face contorting with rapture. "Come up here." He tried to gather her up. "Ride me."

Sara shook her head, but didn't turn him loose, she wanted the full experience. Sucking harder, she touched his sac again. His whole body quaked and a roar of release escaped from his lips. "Sara!" She held on, thrilled by the way he shattered for her, his hips bucking, his breath coming harsh and heavy. His cock jerked in her mouth and a thick stream of cum jetted down her throat. She swallowed, licking gently, loving how he pulsed in her mouth, how his fingers tightened in her hair.

As she released his cock, letting it slip from her lips, she leaned her head against his thigh, unwilling to let him go. "Good?" she asked, needing to know.

Daniel felt as weak as a kitten, but not too weak to show her how he felt. Pulling Sara to her feet, he wrapped his arms around her. "So good. You wiped me out." With closed eyes, he blindly sought her mouth, kissing her deeply.

"I'm glad." She smiled, chewing on her lower lip. "I had no idea I'd get so excited."

"You did?" Daniel asked. "Tell me about it."

Sara blushed. "Well, my nipples got so hard." She rubbed herself on him, letting him feel the stiff, swollen peaks. "And I got all tingly and achy and empty." Daniel made a groaning noise and clasped her hips, pulling her lower body up against his. To Sara's surprise, he was hard again. "How?"

"You," Daniel whispered. "This always happens around you."

Lifting her up, he reversed their positions, bracing her against the wall. Sara wrapped her arms around his neck and her legs around his waist, resting her head on his shoulder as he fitted his cock to her tender opening and pushed in. "Oh, yea, that's what I needed," she exhaled in relief, helpless pleasure swamping her senses.

As Daniel began to hammer home, his hips moving faster and faster, he drank from her lips. In between kisses, he poured out his heart. "You knew just what I needed and you're just what I need. You're my everything, Sara. My everything."

CHAPTER NINE

Daniel stood in the shower, his face lifted to the warm spray, his hands soothing the soap from his body. He was sated. Happy.

Satisfied. Content.

Being with Sara, having her in his life, fulfilled him as nothing ever had. Knowing what the day held in store, he soaped his hands to finish the job of cleansing himself.

She'd given him a blow-job.

He smiled at the memory. The woman was amazing. She'd come into his life and dispelled every doubt he'd harbored.

Daniel didn't think of himself as a weak man. No. He could bench press three hundred fifteen pounds. His body was muscled up, and not just from workouts. He was a cowboy, he worked the land. The hardness of his body wasn't just for show.

Despite the strength of his arms and shoulders, the broadness of his back, the sturdiness of his legs – he'd been more vulnerable than he realized. More susceptible to the sharp tongues and cold hearts of the people who judged him.

Indian. Dirty redskin. Worthless.

His mother hadn't raised him to believe those things. She'd taught her boys that they were as good as anyone else. Valuable. Worthy.

While they were growing up, there had been incidents. Slights. Innuendoes. The Blackhawk boys had been big for their age. They covered the ground they stood on. Most of what was said about them and their father was said behind their back. Sometimes, the cruel jibes reached their ears, and when it did, they found solace in their home, at the feet of their mother who seemed to have a timeless wisdom.

Catherine Thompson Blackhawk had loved their father beyond measure. She'd stood by him, they'd built a home together, been blessed with four boys. Her greatest gift to them, other than daily care and nurturing, was instilling in them self-confidence and a sense of their place in the world. Daniel had held onto these values until they'd been ripped from his grasp by the cruel lies of people who'd focused their flawed spotlight on the things that set them apart. He held up his hand and looked at it. A little darker than some, but just a hand.

Shrugging off the worry, he soaped his chest, his cock stiffening at the memory of Sara's mouth giving him pleasure.

God, how he loved that girl.

After today, she'd know just how much.

Swiping down his body, Daniel cleaned his cock, giving the shaft a few strokes of promise. Soaping his hands again, he cupped his balls to clean them, like he'd done countless times in his life. "Ouch!" A twinge of pain caught him off guard, just like the one he'd felt when Sara had massaged his sac. He frowned, feeling of his scrotum. Was that a lump?

"Daniel?"

Hearing Sara's voice, he pushed the concern aside, figuring whatever it was, was nothing to worry about. "Be right there!"

He rinsed off and stepped out, toweling himself dry.

"Phone call for you! You left your cell in the kitchen. I put it on the bed!"

"All right, thank you, love." He wrapped a towel around his waist and stepped into his room to grab the phone. "Hello?"

"Hey, it's Easy. Everything's set up. The blue one you wanted is on its way from Dallas. By the time you get back from Mason, it'll be spiffed up and ready to go."

Daniel smiled as he pulled a shirt from the closet. "Thanks. This is going to be quite the day. Wish me luck."

"You've got all our well-wishes. We love Sara as much as you do."

With a chuckle, Daniel stepped into his jeans. "Well, I doubt that, but I appreciate all you've done. I know it hasn't been easy, giving us our space."

"Our time's coming, Brother. You're just the first one to take the plunge. Did you pick up the ring?"

"Yea, I did that yesterday. I think everything's all set up."

"Are you nervous?"

"Hell, yes. I'm scared to death. What if she says no?"

"She won't. Have you seen the way she looks at you?"

"I guess I've been too busy looking at her to notice."

"Well, believe me, she worships the ground you walk on."

"God, I hope so. I love her more than anything." Daniel thanked his brother, then finished dressing, he had places to go and a woman to sweep off her feet.

* * *

"Daniel, what are we doing here?"

Sara was trembling and her heart was pounding in her chest. For the past few miles, she'd been talking non-stop, telling Daniel all about the vegetables she wanted to plant in the garden his brothers had promised they would break-up for her and about the idea she had of taking some online classes.

"I love working for your family, but I think I'd like to get a degree. Do you think I'd make a good park ranger?"

"A park ranger? Sure." He wanted her to be happy, but he didn't want her thinking about leaving him, not when he was about to propose.

"Yea, there are dozens of State parks nearby. I could lead tours on Enchanted Rock or at Longhorn Caverns. Or maybe I should be a teacher…" She hesitated, then just said what she was thinking. "You could tell people I can do more than just bake pies."

Daniel pressed his lips together. "I don't doubt that you can do anything you set your mind to. Your value as a person is much more than an occupation or a degree, Sara. You are so smart. You're sweet and kind. Hell, you're flippin' gorgeous."

"You're just prejudice."

Today, the word that so often tormented him, made him laugh. "Damn right, I'm very prejudice about you. I think you're amazing."

"This home belongs to my mother's family, Daniel. What are we doing here?" she repeated her question while Daniel found a parking place.

"Take a breath, sweetheart. I don't know how long since you've been here, but the place has gone through major renovations and they're getting ready to start tours soon."

"If they haven't started tours, what are we doing here?"

"We're just going to look around." Well, there was more going on than that, but making her feel more at ease was his current goal.

Sara didn't know about this. She'd prepared herself to never see this place again. Her mother was out of the picture and her grandparents were dead. "I'm not sure I want to do this."

"Yes, you do." He came around to help her out of the truck, opening the door, then taking her into his arms. "Trust me. You've helped me so much, let me help you."

Sara wasn't sure she knew what he was talking about, but she did trust him. Implicitly. Daniel would never do anything to hurt her. "Okay." Taking a deep breath, she let him lead her toward the stone Victorian house that she'd never set foot in before. "It's beautiful. Sorta cold looking, though, isn't it?"

"I don't know, let's take a closer look."

As they approached the big mansion, Sara's hand tightened on Daniel's. The place was truly beautiful with its gingerbread trim and graceful stone walls. "I can remember things mother used to say about the house, when I was really small. She told me about running on the porches and climbing the stairs, playing hide and seek with a little boy who lived nearby." Clearing her throat, she forced herself to look up to the very tip top of the spire on the cupola. "She said it had twenty-two bedrooms and fifteen fireplaces."

"Wow, that's a lot of rooms."

"Yea, but not enough room for my mother or me." She swallowed nervously. "I called my grandmother, you know. After Doug left, when I found out I was pregnant."

Daniel steered her up on the porch. Instead of going to the front door, he led her to a white, wooden bench flanked by big Boston ferns. "No, I didn't know. Tell me."

"Not much to tell. I called and her housekeeper wouldn't even put the call through, I guess my name was on some type of list." She pushed her hair back over her shoulder. "Now, I know she was sick. My grandmother had a heart condition and my grandfather had cancer. They died within three days of one another...I found out later. My aunt tried to call me, but I was already gone from the quarry."

"How did you find out?"

"The man who bought the business, after the bank repossessed it, he told me. One day, I stopped by to pick up a few things of my dad's that I didn't take with me when I left initially. Just his pocket watch and his dog tags."

"Did you get in touch with your aunt?"

"No. It was too late."

"Honey, it's never too late." He rubbed her shoulder. "What did you do when you left the quarry, before you ended up at Mike's?" Daniel wasn't sure he wanted to know, but he had to ask.

Sara laughed wryly. "I went all over. Austin. Dallas. Waco. I waited tables. I flipped burgers. I didn't live on the streets, but I shared an apartment with seven other girls at one time. Can you imagine?"

"No, sounds crowded."

"Yea, I also spent some time in a shelter. After I found out I was pregnant, I called my grandmother. When I got nowhere with her, I came back to Burnet. Being close to my old home seemed better than the city. I found a job working at a nursing home. It was a hard job, but they gave me a little room and there was a nurse who watched after me when I became sick."

"You were sick?" Daniel felt apprehension skate down his spine.

"I had a rough pregnancy." She shrugged, her hand on his knee, rubbing small circles on the blue denim. "My morning sickness was a little worse than normal, I guess. After my baby died, I wondered if the sickness was an indication of something, if I could've done anything differently. The doctor said it wasn't my fault. I took care of myself as best I could."

"I'm glad you made your way to the pub, so I could find you." Daniel glanced toward the mansion door, wondering if he'd done the right thing by bringing Sara here. He hadn't expected her to get so upset. "Do you want to go inside and look around?"

Sara became stiff next to him. "I guess so. At least, I know there's no one inside but a caretaker."

Well, that wasn't quite true, but he wasn't spilling those beans just yet.

"It's just a house. A beautiful house."

A house that should've been hers, or partially hers, by all rights, Daniel thought. "I know what it represents to you, Sara."

"I do too. This place represents being written off and judged for someone else's shortcomings." She raised her eyes to his. "Just like you were."

The truth of what she said hit him hard.

"I'll go in, Daniel, but I want something from you."

Still stunned from her statement, he could do nothing but nod.

"I want you to understand how wonderful you are and start acting like it." She wrapped her arms around his neck. "When I realized this morning, however illogically, that you thought you were..." she didn't know how to put it, "less, it made me so sad I almost cried."

"I didn't think it, Sara."

"You just thought others did." She tugged on the hair at the back of his neck. "And this morning, with me, for a heartbeat – you imagined I might feel the same way."

He hung his head. "I knew better, I know you. I know you love me."

She tugged at his hair again, not quite as hard, layering her lips to his. "Dang right I do and don't you forget it."

As she kissed him, neither heard the footsteps on the porch.

"Sara?"

Sara stilled, then looked around, still in the shelter of Daniel's arms. The woman standing before her was vaguely familiar, a face she'd only seen in pictures. "Aunt Beth?"

Daniel watched with bated breath while the woman he knew to be Sara's aunt almost crumpled to her knees. "Oh, Sara, I'm so glad to see you!"

Sara shot Daniel one look, a confused, slightly perturbed look. "Are you?"

Beth Christy clasped her hands together, shooting a glance at Daniel for moral support. "I am. I was so glad when Mr. Blackhawk contacted me. I tried to get in touch with you before my mother's funeral."

Daniel could feel Sara's tension. Having set this whole thing up, he knew some of what her aunt was about to say.

"I know."

"Sara, I didn't understand what was going on.

Your mother and I weren't close. Like her, I never got along with my parents and I regret like everything never having had the chance to get close to you."

Beth took one step closer to Sara, who was sitting so near to Daniel that he could feel her tremble like a puppy terrified of a storm, in waves of shimmering shakes. "Hey, it's okay," he ran a comforting hand down her back. "This is a good thing."

"Will you come into the house with me?" Beth asked. "Have a cup of coffee?"

Daniel didn't move, this had to be Sara's decision.

"All right." Sara was going to do this, she didn't know if it was for Daniel or for herself.

Walking a few feet behind, Daniel followed Sara and the only blood relative she had left, into the big ass mansion. Over the next hour and a half, he sat back and watched a miracle take place. The first few minutes were a bit tense, but Beth Christy was a little fireball of positive energy and soon she had Sara laughing. They took a tour of the house and he watched Sara's face as they strolled from room to room. He could just imagine she was thinking how different things could've been in her world. When they climbed the stairs to the third level, Daniel saw how enchanted Sara became over the stained-glass windows and he vowed the house he built for her would have one of its own.

By the time the visit was over, Sara became reacquainted with her roots. She couldn't believe there was a ballroom and a wine cellar. "Did they even have friends to share such fancy things with?" she asked her aunt.

Beth laughed. "Not really, these rooms were as moldy and unused then as they were the day we began renovations." She motioned them to follow her to the backyard. "Do you want to see the topaz fields?"

Daniel did. "You say topaz fields the way a Nebraska farmer might say corn fields."

Heading to the yard, Beth pointed to the surrounding rocky terrain and the stream meandering through it. "They aren't worth as much as a corn field now, unfortunately. Finding a hen with teeth is easier than finding a good size topaz these days." Beth placed a hand on her hip. "Oh, they're still out there, I'm sure. It just takes a good size rain to uncover one. In the past, so I'm told, it was like hunting Easter eggs."

"I guess that makes the gems already on the market more valuable," Sara mused.

Daniel could vouch for that, he'd paid a pretty penny for the one he'd bought a few days ago.

"True. Unfortunately, that doesn't put anything in our pocket. The days of our family making money on the Texas topaz are over." She patted Sara on the shoulder. "Nevertheless, this is our home. Anytime you want to come search for your own stone, you're welcome." In fact, she dug in her pocket. "Here's a key to the house."

"No." Sara backed away. "I don't…"

Beth shook her finger at her niece and put the key into Sara's hand. "I never married. I have no children. I'm not likely to have any at this late stage. You have just as much right to be here as I do." She waved toward the house. "In fact, you can move into one of the rooms now, if you want. When the tours start, which will pay for the rest of the renovations, the third floor will be off-limits to the public. Our bedroom and a private kitchen could be up there, we would be like Elvis's Grandma Dodger living upstairs at Graceland."

Daniel frowned. This wasn't the plan. He didn't want Sara moving out of his house. He was searching for a way to say that, without being rude, when Sara spoke up.

"Thanks for the offer." She handed the key back to Beth. "I'm very glad to be reconciled with you, and I will come visit, but I have a life of my own."

Her aunt seemed to understand. "Of course." She led them back to the house, realizing the younger couple was about to take their leave. "Just remember, you're always welcome. I hope we can get together soon."

Sara hugged her aunt. "You can count on it." She glanced at Daniel. "You're welcome to visit me at Daniel's also."

"Absolutely, please come visit." He shook Beth Christy's hand. "Thank you for everything."

Daniel and Sara were quiet as they left the property. In fact, he was a bit nervous when they'd almost covered the distance to their most important destination and she still hadn't said anything. "Sara? Are you angry at me?"

She wiped her eyes.

"Damn, you're crying. I'm sorry."

"Don't be, I'm not angry. You have given me a great gift. You gave me back my family. Beth may just be my aunt, but I have no one else. No family at all."

"I was glad to do it. From the day you told me about your mother, I attempted to start the ball rolling for this to happen. I talked to your aunt first, of course. If she'd been a bitch, I wouldn't have let her within ten miles of you." He captured her hand. "But know this, what you said about having no family…well, that's just not true. I'm your family. My brothers are your family. Aunt or no Aunt, you'll never be alone again." As he pulled into the parking lot of Garner State Park, the moment was drawing near when he would make his status in her life official.

"Thank you, Daniel." As soon as the truck came to a stop, Sara unfastened her seat belt and went to her knees in the seat to lean over and kiss him. "That was so generous of you, so considerate."

Daniel clung to her, accepting her kiss and claiming a couple of his own. "Will you take a walk with me? I want to show you something."

Sara looked over her shoulder. "Goodness, I was so wrapped up in you, I didn't realize where we were."

He whispered in her ear, "Later, I'll let you wrap yourself around me all you want."

"It's a date." She gave him a loud smack on the cheek. "I loved the few times I've visited Gorman Falls!"

"Good. Me too." He lifted her from the driver's side and held her for a moment before letting her slide down his body. "This time, we'll see them together."

They strolled hand in hand until the trail became steep and narrow, and then he went ahead and pulled her along behind him, insuring that she didn't slip or slide on the slick rocks.

"Beth is nothing like I imagined her to be. She's nice."

"I thought so, I wouldn't have taken you there if I hadn't thought so."

"Just don't go sending envoys to Thailand to track down my mother. She left on her own, if she comes back, she'll have to do it the same way. On her own."

Daniel understood her resolve. "My envoys will remain on the ranch, right where they belong."

"Listen." Sara stopped, tugging on his hand to bring him to a halt. "I can hear the falls."

Daniel cocked his ear, the roar wasn't strong, but the unmistakable sound of flowing water made him smile. "Come on, just a little farther." The last few dozen yards, Daniel carried her.

"Hey, I can walk," she squealed with laughter.

"I know you can, you just don't have to. You've got this big, strong, hunky boyfriend who would carry you to the ends of the earth if you asked."

"Oh, I like the sound of that." She rested her head on his shoulder as he deposited her on the most comfortable looking boulder he could find.

For a few minutes, they appreciated their surroundings. Gorman Falls was the one place in Texas that Daniel always thought looked like it could be located in Hawaii. The spring fed falls fell sixty-five feet over moss colored limestone rock and a mysterious mist rose from the pool of water below.

"This feels magical, doesn't it?" Sara sighed happily.

"Yea, it does," Daniel agreed, although he only had eyes for her.

Sara felt Daniel move and when she turned her head to see where he was going, she found him on one knee. "Daniel?"

He held out a ring. A beautiful blue topaz ring surrounded by diamonds. There was a Texas star cut into the stone, so she knew it was from her family's land. "What are you doing?"

Daniel took her hand. "I'm looking at the most beautiful girl in the world. I fell in love with you the first moment I saw you. Did you know that?"

"No." Sara was finding it hard to speak. She was overwhelmed. "I didn't know that."

"Yea." He licked his lips, nervous as a cat. This was so important. "Damn, my palms are sweating." He wiped them on his jeans. "I was talking to Easy when I looked up and saw you running into the highway to save that baby. God, my feet started moving. If anything would've happened to you…" He paused, shook his head and continued. "Anyway, I told him right then and there I had to get off the phone, that I'd just spotted the future Mrs. Daniel Blackhawk."

"Really?" Sara smiled. "I love knowing that and…I noticed you too," she admitted. "You're hard to miss, Cowboy."

Daniel smiled at her, all the love in the world shining out of his eyes. "Will you do me the honor of becoming my wife? Will you marry me, Sara?"

Sara felt tears gather in her eyes. Holding out her hand, she waited for him to slip the ring on. "Yes, yes, I'll marry you, Daniel."

He put the engagement ring on her finger, then brought it to his lips. "I love you more than life. You do know that, don't you?" he asked. "There's nothing – nothing in this world I love more than you."

"I love you too, Daniel. So much." She went into his arms and surrendered to his kiss. "I can't believe how lucky I am."

"I'm the lucky one. I'll cherish you as long as I live, I promise. Nothing will ever separate us. I want you to be mine forever."

Sara found a home within his arms.

She believed every word Daniel told her.

…On the ride to Kingsland, Sara split her time between looking at Daniel and gazing at her ring. "I am so happy."

"Me too," Daniel assured her. "I can't wait for us to start planning our life together. We'll have to meet with a contractor to draw up a blueprint for our house and I can start laying out fences so we can move some of the herd to our land."

"I think we need to plan a wedding first, don't you

think?"

Daniel chuckled. "Can't be soon enough for me. I'd marry you today, but I want you to have the wedding of your dreams." When he slowed down to stop at an intersection, he reached over to rub a thumb across her cheek. "How about Falkenstein Castle, would you like to have the ceremony there?"

Sara's eyes grew big as saucers. "No. I'm sure that would be way too expensive."

"Your mouth is telling me no, but your eyes are screaming yes." Daniel gave her a smile. "We're only getting married once, so I think we should do it right."

A look of sadness crossed Sara's face. "I wish you were my first."

"I am." Daniel told her in no uncertain terms. "The other wedding doesn't count. The jackass doesn't count."

"I agree," Sara said, ready to turn loose of all the bad memories. "Where are we going now?" She pointed behind them. "You missed the turn-off to the ranch."

"One more surprise, my Sara. I told you this was going to be a big day."

"I don't know how it could get any bigger." She was mystified, until they drove up to the local car dealership. "Daniel, what are we doing here?"

"Picking up your new car, Pet." He beamed at her. "Just yours. You'll never have to haul groceries in a wagon, again."

Sara was overwhelmed. She didn't know what to say. He pulled in next to a light smoky-blue Mustang convertible and she started to cry. "This is too much. I can't let you do this."

"Oh, yes you can. You're mine," he told her, coming around to help her from the truck, "giving you

things, especially things you need, makes me happy."
He kissed her tears away, ignoring the car salesman
standing by with a sheaf of papers. "Now, dry those
eyes so you can see. You've got to drive your new car
home."

* * *

"I ate so much, I may have to stand up to sleep, I don't
think I can breathe lying down." Daniel rubbed his
stomach, which was full of baby back ribs and all the
fixings.

"The food was really good. Your brother could
start his own BBQ business." Sara shut the door
behind her. Retiring to Daniel's room in full view of
his brothers still made her shy.

"I'm not sure how you'd know, you didn't eat
enough to keep a bird alive." He began to unbutton his
shirt.

"I was still too excited to eat." She held out her
hand. "I love to look at my beautiful ring almost as
much as I love to look at you."

Daniel threw back his head and laughed. "I can
see where your eyes are focused."

"Can you?" Sara hid her hand behind her back,
then slowly walked toward him like a lioness stalking
prey.

Standing his ground, Daniel welcomed her
aggression, holding out his arms and pulling her close.
"Did you have a good time today?"

"I'd say this was the best day of my life, so far."
She grinned up at him, completely secure in his love.
"I do expect better days ahead, though – just so you
know."

"Oh, you do, do you?" He leaned her back over
his arm and kissed the graceful line of her neck, loving

it when she giggled with joy.

"I do." After he drew her up for a kiss, Sara let her hand wander down to cup his erection. "Is that too much pressure for you?"

Daniel felt his cock grow at her gentle, expectant touch. "Oh, I think I can stand up to the strain."

"I hope so, you've spoiled me so far." She began to unbuckle his belt. "I'm horny all the time."

"I've created a monster, huh?" He began divesting Sara of her clothing also, enjoying each inch of skin he unveiled for his pleasure.

"Yea, a monster." She nipped the strong, sexy cord of muscle where his neck joined his shoulder. "You're so sexy, Daniel. I could just eat you up." She pushed his shirt open and began licking and kissing his chest.

Daniel thought he'd died and gone to heaven. "Come to bed." They helped one another with the last remnants of their clothing, then lay down together on his big king bed. "Oh, gosh, I am serious about being full, I think you're going to have to be on top tonight. I might crush you with my serious bulk."

"Sounds good to me." She waited for him to lie down, then she cuddled up next to him. "Let me hold you a minute, just for fun."

"Just for fun," he agreed. Facing one another, he rested his head against her chest, finding a home there he hadn't known he'd been looking for.

She kissed his head, caressing his hair. "You're such a good man. I love you dearly. I want to help you fulfill every dream you'll ever have."

He pressed a kiss to her cleavage. "You already do."

Pulling him up, Sara looked him in the eye, undulating just as close to him as she could get. She slipped her leg between his and cupped the side of his face in her hand. "I don't mean just sexual, that's a given. I mean life dreams. Building your ranch. Making a name for yourself in the community, however you choose to do that. And children. I want to have children with you. I loved my little girl so much, I want to share that kind of love with you and the babies you give me."

"I'll give you just as many babies as you want," he promised. "Little Indian babies."

"Papooses." She giggled. "They're going to be gorgeous."

"Yea, if they look like their mama." He nestled close to her. "This is nice."

"Yea, it is." This wasn't their first time to cuddle in bed, of course. They'd slept together a dozen nights or more. Most nights they'd had sex, except when she was on her period and crampy. Even on the nights when they weren't intimate, they'd held one another, snuggled up against each other to sleep. "I feel like you are part of me."

"I am. Inseparable."

"I want us to be like this forever." She closed her eyes and just let herself feel. They were wrapped around one another, their fingers stroking. She could feel his hand on her breasts, rubbing her nipples until they were diamond hard peaks. Needing to touch him, she soothed her palm on his supple skin. He had very little hair on his body, but she loved to trace the happy trail that ran down his stomach to intriguing parts below. When she delved a bit lower, Sara smiled when she found what she was looking for, something iron-hot and wonderfully hard. Thick. Smooth. Pulsing hot in her hand.

"Touch me. Stroke me, baby," he whispered,

catching the lobe of her ear in his teeth.

Sara pumped him in her hand, feeling her own body respond with amazing arousal. She grew hot and tingly, so aroused she couldn't see straight. "I need you now, Daniel, so much."

He rolled to his back, taking her with him. "I'm yours, Pet." His hands slid up and cupped her breasts, weighing them in his palms, kneading and molding the perfect globes, loving that she arched, showing them off, tempting him to pull her down and worship them with his mouth.

Sara was on fire. Moving her hips back and forth on him, she felt like their souls were as entwined as their bodies were about to be. Sara held her breath as one of his hands left her breast to slide down to the spot where she longed to be touched the most.

"I love how wet you are."

"For you."

"For me."

She let him lift her high enough so he could join with her, sinking deep into her body. Two pieces made for each other, fitting perfectly together. Face to face they sat, her draped over his lap, where they could touch and kiss, staring into one another's eyes. Impaled on his cock, Sara could feel him swelling inside of her. With his help, she rose up and eased down, over and over – him bucking his hips, pounding into her again and again.

"Daniel, hold me," she whimpered as her body shook, her breasts jiggling with each thrust. He tightened his arms around her, giving her the connection she needed. Sara could feel her femininity begin to contract, clasping Daniel's staff. She felt as if she was being drawn into a vortex, buffeted by an erotic wind on a sea of sensuality. As he loved her, she felt pleasure rush over her like a waterfall, flowing from her head to her toes, pooling in the apex of her thighs.

"Come for me, Sara!" Daniel commanded as the hold he held on his own control slipped away. The orgasm hit them both like a storm, ecstasy rushing through them, the surge rising and rising until it crashed on some eternal shore. Daniel held her as she collapsed against him, wrapping his arms around her, vowing to love her until the end of his days.

CHAPTER TEN

"I'm engaged!" Sara made the announcement with absolute elation in her voice. Supper was cooking, the house was clean, and she was waiting for Daniel and his brothers to finish their work for the day. When she'd taken a break to enjoy a soft drink, Sara gave in to the temptation to call her new friend.

"Congratulations!" Ryder squealed. "When? Tell me all about it!"

Twirling in a circle, Sara proceeded to share her good news with Ryder. "Daniel is perfect. He planned this special day for me, everything from orchestrating a reconciliation with my mother's family – long story – to buying me a new car. Both of those things pale to the moment he proposed to me at Gorman Falls. He took me up to the waterfall, got down on one knee, and asked me to marry him." By the time she finished her joyous spiel, Sara was crying.

So, was Ryder. "I'm so happy for you! When can we get together so I can see your ring? And your new car?"

"Oh, soon, soon," Sara promised. "I'm just so happy, Ryder, I had to tell someone."

"Well, I'm glad you called me. I'm tickled pink. I'll tell Pepper when I talk to her, she's in Nashville with Judah, he's recording a new album that has some duets with popular country stars."

"Oh, that sounds amazing and yes, please let her know."

They talked a little while longer, discussing some last-minute plans for the pie auction. "I'm ready to get started, I've made a list of flavors that I want to run by you."

"Perfect, email me." Ryder gave her an email address.

Once they finished their call, Sara placed one to her aunt, this was the first time she'd ever reached out to her. To make herself not feel so nervous, she sorted through the items in the dining room hutch. She knew they'd belonged to Daniel's mother and some were dusty from sitting in one place so long.

"Hello?"

"Aunt Beth, this is Sara."

"Sara! I'm so glad you called!"

Sara ran a shaky hand over her face. "I just wanted to tell you how glad I am that Daniel brought us together."

"Me too. There's just the two of us in the family, it would be a shame for us not to be close."

"Yes. Anyway, I just wanted to let you know that Daniel proposed to me yesterday."

"He did?!" Beth exclaimed. "Marvelous!"

"Yea." Sara smiled so wide, her face ached. "He took me to Gorman Falls right after we left the mansion and asked me to marry him there. The ring he gave me is a Texas topaz from our land." Saying 'our' felt funny, but good. When Beth made no response, Sara thought she'd hung up, but then she realized she could hear a slight noise. "Are you crying?"

"Yes." Aunt Beth sniffled. "You two have restored my faith in love and romance."

"Mine too," Sara admitted. "I've had a really hard time."

"Tell me, sweetie."

Over the next half hour, as she hand-washed a cut-glass punch bowl and cups, Sara poured out her heart to her aunt. She told her about the difficulties she'd faced with her father after her mother left. She told Beth about her father's death and the mistake she made in falling for Doug Wright's lies. Finally, she cried and told her about the baby she'd lost.

"Damn him, leaving you pregnant. I hope the devil takes that fool."

Sara giggled sadly. "I doubt it, I'm sure even old Beelzebub has standards."

Her aunt commiserated with her about everything, giving Sara a sense of belonging to a family, something she'd rarely felt until Daniel came into her life.

"We need to get together soon."

"I agree," Sara replied. "Maybe…maybe you could help me plan the wedding?"

"Oh, my God, yes!" Aunt Beth exclaimed. "I would love that! You could get married here!"

"Well, Daniel has suggested another venue." Sara told her about Falkenstein Castle as she dried the punch set and put them back where they belonged.

"Oh, that's perfect, Sara. Daniel Blackhawk worships the ground you walk on, I can tell."

"Yes, he does." There was no doubt in Sara's mind.

She was loved.

"Sara! Sara! Come quick!"

The voice was Benjen, she recognized it, but there was an element of panic in his tone that she'd never heard before. "Oh, Lord." She threw down the dishtowel and sprinted to the door. "What is it?" Once she was through the door, she could see Benjen holding up a pale-faced Daniel. "Daniel! What happened?" One good look told her his jeans were ripped at the thigh and blood was pouring down his leg. "Did you call 9-1-1?" she screamed, but she didn't wait for an answer. Running back into the house, she grabbed a belt and some medical supplies.

The whole process of seeing an injured Daniel and gathering what she needed to help him, probably didn't take ninety seconds – but it seemed like an eternity. Knowing the ranch was some distance for an ambulance to drive, she knew doing what they could now, might make all the difference in the world. "Did you call 9-1-1?" she repeated as she raced out to rejoin the brothers.

Daniel was seated on the edge of the porch and Benjen was standing by him, bent over, and pressing a rag of some sort to the injured area on Daniel's leg. "He wouldn't let me, Sara. I think we need to take him to the hospital."

"Let me see." Benjen moved just enough for Sara to see that blood was still coming from the wound.

Seeing something had to be done quickly, she elbowed in and put the belt around his upper thigh. "Raise up just a fraction," she told Daniel as she moved the belt high enough to be above the wound. He did, wincing, and she quickly tightened it enough to stop the blood from pumping out of his leg with every beat of his heart.

"I'll be all right," he said weakly.

"Let's get him in the truck, Ben, you drive. I'll put as much pressure on the wound as I can."

Daniel didn't argue as they worked with him, leading him to the truck, and seeing that he settled in with Sara beside him. Again, this was all happening fast, but Sara felt like an hour had passed before they were on their way. "How did you do this?" Her voice was tight and chastising.

"It's okay, Pet." Daniel pulled Sara close enough to kiss her forehead.

"Don't. I'm trying to stop you from bleeding to death." Tears were flowing down her cheeks and her heart was skipping beats. The adrenaline rush from seeing him hurt was wearing off and now she felt weak and sick from worry. "How did you do this?" she asked again.

Daniel's voice was low and even. "I was putting some new shingles on one of the hay sheds, I slipped off and landed on a damn piece of tin."

"He got in too big of a hurry and didn't wait for me to get up there and help him," Benjen said tightly. "I swear to God, Daniel…" His voice trailed off.

"Hurry, Benjen, please!" Sara kept the pressure on Daniel's leg, but she let him hug her close, leaning her head back far enough she could kiss him on the cheek. "How dare you get hurt before I can get you to the altar?"

"This is no big deal, you'll see," he assured her.

Sara cried as they raced down the road to the emergency medical clinic in Kingsland. She'd never considered the dangers of living so far from a hospital. If praying could make them cover the distance faster, they would be flying on the wings of angels.

Once they arrived at the modest concrete building, an attendant ran out to help. "I heard your brakes squealing as you turned in," he told Benjen.

"My brother ripped his leg open on a piece of tin."

"Damn."

Sara relinquished her hold on Daniel, but she

hovered near as they took him inside. "You just wait, Pet. I'll be right out, right as rain."

Sara melted into a chair next to Benjen, knowing he was in good hands, but worried all the same.

Inside the emergency room, Daniel threw his head back and winced as the nurses worked over him. "We're just cutting these pants off you."

"I don't want to be damn naked and don't ruin my jeans! I paid almost thirty dollars for this pair!"

"We need to see what we're doing, don't struggle so, I have a pair of scissors in my hand."

The older woman who was tending to him gave him a stern look that he found himself obeying. "Yes, ma'am."

"Your pants won't be ruined, your wife can sew these seams back together."

"I'm not married. Yet." Daniel smiled at the thought of Sara.

In a few minutes, a doctor came in. "Finally, someone I recognize." Daniel jerked as the nurse probed at the rip in his flesh. "How are you, Calhoun?"

"Looks like I'm better than you, Geronimo."

Daniel closed his eyes as his friend school tended to his wound. "Oh, I lost my footing, it's no big deal."

"You need stitches."

Daniel blew out a long breath. "Dammit, I hate needles."

"Tell me his vitals," Dr. Brad Calhoun spoke evenly as he began to stitch up his friend. After the nurse read off the numbers, Brad gave a head nod to the door. "Bring a unit of blood and hook him up."

"Blood? I was planning on finishing that roofing job this afternoon."

"I don't think so." He directed his nurse to pull Daniel's records to check his blood type. "This won't take long though, I'll have you home in time for supper."

"Someone tell my girl I'm okay." Daniel looked to the grumpy nurse. "Please?"

The doctor nodded. "Tell her we'll come get her in a little while."

As soon as the woman left the two men alone, Daniel began to whisper to his old friend. "Since I'm here and you're…down there, I was wondering if you'd take a look at something that's been bothering me."

"I don't do penis extensions, Blackhawk," Dr. Calhoun teased, then grew serious. "What's up?"

"Oh, I'm still getting it up…" Daniel bit his lower lip as the needle punctured his skin again. "I found a lump."

"A lump? Where? Show me."

Daniel turned his head to the side, as if to hide his actions from his own view, then proceeded to lift his cock and move his scrotal sack to one side so the doctor could see the general area where he'd felt the disturbing small knot in his sac. "Right about there."

He closed his eyes and tried to blank his mind as the doctor felt around where he'd never allowed a man's hand to delve, then laid absolutely still until Dr. Calhoun broke the silence.

"Well, there's a lump there, all right." He sighed, then went back to applying gauze to the area he'd stitched up high on Daniel's thigh.

"Well, what do you think it is, man?" Daniel asked with exasperation in his voice.

"I can't tell without some tests. Call my office tomorrow and make an appointment, we're not set up to take care of that type of thing here."

This was no more than what Daniel expected.

God, he hated medical issues! His mind went back to the day his mother told him about a lump in her breast. She'd assured him and his brothers that everything would be fine.

Well, it wasn't. Nothing was ever fine with her again.

"What kind of tests?" He held his breath awaiting the answer as the nurse returned and began to hook up an IV to administer a pint of blood.

The doctor shrugged his wide shoulders. "We'll do an ultrasound to create an image of your testicles, scrotum, and abdomen and draw some blood to test for the presence of tumor cells, or infections."

"Hell." The feeling in his gut was very similar to the one he felt when the jury handed down the guilty verdict so long ago.

"Daniel?"

Sara's voice sounded at the door and a moment later, she was in his arms. "I'm fine, Pet. Just a scratch. The doctor has me all sewn up."

Dr. Calhoun cleared his throat. "That's right. It would take more than a little injury like this to bring a stubborn bull to his knees." He stood and bowed to Sara. "I'm Dr. Brad Calhoun at your service, pretty lady."

Daniel bristled a bit. Brad Calhoun was surfer boy pretty, all the women loved him. "Brad, this is my fiancée, Sara Riley."

"Hello." Sara scarcely saw the medical professional, she only had eyes for the man she loved. "You're giving him blood?"

"Just a precaution," Dr. Calhoun assured her. "If you'll give us a few minutes, I'll finish up what I have to do here. Even though his chart says he's had a tetanus a while back, I'm going to give him another one, just to be sure."

Sara didn't want to go back to the waiting room, but Daniel kissed her hand, and gave her a smile. "I'm fine, just let us finish up here and we'll go home."

As soon as she was gone, Daniel grew serious again. "What does this mean? The lump, the tests?"

"Could be a lot of things, could be nothing." He readied a syringe to give Daniel a shot. "Let's don't cross any shaky bridges until we come to them. After we examine you tomorrow and wait on the test results, just continue living your life as usual until we know more."

Easier said than done.

…At home, Daniel told his brother's the same thing he'd told Sara umpteen times, "I'm fine. I'm fine. Brad says I'll be good as new by tomorrow."

"Well, you're not getting back up on that damn roof." Sam stood over the recliner where Daniel was resting, one hand on his hip, his face grim.

"And I suppose you are?" Daniel pointed to Sam's leg.

"My leg is fine."

"I'll deal with it," Easy told them both. "Quit worrying about the blasted roof and let's just take care of our brother."

"I'll help Easy, no worries," Benjen added, handing Daniel his bottle of pain pills. "Here, take one of these before you pass out from the pain."

Daniel's hand hung to the side, petting the small dog, who could tell something wasn't right in her world. "Stop it." He ignored the bottle of pills. "Look…" Daniel whispered, his eyes cutting to the kitchen where Sara was fixing him some concoction that she thought would make him feel better, "hold it down, she's upset enough as it is. Just act normal." He rolled his eyes. "If that's possible."

They all obeyed his request as Sara came back with homemade chicken soup. "There's plenty in there for all of you." She placed the tray in Daniel's lap.

"I don't have a cold or the flu, Pet." Daniel chuckled, appreciating the appetizing aroma of the food she'd prepared.

"Eat up, chicken soup is good for everything."

As he ate, she sat on the floor next to him, her eyes full of concern.

"Go get you a bowl," he told her, "you're going to need the nourishment."

"Why? Do we need to take you back to the doctor?"

"No." He would be going back, but she would be none the wiser. This was something he had to deal with on his own. "I want to go to bed soon and you're going to need your strength to keep up with me."

As she frowned at him, Sara blushed. "You're not able."

"I beg your pardon? My leg is hurt, not my dick."

She crossed her arms over her chest. "It was pretty damn close and we're not going to risk tearing your stitches open." Nodding her head, once, forcefully, she laid down the law. "So, no sex for you!"

Daniel laughed. "Don't be cruel, love." He sobered. "I need you." She had no idea what he was going through and he didn't want her to know, but he was scared to death. He needed her, he needed to act like nothing was going to change.

"Well…" she softened, "I'll see what I can do. But…I'm in charge. You're going to lie on your back and not move a muscle."

"I did not hear that." Benjen walked through with his hands over his ears and his dog at his heels. "I did not hear that."

While he ate his soup and listened to Easy talk about a cattle sale he attended, Sara relented and filled a cup, standing over the sink while she drank it. She knew Daniel's injury wasn't life-threatening, but she couldn't shake the feeling that something was amiss, something she couldn't put her finger on. Staring out the window, she knew the meadow was directly in front of her, and she tried like mad to make out the form of one of the horses she presumed was grazing out there – but she couldn't make any out, the night was dark and the glass was reflective.

All she could see was herself.

And she looked scared.

"Stop it. There's nothing to be scared about it." Draining the last drop, she rinsed the cup and put it in the dishwasher. "You've got every reason in the world to be happy. Thankful. So, act like it." Putting a smile on her face, she returned to the living room in time to see Easy picking up Daniel's tray to carry to the kitchen.

"He's all yours," Easy mouthed with a wink.

"Yes, he is," she muttered with a smile.

"About time." He was already getting up from the chair when he saw her.

"Hey, careful!" she cautioned him, hurrying the last couple of steps. "I want you to take a pain pill before you go to bed."

"Not until after," he insisted, gritting his teeth. Damn, it hurt like a son-of-a-bitch.

"You are so stubborn." Sara took his arm. "But, I love you," she relented and kissed his cheek.

Moving slowly to the bedroom, Daniel tried to take his mind off unpleasant topics. "So, what did you do today before I tried to julienne myself on a big tin

222

mandoline?"

Sara was still worried, but she remembered the pep-talk she'd given herself in the kitchen. "I called Ryder and Aunt Beth and told them you'd ask me to marry you. They were thrilled."

"Good. What else?"

"I used my phone to look on the internet for house plans. I was going to ask how many bedrooms you think we need." She let out a small giggle. "I guess it depends on how many children we're planning on having."

Daniel's heart sank. "Oh, we'll have to give that some…serious consideration," he teased, turning his answer into sexual innuendo. Why did he feel this way? There was no verdict, no certainty. He could perform and he didn't feel bad, just had a damn twinge. People found little lumps here and there all the time, not every one of them proved to be a problem.

But this was his manhood. He steeled himself. "I need to go to the bathroom."

"Do you need help, big boy?" She put a bit of risqué in her suggestion.

"No." His answer was too quick, he realized – but he…needed a moment.

"Sure," she answered slowly, "I'll use the one in my old room."

They parted for a few minutes, Sara to freshen up and put on her gown, Daniel to sit on the toilet and probe his privates in hope the lump had simply vanished since coming home from the hospital.

It hadn't.

He slipped off his clothes and chunked them into the hamper, ignoring the slight pain in his thigh. Instead, he took a moment to think about Sara. How ultra-feminine she was, all softness and curves. Those perfect tits that he loved to suck, the sweet, sexy place between her thighs that he lived to fill with his cock. He loved the way she looked at him like she wanted to eat him up, the way she'd lick her lips when she was a little nervous – God, everything about her made his body tighten with pure lust. When she touched him, any way she touched him, made him so hard and horny that he couldn't breathe.

Daniel touched himself, moving his foreskin up and down his stalk.

He was hard for her and he was ready for love.

Out in the bedroom, Sara waited. Shivers of left over fear coursed through her veins when she remembered walking out and finding Daniel leaning on his brother, blood running down his leg to his cowboy boot.

"What's taking you so long?" she called out through the closed, wooden door.

Suddenly the door opened and he was there – that massive, comforting, panty-wetting presence – all six-foot five inches and two hundred fifty pounds of him. Pure muscle.

Her man.

Sara's heart skipped a beat when she saw the patch of white bandage on his thigh. "Okay?" She looked from his leg to his face.

Daniel chuckled. "Don't I look okay?" He pumped his cock, pushing his hips forward. "Did you somehow miss all this manly beauty waving at you?"

Sara grinned. He was so cute. Devastatingly handsome. Sexy. "No, I don't think anyone could miss all of that." The miracle that she was here with him never escaped her. Every now and then, she halfway expected him to come to his senses, to see her for what she was – just Sara, plain Sara Riley. She wasn't sexy enough, her boobs weren't big enough, she didn't have all the audacious curves that men liked on their women.

Yea, the only thing that kept her from melting into a Sara-size puddle of self-doubt was that Daniel Blackhawk had never missed an opportunity to make her feel like the most cherished, desired, loved person in the world.

"Good thing, because I need you right now."

Sara locked her gaze with Daniel's, his eyes had narrowed and his face had hardened, his jaw clenching. This was a look she didn't recognize. Oh, it was a good look, the intensity didn't make him less appealing – it made him more. A thrill shot through her and she held out her hand. "I'm here. I'll always be here."

Daniel didn't take her hand, he captured her wrists, one in each hand, crowding into her space, towering over her, staring at her as if he'd never seen her before. His body brushed against hers as he backed her toward the bed, her breasts skimming against his chest. They made it to the bed and he eased onto it, settling in the middle of the bed on his back.

"Ah, now I've got you where I want you," Sara teased, carefully coming over him, straddling his mid-section, still protecting his thigh. "I'm going to kiss you now, Blackhawk."

"Well, get after it, I'm not getting any younger, you know."

One breath he seemed so serious, the next he was teasing, he was making her dizzy. Before she could commence her own brand of seduction, Daniel raised his head and fit his mouth to hers. As soon as the electric connection was made, every inch of her skin came alive. Just that fast, he took control, his kiss overwhelming and hungry. This was no tentative joining of lips, their mouths meshed together in passion, his tongue surging up into her mouth and dominating the kiss.

"You're so good at this," she whispered as she ate at his mouth.

"Undress, I want to smash."

Sara laughed at his happy face, loving how much fun he was having. She skimmed the sleep shirt over her head, she wore nothing underneath. "I'm going to do all kinds of things to you. You're at my mercy."

Her mouth came down on his again and Daniel felt himself being carried away. This was what he needed, a lifetime of this. As she kissed him, her lips moving over his face and neck, and down to his shoulders – light kisses, darting tongue, seeking mouth – his hands moved over her, memorizing every delectable inch of her soft, silky skin. "Show me no mercy, Pet. None."

His voice had turned midnight dark – mesmerizing and sensual. The tempting tone bid her to show him how much she desired him. Settling to one side of his big body, she began to make love to him with her mouth and hands, kissing his cut chest, licking lacy patterns of ecstasy on his warm skin. Daniel was not merely a recipient, he was an enthused participant – touching her breasts when he could reach them, running his hand over her hip, dipping between her legs when she was near.

Sara wanted to touch him everywhere, give him the pleasure he craved, so she was drawn time and time again to his rigid erection. Her heart hammered out an excited rhythm as she beheld his straining cock.

"Touch me," Daniel begged, "my cock, not my balls," he added quickly.

Too lost in her own haze of euphoria, she didn't question his request, her only desire was to please. With her tongue darting out to dampen her lower lip, Sara gripped his cock and began to pump it in her palm, gratified when her touch drew a moan from his lips.

"Good, Pet, so good." His whole body hummed with a greedy energy, he wanted more and more of her – as much as he could get. As she took him in her mouth, he pushed in deep, his hand cupping the nape of her neck as the tip of his cock found the soft, sweet spot at the rear of her throat. While she pleasured him with her mouth, her head bobbing as her lips slid over his aching shaft time and time again, he smoothed his palm down her side and over her thigh. When his hand found her pussy, she was so soft and wet. "You're always ready for me," he murmured in wonder.

Sara didn't release his cock to answer, but he was right. All he had to do was walk into a room and she wanted him. She trembled at his touch when he played with her clitoris, the swollen bud was throbbing with excitement as he swirled his finger around it, applying just enough pressure to drive her insane.

Every draw from her lips, every swipe of her tongue, brought him closer and closer to the pinnacle he craved. Pure unadulterated ecstasy coursed through him, causing his body to quake and shudder. He couldn't last, this felt too good. As she sucked, he stretched his legs, muscles tensing, toes curling. "God!" He was cumming and cumming, filling her mouth with his seed. Daniel felt her swallow around him, using her lips and tongue to bring him ease. Even as she brought him down, he kept rubbing her pussy, wanting to give her the same amount of pleasure she'd given him.

"Oh, Daniel!" Sara cried, as the sweet pressure built, bubbling up like effervescent champagne once the cork is popped. Her breath came in pants, not only from having him in her mouth, but from the orgasm he coaxed from her body. Sated and happy, she dropped her head to rest on his abdomen.

"Give me your mouth," he asked, his head rising to meet hers when she moved close enough. His tongue pushed between her lips, mating with hers. Daniel kissed her so deeply and so long, there was no time to breathe. Sara didn't miss it, she didn't need air, she just needed him.

Once their breathing quieted and their blood pressure returned to normal, she lay beside him, with her head resting on his chest. When she glanced up at his face, it was to find him looking down at her. "What is it? I should get your pain pill for you." She began to wiggle away from him.

"Hush." Daniel tightened his arm around her back, drawing her more tightly to him. "I just want to memorize this moment, I want to always remember how beautiful you are after I've loved you."

A shiver ran down her spine. What he said seemed to contain a hint of finality. But that was silly. Their future together was just beginning. "I'm not going anywhere, you know."

"I know." He kissed her head. "The only place you're going is to sleep."

* * *

The next day, Daniel placed the call to Brad's office. The earliest appointment he could get was late afternoon. For the first time, he found himself stretching the truth with Sara. He'd hid things from his brothers before, not often, their father had always insisted their word was their bond. Lying, even about something like this, didn't sit well with him. When he found her in the kitchen, she was elbow deep in dough. He found he couldn't look her in the eye. "Hey, I'm heading into town to the feed store. Are you making dumplings?"

"I am." She gave the flour and lard mixture one last pat and rinsed her hands in the sink. "I thought you might like chicken and dumplings for supper."

Daniel wasn't surprised, she was doing everything she could to pamper him. "That sounds good."

"I'm glad to see you." She came to him, draping her arms around his neck, careful not to bump his thigh. "How are you feeling?"

"Better now." He accepted her kiss, his body reacting to her touch. "I have to pick up some calf wormer, can I get you anything while I'm there?"

"Uh, yea!" She gave him a dazzling smile as she ran her fingers through his hair at the back of his neck. "If you go anywhere near a drug store or someplace like that, pick up a couple of bridal magazines. I want to start getting some ideas for our wedding."

Despite his worries, Daniel chuckled. "You want this big, tough, redskin cowpoke to walk up to the counter with bridal magazines in hand?"

"And some tampons, the absorbent kind."

He choked at her teasing. "What?"

"Don't tell me you're embarrassed?"

"Well, no." He wasn't, he'd just never purchased feminine products before. "Do you want the winged ones?"

Sara giggled. "Tampons don't have wings. I'm kidding, Daniel, I don't need any. I'm just giving you a hard time." She went on her tiptoes to kiss him. "The magazines will do."

Letting go of his worry, Daniel cupped her bottom and hauled her close. "I'm the one who is supposed to give you a hard time."

"Oh, you do. You do." She held him tight. "I had a good time last night."

"Me too." He kissed her once more. "I'll try for an encore performance tonight, so get ready."

"Always." Sara walked him to the door. "Be careful. I'll be waiting."

Daniel lifted his hand in farewell as he pulled out of the drive and headed into town.

…The tests took longer than he'd anticipated, he was rushing like mad to buy the magazines and calf medicine. If Sara or his brothers questioned the length of time he was gone, he was prepared with an answer. Brad had changed the dressing on his wound and Daniel figured he could concoct some story about forgetting a follow-up visit.

Daniel let out a huffed breath, attempting to release some of the tension stored in his body. He'd questioned the doctor about possible outcomes, his old friend had cautioned him about jumping to conclusions, saying that even if the worst scenario proved true, there was various things they could do.

"I won't lie to you, we could be dealing with a slight problem here, but there are treatments and options that can allow you to survive and thrive."

"How about…sex?"

"Oh, yea, most men pick right up where they left off. Good odds."

Daniel had barked out a wry laugh. "Most men? Good odds? What kind of doctor speak is that?" He didn't always have the best luck and he needed a bit more reassurance.

"Until we get the tests results back, there's no way of knowing."

"And when will that be?" He didn't know if he wanted it to be sooner or later.

"Soon. A few days. I'll put a rush on it for you." Brad clapped Daniel on the back. "Chin up. There's no need to worry before you have something to worry about. Go home, make love to that beautiful woman of yours and we'll face what's coming together."

Looking back, he realized neither man had put a name to the threat he might be facing.

Once he was on the road home, he noticed the bride on the front of one of the glossy magazines seemed to have a sad look on her face. "No, no," he chided the oversize periodical, "don't look at me like that. Everything is going to be okay."

* * *

Soon. A few days.

A waiting game.

Sara didn't know what was up with Daniel, but something was definitely amiss. She tried to put her finger on what had changed and she had a hard time doing it. He was considerate. Polite. Attentive in bed...but distant everywhere else.

Yea, distant.

When they talked, he didn't look at her anymore. When she asked him what was wrong, he said, 'nothing'. She didn't think it was his leg, the injury appeared to be healing nicely. No, it was something else. She just couldn't put her finger on what.

His brothers noticed it too.

"Hey, Daniel, do you want to take a ride to look at the horses?" Sam asked, glad to be back in the saddle again. "We need to decide which ones we're keeping and which ones we're taking to the sale."

"No, thanks. Take Easy with you. I have some paperwork I need to do."

Sara didn't think he was telling the absolute truth. Last night, when she'd taken a slice of his favorite Almond Joy pie to his office, she'd caught him staring into space. The computer hadn't even been turned on. He'd offered no explanation for why he was hiding in his office and she hadn't asked for one.

"When you finish, would you like to see what I found in those magazines you brought me?" Sara gave him a hopeful look. "I would like your opinion on colors and decorations."

Daniel gave her this wan smile. "I'm not any good at those things. My opinion isn't worth much."

"It's worth a lot to me," Sara told him. When he didn't answer, she tried another tactic. "I think I'll go take a long bubble bath. After you finish, come to the bedroom and I'll give you a surprise."

"A surprise?" He finally looked straight at her and Sara was relieved to see a hint of sparkle in his eyes. "What kind of surprise?

"I ordered some adventurous lingerie for our honeymoon. I'm saving most of it, but there's one outfit I'd like to take for a test drive." She gave him a sultry smile. "That is, if you're interested."

Interested? "Hell yeah, I'm interested." By the time he finished in his office, he'd need a distraction. Daniel was torturing himself, researching what might be in store for him. Worst case scenarios. He wished he could just let it go, wait for the final verdict, but he couldn't. He leaned in to give Sara a kiss. "Enjoy your bath, Pet. I won't be long."

Sara took him at his word, finishing her work, then preparing herself for bed. The short, red, baby doll pajamas she'd bought to tempt him was really a gift to them both. She longed to please him, and when she succeeded, the reward was worth everything.

As Daniel proved a few hours later.

"One more," Daniel whispered against her neck as he pumped into her. They'd just cum together, but his cock was still stiff and he was insatiable.

He needed more.

More orgasms. More time. More her.

"Oh, baby, I don't think I can. You've wiped me out," she moaned, even as her arms came around his neck and her hips rose to seek his. The baby doll pajamas had done their job.

"You want me."

She did. "Always."

"One more," he spoke through gritted teeth. He wanted another and another, he wanted to make this night last. What if the test results came back positive? What if he lost his…

STOP!

Daniel tried to control his brain, even as his cock ruled his body. She'd belonged to him for too short a time. He wasn't ready for this to end.

DON'T EVEN GO THERE!

But what if…

What if he couldn't get hard anymore? What if they cut off his…

STOP!

Oh, God, what if he couldn't give her children?

"What's wrong?" Sara clutched his hair, making him look at her.

"What?"

"You stopped." She kissed him. "Don't stop. You've got me all worked up again."

"I won't stop." He rose over her and began to

pump in earnest. He was determined to enjoy every moment. Daniel wanted to relish and remember every iota of delicious pleasure he could share with her. He needed to save each smile, each touch, each kiss, save them like time in a bottle.

How much he wanted her.

How much he cherished her.

How much he loved her.

All he wanted to do was immerse himself in her, satiate himself. Do this amazing, God-given thing with the woman he loved, that might be taken away from him forever.

"More baby, give me more." She clung to him, her body completely in tune with his, her desire as great as his own.

"God, yes." He closed his eyes and gave her what they needed – time after time. As he moved feverishly within her, Daniel marveled that she never pushed him away. He knew she had no idea of the storm rising on the horizon, but she accepted him, craved him, welcomed him every time he reached for her. Even with his ravenous appetite, sometimes she came to him and he never, God help him, he never turned her away.

"Oh, Daniel, right there, baby," she whimpered, arching up to him, curving one leg around his hips. He angled up, riding her high, grinding against her clit in the way he knew she loved. "God, yes!" she cried and he closed his eyes, immersing himself in the perfection of the moment, never wanting to forget how it felt to be inside of her, cherishing the way her pussy fluttered around him, clasping him so tight she might never let him go.

Her climax triggered his own, and he surrendered. Perfect ecstasy rushed down every nerve ending, exploding in his balls and he was cumming and cumming, shuddering and shaking so hard that he collapsed against her.

"Please," he said, praying the last silently, *don't let this end.*

"Please what, baby?" she asked with a sleepy yawn.

"Nothing," he whispered, kissing her eyes closed. "Everything's fine. Everything's perfect."

CHAPTER ELEVEN

"Would you like for me to pack a picnic lunch and meet you by the river? We could eat together and talk about this weekend." She touched his chest, fingering a button on his shirt. His birthday was coming up and she needed to probe a bit and make sure her plan was going to work.

"Sorry, Pet, I have to run into town." He drained his coffee cup and stood from the table. "Here, you beggar." Bending over, he gave his last bite of bacon to Hope.

"Oh, that means no one will be around. I made sandwiches for your brothers to take with them."

"Yea, they're bringing the calves in for their shots." With eyes on the floor, Daniel was actually measuring the distance to the door. Four steps and he'd be out of here, away from the questions that were haunting Sara's eyes.

"Could I go with you to town?"

Her question took Daniel by surprise. "Uh, no."

His short negative answer stunned Sara. "Oh. Okay."

Shaking his head, Daniel tried to soothe things over. "I'm going to be busy. I, uh, have to see a man about a horse." He winced over the lame old punchline.

"Sure." Sara attempted to laugh it off. "I have plenty to do here. I'll darn socks or knit a sweater or something." Truth was, she was caught up with everything. "Maybe I'll bake some cookies."

"Sounds good." Daniel gave her a quick kiss and almost ran from the door.

Sara sighed, wondering what she'd done wrong.

…At the doctor's office, Daniel sat across from his friend, a wide desk separating them. "It's bad, isn't it?"

He could tell from the look on Brad's face that the news wasn't what he'd hoped.

Brad cleared his throat. "Don't jump off the end of the pier until I explain things."

"Fuck."

"You have testicular cancer."

You have testicular cancer.

You have testicular cancer.

The four words reverberated through Daniel's brain. Thoughts began to ricochet through his head. "What does this mean, exactly?" Surely the truth wouldn't be as bad as his imaginings.

"This is treatable. My usual recommendation would be that we remove one testicle, then start a round of chemo to insure no stray cells metastasize anywhere else in your body. You'll be able to function normally…"

Daniel had stopped listening.

Remove a testicle. Chemo. Cancer.

A widespread disease, affecting millions. Lung. Liver. Stomach. Skin.

None of it was good, but his was in the one part of him that defined his whole life.

His manhood.

"What if I don't?"

"Don't what?"

"Have the testicle removed."

Brad Calhoun sat up straighter in his chair, eyeing the big man across from him. "You'd be a fool. We can stop this cancer in its tracks. You let it go, let it spread, you'll be writing your own death sentence. This type of shit doesn't go away if it's ignored."

"I need to think."

"No. You need to schedule surgery."

Something inside Daniel forced him to fight. "You didn't even do a biopsy. How can you be sure?"

Shaking his head, the doctor tried to explain. "We run too big of a risk spreading the cancer if a biopsy is performed."

"So, how do I know I have cancer to spread, if there's no biopsy?" He expected Brad to give him some pat answer about trusting your doctor, but he didn't.

"Well…" Brad took out a chart to show him how the test worked. "We used the ultrasound to produce an image of your testicle. A wand-like transducer gives off sound waves and picks up the echoes as they bounce off organs, then a computer creates an image on a monitor from the pattern of the echoes. We can distinguish a pattern from those echoes and we know a solid tumor is most likely cancer. Most testicular cancers produce high levels of certain proteins, such as alpha-fetoprotein and human chorionic gonadotropin. Tumor markers. When we see these proteins in the blood, we know the tumor is cancerous."

"We know this," he repeated, not sounding convinced.

"Feel free to get a second opinion, but don't wait long. Cure rates and survival rates are highly dependent on early detection and complete eradication."

"All right." Daniel cleared his throat, feeling sick. "If we do this, describe to me what will happen."

Brad looked at him with sympathy in his eyes, but he continued his explanation in a clinical monotone. "The operation is called a radical inguinal orchiectomy."

"Radical, huh? Apt description."

"I'll make an incision just above the pubic area and remove the entire tumor along with the testicle and spermatic cord. This is important, because the spermatic cord contains part of the vas deferens and blood and lymph vessels that can act as a path for the cancer to spread to other parts of the body. To decrease the chance the cancer cells can spread, we'll tie these vessels off early in the procedure."

Daniel was sweating. "So, basically, you're going to neuter me. Like a dog."

"You'll still have one testicle, Daniel. You can still get hard, have sex, and father children."

"I read some accounts on the internet of men who weren't so lucky, they couldn't get it up afterward, couldn't perform."

"I'm sure some of those cases were psychosomatic, the cause of their impotence wasn't physical."

"Impotence." Just hearing the word made him feel like he'd been kicked in the gut.

"Daniel, I can almost guarantee this won't happen to you." Brad stood, took off his reading glasses and chunked them on his desk. "I can only imagine what you're going through, but inaction isn't the best choice in this case."

"An almost guarantee isn't very comforting."

"You know I can't offer a guarantee..." He grinned at Daniel. "Shit happens."

Daniel laughed and shook his head. "I can't believe they give people like you a medical degree."

"Look, there's one thing I can do, it's not really recommended, but we can do it."

"What's that?" Daniel felt a bit of hope rise in his chest.

"When I get you on the table, I can do a biopsy then, before I snip-snip. If there's no cancer, I'll close you up with your ball still attached. If cancer is present, I'll continue."

"If I decide to go through with it, that seems like the best option."

"I strongly advise you to go through with it, those markers in your blood are a good indication there's a problem."

"But we don't know how much of a problem."

"Right. When we do the surgery, if there is cancer, we'll perform a number of scans later to determine if its spread. If it has, we'll do chemo."

"All of this 'we' stuff implies a greater level of involvement than you're planning on."

"I can't do it for you, no. But I can be there with you. Between me, your brothers, and that beautiful fiancée of yours, you have all the support you'll need."

Words meant to provide solace, brought despair, instead. There was no way he could tell Sara about his problem. Not now. Maybe, not ever.

"Like I said earlier, let me think about this."

"Fine," Brad spat out the word, disgusted with his friend and patient. "Just realize that you don't really have much choice in this matter. You either deal with the damn thing now, or deal with something much worse later."

Daniel thanked him, paid his bill, and left.

* * *

Sara sat on the porch swing, holding a hassling Hope next to her. "I see a cloud of dust coming. Who do you think it is?" Hope perked her ears up and tilted her head. "Is it Daniel?" They received their answer when the familiar white pickup came into view. She was so glad to see him, the familiar thrill shot through her as he climbed from the truck. Hope jumped down and scampered ahead of her. She wasn't far behind, running to him with open arms.

"Hey! You're home!" Sara plastered herself against him and wrapped her arms around his neck. "I missed you so much!" She held up her face for a kiss, but his response surprised her – he gently extricated himself from her embrace, clasping her arms, and pulling them down. "What's wrong?"

"Nothing. Just ready to get in the house and take off these damn boots." He stepped aside to move around her and headed into the rock house, leaving Sara standing where he left her.

As he moved away, Daniel could feel the confusion and pain coming off her in waves. God, he would burn in hell for this. He knew it. The trip home had given him a chance to think. He still needed more time, he wasn't ready to throw away the most precious thing in the world to him – but he had a choice to make, and he knew it.

Eventually, Sara moved, her feet as heavy as her heart. What could've happened in the last twenty-four hours to change Daniel so much? Last night, he worshiped her with his body. Today, it seemed he couldn't bear to look at her. Squaring her shoulders, she took off after him, determined to learn why he was treating her so coldly.

Upon entering the house, she searched for Daniel, finding him standing at the sink in the kitchen. Any other time, she would've felt completely welcome to run up behind to give him a hug, to place a kiss in the middle of his back. Now, she felt unsure and unwelcome and she didn't know what she'd done to make him so distant. "Supper is keeping warm. I made a pork roast, stuffed with boudain. Sweet potatoes. Butter beans. Chocolate cake."

Daniel didn't turn around, he closed his eyes as a hot shaft of pain lanced through him. He loved Sara to the depth and breadth of the ocean, she meant everything to him. Yet, the thought of seeing the light die in her eyes when she learned of his problem...well, he couldn't handle it. Daniel really couldn't see a way out of this for them. Brad Calhoun's belief that he would make a full recovery after the surgery, that his cock would work like it was supposed to, wasn't assurance enough. Daniel knew Sara. If he became ill with cancer, Sara would stay with him. If his dick turned into a limp noodle, Sara would stay with him. If he couldn't give her children, or satisfy her – Sara would stay with him.

Out of love and out of pity.

And he didn't want that.

He wanted Sara to have a full and happy life with a man who could give her everything she needed and deserved.

"I'm not really hungry."

Not hungry? Since when? "What's wrong? Is there anything I can do?" Sara was panicking. "Are you sick?"

"Yea, I'm sick of you asking me stupid questions," he said, spitting the words out at her like bullets.

Sara staggered like she'd been shot. Daniel had never raised his voice to her before, never spoke to her with such bitterness in his voice. "I'm sorry." She didn't understand. Just a few days ago, he'd begged her to marry him. Just last night, they'd made love – over and over again. Had he changed his mind about them? Did he realize he'd made a mistake? "What's going on, Daniel? Talk to me," she begged, moving near enough that she could lay a pleading hand on his arm.

"I don't want to talk. I'm going to bed. I'm tired. Sleep in your own room tonight, okay?"

He was there one minute and gone the next. Sara didn't know what to think. She ached all over. Only the sound of his brothers coming in the back kept her from sinking to the floor and crying her eyes out. Quickly, she set the food on the table, then excused herself, explaining that Daniel was resting. They presumed she was hurrying away to be with him and she didn't correct their erroneous conclusion.

Once she was behind closed doors, Sara threw herself on the bed and cried.

In his room, Daniel stared out the window into the darkness. The shadows and gloom matched his mood. What in hell was he going to do? Was he making a mistake that he'd regret for the rest of his life? Maybe he should get a second opinion before he tore his life and Sara's to smithereens. Before going to bed, he slipped out to his office and got on the computer. In a few minutes, he'd found a urologist in Austin. Tomorrow, he'd call for an appointment. "Yea, that's what I'm going to do." Finding a measure of peace, he went back to his lonely room and crawled into his lonely bed.

Across the house, Sara sat on the edge of the window seat, staring at the floor, her heart aching.

Three hours later, she was still sitting there, reliving every moment they'd shared, every tender word he'd spoken, every kiss he'd placed on her lips.

"No, what we've shared has been real and wonderful. Something is bothering him and I intend to get to the bottom of it. Hiding here in the dark isn't going to fix anything." Rising to her feet, she slipped out of her room and padded barefoot to his.

Taking the knob in hand, Sara halfway expected to be locked out. She breathed a sigh of relief when the door opened. The room was so dark, it took a moment for her vision to adjust. When it did, she saw Daniel in bed on his side. The spot next to him, the one she'd occupied for the past couple of weeks, was empty, like he'd been saving her place. With quiet footsteps, she moved closer, trying to see if he was awake or asleep. When she drew near, Sara could see his beautiful face was relaxed, he looked peaceful. His breathing was even. Whatever was bothering him had been forgotten while his body rested. Watching him, so incredibly dear, made her ache with longing. "I'd do anything in the world for you, don't you know that?"

She remained there, staring at him, until she grew chilled. With the anticipation of sleeping alone for the first time in forever, she'd worn a simple T-shirt. Chafing her arms, Sara admitted there was little about her to entice. Even when she was wearing sexy clothes, she always felt like an imposter. Her lack of sophistication made Sara wonder what Daniel ever saw in her. She shivered at the uncertainty she felt. What would he do if she just crawled in next to him? Would his true feelings emerge? Would he welcome her with open arms or push her away? Needing to know, she eased the covers back and slid in next to him.

In his dream, Daniel was so lost and alone. He'd come in from working the ranch and found the house deserted. No one was about. Not his brothers. Not his parents. Not Sara. No one. He felt lost. "Sara!" As he stormed from room to room, there were only cobwebs and shadows. When he came to his bedroom, he threw the door open and a golden light streamed from within. He stepped inside and saw Sara lying on the bed. She looked like everything he'd ever dreamed of – wanted – ached for. "I need you." When he tried to go to her, his feet wouldn't move, the air was too thick to breathe.

Struggling, Daniel rolled over, his hands reaching out blindly. When they came into contact with Sara's warm skin, he exhaled in absolute relief, pulling her body tightly against him.

"Daniel?" she whispered, thinking he was awake. When the only answer she received was his even breathing and the near-desperate clutch of his fingers at her back, she relaxed in his arms. He was still asleep, his reaction was instinctual. She let out a long, weary breath. This felt so right. If he was so angry, how could he hold her this way? Finding no answers in her heart, she gave herself over to him, nestled against his chest, thankful for the steady beat of his heart beneath her cheek.

They stayed that way until the first light of morning broke the eastern sky. Sara pulled herself gently from his embrace to stand, pulling the covers back over his broad shoulders. She still didn't know what yesterday had been about, but after sleeping all night in his arms, she hoped today would be better.

* * *

When Daniel awoke, his first thought was of Sara. He'd dreamed of her, dreamed he held her in his arms. Waking alone seemed like an omen. His eyes went to her empty pillow, seeing the slight indention where her head last lay made his heart ache. What had he done? Closing his eyes in anguish, he wondered at the impossible turn his life was taking. Finding Sara, loving her, was like being reunited with the missing half of his soul. And now – he'd pushed her away.

The turmoil roiling in his heart and mind made it hard to think. He'd erected a barrier between them last night, one meant to give him time to make this impossible decision. Knowing Sara, she wouldn't believe him if he just up and told her it was over. No, he had to make her believe it. Until he could get this the second opinion, until he knew for sure, one way or the other, he needed to keep the barricade in place. If he let her back in, Daniel knew he'd never have the strength to let her go again.

Rising from his bed, he readied himself for the day, dreading the moment he had to face Sara again. As he dressed, he damned himself for the coward he'd become. Was he doing the right thing? Trying to protect her? A tidal wave of pure love swamped him. Every fiber of his being demanded that he go to her, hold her, love her – tell her the truth and know that she'd stand by him. But what kind of price would she pay for such loyalty? She'd already been through enough, she didn't deserve a husband who might end up being a burden, one who might not be able to give her pleasure, one who couldn't give her children. "Fuck," he whispered in disgust, realizing his plan had to stay in place. He'd get his second opinion. If it was good news, he'd get on his knees, tell her everything, and beg for mercy. Yea, he smiled wanly, they'd have a good laugh about it all. The smile on his face faded. If the second opinion confirmed the first, he'd do whatever it took to make Sara believe he didn't want her.

Once he was dressed, he put his Stetson on his head and a mask of indifference on his face. Who knew he could be such a damn good actor?

In the kitchen, Sara was putting on her own performance. As far as Daniel's brothers were concerned, she didn't have a care in the world. "So, you hid a rubber snake in his lunch box?"

"Yea, I did," Sam admitted. "Easy is phobic about snakes."

"What did he do?" Sara asked as she poured more pancake batter on the griddle.

"I'll tell you what I did," Easy said, a perturbed look on his handsome face, "I did what any man would do. I took that rubber snake out of my lunch box on the end of a stick, then I laid it on the ground, and proceeded to kill him with a shovel."

"But he was rubber," Sara giggled, "and you knew he wasn't real."

Easy pressed his lips together and shook his head. "Yes, I knew the snake was rubber. It was the principal of the thing – I hate snakes."

Sara knew when Daniel came into the room, the atmosphere changed, became electric. "How many pancakes do you want, Daniel?" she asked in an even light tone.

"Two and some bacon. I'll make a sandwich to go." He slapped Benjen on the shoulder. "How about following me over to Perry's. He wants to borrow the tractor again and I'll need a ride back."

"Sure thing," Benjen agreed. "I'll go get the truck.

I need to unload some stuff from the front seat, so give me an extra minute or two." He stood and snapped his fingers, heading for the door. "Come on, Hope. You can ride with us."

"I'll have this ready for you in just a second, Daniel." Sara flipped his pancakes, her back still to him, her body tense. Should she make him talk to her, or just let him continue with this charade? Chewing on her lower lip, she decided to stand up for what she wanted. "Before you go, could I speak to you for just a second?"

Daniel felt trapped. Sam and Easy were watching his every move like two buzzards keeping an eye on roadkill. "Sure." What else could he say? He didn't want to play out his drama in front of his brothers, not until he had to. He cut his eyes to the woman he loved. Dressed in jeans and a cream lace camisole, she looked so beautiful, he wanted to scream.

Removing the pancakes from the griddle, she placed them on a plate. Turning, she could see Sam and Easy were finished eating, they were just finishing up their coffee. "Could you two excuse us?" She gave them a wink.

"Oh, yea, come on, bro." Sam stood and grabbed his hat.

Easy picked up another slice of bacon and brought it to his lips. "We'll get out of your way. Don't want to get in the middle of a make-out session, or a lover's quarrel." He held Daniel's gaze for a second. "Don't do anything stupid," he whispered.

Daniel didn't respond. He just wondered if he was so transparent, or if his brother was just perceptive.

Sara hesitated for just a second, calling upon a reserve of strength. How odd this felt, to be so wary of him. From the very first, she'd never felt safer with anyone in her life. He was a big man, but she didn't fear he would hurt her with his fist, he wasn't that kind of man. What he could do was shatter her with a word, with a look. Still, she had to try. Something told her their very future was on the line. Pasting a happy smile on her face, she picked up the plate and faced him, holding it out. "Here you go." She almost tacked the word 'baby' on the end, but she couldn't.

"Thanks." Daniel's hands shook as he took the plate from her, setting it on the table in front of him.

"Daniel." Sara threw caution to the wind. "I love you, Daniel." She went on tiptoe and leaned against him, waiting for him to wrap strong arms around her and hold her close.

He raised his arms to hold her, then dropped them. He raised them again, and dropped them again. The only concession he made was bending down just enough to…almost touch her hair with his lips. The words 'I love you' were on the tip of his tongue, but if he said them – all his resolve would be for nothing. If he told her he loved her now and his worst fears were realized, she'd never believe him when he told her that he didn't love her later. "I've got to go."

Sara was devastated by his lack of response. Standing near him always made her feel warm, like his big body was a comforting furnace. Now, she just felt cold. Lowering her arms, she slowly backed up. "Daniel, what's wrong? Please talk to me."

Daniel swallowed the huge lump of sadness in this throat. Shaking his head, he gave her what he could. "I'm just going through something. Give me a day or two to sort things out. Okay?" He cleared his throat. "Please?"

Sara nodded. "Okay." Looking up at him with sad eyes, she tried to read his stoic face. Staring at him, it scared her to realize that this Daniel didn't even look familiar to her.

"I just need some space."

Backing up a step, she gave it to him. "All right." Sara held up her hands in surrender. "I'll give it to you." She almost asked him if he wanted her to leave the ranch. But she didn't.

She was too afraid to hear the answer.

Daniel left the room as fast as he could, his feet unsteady beneath him. Once he was outside, he doubled over with pain, he thought he would lose his guts in the grass. Taking deep breaths, he calmed himself. Lying to Sara, treating her like shit, made him feel like the biggest asshole in the world. Raising up, he leaned against the side of the house. With shaking hands, he took his cell from his pocket and placed the call to schedule an appointment for the second opinion.

* * *

The next several days were surreal for Sara. She did her job, shopped for groceries, and went through the motions of maintaining a relationship that she wasn't sure even existed anymore. In front of his brothers, Daniel acted halfway normal. When they weren't around, neither was he. By now, she'd heard every excuse in the book from him. Sitting at the dining table, she turned the ring he'd given her around and around, slipping it off, then sliding it back on. Her stomach felt upset, sour, like she had persistent heartburn. Heartbreak, more likely.

A light scratch on her leg caused Sara to look down, finding the small dog looking up at her. She could tell something was wrong with her human friend.

"Hey, girl. I'm so sad."

A slight whimper was the dog's offer of consolation.

"I don't even know where he is today, Hope. He left the ranch and he didn't tell me where he was going. Something is wrong and I don't know how to fix it." She didn't even think he realized that today was his birthday. The cake she'd baked set in front of her and the gift she'd so carefully chosen was hidden and awaiting the moment when she could present it to him. "I love him so much, I don't know what I'll do if…" She stopped speaking and she stopped thinking. She didn't even want her doubts to congeal into a thought.

…In Austin, Daniel sat in front of another doctor's desk. Dr. Patel wasn't familiar to him, he didn't look at him with pity in his eyes – not like Brad. As a bonus, this guy was supposedly the best urologist in the area, the expert who knew more about treating and diagnosing testicular cancer than anyone else.

"Well, what did you find?" He was a man, he kept his voice even. The only tell-tale sign of his anxiety was the tapping of his boot heel on the floor.

"Mr. Blackhawk, I've reviewed the results of your tests and I concur with your previous diagnosis. You have testicular cancer."

Daniel blinked. He'd heard the words, but the doctor's voice sounded as if it were coming from far away. A fog seemed to have settled over him.

"Did you hear me, Mr. Blackhawk?"

After a prolonged exhale, Daniel answered, "Yes, I heard you."

"The scans that we did, show no spreading of the cancer at this time. My recommendation to you differs slightly from the other doctor. I would like to do the procedure to remove the testicle and the spermatic cord, but at this point I don't know if the chemo will be necessary. Let's get rid of the tumor, then retest you again before going any further."

Daniel raised his head. "No chemo? I thought that was inevitable."

"Chemotherapy has its place, but I like to avoid it if there's a way to possibly do so." The doctor shrugged. "There are other things we can do."

He'd heard the horror stories of chemo and he didn't relish the awful nausea – or losing his hair. "So, there's no way this is all a mistake?"

"No, we need to act soon. The longer the delay, the more likely the cancer will metastasize. When it does, your options will decrease rapidly."

Options. He was running out of options where Sara was concerned. He rubbed his palm over his aching chest, wondering if he was having a heart attack. "Well, let's do it."

"Good. I'll make the arrangements for the surgery and my nurse will inform you of the details."

Daniel rose, picked up his hat, and left the doctor's office. Every step he took seemed like a step toward an executioner. As he walked blindly to his truck, he tried to sort through what he was about to do. One last time, he considered the facts. Clearly, there was no good choice. If he told Sara the truth, she would stick by him through thick and thin, no matter if he was a burden or not. If he lied to her, if he broke her heart – she would never forgive him.

What choice do you make, when it seems you have no choice?

As he drove toward home, he remembered the first time he saw her. A beautiful woman risking her life to save a child. Daniel also remembered the day the lightning struck, how she'd gotten him out of harms' way by sheer will alone. When Sara came into his life, she'd brought the sunshine with her. The music of her laughter would forever ring in his ears. He recalled her smile, the sweetness of her lips, and the ecstasy of her touch.

Picking up his phone, he made a call to someone he'd never expected to contact again. He needed help convincing Sara they had no future. Daniel wasn't going to just lose her, he was going to push her away. He was going to hurt her so badly that she walked away and never looked back.

* * *

Benjen was the lookout, once he saw Daniel's truck, he forewarned everyone else. "Here he comes, here he comes, get down."

They all found a place to hide. Sara was kneeling behind the love-seat. Sam was behind the door, while Easy and Benjen were hunkered down behind the couch. Only Hope refused to cooperate, she was standing by the door, ready to welcome Daniel home.

When the door opened, they all jumped up and yelled in unison. "Surprise! Surprise!"

As Daniel stood there, stupefied, Sara ran to the kitchen and came out with the cake, leading his brothers in song. "Happy Birthday to you. Happy Birthday to you. Happy Birthday, dear Daniel." Of course, his brothers substituted less than complimentary titles instead of dear Daniel – like fart-face, dipshit, and ass-hat – but the sentiment remained. "Happy Birthday to you!"

As he watched his family and the woman he loved, standing there with smiles on their faces, he wished he was anywhere else in the world than here with them. Even in the midst of the excitement, he could tell Sara's smile didn't reach her eyes.

"What all this?"

"Your party, birthday boy! How does it feel to be so old?" Benjen blew one of those stupid birthday horns right in his face and Daniel had to force his fist to stay at his side.

"Come on, open your presents so we can have some cake!" Sam urged him away from the door, herding Daniel toward his recliner. As soon as he took his seat, several packages were laid in his lap.

"You all shouldn't have." Really, they shouldn't have. He began to open one, his attention split between the gift and the woman who hovered so hesitantly in the background. Daniel wanted to scream, he wanted to drag her into his lap, wrap his arms around her and never let her go. God, he should be horsewhipped. "Tickets!" He held up a pair of concert tickets from Sam.

"Yea, why mess with tradition," Benjen handed him a brightly colored envelope.

"More tickets!" Daniel knew by the time he opened them all, he'd have tickets to several events coming to Austin in the near-future.

"Wow, that cake looks good, Sara." Easy came in carrying a tray of saucers and forks, so they could eat cake once it was cut.

"Thanks, I hope it's good," Sara whispered as she used a fireplace lighter to bring the candles to blazing life. "Are you ready to make a wish?" she asked Daniel in a low, uncertain voice.

"Yea, sure." He stood and came to the table, closing his eyes. The wish he made didn't have a chance in hell of being fulfilled. He sent it anyway, winging its way heavenward. *Please, give me back my life, I don't want to lose her.*

As soon as he blew out the candles, his brothers dove on the cake like chickens on corn. "You heathens," he muttered good-naturedly. Their preoccupation forced Daniel to share a few moments with Sara. He could feel her eyes on him as he searched for something to say.

She beat him to it.

"I have something for you too." She reached behind him and brought out another gift. "I bought it with money from the food truck, I didn't want you to think…you paid for it yourself."

Daniel didn't know what to say. He took the gift, because he didn't know how not to. "Thank you." How pitiful his stilted gratitude sounded. Daniel wished a hole would open up in the earth and just swallow him. Anything would be easier than the slow excruciating death of all he held dear.

Sara nodded, her heart breaking. "You're welcome. I hope you like it."

None of this was going as planned. Daniel was miserable, absolutely miserable. She could see his torment written all over his face.

"Hey, Daniel, open it up. Let's see what you got." Easy encouraged him, but Daniel didn't want to open it, not in front of the others.

There really wasn't time.

When his phone rang, he let out a breath of something that resembled relief. It was the same feeling a person gets when the worst happens and you don't have to dread the suspense anymore, waiting for the axe to fall. Glancing at Sara, he lifted his cell. "Excuse me, I have to take this. Fiona is on the phone."

CHAPTER TWELVE

Sara reeled from the shock his words sent her way. She felt as if a hydrogen bomb had been dropped and the energy blast almost swept her into oblivion.

No wonder Daniel was acting strange. Trapped.

He was seeing someone else!

"What the fuck?" Benjen asked, looking from his brother to Sara and back.

"It's okay." Sara held up one hand, while grasping for the couch with the other. She found a seat, putting a brave smile on her face. "They're old friends, she probably called to wish him Happy Birthday."

"Dumb shit." Easy went to the kitchen to pour Sara a glass of water. "I've a mind to take my brother out to the wood shed."

"No, really, this is no big deal." Sara strove to put on a good front. "Please don't say anything to him. I don't want him to think I'm jealous. Everything's fine." She had no wish to embarrass herself by acting like this mattered. "Let me sip this, then I'll go finish supper."

In his office, Daniel had already hung up the phone. His ruse worked. Fiona had called, but just so he could give her a quote on a horse that she'd been warting him about buying. Pacing back and forth across the room, he put off returning to the living room as long as he could. He expected his brothers to come barging in any minute, he'd seen their faces when he dissed Sara, leaving her just as she gave him her gift. Damn, he hated this.

"Daniel?"

Oh, hell.

"Daniel, could I speak to you a moment?"

This was it. There was no use putting it off. He had cancer. There were no guarantees and he loved her too much to put her through any more of this shit. Better to rip the band aid off now, than to hurt her more later.

Before he turned to face her, Daniel prayed for the courage to send her away.

He prayed for the courage not to fall on his knees and beg her to stay.

Sending her away would be the hardest thing he'd ever do.

"What is it, Sara?" He purposely made his voice even and lacking emotion.

Sara came into the room, her palms sweaty, her nerves jittery. Never had she expected to feel this way in Daniel's presence – unwelcome, an intruder. "I don't know what happened to us, but I know something's…broken. We've…drifted apart. Is there anything I can do to fix this? I love you, you know."

Daniel shut his eyes, gathering strength before he turned to face her. He counted to five, then whirled around, his heart sinking to his stomach when he saw her beautiful, stricken face. "I'm sorry, Sara. This is my fault. I made a mistake."

"Mistake?" Sara's knees almost gave out with relief. She grasped the door facing to stay upright. "That's okay, I understand."

"No, that's not what I mean." Daniel forced

himself to remain still, when all he wanted to do was run to her and catch her before she fell. "Yes, I made a mistake. I hate to hurt you, but I can't go on like this. The sex was great, but I'm just not ready for commitment. I thought I was, I was wrong." He ran a finger around his collar. "I feel like I'm choking, the noose is tightening around my neck. I need a clean break."

"I see." She licked her lips, her heart and mind going numb with agony. "Well, I guess I'd better go." Staring at the floor, she attempted to get her bearings. Looking at him was just too painful. "I don't understand any of this, Daniel. I love you so much."

"Sara, please."

"Here." She pulled off the ring and held out her hand.

"No, keep it." He couldn't bear to take the ring. Turning his back on her, he prayed this moment would end soon. God, he was dying inside. "I don't have any use for it."

Ping! She dropped the ring to the floor. "Neither do I."

Sara backed out of the room and ran. She held back the sobs until she was in her room, where she shut the door and locked it, sliding to the floor. Sara cried like the world was ending. Benjen and Easy came to the door, but she asked them to go away. They stood there for a while, she could hear them speaking to one another in low tones. Finally, they left and she rose to go to the bathroom, her arms wrapped around her middle. She barely made it before she began to throw up, sinking to her knees in front of the toilet.

Sara felt like her world had ended. He didn't love her anymore. If he ever had.

As she rose slowly to her feet, Sara faced the sad

fact that everybody she loved left her.

Her father had died.

Her mother walked away.

She'd lost her baby, Faith.

And now…Daniel.

She wouldn't put Doug Wright in this category, but she wasn't good enough for him either. He'd just taken from her and left.

"Oh, God."

So, had Daniel.

She'd given him her heart and her body and neither was enough to make him stay.

After washing her face and wiping her eyes, Sara began to pack. She didn't have much, so it didn't take a long time. Seeing the keys to the Mustang, she knew she wouldn't be taking the car. She'd only driven it once, hopefully he could sell it for a good price. For a few moments, she considered where she was heading. The hour was late and she refused to take any of the money Daniel had given her, even if she'd earned it. If he wanted a clean break, she wanted no ties to him remaining.

None.

Asking for help was hard, but she had no choice. Finding her cell, she called the Callum mansion.

"Aunt Beth? Would you come get me? I need you."

* * *

"Have you lost your ever-loving mind?" Easy got right into Daniel's face. "What's got into you?" He pointed to the door. "You just let the best thing that ever happened to you walk out of your life."

"I don't want to talk about this now, Easy." He just wanted to be alone, he was dying inside. Doing the right thing hurt like hell. "Move." Daniel tried to step around his brother.

He didn't get very far.

"She left her car! Did you take her car away from her?"

Daniel frowned. "No, of course not."

Benjen joined them. "You broke Sara's heart for Fiona? Are you nuts?"

Sam pushed his way into the huddle. "He has to be. Sara's a doll, Fiona's a damn barracuda."

"Look, this is for the best. I'm doing this for Sara's own good."

"What in the hell are you talking about?" Easy grabbed Daniel's arm as he tried to move away from him.

"Unhand me, Ezekiel!" Daniel growled. "I'm in no mood for your shit."

"I'm not the one who's pulling shit, that's you." He spun Daniel around and gave him a little push. "Now, talk to me, idiot."

Daniel lost it. He'd just broken the heart of the only woman he would ever love. Breaking his brother's head might make him feel better. Lunging across the room, he knocked Easy to the floor. "Mind your own damn business!"

They rolled across the floor, bumping against a table, and knocking over a lamp. Ending up on top, Daniel landed a blow. Easy pushed him off and landed one of his own. "You are my business, you jerk!"

"Hey, what is this? Are you two crazy?" Benjen waded into the middle of the conflict. "Sam, help me!"

By the time the fourth brother was involved, Daniel and Sam stood on one side of the room while Easy and Benjen ended up on the other.

"Daniel, talk to us." Benjen came toward him. "I

know you. You love Sara. You can't stand Fiona. What's going on?"

Daniel dropped his head. There was no use hiding it, they were going to have to know sooner or later. "I do love Sara."

"Explain." Easy panted, wiping a spot of blood from his lip.

"Fuck!" Daniel yelled, making a fist and slamming it against the wall. "I have cancer."

"What?" The same word was voiced in abject horror by all three brothers.

"What kind of cancer?"

"When did you find out?"

"How bad is it?"

Daniel walked to the window, a shaft of pain piercing his gut when he saw Sara's car parked outside. He could still see her happy face when he presented her with the keys. "I have testicular cancer. A tumor on one of my balls. They're going to take it."

"Take it?" Easy asked, "Take what?"

"They're going to cut my fuckin' ball off."

"Shit," Benjen said what they were all thinking.

"That sucks," Sam admitted freely. "But why lie and hurt Sara? She would die for you, Daniel."

"Exactly."

"You'll get well, though. Right?" Easy's voice had dropped almost to a whisper.

"Maybe," Daniel said, evenly. "There's no guarantees. They say the cancer hasn't spread. They say I'll still function as a man. They say I'll still be able to father children." He looked up at his brothers with pain in his eyes. "But what the hell do *they* know? Nothing's for certain!"

The room grew very quiet. All of the anger had dissipated.

Finally, Benjen came forward to hug his brother. "Daniel, I'm so sorry. Everything will be okay. It has to be."

Daniel accepted the hug. "I know. I know," he whispered the words more for Benjen's benefit than his own.

The others followed suit, comforting their brother the best they could.

"I still think it was a stupid idea to break Sara's heart." Easy crossed his arms over his chest and glared at Daniel. "You're going to be okay. You're going to live and be just like you've always been. The only thing you won't have is the love of your life."

"I agree," Sam chimed in.

"Ditto." Benjen squatted down to pet his dog, who was dancing around at their feet, trying to get anyone's attention.

"Sara is the most unselfish person I know," Daniel said quietly. "I'm protecting her in the only way I know how."

With a heavy heart that felt like it would break in two, Daniel grabbed his Stetson and started for the door. "I'm going for a ride."

* * *

"This is great, Aunt Beth. I'll be fine." She moved around the beautiful bedroom slowly, running her hand over the antique cherry wood dresser "Thank you so much for letting me barge in on you like this."

"Oh, sweetheart, I love having you here." She pulled Sara into her arms. "I just hate it's under these circumstances. You and Daniel seemed so perfect together."

"I know!" Sara began to cry again. "I don't understand what went wrong."

"Well, you're here now and I'm going to enjoy having you." She patted her niece on the back. "Don't give up hope, sometimes these things work themselves out."

Sara moved out of her aunt's embrace, wiping her eyes. She wasn't ready to hear platitudes. "I don't think this will be one of those things. He doesn't love me." Even as she said the words, something about them didn't ring true. Shaking her head, Sara forced herself to face the truth. "We rushed things. Got carried away."

"Don't make excuses for him. Sometimes men do stupid things." Her aunt went to the window to straighten the curtain. "I was married three times. Believe me, I could write you a book."

"I'm sure you could." Sara really wasn't in the mood, but she wouldn't be rude. She needed her aunt. Picking up her bag off the floor, she proceeded to take out her clothes to put them away. "I'll start looking for a job tomorrow. I don't know how long it will be before I can afford a place of my own, but I'll start working toward it as fast as I can."

"Don't you dare worry about it." Beth came to help her, handing Sara a few hangers from the closet. "Callum house is partly yours. In fact, I'll make that legal as soon as I can."

Sara felt overwhelmed. She sat down on the bed and bowed her head. "Thank you so much. I don't want to be a burden. So, whatever I can do to help around here, please let me know."

"I think you should rest now." Her aunt gave her a kiss. "You have the run of the house. The refrigerator downstairs is fully stocked, if you get hungry. We'll work together to get everything set up in the days ahead."

"All right." Sara gave her Aunt Beth a wan smile. "I am so grateful to you. My life fell apart today and you were there to pick up the pieces."

"Everything will be fine," her aunt assured her. "You'll see."

Once she was alone, Sara curled up on top of the bedcovers in a fetal position. She hadn't even bothered to turn off the overhead light.

"Oh, Daniel, why? Why?" More tears began to flow. "How could you do this to us?"

She relived the moment he went to his knees to propose. She remembered the first time they made loved and the last time. "I didn't imagine those things, they were real." If Daniel didn't love her, he must be a consummate actor.

As she laid there, Sara was sore, like she'd run a marathon. Her head ached and she felt like a thousand-pound weight was pressing her down into the mattress. Each time she closed her eyes, all she saw was Daniel's face. She wished she could hate him, but Sara knew that wasn't possible. She would love him until the end of her days. Why he did what he did, she didn't know.

Sometimes men do stupid things, her aunt had said.

As she drifted off into a fitful sleep, this statement haunted her.

Sometimes men do stupid things.

…About fifty miles away, Daniel sat on his horse, high on a ridge overlooking the Llano River. Packsaddle Mountain loomed over him. The lights from the ranch flickered behind him. He'd never felt more hopeless and alone in his life. Even when he was in shackles, being led from the courtroom, facing time in prison – he'd never felt like this.

God, all he could see was Sara's face when he told her it was over. "I'm so sorry, Pet." Her love was pure and he'd been the luckiest goddamn man in the world. He lifted his face to the night sky. He wanted to rage against the heavens. "Why? Why did you have to give me cancer? What did I do to make you hate me so much?"

Daniel waited for some still small voice to answer him, but he heard nothing. The only noise to break the silence of the darkness were the distant sound of cars traveling on the highway and the howl of a lone coyote. In disgust, he headed his horse toward home.

There was nowhere else for him to go.

He hoped his brothers were in their rooms, Daniel didn't feel like rehashing any of this with them. He didn't know which was worse – their sympathy or their anger. Having never been in his position, they couldn't understand why he'd chosen to end things with Sara. "Giddy-up!" Urging his mount into a canter, Daniel felt a sense of panic rising in his chest. Just the thought of seeing pity in her eyes made him crazy. What if he couldn't perform? Hell, he didn't think he could perform now.

His emotions were shot, some damned self-fulfilling prophecy was taking hold and swamping him with doubt and despair. "Get a grip, asshole," he chastised himself. "You're going to have to deal with this one way or the other."

As he galloped home, he made plans. Tomorrow, he'd hear from the doctor. There was no use delaying the inevitable. He needed to face what lay ahead of him like a man. His brothers could pick up the slack until he was back on his feet.

After settling his horse for the night, Daniel made his way back to the rock house. Even though his brothers would be there, he knew the house would feel empty.

Without Sara.

He was right. As soon as he entered the front room, the dog came to him, her head hanging low, her tail wagging weakly. "You know she's gone, don't you, girl?" Daniel knelt down to pet Hope. "Come on, sit down with me." He went to his regular chair, the worn recliner by the fireplace, settling the dog next to him. His eyes fell on the gift Sara had given him for his birthday. The package still lay on the arm of the chair, unopened. He picked it up and held it in his hands, soothing the paper with his fingers. She'd wrapped this herself, he could feel it. With tears in his eyes, he ripped off the paper and found a square box. Swallowing nervously, he opened it, curious as to what it might be. To his surprise, he found a cuff bracelet. Silver. A thunderbird was etched on the top and there were turquoise inlays on either side of the Native American symbol. "Oh, Sara." He knew exactly what she'd intended. "Pride." She was intent on instilling pride within him, pride for who he was, for what he was.

Rubbing his thumb on the inside of the bracelet, he noticed a rough spot. Turning it over, he found an inscription. Pain and love rose within his breast as he read the words: *I love you just the way you are. Forever and always, Sara.*

"Oh, hell, baby."

There was no doubt in Daniel's mind what he was.

An idiot.

* * *

"Are you sure you want to throw these away?"

Sara knew what her aunt was asking. She'd found

the bridal magazines in the trash. "I know it seems like a waste, but they make me sad to look at them."

"Well, maybe I'll save them." Beth held them tightly to her chest. "Perhaps the library would like them."

"Okay." Sara could see her point.

She tried to focus on what she was doing. Making pie crust was second nature to her, she didn't know why the task suddenly seemed insurmountable. "Just as soon as I finish here, I'll help you polish the silverware."

"I'd much rather you were baking, dear. Once we start tours, you could sell pies again, if you'd like that. We could set up a gift shop in the parlor." Beth had been rubbing the same fork so long, she was about to polish a hole in it. "You don't have to, of course, I want you to be happy."

Sara rinsed her hands, then dried them on a towel. "I like the idea, but I need to find something to do that pays a little better than selling pies by the slice." She reached over and rescued the fork. "Stop worrying about me, Aunt. I'll be okay."

Eventually.

"I know you will."

Honestly, Sara wasn't so sure. She'd never realized a person could function, act normally, and be in so much pain at the same time.

Not a moment went by that she didn't think of Daniel.

Try as she might to be angry, all she could manage was misery. She missed Daniel – with every breath she took, she missed him. She missed taking care of him. Sleeping with him. Loving him. She missed his brothers. Heck, she missed the dog so much that she thought about calling her during the day when no one was home, just to leave Hope a voice message. She'd seen how the little animal would listen when someone would leave one on the ancient answering machine that Daniel kept, preserving his mother's voice: *This is the Blackhawk residence. We're glad you called. Leave a message at the tone, please.*

Glancing at the clock, she imagined what Daniel might be doing at this moment. Probably working his fingers to the bone, fixing a fence, or shoeing a horse. She hoped he'd eaten a good breakfast.

...In Austin, stretched out on a gurney, Daniel was being wheeled into surgery. The anesthesiologist had put something in his IV and told him that he'd feel drowsy in a moment. He was glad. He certainly didn't want to be awake for the operation. Last night, he'd tried to rub one out for old time's sake. He couldn't. Only Sara turned him on and thinking of her now, just made him ache – but not in a good way.

Ironic.

The impotence he'd feared was upon him and the knife was still to come.

"Are you ready for this?" A too cheerful nurse walked beside him.

"Oh, boy!" He gave her a sardonic smile. "Can't wait!"

Apparently, sarcasm was lost on her. "You'll be up and out of here before you know it. Good as new."

Well, not quite as good as new. Unless a miracle occurred when the doctor performed the biopsy, he'd have a half-empty ball sac. Oh, no – he'd forgotten the form he signed. When he emerged from the operating room, he would be the proud owner of a prosthetic testicle. Size large. Damn straight. Firm. Gel based. Guaranteed to fool the most discerning blow-job giver.

God, he felt woozy.

Blinking his eyes, he became mesmerized by the lights passing overhead as he was pushed toward the operating theater. Daniel chuckled. Theater. Wonder what was showing? Les Misérables? Well, he'd never seen it. He hated foreign films. Especially musicals.

Finding it hard to keep his eyes open, he closed them. "Sara," he whispered, "I love you." This was the last coherent thought Daniel was able to process.

* * *

"Look on the bright side, Daniel, it's over with." Easy handed his brother a glass of ice chips. "The doctor said the chemo is just a precaution."

"Yea, but he said I wouldn't have to have it," Daniel grumbled. "He lied."

"Once he got in there," Benjen pointed at Daniel's groin and swirled his finger in the air, "I guess he changed his mind."

"You have something called seminoma, Stage 0, which has to be good," Sam informed him. "Zero is a mighty small number. The chemo will be a one-shot deal, you probably won't even notice it."

Daniel sat up in bed, licking the ice cream cone his brothers had brought him. "This wasn't a tonsillectomy, you know." He held up the cone and waved it at them.

As if making a toast, each brother held up his own cone.

"There's no bad time for ice cream," Easy said, matter-of-factly.

"Are you ready for us to call Sara and explain things for you?" Benjen asked, stepping a little closer to the door, just in case Daniel decided to throw a bedpan at him.

"No!" Daniel was emphatic in his objection. "I do

not want you to tell Sara anything. Got it?" His brothers all stared at him. "I'm serious, guys. Do not fuck with me on this. I do not know what's going to happen to me and I do not want her involved. Under any circumstances! Do you hear me?"

"Hey, hey, everybody on this floor hears you." Dr. Patel came into the room with a frown on his face. "Could you all excuse us. please? I'd like to examine my patient."

"Sorry." Daniel offered the one-word apology reluctantly.

"Sure, we'll be in the waiting room." Sam pointed down the hall rather lamely. "Waiting."

"Do not call Sara!" Daniel said again, not nearly as loudly this time.

Easy just waved at him as they went out the door.

"Are they giving you a hard time, Mr. Blackhawk?" the doctor asked as he lifted the sheet and began to probe around Daniel's private parts. "Does it hurt when I do this?"

Daniel winced. "Yes. Don't do that, please."

"Good."

"Good?"

"That means you have feeling down there." Dr. Patel gave him a sideways grin. "I didn't cut any important nerves in two or anything."

Daniel frowned. "You're not instilling me with a great deal of confidence, Doc."

"Oh, you'll be fine." He typed something into the tablet he was holding. "The biggest hurdle you're going to have to face is in your head, not your cock."

Hearing the doctor use the slightly crude word surprised Daniel. "What do you mean?"

"Everything should work properly, if you'll let it."

"Well, I'm certainly not going to do anything to discourage it." Daniel was still a little loopy. He knew the drugs would wear off soon and his balls would hurt.

Correction.

His ball would hurt. Singular.

"As soon as you're feeling a little more up to it, there's something I want you to do for me."

"Great. Homework."

The doctor chuckled. "At least you didn't lose your sense of humor during the process."

"Hey, I lost enough. So, what do you want me to do? Sing? I used to have a bass voice. I might be a tenor by now."

"Nah, you still have one nut. You're probably a baritone." The doctor pulled up a stool and sat down. "I want you to go to therapy."

"Hell, no. I'm not going to some damn shrink. I've lost a ball, not my fucking mind."

"Calm down, Mr. Blackhawk, you misunderstand. I'm not talking about a psychiatrist, this is more like rehab. I shouldn't have called it therapy. This is a support group, if you will."

"A support group for eunuchs? I've heard of the empty stocking fund. Would this be the empty sack society?"

Dr. Patel wagged his finger at Daniel. "Oh, you're a funny one. And you aren't a eunuch, obviously. Once you heal, you're not going to know the difference. Your sex drive will be undiminished and I expect you to name your first son after me."

"What's your name?"

"Balthazar."

"Balthazar Blackhawk? I don't think so." Daniel cringed a little at the thought. Kids were probably just a pipe dream now, anyway. Without Sara in his life, any thought of a family seemed futile.

"Oh, well, my middle name's Horatio if that appeals to you more."

"It doesn't. So, what do you expect me to do? Lift weights with my cock, I've seen a video of that before."

"No, nothing so demanding. There's a program at the hospital nearest you run by a man named Jaxson McCoy. Do you know him?"

"Yes." Daniel nodded slowly. "I do. He's a rancher, up close to Lake Buchanan. I know he leads some type of sit-in-a-circle-and-talk-about-yourself group, but he's an amputee." Pausing for a moment, Daniel thought. "Ah...so am I, in a fashion."

"Coping with a loss of any kind is difficult to deal with."

Daniel shifted in the hospital bed. His lower regions were beginning to awaken and the feeling wasn't pleasant. "Look, Dr. Balthazar, I don't intend to sit there and discuss how I feel about being half a man."

Dr. Patel frowned. "All right, that's enough. I could put you in a wheelchair now and roll you down the hall and show you twenty people who are really suffering. Who've lost more than one teste. Some are going to lose their life." Standing, he pinned Daniel to bed with a stare. "If you'll pull your head out of your ass, you'll realize the only thing you're apt to lose are friends if you keep acting like such a doofus."

Doofus? "I can't say much for your bedside manner, Doc." Daniel winced. "I'll think about it. What I'd like is a pain pill if you can spare one."

"I'll call the nurse for you." He started out the door, then paused. "Do you want me to send your brothers back in or should I tell them you're resting?"

"Send them in." At least if they were where he could see them, maybe he could keep them from doing something foolish – like calling Sara.

A wave of sadness washed over him. The doctor was right about the difficulty of coping with a loss.

The loss of someone you love was devastating.

* * *

"I like this one." Sara pointed to the blue flowered wallpaper sample. "I think it looks more like the pattern I saw in the old photographs than the others do."

"I think you're right." Beth marked the pattern number on the order chart. "Thank you. I think this will look perfect."

"Great!" Sara glanced out the window. "If it's okay with you, I think I'll take a walk."

"Sure." Her aunt waved her hand in the air absentmindedly. "You go on ahead and I'll add some vegetables to the pot of soup I'm making to go with that luscious pie. What did you call it?"

"Almond Joy." Just saying the name of the pie reminded her of Daniel. She'd made it as a cleansing exercise, sort of a wash-that-man-right-out-of-your-hair move.

It didn't work.

She still thought about him every minute of every day. Angry thoughts. Sad thoughts. Wishful thoughts.

Sara wondered if Daniel thought about her at all.

"Scrumptious!" Beth headed toward the kitchen. "Watch for snakes!"

"Ewww," she hissed. She hadn't thought of snakes. At least not the no-leg variety. Exiting through the back door, Sara took a minute to admire the expansive porch. She could just imagine fancy tea parties being held out here, or seeing the wide verandahs decorated for fall, with large pots of mums, stacks of pumpkins, and hay bales. "This is going to be a beautiful place." As she moved toward the steps leading to the ground, she happened to catch a glimpse of the bench where she and Daniel had rested, the day he'd brought her here to meet her aunt. Confusion muddled her mind. How could he have been so considerate if he cared nothing for her? Time and again since their break-up, she'd dissected each and every moment they'd shared, every sweet word he'd whispered to her, every kiss he'd placed on her lips.

If none of that was love, what was it?

Unhappy and frustrated, she stomped out into the yard and cut across the field. The sun was shining brightly, so Sara kept her focus on the ground. She might as well keep her eyes open for a topaz, the stones would catch the bright rays and glint like blue fire. Sara much preferred these stones to clear, hard diamonds. To her, they were warm and full of life. She couldn't help but remember the engagement ring she'd worn with such joy. The chance to marry a man like Daniel had been a dream come true.

A dream proven to be flawed.

At least, he'd come to his senses before the wedding. She wouldn't be visiting another lawyer, trying to find a way out of a marriage that never should've happened in the first place.

Every step she took, a different memory plagued her heart. She remembered playing in the water with Daniel at the Slab, riding cradled in front of him on his horse, and holding hands at the movies. Sara hadn't known it was possible to feel so close to someone. When she cried over her lost baby, he'd held her in his arms and offered her his strength. When she needed to be free of a man who used her, he made it possible. When she needed a place to go and someone to protect her, he'd been her rock. There'd been no doubt in her mind then, Daniel Blackhawk was a good man.

So, how could he have changed so much in so short a time? How did he go from being warm and giving to being so cold and selfish?

As a flash of reflective light caught her eye, the truth hit her.

He couldn't.

Daniel Blackhawk's heart didn't change so fast, it was impossible.

Going to her knees, she dug among the rocks until she held the rough topaz in her hand. This was a find. A treasure hidden among rubble. All she'd had to do was be willing to look for it.

Something told her there was more to Daniel Blackhawk than she was seeing, if only she was willing to look.

CHAPTER THIRTEEN

"An interview? Why didn't you tell me?" Sara rushed around trying to dust the furniture before their company arrived.

Beth straightened some finials on the mantle of the fireplace. "I did tell you. Last night. You nodded like you were listening, but I don't think you were."

"Sorry." Her aunt was probably right. Once she came back from her walk, she couldn't get Daniel off her mind. Slipping her hand in her pocket, she rubbed the topaz she'd found between her thumb and forefinger, like a worry stone. "I guess my mind was elsewhere."

"And where would this elsewhere be, eh?" her aunt asked with a mischievous glint in her eye.

Sara was saved from answering by the ringing of the doorbell.

"Well, let him in!" Aunt Beth clapped her hands. "I adore company!"

During the next half hour, it became clear to Sara that the journalist had found something else to focus on other than the renovation of the historical landmark of Callum House.

"I remember you!" the man exclaimed with a grin. "You're Sara Riley, the woman who saved the child in front of Rev. Mike's Dam Pub a while back. So, you didn't know you were an heiress?"

Sara blanched, looking to Beth for help. "I'm not an heiress. I'm merely helping out my aunt."

"She's oversimplifying things," Beth explained. "Our family was estranged for some time, finding Sara again is an answer to a prayer. When you use a word like heiress, you're assuming much. The value of Callum House lies more in its historical value than in any wealth associated with it."

The journalist did not seem to be put off by the account he'd received. "Let me get a picture of you next to the stained-glass window, Sara."

"Oh, no. Take my aunt's photograph. This renovation is her dream. I'm just…here."

Sara's reluctance didn't do her much good. "Both of you, then." He herded them into place and took his pictures. After that, Beth insisted he see some of the family scrapbooks for information on the past grandeur of the estate and the former richness of the topaz fields.

While they were thus engaged, Sara wrote a note to her aunt. There was an errand she could not put off. Finding the keys to the car Beth had put at her disposal, Sara set out for Blackhawk Ranch. She wouldn't be satisfied until she looked Daniel in the eye and asked him some extremely pointed questions.

As she traveled south toward Kingsland, Sara tried to rehearse what she would say to Daniel once she got there. "Daniel, I've been thinking…no, that's stupid." She huffed out a breath. "Daniel, I want you to explain to me…you sound like a schoolteacher." Pulling over to the side of the road, she rolled the windows down to get some air. "Maybe, this is a dumb thing to do. What if I'm imagining all of this?" When several cars passed by and the passengers stared at her, she grew worried someone might stop to see if she needed help. "I probably do need help, I'm a mental case."

As she started the car to continue her journey, Sara couldn't help but replay Daniel's speech in her head when he told her it was over.

I made a mistake. I hate to hurt you, but I can't go on like this. The sex was great, but I'm just not ready for commitment. I thought I was, I was wrong." *He ran a finger around his collar. "I feel like I'm choking, the noose is tightening around my neck. I need a clean break.*

She tried to remember his face, the timbre of his voice as he delivered those painful words. Had he been speaking from the heart or was there something else going on?

She wouldn't be satisfied until she knew for sure.

By the time she could make out Packsaddle Mountain in the distance, Sara was as nervous as a cat.

When she arrived, it was right at five. Knowing Daniel's habits, she knew he would be coming in from a hard day on the ranch to clean up and get ready for the evening meal. Even if he were eating out, he'd still come in to clean up before going into town. Sara's heart sank when she didn't see Daniel's pickup. Oh well, maybe she was a little early or he was running a little late.

Pulling in next to the Jeep, she saw the blue Mustang parked in its usual place. Her heart leapt when she realized he hadn't sold her car. This had to mean something, right? On unsteady legs, she made her way slowly to the rock house, wondering if Hope would be glad to see her.

Bark! Bark! Bark! Bark!

Sara smiled, that question was answered in a

wonderful way. "Hope!"

The screen door opened and the little dog came running as hard as her little legs would carry her.

"Sara!"

Sara stood up, holding Hope, who was licking her face madly. "Hello, Benjen. Is Daniel home?"

To say Benjen looked startled was putting it mildly. Clearly, her unannounced arrival was causing more than a normal amount of surprise.

"Uh...uh...he's not here."

"Aren't you going to ask her in, Miss Manners?" Easy came up behind Benjen and popped him on the back of the head with the flat of his hand.

"Sure, sure, come in." Benjen and Easy stepped back to allow her entry. Sam stood just inside the door.

"Hey, Sara." He came forward to hug her. "It's good to see you."

"It's good to see you all too." She received hugs from the other two brothers. "Could I have a glass of water?"

She felt odd asking, but she felt a little faint. Probably excitement.

"Oh, yea, hold on." Easy took off to the kitchen to fetch some for her.

"Come on in, sit down." Benjen gestured toward the living room.

Sara knew they were being perfectly polite, but they were also acting extremely odd. Like they felt...guilty about something. "Thank you. Where is Daniel? Will he be home soon?"

Benjen and Sam looked at one another, their eyes going wide. Obviously, lying was not their strong suit. Admirable.

"Here you go, Sara." Easy handed her the water. "Daniel's in town."

"Oh." The way he said it, she presumed he meant that Daniel was in town on a date…with Fiona.

Sara took a big sip of water, wishing it was something stronger. "How is he?" she asked once her thirst was quenched.

"Better," Benjen said with a nod, then he jerked when Sam elbowed him. He quickly added an additional bit of information. "I mean, fine, he's fine."

Sara narrowed her eyes, wondering at their apparent nervousness. "I know my coming here out of the blue is strange, but I've been looking at the big picture and I just wanted to make sure…" She shook her head, rising. "I don't know why I came. It was stupid. Daniel's not here. He's on a date with Fiona, isn't he?"

Again, the brothers just exchanged looks.

"You're protecting him, I can tell." She held up her hands. "I'm sorry I came. Tell Daniel that I was here." Sara started for the door, giving Hope a pat when the small dog began to jump at her feet. "No, on second thought, don't bother telling him anything. My thinking something weird was going on with him, it was just my imagination."

"Sara, are you okay?" Sam asked with concern. "You're pale."

"I'm fine, I just haven't been sleeping very well."

"Neither has Daniel," Benjen offered, earning himself an ugly look from Easy.

Seeing how they were passing looks between them, Sara felt like a complete outsider. "I'll be going now. I just wanted you to know that I've missed…all of you and I…I wish you well." She nodded her head, affirming what she'd just said. As they all stood there watching her, she had no choice but to leave.

"Bye, Hope." She blew a kiss to the terrier. "See

you guys later."

She'd barely made it halfway across the yard before Benjen caught up with her. "Sara, wait."

Sara froze. "What, Benjen?"

"Don't give up on him, Sara."

"What do you mean? He's clearly made his choice. I was wrong to hold out, hoping for something different."

"Just don't give up on him, Sara. Please."

With those odd words, he returned to the house and Sara was left more confused than ever.

…At Seton Highland Lakes Hospital in Burnet, Daniel sat in a room filled with recliner like chairs. At his right, an IV pole stood with a bag attached, dripping a cocktail of bleomycin, etoposide, and cisplatin into his veins. Looking around at the other people seated with him, he could tell some were sicker, some looked almost too weak to sit upright. He glanced down at his arm where the needle was stuck into his skin. None of this was comforting by any means, he felt vulnerable as hell.

While he waited, he tried to look at a magazine, but he found himself reading the same sentence over and over again. Finally, he just raised the footrest and closed his eyes, not waking up until the nurse came and removed the needle from his arm nearly three hours later.

Before he left, the nurse gave him a little pamphlet and some instructions. "You may experience some side effects with this dose. Nausea, sores in your mouth, tiredness, and you may lose a little hair." She brushed a lock off his forehead. "I don't expect you to lose much, if any, not with only one round." She gave him a card. "Come back on this date so we can redo the scans and blood tests. If necessary, at that time we'll schedule another round. Okay?"

God, he hoped not. "Okay, thank you."

Daniel left the treatment area as quickly as possible. He'd started to head to his truck when he remembered his promise to Dr. Patel. "Oh, well, it's not like I have any reason to hurry home."

His Sara wasn't there.

He wondered, for he hundredth time that day what she was doing. Was she happy? Did she hate him? Did she still love him?

"Hell, I hate my life."

Feeling down, he questioned the wisdom of signing up for Jaxson's group. Would it do him any good? He wasn't the type to talk about his feelings. Oh, heck, he'd just check it out, get a brochure or something. Turning down a long hall, he checked out the room numbers until he found the right one. There was no one inside except a young woman manning a reception desk. "Can I help you?"

Daniel puffed out a breath. "I'm thinking about signing up for Jaxson McCoy's group?" He knew he'd phrased the comment like a question, which conveyed the meaning that he wasn't really sure about doing it.

"Great!" The receptionist didn't notice or pretended not to notice his hesitation. "Jaxson is an amazing facilitator for the group. He knows what it's like to almost give up. I've seen him relate to people with all kinds of problems, not just amputees."

"Wow, I take it you're a fan."

She sobered, glancing down. "He helped me." She touched her chest. "Breast cancer."

Daniel read between the lines, thinking she might have had a mastectomy. Wow. Did he feel like a dork. "I'm sorry. I'm sure I can benefit from the sessions." He filled out the forms and took note of the meeting times. "Thanks, I appreciate your help."

On the way home, he tried to analyze how he felt. Daniel had no idea how soon he'd start to feel the effects of the chemo. Hopefully, he wouldn't notice anything.

By the time he drove under the ranch sign, he knew he wasn't going to be so lucky. Nausea was causing his stomach to do flip-flops. His skin was wet with sweat and he felt like he'd run from Burnet instead of driving. Taking it easy, he trudged to the steps, holding the railing to climb slowly up to the porch.

"Hey, you're home!" Easy met him. "Damn, you look like shit."

"Thanks."

"I knew we should've driven you," Sam said, his concern evident. "How'd it go?"

"Fine. I'm fine." He staggered into the house and aimed for the recliner. "You needed to work, we can't all have an afternoon off."

"I don't think this really counted as an afternoon off, did it?" Benjen came to kneel next to his brother, holding Hope back from trying to climb up into his lap.

"Probably not." Daniel laid his head back, trying to get his breath and stop his head from spinning. "What's been going on here?"

When his question was met by a suspicious silence, Daniel opened one eye.

"What aren't you telling me?" Seeing the looks the men were exchanging, he raised his head. "Is something wrong with the cattle or the horses?"

"No," Benjen spoke up. Taking a deep breath, he spit out the words quickly. "Sara was here. She came to see you."

"Really?" Daniel raised up, his heart racing even

harder. "What did she want?"

"To see you." Easy repeated Benjen's words. "She was asking all kinds of questions. I think she suspects something."

"How could she?" Daniel raised his voice. "Did you tell her anything about my surgery?"

"No," they all answered in unison.

"She assumed you were on a date with Fiona and we didn't correct her," Sam informed his brother.

Benjen pressed his lips together and said nothing more.

"Damn, damn, damn." Daniel stood up. "I'm going to bed. I feel like shit."

"Are you all right?" Easy asked, putting a steadying hand on Daniel's back.

"This is normal, I just need to lie down."

They let him go and Daniel slowly made his way to his room. Hearing that Sara had come to him, made Daniel feel sad and happy. He kept a hand on the wall, hoping to hell that he didn't fall down. For a moment, he imagined that Sara would be waiting for him in his bed. Lord, it would be amazing to fall asleep in her arms. Talk about a good dose of medicine, she would make all his ills bearable.

Once he was in his bathroom, Daniel pulled off his clothes. The dressing over his incision had come off a couple of days before. He hadn't really taken a good look at his business since then, he'd been afraid to look. Bruising wasn't something he'd really anticipated, more fool he. Sitting on the closed toilet lid, he took a gander at his poor johnson, staring at the two lumps in his sac with an uneasy fascination. One didn't really look much different than the other. He couldn't bring himself to touch it, he was probably still too sore. Of all the places on his body that could be injured or require surgery, this was the one area he'd rather remained healthy and untouched by problems. Daniel guessed there wasn't a man in the world who would feel differently.

After performing the minimum amount of bathroom duties he could get away with, he made his way to bed. "So, my beautiful Sara came to see about me today." Easing under the covers, he let out a relieved sigh when he was flat on his back. "As much as I miss you, Pet, I sure am glad you can't see me like this."

Daniel closed his eyes and shut the world out of his sight.

* * *

"I can't believe this." Sara tossed the newspaper onto the table. "He barely talks about the house at all."

"There are a couple of nice photos." Beth reread the article. "And he mentioned all of the beautiful antiques we have."

"I don't like it, he turned the article into sensationalism. He makes it sound like I'm part of some romantic rags-to-riches story." Sara knew she was probably overreacting. If anyone read the piece today, they probably wouldn't remember it tomorrow. No, her bad mood was due to her visit to Blackhawk ranch the day before and the realization that Daniel had moved on with his life. Her feeling that he might regret their break-up was no more than wishful thinking on her part.

With a heavy heart, Sara returned to her project of planting pansies in the front beds. Their beautiful blooms did little to lighten her mood.

…At the Blackhawk Ranch, Daniel folded the newspaper and put it aside. After lunch, when he felt better, he'd clip the photograph of Sara from the newspaper and put it away somewhere safe. He regretted that he hadn't taken photos of her while she was with him. Neither he nor his brothers were big on selfies or scrapbooking. At least he'd have this one to take out and look at and remember. Although, there was zero chance he would ever forget her beautiful face or how it felt to be with her.

As a surge of nausea struck, Daniel jerked to his feet and made for the bathroom. After he'd emptied his stomach, he sat down by the toilet and took stock of his sad situation. He couldn't get over the fact that Sara had come to him. A faint smile played around his lips. Leaning back against the wall, he let his mind wonder to what might have been. If he hadn't found the lump, if he'd never said those cruel lies to her, they would be planning their wedding and looking at house plans. Picking out names for their children. Instead of bringing comfort, these thoughts brought him pain.

A weak groan slipped from his lips as he stared up at the bathroom ceiling. So, this was what the view from the bottom of the barrel looked like. He missed Sara like hell, but he'd made the right decision. If what he'd read in the article was true, Sara was going to be just fine.

…Halfway across the state, someone else was reading the newspaper article. "Well, little Sara, what have we here?" He smirked, holding the photo closer to his face. "Looks like you've come into some money." After draining his coffee cup, he rose to his feet. "You look a little lonely in this picture, sweet wife. I think it's time your husband paid you a little visit."

* * *

The next day, Daniel was feeling somewhat better. He wasn't ready to resume ranch work just yet, but after a reminder call from Dr. Patel's office, he couldn't think of an excuse to miss the group session at the hospital.

As he passed through the double doors and into the cool interior, he was conscious of how loud his footsteps were on the tile floor. Everyone else wore rubber sole shoes, it seemed. Suddenly, he felt out of place in his standard cowboy get-up. As he eased down the hall, trying to step lightly in his Justin boots, he noticed several pretty women staring at him. In day's past, he'd take their smiles and pointed glances as interest. Now, he rubbed his hand over his forehead, making sure there wasn't a sign plastered there that read *Broken* on it.

When Daniel drew near the meeting room, he saw at least a dozen people milling about. Some were on crutches, some had prosthetics, others showed no visible sign of injury at all. Like him, he realized. Sometimes you just couldn't tell by looking at a person what they were feeling inside. A deep rumble of a laugh at the front of the room drew Daniel's attention. Looking that way, he saw Jaxson McCoy leaning on a podium. Well, at least he wasn't the only cowboy in the room. Just looking at the big rancher, no one would ever know he only had one leg.

Daniel found an aisle seat near the back of the room. He didn't want to draw attention to himself and he hoped like hell he wouldn't be asked to get up and talk about his problem or how he was feeling about it all. A man who looked even more unapproachable than Daniel sat down next to him. They nodded to one another, that brief male acknowledgement that men give when they'd rather not communicate any more than necessary.

He didn't expect to be recognized by McCoy. Even though they lived fairly close, they existed in different worlds. When the meeting began, Daniel felt himself go tense, wishing like hell he'd elected not to come.

"Good afternoon everyone," Jaxson began, "I'm pleased to see such a good crowd today. This group is made up of all first timers." He held up a handful of papers. "I reviewed all of the information you gave me and…" he laughed lightly, "we're a motley crew." He held up his leg. "For those of you who don't know, I lost my leg in an accident a while back." Jaxson stepped away from the stand and moved out in front of it. "I won't beat around the bush. I thought my life was over. I even considered taking my own life."

Daniel stiffened in surprise. McCoy considered committing suicide? The man had it all. A big family who loved him. Land. Money. Looks.

"I know," Jaxson held up his hands, "some of you might wonder at my weakness. You might be sitting there dealing with something much more devastating, truly life-threatening. The only excuse I can offer is my ego. My pride." He began to walk slowly back and forth across the room. "I thought my life was over because my body changed. I thought losing one part of me meant losing it all. I don't know about you, but I was an active guy. Rodeo. Horses. Rock-climbing. You name it, I did it." Suddenly, his face broke into a smile. "Guess what? I can still do some of those things. Maybe not so fast, maybe not so good – but I had to learn that my life didn't end with my accident. My value as a person didn't change when I went from two legs to one. Our worth isn't measured by the sum of our body parts or whether we fit society's definition of perfection."

At some point, Daniel stopped listening, not because he wasn't getting anything out of McCoy's talk – but because the point he was making hit so close to home. He hadn't lost a leg, he'd lost a damn testicle. Part of Daniel felt ashamed that he even equated the two. The man was right about one thing, Daniel's self-worth was wrapped up in the idea that his masculinity defined him as a person.

When a woman up front asked a question, Daniel took the opportunity to slip out. He walked quickly out of the hospital and on to his truck. Even though McCoy had hit the nail on the head, he hadn't said anything to banish the demon. The doctor had told him there was no physical reason that he couldn't perform – get hard, ejaculate. Maybe, it was time to test out his equipment. If all his plumbing still worked, he might could get it in his head that he had a future worth living.

At home, Daniel shut himself in his office. There was no one in the house but himself and the dog. She was scratching at the door, but he ignored her. He had more serious business to attend to. Sitting down at his desk, he lifted the lid to his laptop and accessed a porn site. This wasn't his first time to visit one, but it had been awhile. Falling in love with Sara had more than fulfilled his needs. In fact, there was no comparison. One was plastic, a substitute, a stand-in for something real. Being with Sara was meaningful, fulfilling. Sara was everything.

But Sara wasn't here. He'd seen to that.

Calling up a video hailed as a hot, intense cream-pie, he pressed the play button. Soon, the image of a man and woman came into view. He watched as they got right to it, very little foreplay, him flipping her over and nailing her from behind. The guy made no noise other than a few grunts, but the woman began caterwauling almost immediately. As he watched her breasts jiggle, watched the man's cock slide in and out of the woman's perfect pussy, he unzipped his pants and began stroking his dick.

His eyes followed their movements, the joining of a male and female body in the act of coitus. Daniel was thirty-one years old, he'd been jacking off since he was twelve. He knew the drill – his heart rate would elevate, blood would flow to his cock, pleasure would begin to build. The couple in front of him moaned their enjoyment, changed positions, and he began to fuck her missionary. She clawed his back as he sucked her tits. Daniel leaned in, trying to put himself in the guy's shoes, to imagine what he was feeling, how his cock was being massaged by the woman's tight sheathe.

Shit.

Nothing.

Daniel looked down at his limp member.

Traitor.

"Daniel! Daniel! Are you in there?" The knob rattled as Benjen tried to open the door. "Why did you lock the door? What are you doing in there?"

He slammed down the lid to the laptop.

"Nothing. Absolutely nothing."

* * *

"I can't believe everything is ready for tours." Sara turned in a circle, admiring the restored grand entrance. "This place looks amazing."

"I agree." Beth patted Sara on the shoulder. "I have to say, that newspaper article might have focused on you, but it certainly did its job. We're booked solid for the first month."

"I'm glad." Sara tapped her bottom lip with her

forefinger. "Our quarters upstairs will be off-limits, though. Right?"

"Of course, I told you that from the beginning."

"It's just going to be odd. People coming in and looking all around." She'd just begun to feel comfortable in the mansion. Sara couldn't say it felt like home, not the way she'd dreamed of a home making her feel – but it was all she had.

Ding! Both women jumped a bit when the doorbell rang. "Oh, my goodness. Who could that be?"

"I don't know. We don't have any appointments scheduled or anything, do we?" Sara started for the door. A flash of hope pierced her mind. What if it were Daniel? When she drew near enough, she glanced out the front window to see Ryder Duke waiting to be greeted. Disappointment spiked in her breast. Opening the door, she forced herself to smile. "Why, this is a surprise! Come in." Sara was glad to see her, she'd just rather her visitor was Daniel.

"Thanks." Ryder's eyes immediately began to rove around her surroundings. "Wow, I've always wondered what this place looked like inside. This is just like stepping back in time."

"I know what you mean, sometimes I expect to see women in hoop skirts come strolling down the stairs." Sara stepped over to her aunt. "Aunt Beth, this is my friend, Ryder Duke. Ryder, this is my Aunt Beth. Beth Christy. She's my mother's sister."

"I'm so pleased to meet you." Ryder took Beth's hand. "Your niece is an amazing woman." She leaned in and whispered, "The best pie maker in the country."

"Yes, our auction is fast approaching, isn't it?" Sara had begun making preparations. "I have all the crusts made and in the freezer."

"Great. If you have time, let's sit down and go

over some specifics."

"Sure. How about we go to the kitchen and I'll make some coffee?" Sara invited Ryder to go ahead of her with an outstretched hand.

Beth put her hand up to cover her mouth, stifling a yawn. "While you two girls work, I think I'll take a nap. When you get to be my age, a siesta is more fun than a fiesta."

Sara frowned at her aunt's weird sense of humor. "Sleep well, Aunt Beth."

Ryder waited for Sara, then accompanied her into the newly renovated kitchen. All the appliances were state of the art, but they were fashioned to fit in with the turn of the century décor.

"I can't get over this." Ryder turned in a circle, looking at everything. "I don't think I ever told you, but I was raised in an honest-to-God southern plantation called Belle Chasse."

"Really, I bet its beautiful." Sara took down two coffee cups and punched a K-cup in the Keurig. "Where is it located?"

"It used to be located in South Louisiana, it doesn't exist anymore, Hurricane Katrina saw to that."

Ryder's voice was even, but Sara could hear the lingering sorrow in her words. "I'm sorry."

"Yea, I lost my mother too. She stayed behind to secure the house, despite promising my father she'd leave in time. The storm turned and she was swept away in the storm surge."

"God, Ryder, how awful." She'd lost her mother too, in a way. But there was always the chance she'd come home, change her mind about wanting to be her mother. Ryder didn't have that hope.

She shrugged. "It was a long time ago. We've all grown up and moved on." Taking a seat, she patted the table, indicating Sara should join her. "This is the plan." She opened a portfolio and displayed the itinerary for the auction. "It's going to be an old-fashioned BBQ. We've invited all the right people, so money should flow like water. My brothers will grill up a storm and Judah is going to entertain us. After the entertainment, we'll auction off your pies. Are you still going to be able to make four dozen?"

"Easily. I'll still need help getting them baked. Although," she pointed to the double ovens behind them, "this kitchen will certainly come in handy. It's bigger than the one at…"

When Sara's voice trailed into nothingness, Ryder cleared her throat. "So, tell me what's going on with you? I know we've been emailing one another, but if I hadn't seen that newspaper article, I wouldn't have known you…moved!" She said the last word with emphasis. "What happened to you and Daniel?" She picked up Sara's hand. "And where's your engagement ring?"

A wave of embarrassment and sadness cascaded over her. "The engagement's off."

"Really?" Ryder appeared perplexed. "I know you better than this, but your breaking up with him wouldn't have anything to do with the fact that Daniel was in the hospital recently. Would it?"

"Hospital?" Sara was startled, instantly upset. "What do you mean? Why was Daniel in the hospital?"

"I don't know, I didn't ask any questions. Jaxson works with many different people in many different circumstances. I help him when I can, but I don't probe."

Sara's eyes darted back and forth. "He's been ill? Or hurt? And I didn't know it? Why didn't they tell me when I visited?" She felt paralyzed, numb.

"Why did you two break up?" Ryder asked quietly.

Holding her face in her hands, Sara tried to catch her breath. "He broke up with me. He's seeing someone else, an ex, Fiona Meadows."

"I know Fiona Meadows..." Ryder spoke slowly. "And she's seeing someone, but it's not Daniel. I think she just moved to Dallas to be nearer to the guy."

Sara sat there, silent, assimilating what she'd heard. Daniel at the hospital. Fiona gone. Benjen's plea – *Don't give up on him, please.*

Standing to her feet slowly, Sara reached for her purse on the counter.

"Ryder, I'm sorry, but I have to go."

* * *

Daniel stepped into the shower and began to soap up. He was feeling stronger, more like himself. No nausea. The sores were gone from his mouth. The fatigue he'd been experiencing was a thing of the past. He even dropped his hand and cupped his sac, rolling the balls between his fingers. One felt a little different, but not too noticeable. He wasn't sore down there, that was something. Now, if he could just get a damn erection.

Stepping under the spray, he rinsed off the soap, still deep in thought. Tomorrow, he planned on making an appointment for the scans. He needed to know if the chemotherapy had done its job.

"What was that?"

He flipped off the water so he could hear better. There was a noise in the hall. "I'm in the bathroom! Be out in a second!" he yelled to whichever brother had come home early.

In spite of his announcement, Daniel heard his

bedroom door open. Making a grab for his towel, he held it in front of him. "Hey! What are you barging in for? Can't a guy have some privacy?"

"Privacy?" a female voice spoke softly. "You used to love it when I joined you in the shower."

Daniel made a grab for the frame of the shower door. He was floored by who stood before him, looking more beautiful than any woman had a right to look. "Sara? What are you doing here?"

CHAPTER FOURTEEN

"What am I do doing here?" Sara asked, her eyes scanning his body hungrily. The small towel hid very little, he was just as magnificent as ever. "I heard you've been in the hospital, is that true?"

"Where did you hear that?" Daniel was thrown by Sara's sudden appearance. He was tempted to draw her into his arms and beg her forgiveness. Beg her to stay with him, to forget everything that had gone before.

But he couldn't.

As far as he knew, nothing had changed.

She didn't give him a direct answer. "Doesn't matter. Is it true?" She moved a step closer and her nearness affected Daniel so profoundly that he backed farther into the shower. "Running from me?"

Daniel didn't have to glance around to know Sara had him blocked in. His foolish heart was pounding and he ached to hold her close. "I'm not running from you."

Sara smiled a sad smile. "You're not talking to me either. Why not? What are you hiding?" When he didn't answer, she persisted. "You might as well tell me, I'm not going to leave this time just because you're feeding me some line." Bravely, Sara reached out and touched Daniel's face. When he closed his eyes and leaned into her palm, she knew she was right.

"You weren't cheating on me with Fiona, were you?"

"I never said I was." Daniel had to move, he had to get away from her. Now. Or he was going to lose it. "Excuse me." Gently, he attempted to push by her. He was trembling, chill bumps had broken out all over his body.

"Not so fast."

It didn't take much, she just stepped so close that her breasts grazed his chest. "Why did you send me away, Daniel?"

"It wasn't working," he muttered lowly.

She leaned her head the mere inch necessary to kiss his chest. "It was working for me."

"Don't, Sara." He swallowed hard. "Stop."

She kissed him again, her tongue trailing on his skin. "I don't want to stop. I want you, Daniel. I still want you."

Her admission set off a chain reaction in his body. He felt too much. Need. Doubt. Panic. "I can't. Don't you understand?!"

When he shouted at her, Sara flinched. This time, he pushed by her with force and she had no choice but to let him pass.

Daniel left the room like a rampaging bull, wanting to put as much distance between him and temptation as he possibly could. He didn't stop until he was in the laundry room, where he leaned against the dryer, his arms stiff, his head bowed.

God, what she did to him! His blood was rushing through his veins like hot lava.

And that was when he realized—he was hard.

Blessed. Fuckin'. Rock hard.

Sara fled the bathroom, tears flowing down her cheeks. She'd let him do it to her again. "Damn you!" she cried. "How dare you treat me this way!" Without thinking, she raced through the house, knowing he couldn't have gone far without clothes.

Daniel, dazed in his newfound aroused state, made his way back through the kitchen, dressed in clothes he'd found in the dryer. Blinded by impossible hope, he collided with the object of his desperate desire.

"There you are!"

Like a small tornado, Sara swirled around him. She whirled around his side, before facing him with eyes blazing. "Daniel, I demand that you tell me what's going on!"

"I told you, things weren't working between us." This time, his words held no conviction. His declaration sounded very much like a question.

"I don't believe you. And do you know why?" She stomped her foot and glared up into his face. Not giving him a chance to answer, she continued in her passionate tirade. "I went back over every moment we've spent together – every touch, every kiss, every tender word. And do you know what?"

"What?" Daniel was mesmerized by her. His cock was equally intrigued.

"You once told me I meant everything to you." Sara faced him like a spitting kitten. "You weren't acting before, when you were good to me, you're acting now. You love me."

How could he resist her? Daniel didn't know if he was surrendering to her demands or his own needs, but he reached out, grasped her shoulders and pulled her to him. "You're damn right I do." He stared deep into her eyes for one long moment, before crashing his mouth to hers, drinking from her lips like a man dying of thirst. Her arms crept around his neck and she melded her body to his, clinging to him like he was the only life raft in a raging sea. One kiss wasn't enough, he feasted on her mouth, like he was trying to make up for lost time.

"Why?" she whispered, when they parted for breath. "What was all this about?"

Daniel buried his face in her hair. "I…" God, he still couldn't say it. "I found a lump." When she tensed in his arms, he just blurted it out before his lost his nerve again. "I went to the doctor. I had, I have, hell – I had testicular cancer. They operated and removed one of my…boys. I took a round of chemo. And now here I am."

He waited for her to react, for her to say something. But when her response came, it was nothing like he'd expected.

She jerked back, eyes wide and mouth open, tears pouring down her cheeks. "And…you didn't tell me?!" She took one small fist and pounded him on his chest repeatedly. The blows were like cotton balls bouncing off an oak tree. "Why didn't you tell me? You were sick! And you let me think you didn't want me anymore…instead of letting me love you through it!"

Daniel absorbed her tiny blows like they were air brushes. He didn't know what he'd expected, but this wasn't it. She was furious, gloriously furious at him – with him – for him. "I didn't want to hurt you, Sara."

"You didn't want to hurt me? What do you think you did?" She closed her eyes and took a deep breath, swaying a little. "What does the doctor say now?"

"I was Stage 0, which is the lowest risk, so the chemo should have eradicated any problem. I need to go back for scans next week to determine if it worked." He kept his eyes on her stricken face. "I thought I might be impotent…" he glanced down at his bulging package, "but it looks like you cured that problem."

Her lips and chin trembled as she raked her eyes over him. "Don't you know I would've done anything for you? I would've taken your place if I could have," she narrowed her eyes at him, "you big dummy!" With that sharp retort, and one more hard stomp of her foot, she turned and took off.

"Hey, where are you going?"

"I can't look at you right now!" She blazed through the house and out the door.

Daniel delayed only a second. "Wait!" By the time he made it to the front, she was running across the yard. She didn't head toward the car she'd arrived in, she was making for the barn. "Sara!"

Sara hoped there was no one about, she needed to be alone. "Go away!" she yelled back at Daniel. "Don't follow me! Pretend I'm not here, that's what you wanted, isn't it?"

How the hell did he ever think he could exist without her? She was his lodestone, his center, his footsteps were drawn as irresistibly to her as a moth to the flame. "I was trying to protect you!"

"Piss poor job, Blackhawk!" She slammed open the barn door and fled inside. "Everybody who says they love me leaves me, Daniel! You just confirmed my worst fear." He was right behind her, but she darted into the shadowy building, flitting from room to room like a ghost.

"Stop! Please! Wait on me." He checked in each stall. There were no animals in the barn, they were all out in the paddocks or pastures. "I just want to talk."

"Not now, please." He could faintly hear her voice. "I don't want you to see me cry."

Daniel slowed his steps. He had no intention of turning his back on her, not again. "I was scared, Pet.

I knew you'd stay with me, even if the worst happened."

"Well, of course I would have," she sobbed in earnest. "That's what you do when you love somebody."

The sound broke his heart and the gift of her words mended it. "Would have?" He came a little closer, nearing the bottom of the ladder to the hay loft. "Past tense? Can't you forgive me for being stupid?"

She said something, but he couldn't hear, didn't understand. The noise was too muffled. Taking hold of the ladder, Daniel began to climb. As he ascended higher and higher, the fog that had clouded his mind seemed to lift. He'd been wrong, so wrong. He'd hurt her senselessly.

When he arrived at the top, he could see her huddled next to the open bay, cuddled down into a deep pile of hay. "I couldn't hear what you said." He began to move nearer, coming close enough to lie down next to her. "Can you forgive me?"

"Oh, Daniel." She turned into his arms and buried herself against his neck. "Forgiven. I forgave you for everything you've ever done or will ever do when I fell in love with you." Another sob broke her voice. "That's what love does."

Daniel gathered her close. "I'm so sorry, Pet. I made a mistake. When I found that lump I panicked."

Pushing away a fraction, Sara began to run her hands over him – from his face, to his shoulders, pushing her way under his shirt. "Are you okay now?" She skated her palms over his hips and down his thighs. "Shouldn't you be resting or something?"

Daniel knew she was touching him to assure herself, not to arouse him – but that was exactly what was happening. He was amazingly aroused. "I think

I'm improving quickly." He pushed her back in the hay and covered her sweet lips with his, kissing her senseless. Over and over. Drugging kisses. Searing kisses. They were both so hungry for the other that nothing else mattered.

"I thought I'd lost you." She ran her palms up his chest. "Don't ever do me that way again. No matter what's wrong, you let me be there." She laid her lips over his, inhaling his breath. "I can always make things better."

"I don't have an excuse other than I was scared. I don't think I would've reacted this way over anything else." He captured her mouth again, his tongue prowling lazily inside, pouring all the hunger he'd felt for days into the kiss.

"I know, baby," she whispered, "I understand." She began to unbutton his shirt, kissing his chest feverishly. "But what you've got to realize is that you're so much more to me than just this." She nipped him, making him shudder. "As much as I love your body. As much as I adore having sex with you. It's only good because it's you." She licked a path around one of his nipples. "You are what's important to me." She rubbed her face against his chest. "You. Just you. Do you understand?"

Understand? Hell, he was past comprehending anything but his need for her. Because she was awaiting an answer, he gave her one. "Yes, baby, yes." He was out of his mind for her. A hot surge of lust lit up his body. If he didn't get inside of her soon, he would die. "I need you. Now." Daniel fumbled with her clothes. "I can't wait."

She helped him, ridding their body of the offending garments keeping their skin from touching. When they were naked, he cupped her bottom, pulling her close enough that he could notch his cock in the sweet place between her thighs. "I missed you so," he told her.

"Good. I'm glad." She leaned in and bit his chin. "Don't you ever think of doing something like this again. What if I did it to you? Pushed you away because I was in trouble? How would you feel?"

A sense of helplessness washed over him. "I'd die. So, don't do it. Ever." As he took her mouth again, a deep possession, she didn't resist. Daniel felt like he'd go crazy if he didn't reclaim her soon. "God, I love this. I love you." He pressed himself to her, her every perfect curve fit him to a tee. Her swollen nipples were stabbing his chest, her tongue curling around his – seeking and soft as he ravished her lips with another scorching kiss.

"I love you, Daniel. I want you so much."

Blazing fire charred his vein as he pulled one of her legs around his hips. His famished cock had turned to stone. Taking her wrist, he guided her palm to lay over his erection. "See how much I want you."

She tried to jerk her hand away. "I don't want to hurt you." She remembered how he'd flinched when she'd touched him before.

"The pain's gone, I'll only hurt if you don't touch me."

She understood how entwined a man's self-value was with his sexual prowess. Sara let her eyes drift shut, enjoying the contact. He was so hard, thick, long, so much a man. Heat and need shimmered through her body. "I don't want you to hurt. Ever."

Daniel nudged her thighs farther apart, covering her, his breath feathering along the side of her graceful neck. Sara shivered as sparks of awareness tingled down her spine. Her sex clenched in on itself, showing how lonely she'd been, how she ached for him. Daniel's hand dipped between them, tracing her thigh, testing her readiness, finding her wet and blooming open. When his fingers caressed her, cupping her mound, she arched her back, whimpering at the electric spark his touch rekindled. "You're ready for me."

"Oh, yes, Daniel, oh yes," she gasped, shivering with erotic anticipation. The desire she felt for this man was overwhelming. Sara was drowning in sensation as he played with her, ensuring his place within her. Her body throbbed with desperation, she'd longed for him so much, and now that he was here, she could only beg him to hurry. "Please, baby, don't make me wait any longer."

"Easy, love, soon." Daniel wanted to reacquaint himself with the body of the woman he loved so well. "How can I take my pleasure without paying homage to these beautiful breasts?"

When he bent to lick, kiss, and suck her nipples, Sara cupped his head, running her fingers through his hair, tightening her clasp on his head to hold him in place. This was her man – big, powerful, with more testosterone in his little finger than most men had in their whole body and soul. "You are my pleasure, every bit of you, Daniel Blackhawk."

He needed no further invitation. Covering her mouth with his, he mounted her, wedging his hips between her thighs. As his tongue delved between her lips, Sara hummed her happiness as she welcomed every hard, sublime inch of him deep within her.

Daniel groaned with ecstasy as his head jerked back, his eyes closing, his teeth catching his lower lip. God, how he'd missed her, missed this.

"Look at me, Daniel," Sara asked as she moved

with him, every thrust sending a flame of fire directly to her clit. The throbbing between her legs increased with every powerful thrust of his hips. At first, his eyes were unfocused, lost in the pleasure of the moment. "Look at me and know I'm yours. All yours, Daniel. Just yours." As the words sank in, his dark gaze melded with hers. She'd never felt so connected with him, every beat of his heart, every breath he breathed, was familiar and more dear to her than life.

Daniel fought for control, sucking in a deep breath, trying to keep his head clear. He wanted to relish every second. Almost wild with relief, he was back where he belonged, loving the woman who loved him enough to get in his face and make him see reason. "God, I love you, love you, love you," he chanted as he plowed into her over and over.

"And I love you, Daniel, so much." She gave him a beautiful smile as he sat up and grasped her thighs, lifting them over his. The movement caused him to partially withdraw and to his delight, her tight sheathe tugged at him, clenching hard enough to make his eyes roll back into his head.

"Fuck, you're sweet," he muttered, sliding back in slowly. She welcomed him, her hips rising, her palms kneading his forearms as she held her head up to see where they were joined. "Look at us, perfect." Sweat rolled down the side of Daniel's face. He didn't know how long he could endure this incredible pleasure, this sensual torture, without surrendering to the orgasmic tide rolling up from his…balls. The thought made him bark out a laugh. Thank God, he was going to be all right.

"What's so funny?" she panted, not really able to do anything but languish in the fierce need building in her core.

"I'm okay, everything is going to be all right." The demands of his body kept his hips pumping, yet he couldn't help but appreciate her beauty – the softly flushed face, the round globes of her breasts, bouncing softly, her small waist and beautifully flared hips. "You're exquisite, Pet."

Sara didn't reply, the ecstasy was rising, becoming so intense, that she couldn't concentrate on anything else. "Daniel, I'm coming," she whispered, clutching his shoulders to pull him down. "I want to feel you." She needed his weight to press her down, to cover her, to make her know he was there and he wouldn't be leaving her again. "Closer," she demanded, wrapping her arms around his neck as he impaled her again. Of all her senses, touch became supreme. White starbursts blinded her, her blood roared in her ears, nothing seemed to register except the orgasm that rocked her world.

Daniel could feel her shatter, shaking and flying apart as she clung to him. He absorbed her pleasure, his own feeding off hers. The sounds she made, the way her body milked his cock was mind-blowing. He endeavored to keep the cadence of his strokes going, giving them both what they needed, what they'd missed, what he'd doubted to ever have again. "I love this, Sara. Being inside of you is fuckin' heaven."

Sara screamed as another orgasm tore through her. Daniel increased his pace. Pounding. One deep, long stroke after another. Seeing her desperate pleasure only fueled his own. "God, this is good, so good."

Shaking her head back and forth, she bucked and thrashed underneath him. Daniel rode her, reveling in her response to his possession. "Yes, Daniel, oh god, yes! Don't stop, please, don't stop."

Her hands clawed in the hay, finding little purchase as he ground into her, fucking her hard. He gloried in the euphoric labor to satisfy them both. Every nerve ending was alive, every cell in his body was on fire – he held himself up on his arms and thrust and thrust and thrust. "Sara!" Perfect, amazing bliss raced through his veins, rushing through his bloodstream as his climax exploded, detonated, lighting up his world as everything he knew about love and pleasure was redefined. He bellowed and shook as he jetted his essence deep inside of her, "Yes, fuck, yes!"

Holding Daniel as he quaked, she coaxed him down, until they collapsed together in the hay. She peppered tiny kisses over his neck and chest. "That's the way it should be." She wove her fingers in his hair, holding his head steady so she could look into his eye. "This is us. This isn't going away." She kissed him on the nose. "So, don't ever think about pushing me away again…or I'll hurt you. Understand?"

Daniel began to chuckle. "Got it." He reached behind him to brush off his naked ass. "I think I have hay in places where it doesn't belong."

Sara sighed. "I don't care. I'm back where I belong and that's all that matters."

Daniel held her close.

She was right.

* * *

Sara was a little nervous, wondering how his family would react to her reappearance.

"Are you kidding? They didn't approve of how I handled this at all. They thought I was crazy," Daniel explained as he pulled on his clothes.

"Well…" she said, teasingly, as she fastened her

bra. It was heady, dressing in front of him, watching him watch her. "I'm still mad at you, you know."

"You are? Why?" Daniel was just glad it was all over. Yea, he still had to have some tests, but he just had this bone deep feeling that everything would be okay.

"For not having enough faith in me to think I could handle this."

"You're wrong, sweetheart." He started down the ladder and held out his hand. "My faith in you was unswerving, I knew you'd stick by me no matter what – that was the problem. I didn't want you shackled to someone who couldn't make love to you, who couldn't give you children, who might just get sicker instead of better."

She let him help her to the ground. "Do you still want to marry me?"

Her question took him by surprise a little. He'd brainwashed himself since finding the lump, thinking his life was irrevocably changed, and not for the better. Having Sara set him straight was a revelation – and the hard-on she gave him went a long way in his acceptance of the epiphany. "As soon as I get the results of those scans, we'll make plans."

"I pray the scan results are good, but whatever the results are, they have no bearing on whether or not I want to marry you." Sara stood before him, her arms crossed over her pretty breasts. "The vows that we take will say for better for worse, for richer for poorer, in sickness and in health, as long as we both shall live. Right?"

God, he loved her. He tugged her to him. "Right." Smiling with happiness, he whispered in her ear, "I think there's also some language in there about you worshiping me with your body and obeying my every whim. Ow!" Daniel broke out in laughter when she nipped him on the chest again. "I love how feisty you are. I think I'm going to keep you."

"Good." She linked her arm with his and started out of the barn. "Do I still have a job here? Or do you want me to go back to Callum House?"

Daniel frowned. "I'll provide anything you need. You belong to me. Call your aunt and tell her what's going on. I'll drive her car back and you can follow me in yours."

"You didn't sell my car." She gave him a sideways sassy glance.

"No and I didn't pawn your engagement ring. As soon as we get in the house, I'm putting it back on your finger where it belongs."

Sara leaned her head on his shoulder, then raised it abruptly. "I just now realized what's missing. Where's Hope?"

"With Benjen. Since…you weren't here, she wasn't happy staying at home alone. She's been riding shotgun with him wherever he goes." He winked at Sara. "They went on a date the other night…with a girl."

"Benjen had a date!" Sara was happily surprised. "I've known Easy and Sam to socialize a little, but this is new. Isn't it?"

Daniel shrugged as he ascended the steps to the house, guiding her with a palm to her back. "Not his first date by any means, but Benjen isn't exactly a Lothario. When he falls, he'll fall hard, I'm sure."

"Like you did?" She wiggled out of his grasp and danced out ahead of him.

"Yea, like I did." He walked to the bookcase and opened a small wooden box. "For you. Give me your hand, let's make this official."

Sara melted as the big man went to his knee once more.

"Will you wear my ring, beloved?"

Holding out her hand, she held her breath as he slipped the ring on her finger. "The answer is yes, it will always be yes."

…During the next few hours, Daniel's world righted itself. Sara informed her aunt of their reconciliation and Beth did not seemed surprised. His brothers returned home and rejoiced that Daniel had come to his senses. They didn't let her lift a finger in the kitchen that night, the guys pitched in and prepared a feast of cowboy chili with beans, cornbread, and homemade ice cream.

"If I'd known you fellas could cook like this, you would've been doing it at least once a week," she told them after helping herself to a second helping of peach ice cream.

"Ah, we have to have some secrets, some mystery, to keep you girls guessing," Easy teased her. "Isn't that right, Daniel?"

"Maybe." The greatest mystery to him was how'd he managed to survive without Sara for as long as he did.

By common agreement, the Blackhawk brothers made themselves scarce after supper and Daniel and Sara found themselves alone. They drifted to the front porch and cuddled in the swing.

"I'm so happy to be back with you," she confided in him, her head on his shoulder. "I don't want this to ever end, Daniel."

"It won't, we'll be sitting here and holding hands when you're ninety."

Sara giggled. "And how old will you be?"

"Hush." He calculated. "Good, Lord. A hundred

and one."

"And still as virile as ever, I bet." She crawled up into his lap to straddle him. "I don't care how many years we're together, Blackhawk, I'll only love you more each passing day."

Daniel buried his face between her sweet breasts. She was the one. "I'd lay down my life for you in a heartbeat, Pet."

"Don't lay it down, Daniel, live it…for me."

He didn't answer. What could he say? If he tried to talk now, he'd embarrass himself. To keep Sara from seeing a grown man cry, he picked her, carried her to bed and loved her all night long.

* * *

The day of the pie auction dawned bright and clear. Sara, on the other hand, was a little rain storm threatening to happen. "I don't know how I'm going to do it all!" she squealed in a high, desperate little voice.

"Relax, baby, we've got this." Daniel came up behind her with his three siblings in tow. "You just tell us where you need these pies to go for baking and we're on it like white on rice."

"Oh, thank you," she murmured, "Ryder and Pepper are on their way to pick up a couple of dozen, but I need this group," she pointed to an assortment of fruit pies on the counter, "to go to Callum House."

"Done," Easy said as he and Sam picked up two each and headed out the door.

"What can I do?" Benjen offered.

Hearing a woman's voice, Sara knew Ryder and her sister had arrived. "You can help Ms. Duke and Ms. James load the pies sitting on the dining room table and atop the buffet."

"Got it."

She took time to greet her visitors, assuring them that all the pies would be at Highlands Ranch by six pm that evening. "We'll be there with bells on."

"I'm so glad you two got back together." Ryder gave her a hug. "And I hope everything works out well with Daniel's treatment."

Sara thanked her, sending up her own prayer with her friend's wishes. "See you tonight." The task of loading the pies into the two SUV's that Ryder and Pepper had driven went fast when Daniel pitched in to help Benjen. Once they were through, Ben set out to finish the ranch chores while Daniel returned to the kitchen. "Okay, what can I do? Put me to work."

"I'm on the last dozen," she informed him as she rinsed a big bowl to use again for a different filling. "These are going to be bourbon pecan fudge, so if you'll help me measure out the pecans, I'll finish the praline filling."

"Gladly." Daniel pitched in, enjoying working next to Sara. He was glad of the task to take his mind off the appointment he'd made with the lab for testing on Monday. What would he do if the news was bad?

"I love doing this with you," Sara confided as she measured out the sugar and poured it into a bowl. "You make everything seem so much easier."

And there was his answer. If the news was bad, they'd deal with it together. "Yea, together we can do anything, can't we?"

"Yea." She leaned over for a kiss. "Absolutely. We're a great team."

When the pies were put together, Sara slid four of them into the oven. "Great. Now, all we have to do is wait."

Daniel pulled out a chair for her to sit down in.

"Here rest, let me pour you something to drink." He did so, then was about to join her when his cell rang. Seeing it was Zane, he frowned. "I wonder what he could want?"

"Who?" Sara asked.

"Zane Saucier. Hold on." He walked to the window as he hit 'accept'. "Blackhawk, what's up?"

"Hey, how are you?"

"Good." He didn't take time to go into his recent problems.

"Great. I called to give you a little news. My investigators have a lead on Doug Wright. His real name is Vaughn Bell and there's several arrest warrants out on him in three states. Assault. Sexual Assault. Not to mention fraud. Our boy's been pretty busy, seems like he makes his living scamming people, especially vulnerable women."

"Well, we knew that, didn't we?" Daniel's guts felt like they were tied up in a knot. "Any idea where he is?"

"Nope." Zane scoffed. "We got a bead on him in Odessa, but by the time we alerted the authorities to round him up, he was gone."

"Well, hell. I'd love to see him pay for what he did to Sara." Daniel's fist clenched at the thought.

"At least we know he doesn't have a reason to return here. He got what he wanted before he left."

Zane's comment was made offhandedly, he had no idea what the words meant to Daniel, who knew exactly what the jerk had taken from Sara. "If he knows what's good for him, he'd better not be stupid enough to show his face around here, that's for sure."

"I just thought you'd want to know," Zane stated evenly. "I'll keep you informed if we learn anything more."

"Thanks." Daniel pocketed his cell phone. When he turned to speak to Sara, he found she'd stepped away. He could hear her in the living room, playing with Hope. Daniel was glad she hadn't overheard the conversation. He didn't want her to worry.

* * *

By the time six rolled around, Sara was more than relieved for the day to be winding down. "I don't think I ever want to see another pie," she said, leaning her head back on the headrest as Daniel drove her and the last batch to Highland Ranch.

"Oh, don't say that, I was hoping for at least two pies a week and if we're married fifty years, that's – uh – uh…"

"Two thousand six hundred." Sara did the calculation in her head. "Is that all? Doesn't sound like enough to me."

"I can see a fat old man in your future, Pet." Daniel laughed, reaching across to hold her hand. "Your cell is buzzing."

"Oh, dang," she reached for it, "you're so distracting."

This pleased Daniel, who put on his blinker to turn off Highway 29 and head up north toward Lake Buchanan. While he drove, Sara spoke to her aunt.

"Are you ready for the tours to start next week?"

"I think I am. The help I've hired is working out well. Her name is Sharon and she seems fairly competent. I do want you here for a couple of the first tours, if you can spare the time."

Sara glanced at Daniel. "I wouldn't miss it. I can't be there Monday, Daniel has an appointment and I'm going with him." She met his eyes and widened hers, affirming her assertion. He wasn't about to talk her out of being with him when he went for the scans and lab work to determine if the chemo destroyed all signs of the cancer.

"Of course, you need to go with him. I wouldn't dream of asking you to miss that. You come here and be with me when you can, anytime is fine."

"I'm looking forward to taking part, I have my spiel all memorized when I show people the topaz fields." As soon as she said that, she remembered the topaz she'd found the day she'd come to her senses about Daniel. She smiled thinking that it would look nice set into the handle of a custom knife or in a piece of jewelry.

"A man came by today, he was asking for you, said he read about you in the newspaper article."

"Oh, really?" Sara was curious. "Who?"

"I didn't talk to him, I was arranging flowers. Sharon came to ask me what to tell him and I said you'd be at the hospital pie auction at the McCoy's today, if it was important. Was that all right?"

"Sure." Sara shrugged. "I can't think who it would be, maybe someone I met at the pub."

Daniel was waiting to question her about the conversation, but while she talked he was putting on his brakes to avoid hitting a cow and a calf that was meandering across the road. "Good grief, they're going to get run over if someone doesn't herd them back to where they belong."

Sara, who'd just ended the conversation with her aunt, phoned Ryder to tell her about the stray cattle. Daniel did his best to steer the nervous beasts back toward the fence line, but without knowing where they'd escaped, it was hard to know which direction to take them. In a few moments, Gideon Duke came riding up on a horse and took control of the situation.

By the time Daniel was back in the truck, time was drawing near. "We've got to hurry, Daniel. I want to get these pies delivered before the crowd arrives."

Daniel nodded and they set out, easing back into the highway carefully. "We don't want to knock the pecans off, do we?"

"No." She gave a nervous shrug. "I hope everything tastes good. People are going to pay big money for these pies. They're doing it for a good cause, I know that, but I still want them to be special."

"You have nothing to worry about," he told her. "Your pies are almost as sweet as you."

As they drove onto Highland Ranch, an attendant directed them where to park to unload. Making their way through the gathering crowd, neither noticed the man standing to the side, his eyes watchful, a smirk of anticipation on his face.

CHAPTER FIFTEEN

"Put them on these tables, Lydia will take care of them." Ryder motioned to the caterer who was in charge of the meal.

Sara nodded to the middle-aged woman who didn't seem to be harried, despite the rush of activity. "Nice to meet you, Lydia, I'm Sara Riley."

"You've made some beautiful pies, Miss Sara. I daresay they're going to outshine the peach cobblers I made for dessert to be served with the BBQ."

"I don't know, it smells good in here." Sara surveyed the large outdoor pavilion. "I've never seen a place like this before," she told Daniel, who was handing Lydia pecan pie after pecan pie from the special box he'd constructed to transport the desserts safely from Blackhawk Ranch to Highlands.

Daniel followed Sara's gaze as she took in the large covered area, with its arbors, skylights, trellis, and extended patios. "This is what money can buy, if you have enough of it. The McCoy's have always known how to throw a party. They're down-to-earth as you could want, but they don't stint on the things they enjoy."

"I can see that." She'd known Ryder and Pepper came from money and Ryder had married billionaires, but until this moment the differences in their stations in life hadn't really hit home. As they'd driven in, they'd passed limousines, fancy foreign cars, and even a helicopter or two landing on the property. "I don't think I fit in here."

Daniel winked at her as he handed Lydia the last pie. "You fit in better than me, Miss Heiress."

"Stupid newspaper article," Sara grumbled. "The guy didn't know what he was talking about. He made it seem like a lot of wealth came with the estate, when Aunt Beth will tell you that Callum House is definitely a money pit."

"How much money you have or don't have doesn't seem to matter to your friends." Daniel nodded toward the married McCoy sisters.

"You're right. Ryder and Pepper are great. They invited me on a shopping trip into Austin soon."

"Great. You can start looking for your wedding dress."

Sara shivered with happiness. "I guess we should start making plans."

"And we will..." he began, then let his sentence trail off.

He didn't have to finish the rest of the sentence for Sara to hear it in her mind. They would start making plans as soon as he received an all-clear on the test results. "Nothing is going to keep me from marrying you, Daniel Blackhawk." She went on tiptoe to kiss him on his cheek. "Nothing."

"Hey, Sara, there's somebody I want you to meet!" Pepper called as she came through the crowd, accompanied by two pretty women.

"Looks like you're about to make some new friends." Daniel squeezed her shoulder. "While you do that, I think I'll mix and mingle."

"Don't go far," she said, brushing a speck of lint

from his chest, "I don't want to lose you in this crowd."

"I won't," he assured her, "I'll be back before you know it."

As he walked away, Sara was quickly pulled into another conversation.

"Sara, I'd like for you to meet my sisters-in-law. This is Cato and Molly McCoy. Cato is married to my brother, Heath, and Molly is married to Tennessee. Girls, this is my new friend, Sara Riley. She baked all the pies that we'll auction off for the hospital today."

Meeting new people wasn't always easy for Sara. She'd read a book a few years back that laid out a guideline of making others feel important. Get folks to talk about themselves and they'd be drawn to you. "Hello, Cato and Molly, nice to meet you. This is a beautiful place. Do you live on the ranch?"

"Part of the time," Molly told her. "Ten and I have a place in Marfa, down in Big Bend country. We run a wind farm down there."

"Heath and I run Eagle Canyon resort near here, you'll have to come check it out," Cato began, then snapped her fingers. "In fact, I'm hosting a little get-together, girls only, in a couple of weeks. A spa day. Why don't you come?" She pulled a lock of Molly's hair. "We'd love to get to know you better."

Pepper stepped between her brother's wives and linked arms with them. "Do it, Sara. These two women are crazy, you'll have a blast."

"Sounds great." Soon, they were deep in conversation and Sara realized what a huge turn her life had taken since meeting Daniel. No more sleeping on a cot in the storeroom of a bar or pulling a wagon by hand for miles to haul her groceries. Now, she had friends, a family, and a man who loved her. The confidence he'd given Sara in herself was invaluable. She only hoped that she'd returned the favor in some measure, making Daniel realize his own worth.

"Hey, you ready to eat?" His voice in her ear made her smile. She turned in his arms for a kiss, then introduced him to her new friends.

"I've seen you around, somewhere. You look familiar," Molly said, shaking Daniel's hand.

"Yea, I brought a load of hay out that your husband bought from us. When I unloaded it at the barn, you were there with your twin girls."

"Ah, okay." Molly nodded, "that's right, I remember now."

"You ought to." Cato elbowed Molly. "Heath and I were taking a moonlight stroll later that night and caught Ten and Molly taking a roll in the same hay."

Sara blushed, remembering what she and Daniel had done a few days prior.

"Hey, don't knock it until you've tried it." Molly giggled. "I'm a firm believer in enjoying the great outdoors."

"Molly met Ten while they were performing a rescue of a hiker who'd fallen off a cliff in Big Bend Park, she's the athletic type, unlike the two of us." Cato indicated her and Pepper. Our idea of an outdoor adventure is putt-putt golf."

"Don't listen to her," Molly protested. "Cato works for the Texas Cultural Society. One day she might be exploring an archaeological dig and the next she's taking a balloon ride over the lake to look for an eagle's nest."

"I'm impressed," Daniel admitted, although he'd rather be enjoying some alone time with Sara. "If you're interested, come explore our Packsaddle Mountain one day, it has an interesting history, being the site of the last skirmish in Texas between the white man and the local Native American tribe. We're pretty proud of owning a piece of history."

"Great, I'll do some research, thanks." Cato shook his hand. "I'm always looking for new material for the magazine."

Sara was glad to see Daniel thinking of the past without letting it define him.

When they broke away, Daniel led Sara to the buffet line. After they'd filled their plates with Texas BBQ and all the fixings, he led her to a table overlooking the lake. "This is one beautiful piece of land. Can you imagine having a view like this outside your window every day?"

"Oh, I don't know," Sara mused. "I think the view from our new house, will be just as pretty. I prefer more rugged vistas," she winked at him, "like I prefer rugged men."

"Oh, you're cute." He chuckled. "I like your new friends."

"Yea, me too," she admitted, "Cato invited me to a spa day."

"Oh, wow." Daniel grinned mischievously. "Are you going to get your pink parts waxed?"

Sara fidgeted in her chair. "Gee, I haven't thought about it. Would you like that?"

"I'm going to love you anyway I can get you, but it might be fun."

"For you." Sara grimaced. "I'm not so sure it would be fun for me. I've heard it hurts like heck."

Daniel leaned over to whisper in her ear, "I promise I'll kiss it all better."

Sara laughed, glancing around to see if anyone could hear them. "Keep on, you might persuade me that the torture would be worth the reward."

"Oh, I'll reward you either way, it's up to you." Daniel cut up his brisket with a fork. "This stuff is tender. I checked out the McCoy's fire pit, they've got a big set-up over there. I think they can cook twenty briskets at the same time."

"These folks do know how to entertain." She looked around at the people eating, talking, and dancing to the live band music. "Who did you see when you wandered off?"

A cloud came over Daniel's face. "I talked to Jaxson about the support group thing."

"Oh, really?" She knew he was still worried. "The tests are going to come back negative, Daniel. You're going to be okay."

He nodded his head. "I know. As far as cancers go, this type is one of the easiest to beat."

"And one of the hardest to deal with, from a guy's perspective, I'm sure." Sara reached out and covered his hand. "But you're good, your libido is as strong as ever."

Daniel nodded, relieved. "You'll never know how much I worried about that. Before you came along and proved me wrong, I thought I'd lost the most important part of me. I even tried watching porn, nothing worked."

Sara frowned. "Porn! Really?" She whacked his arm with her napkin.

"Well, it didn't work. Only you turn me on, Pet," he murmured in a cajoling tone. "Besides, don't tell me girls don't look at porn too, sometimes."

"Probably," Sara admitted, reluctantly, "I'm sure they do, but the only thing I've ever watched is late-night shows that suggest sex, soft-core stuff."

"Well, I guess you're just a natural," Daniel teased, "cause you sure as hell know how to turn me on."

"Stop it," she protested, "my nipples will start poking out and we're surrounded by people."

Daniel groaned, "That's not the only thing that's going to be poking out."

Sara laughed. "Save this until we get home where we can do something about it."

"Spoilsport." Daniel loved picking at Sara and he was thankful that his body could respond the way it did. A person didn't know how to be grateful for their health when they had it, he knew he'd never take his for granted again.

By the time they were finished, Judah James took the stage to perform. Everyone was enthralled to hear the world-class sensation in person. "I can't believe Pepper is married to that guy," Sara said with amazement in her voice. "He's good."

"Better than me?"

She cut Daniel a glance. "I didn't know you could sing."

"I don't, I just meant…in other ways."

Fragile male egos. "Daniel, Judah is a good-looking guy, if you like that type. He's artistic, got that unruly mane of long hair." She heard Daniel growl. "While you, on the other hand…" she leaned in closer to him, "make me wet every time I look at you. This face…" she whispered, "these shoulders and chest…" she rubbed her palm over his pecs, "you're the sexiest man in the world to me."

"Let's go home."

Sara grinned at him. "We can't, not yet. Soon."

They held hands while Judah sang, then came the time for the pies to go up for sale. "Oh, God, I need to hide under the table," Sara muttered when Ryder called out her name. Reluctantly, she stood up and waved to the crowd as they applauded her efforts.

"We've gathered together to raise money for a worthy cause. My brother," she motioned to Jaxson, "has devoted a great deal of his time and effort in helping people cope with loss. Life doesn't have to be over, just because a change comes to our world. He works to make people believe that they have every reason to live and love and look forward to what each new day might bring."

Jaxson received a standing ovation, but he chose to let his sister speak for him. "You know he's really not an outgoing guy," Daniel observed. "I'm really surprised he has chosen to take on this type of work."

"It must mean a great deal to him, I guess," Sara said, her eyes on Pepper who'd come forward with one of her pies. She closed her eyes and held her breath, not knowing how all of this would go down.

"I can guarantee these are the best pies you'll ever sink your teeth into, folks. So, let me hear a bid – for a good cause and a great dessert!"

"I think these McCoys could sell anything, they certainly have a winning way about them." Daniel observed as the dollar amounts thrown out from the pie rose into the thousand-dollar range quickly.

"Oh, my goodness." Sara bowed her head, afraid to look. When the bidding ended, her first pie brought ten thousand dollars. "I'm going to faint." Things didn't get any easier when the lucky buyer announced he'd share his prize with anyone who wanted a taste. Soon, people were raving over her pies as they sold for astronomical amounts and Lydia handed out plates and forks so everyone could share.

"See, you had nothing to worry about." Daniel pushed her hair over her shoulder. "Your pies are a mega hit."

She was amazed at the amount of money the auction raised so quickly. Yes, she knew the participants were the richest people in the hill country and that they weren't really buying her pies, they were donating to a good cause – still... "A half-million dollars is a lot of money, isn't it?"

"Yea, it is." Daniel kissed her. "Congratulations."

"I think I need to go to the restroom," Sara told him. "I've held it as long as I can."

Daniel chuckled. "Pea bladder." Pointing over her shoulder, he indicated the doctor who'd stitched up his wound the day he'd slipped off the roof onto the piece of tin. "I'm going to go speak to Brad Calhoun. I feel bad since I ditched him for Dr. Patel."

"I'm sure he understands, Brad is a GP and Dr. Patel is a specialist."

"Yea, you're right, but he's an old friend."

"Sounds good to me. I'll be back before you know it." Sara gave him a kiss and headed toward the cabana-style facilities. Weaving her way through the crowd, Sara spoke to a few people that she recognized. Many thanked her for the pies, making her blush. When she came to the cabana, she slipped in to freshen up.

When she emerged, Sara was looking down and didn't notice the person stepping in front of her – until she barreled right into him. "Oh, excuse me. I didn't see you."

"It's been a long time, wife."

The familiar, hated voice stole Sara's breath. "Doug! What are you doing here!"

"I hear you've come into a bit more community property that we need to split between us."

"I'm not your wife anymore, the marriage has been annulled." Sara backed up, trying to get away from him. "I was told Doug Wright isn't even your real name."

"Who told you that?" Doug approached her slowly. "And I don't believe our marriage has been annulled, I didn't sign anything."

Sara glanced over his shoulder, trying to see if anyone was close. She'd never really feared Doug, but there was a menacing light in his eyes that she'd never seen there before. "You need to leave. I'm with someone else now. You took everything I had that was worthwhile and I'm not giving up anything else."

"Well, we'll see about that, won't we?"

"I'm going to scream!" She opened her mouth when the man lunged at her, placing his big hand over her face. Sara struggled and cried out, but any noise she made was muffled.

"Hold still, Sara. We're getting out of here where we can talk."

Sara didn't intend to cooperate. She wanted Daniel. She tried to scream, to no avail. The only thing she could do was kick and bite down hard on his hand.

"Bitch! If that's the way you want to play…"

Sara didn't hear more, because he slung her around, one hand choking her neck and the other balled up in a fist as he knocked her unconscious with one blow to the head.

* * *

"I'm just glad you had the surgery. I'm sure you'll be fine. The chemo they gave you was the best possible combination of drugs. I would be surprised if you have a problem after this."

"I hope you're right, Brad." Daniel clapped his old friend on the back. "When you have time, come out to the ranch. There's a couple of great fishing spots on my land."

"Hey, thanks, I might take you up on the invitation. I've been needing a breather, I broke up with my long-standing girlfriend last week."

"Oh, really? Sorry to hear that."

"Don't be. She cheated on me."

Daniel frowned, commiserating. "You need to find you a good woman."

"Like yours?"

"Yea, like mine. They're few and far between though, so good luck."

Feeling better after mending what he feared was a broken fence between him and the good doctor, Daniel went to find Sara.

He looked and looked, but she seemed to have vanished into thin air. He checked with Pepper and Ryder, with Cato and Molly – nothing. He walked the entire grounds, even heading up to the main house to see if she'd gone there. Daniel could feel a rising panic in his gut. Something was wrong, this was totally out of character for Sara. He began to walk faster and faster, asking everyone he ran into. "Have you seen Sara, the pretty girl who made the pies?"

No one had – until he ran into Lydia.

"Yea, I saw her. This guy said she got sick. He was carrying Sara, said he was taking her home."

Daniel felt like a rug had been snatched out from under his feet. "A guy? What did he look like?"

Lydia described him. "Not as tall as you. Sandy blond hair. Nice-looking."

"Thanks." Her description didn't really help. "I need to find her." As he ran toward the truck, he called Ryder to tell her what was going on. She said that she'd check with her family to make sure none of them had seen Sara. Next, he called home, thinking someone might have carried her to Blackhawk.

"Easy, have you seen Sara? Has anyone given her a ride home?"

"Nope, we haven't seen anyone, Daniel. What's going on?"

"Sara has disappeared from the auction. She went to the bathroom while I was talking to Brad Calhoun. When I finished, I went to find her and she's just not here. A woman saw a guy carrying her out who said she'd taken ill and he was carrying her home."

"Fuck, man. Did you call her aunt?"

"I'm about to, that's my next call." Daniel was breathing hard as he continued to search the grounds of Highlands Ranch.

"Let me know what you find out and just tell us what to do, we're ready to help you."

"Thanks, man. I will."

He hung up and dialed her aunt. "Beth?" He was almost out of breath. "Have you seen Sara?"

"No, what's wrong?"

Daniel explained things to her in the same way he'd explained them to Easy. "She left with some man, I don't know who. I'm scared, she might be sick."

"Odd. There was a man here asking for her earlier. I told Sara about it when she called me a few hours ago."

Daniel winced. He remembered the conversation she'd had with her aunt right before he'd stopped to deal with the stray cattle on the road. "Did he give you a name? What did this man look like?"

"I don't know, Daniel. The woman who spoke to him said he was a nice-looking blond fella."

Shit. A queasy feeling was growing in Daniel's gut. What Zane Saucier had said about Doug Wright or Vaughn Bell – whatever the hell his name was –

came back to haunt him. What if? "Fuck!" he growled as he made a run for his truck. He had this sinking feeling that he knew who took Sara. But where? Where would home be?

As he climbed into the truck, it dawned on him.

Sara had been taken to the quarry, the place where her father had died.

…Her head was swimming, Sara didn't understand where she was, or what was going on. She reached out to her side to lever herself up and found cold limestone rock beneath her fingertips.

"Did you finally wake up, Sleeping Beauty?"

A rush of reality swept in and she sat up quickly, her head aching. "You hit me," she said accusingly.

"Yea, sorry about that, you were about to call out for help. I couldn't let you do that." Doug squatted next to her. "I needed to get you somewhere we could be alone, so we could talk."

Sara looked around frantically. "I can't believe you brought me here." She was sitting on the edge of the highest cliff, a sheer drop-off to the deep quarry lake was mere feet away.

"Yea, the place is deserted now. The new owner went bankrupt. I thought it would be a fitting place for a reunion."

Sara's skin crawled. Why she'd ever thought this man was appealing was a mystery to her now. "I have no desire to reunite with you in any capacity. You lied to me, you stole from me, you pretended to care about me, then you abandoned me." She refused to tell him about Faith, Sara didn't want this bastard's words or sneers to soil the memory of her little girl. The little girl that she'd only been privileged to keep for a few days.

Doug sneered, then laughed. "Sorry about that, I

guess you could say I got what I wanted." He reached out and stroked her cheek. "I see you found yourself a man, little Sara. Are you any better of a lay now than you were when I popped your cherry?"

Sara jerked back from him. "I'm leaving." She only made it one step before he jerked her down – hard.

"You're not going anywhere until I get what's coming to me!"

She certainly wanted him to get what was coming from him…but she knew he meant something else entirely. "I don't know what you want from me."

"I read the newspaper article and I visited that damn big house today. You've been accepted back into the Callum fold. Your mother's fortune was the reason I wormed my way into your life. You can imagine my disappointment when I learned your father didn't have two nickels to rub together. The handful of change in the bank accounts was barely worth the trouble of deflowering you."

Being this close to Doug made her feel sick to her stomach. This was the man who'd been asking about her. He'd only returned because he thought she'd come into a lot of money. "There is nothing to give you, every bit of cash in the estate was poured into the renovations of the house."

"How about those topaz fields? They must be worth millions!"

"They're picked over, empty. More of a conversation piece nowadays than anything else."

Her matter-of-fact words infuriated him. "I don't believe you!"

"It's the truth." She shrugged with a sneer. "And even if I did have something, our marriage was never real to begin with. Your name isn't Doug Wright, you used a fake identity."

Doug didn't argue with that point. "The marriage was real, we stood before a JP, repeated vows."

"I went to a lawyer, and he went through a series of legal steps to ensure the dissolution of the marriage."

"What steps?"

Sara swallowed nervously. "He ran an announcement in a bunch of newspapers, an official notification informing you of my intent to legally separate from you."

"Who reads a damn newspaper?" Doug chunked a rock over the side and Sara counted the seconds until she heard the splash far below.

Eight seconds.

"Sorry, it was just a formality. You didn't want to be married to me, if you had, you wouldn't have left me behind. No phone number, no phone call." She bit her tongue to keep from blurting out about the baby. "You left me penniless and alone." Jumping to her feet, she intended to make a break for it. "I owe you nothing!"

He jerked her back by the hair of her head. "Not so fast. You owe me."

"I do not!" she screamed. "I have nothing of value to give you!"

"Oh, I think you do. If there's no money to be had, you can at least give me a taste of what that Indian's been getting."

Sara struck out at him. "No! Daniel won't let you get away with this, he'll come for me!" She really didn't have any hope that he would, Daniel had no way of knowing she'd been taken.

"Are you sure you're worth the trouble?" He pulled Sara down to the ground. "Let's see if you're any better at sex than you were. The time I took you, you laid there like a dead codfish."

Sara kicked out at him, trying to keep the disgusting creature from pinning her down on the hard ground. "I'm not a dead codfish now." One of her blows landed right in his balls and he collapsed in a heap on the ground.

Taking the opportunity, Sara made a run for it, skating along the side of the quarry, back toward the front of the property where the house and shop were located. Her breathing was erratic, her adrenaline running high. "Daniel!" she screamed, even though she knew he couldn't hear her. She tried to think how far she'd have to run to get to a place where someone might see her and help her. Hearing the footsteps behind her, she knew the distance was too far to matter.

She didn't stand a chance.

Sara began to cry. "No! What do you want from me? Haven't you done enough?"

"I haven't done nearly enough! No court in the world will recognize your annulment, not when I show up with our marriage license. Getting rid of your father was no problem, now I'll just get rid of you. Once you're gone, I'll just step in and collect what's rightfully mine."

The horror of Doug's words finally registered with Sara about the same time that he caught up with her and snagged her arm, hauling her against him. "You got rid of my father?"

He laughed, an evil sound as he dragged her toward the edge of the quarry. "Yea, it was just a matter of messing with the steering and brakes on that old track-loader. Once he was at the right angle, I just gave him a little push."

Sara was horrified. "You murdered him? For what?!"

"Very little, it turns out. Maybe I'll have better luck this time." With that angry retort, he yanked Sara closer to the edge. "The water's not very deep here, you'll hit the rocks. Hopefully, it'll knock you out and you won't know you're drowning. It will be easier that way, for you." He patted his pocket. "If not, I've got a pistol in here, I can do a little target shooting. I've always enjoyed shooting at things in the water."

"No!" Sara fought him for all she was worth. But he was bigger. Stronger. Her feet slid on the ground as she tried to forestall the inevitable. "No! Please!" She didn't want to die this way. She wanted… "Daniel!"

"I'm here, Pet." The quiet voice was a direct contradiction to the mountainous angry man who charged in and picked up her attacker by the neck, holding him aloft. "Step back, baby. Call 9-1-1." He tossed her his phone.

Doug's face turned red as Daniel held him out in mid-air, dangling him over the cliff. "How does it feel, asshole, to have your life threatened by someone bigger than you?"

Crying and gasping, she gave the dispatcher their locale and told them a man had tried to kill her. When she saw Daniel's face, she knew he was angry enough to hurt the man. "Daniel, don't." she pleaded. "He's not worth it."

Understanding, Daniel pulled him back from the brink and threw the man to the ground. Like a rabid dog, Vaughan Bell aka Doug Wright – sprang from the ground and rushed Daniel. He welcomed the battle, going wild Indian on the idiot. "How dare you attempt to hurt what's mine!" He ground out the words as he pummeled the conniving thief.

Sara stood back, her heart in her throat as the two men wrestled and fought. "Be careful, Daniel!" In the midst of the confusion, she'd forgotten an important detail and it wasn't until she saw Doug's hand slip into his pocket, that she remembered. "A gun! Daniel, he has a gun!"

Daniel saw the glint of metal, he saw the raising of the man's arm. "No!" He made a grab for it, realizing that Bell wasn't pointing the gun at him, he wasn't pointing it at Sara. "Hell, no!"

BAM!

Just as the gun went off, Daniel threw himself in front of Sara, daring the offending bullet to come within an inch of his beloved. A searing pain ripped across the fleshy part of his arm, but he paid the pain no mind, barreling forward to take the gun from the idiot before he fired again.

"Daniel! Daniel!" Sara thought she would die if anything happened to him.

"You've caused enough trouble, you scum!" He wrestled the gun from Bell's grasp and jerked him to his feet, just as the sound of sirens could be heard.

Sara was weak with relief when she realized help was arriving. Daniel could handle himself, she knew, but he was hurt and she needed to find out how badly.

"Are you all right? Tell me!" she demanded as the police arrived on the scene. Weak with worry, she hovered near him until Doug was led away in handcuffs. "We need an ambulance!" she cried, seeing the blood running down his arm.

"It's a scratch, Pet, just a scratch," Daniel assured her as he gathered her close. "Nothing to worry yourself about." As her body touched his, he felt a wave of relief cascade over him. "No more bathroom breaks for you. I'm never letting you out of my sight again."

Sara was careful not to bump his arm, but touching him was the only thing that allowed a full breath into her lungs. "You can't be hurt, I won't allow you to be hurt," she crooned, kissing the side of his neck again and again.

"I'm fine," he repeated, even as an EMT arrived on the scene.

As the medical technician bandaged Daniel's arm, Sara turned away their attention. All she wanted to do was get to Daniel. As soon as he was free, the policeman told Daniel they needed to come to the station to make a statement. "I've called my lawyer, Zane Saucier, he'll send someone promptly. This man has outstanding warrants and Zane has all the information. I need to get Sara home, but we'll come down tomorrow and tell you everything we know."

Sara was shaking with shock by the time Daniel finished speaking, the reality of what had almost happened hitting her like a ton of bricks. "He murdered my father, he admitted it."

The cop looked surprised, then made a note. "We'll need you to tell us everything you know, but tomorrow will be soon enough."

"Thank you," Sara muttered, "I don't think I could deal with anymore tonight." All she wanted was to be held in Daniel's arms.

"Let's go home." He took Sara by the hand and led her to the truck. "I'm so sorry about your father and I'm sorry I didn't see this coming. I should have. Zane called and told me they'd found out Bell was wanted for assault."

"Bell?"

"Yea, that's the assholes real name, Vaughn Bell. They also traced him to Odessa, but he'd disappeared by the time they got there." He lifted her into the truck, then laid his head in her lap. "I should've protected you better."

Sara ran her fingers through his hair, rubbing his head, comforting herself as much as him. "There's no way either one of us could have predicted this, Daniel. My aunt had contact with him today too, but we're not evil, we just don't think the way he does." She leaned forward and kissed his hair. "You came just in time to save me. Just in time. You're my hero."

Daniel didn't feel like a hero, he felt weak in the knees and he was shaking like an Aspen leaf in a windstorm. "If I'd lost you, Sara, I don't know what I would do. You're my life, baby." He took her in his arms and kissed her gently.

"And you're mine, that's why I couldn't stay away from you."

"I'm glad you didn't. We belong together." He gave her one last kiss, then came around to get behind the wheel and drive them home.

"In good times and bad," she whispered, knowing they still had another mountain to climb.

...At Blackhawk Ranch, the brothers were waiting. "Why didn't you call?" Sam demanded. "We've been pacing holes in the rug."

"Daniel saved me from my crazy ex-husband." Sara let them all pull her into their arms, nearly being smothered in the process. Even Hope got in on the act, raring up to be noticed. "Hey, girl, I'm glad to be home."

"We're glad you're okay, for sure." Benjen embraced Sara, then pulled Daniel into the hug. "I guess you two just take turns saving one another, don't you?"

"That's how being in love works, little brother,

that's how it works." Daniel couldn't take his eyes from Sara. Just the thought of someone hurting her and taking her from him was intolerable. "Sara and I will enjoy watching each one of you fall hard. One of these days you'll meet someone who'll turn your world upside down."

"I don't know, I'm not sure there's a woman out there desperate enough to fall for Easy," Sam teased, punching his brother playfully on the arm.

"And do you think you're some type of prize?" Easy turned the tables on Sam. "Benjen acts like he's allergic to women, but you seem to collect them, yet we never get to meet any of your harem."

"I'm too smart to bring any woman around the likes of Ezekiel Blackhawk, your name says it all, Easy." Sam emphasized Easy's name.

Benjen didn't say anything, he was strangely silent during their light-hearted exchange.

"Enough, guys," Daniel said, waving his brothers off. "Thanks for waiting up for us, but I'm taking my baby to bed. She's had a big day, her pies raised a million dollars for the hospital."

"Wow, congratulations," Benjen offered, finally speaking up. "I'm glad we don't have to pay that much for your desserts."

"I love taking care of all of you," Sara confessed as she leaned on Daniel's chest.

"Come on, before I get jealous." Daniel led her toward his room.

Once they were in bed, the enormity of the situation hit home. Daniel turned on his side to face her. Running his fingers over her cheek, he pushed her hair away from her face. "Promise me something."

"What's that, handsome?"

"You are so precious to me. Promise me that

you'll take care of yourself, no matter what happens."

His low, heartfelt whisper made Sara's chest ache. She knew what he was saying. "I'll be fine, Daniel. I'll be fine because you'll be here to take care of me, just like you did today. For always."

"I pray that to be so." He took her in his arms, the love he felt for her rising within him to an overwhelming level. "While I'm alive and well, there's one thing that will never change," he whispered as he made a place for himself between her thighs.

As she accepted him inside of her body, Sara found his lips and claimed them in a kiss. "What will never change, beloved?"

"This wanting. I don't see an end to my wanting you."

He began to thrust, filling her need for him, time and again. Sara brushed her lips over his. "Be assured, the wanting is entirely mutual." She held him tightly to her, repeating her own version of his mantra. "You're everything I've ever wanted, Daniel, everything I'll ever need."

EPILOGUE ONE

Two days later, Sara and Daniel sat in Dr. Patel's office, awaiting the results of Daniel's tests. "When we finish here, why don't we go bowling?" she suggested with a grin.

"Bowling? Do you even bowl? I've never heard you mention it before." Daniel knew what she was doing, trying to get his mind off what was coming.

"No, but you could teach me, show me how to stay out of the gutter."

He tugged on a lock of her hair. "I like for your mind to be in the gutter. Makes for more excitement between the sheets."

"Oh, like I did last night? With the chocolate sauce?"

Daniel groaned, "Yea, the chocolate sauce. Wow."

"It was the recipe I found for fudge dipped bananas, that did it. I just couldn't resist coating your…"

"Sounds like I'm interrupting a juicy conversation. Glad to see you two are in high spirits."

The doctor's remark jerked Daniel out of his lighthearted reverie. "Why? Do we need to be in high spirits to deal with what you're about to tell us?"

"No beating around the bush with you, is there?"

The doctor observed the man and woman sitting in front of him. "You two make a cute couple."

Sara could see Daniel was about to crawl out of his skin. "Doctor, please…" *Please tell us good news. Please don't break my heart. Please tell me the man I love will be okay.*

Daniel held his breath, his hands clenched into tight fists. "Did you find any cancer markers or whatever you call them?"

"You'll need to have the tests annually, for at least five years. But right now, you're in the clear."

"Oh, God, thank you." Daniel exhaled loudly, feeling like a million-pound weight was being lifted from his shoulders by unseen hands. He reached for the most important person in his world, pulling Sara to her feet and into his lap. "I'm going to live, Pet, I'm going to live."

"Yes, you are." Sara smiled with absolute elation, as she framed his face and stared into his eyes. "And I can't wait to share every moment of my life with you."

EPILOGUE TWO

"This place is straight out of a fairytale, isn't it?" Sara stepped from Ryder's SUV, her eyes soaring up to the spires of Falkenstein Castle.

Six months had passed since Daniel had received a clean bill of health. Six months since Vaughn Bell had gone to prison for the murder of her father.

"I think this is the perfect place for a wedding." Ryder picked up the train of Sara's gown and folded it over her arm. "And you're a beautiful bride."

Sara laughed. "I just hope I don't throw up on this gorgeous gown." It had been six weeks since she'd discovered she was pregnant with Daniel's child. Keeping the news from him had been hard, but she planned on telling him today. This would be his wedding present. For him to learn he could father a child after the ordeal he'd been through would just put the icing on the cake. Speaking of… "Did the wedding cake make it here in one piece?"

"Everything is going to be perfect, you don't have to worry. As your matron of honor, I've delegated all the necessary tasks to the right person. Pepper, a master of organizational skills, she has monitored every minute detail. I can promise you everything will be as perfect as your beautiful dress and the fabulous cake."

Sara nodded. "I'm honored to have you and my amazing team of bridesmaids. You all have taken care of everything." She took one step forward toward the summerhouse where she and her attendants would await the moment when the ceremony would begin.

"Gideon and I are going to carry all this stuff in." Samson began unpacking the cases of makeup, shoes, and other wedding paraphernalia that the women would need to make the moment perfect.

"Thanks, sweetie." Ryder kissed one of her handsome husbands. "Help us down there first, though, these heels and rocks don't mix very well."

"Sure thing. Gideon! Hold off on the mule duty, let's play escort first."

Sara giggled at the sight of the two mega billionaires making sure their wife's every need was being met. She was just grateful to be included in their attentiveness. "I wonder if Daniel is nervous."

"Oh, I'm sure he is," Gideon muttered as he offered Sara his arm. "You should have seen the two of us. We were fit to be tied. I never told Ryder this, but I broke out into hives and Samson put on his tux so early, he had to change into a fresh one before the ceremony."

"I'm surprised you two had pre-wedding jitters, Ryder has told me how long you pursued her."

"Oh, what we suffered from wasn't pre-wedding jitters." Gideon chuckled at the memory. "We were afraid she'd change her mind about marrying us." He squeezed Sara's arm. "Don't worry, I'm sure Daniel is in the same boat. He's got to be worried that a beautiful woman like you will have second thoughts."

"Not a chance." Sara smiled serenely. "Daniel's perfect. I'm the luckiest woman in the world."

…Daniel wasn't feeling so perfect. "I'm not going

to remember those vows and the speech I wrote. I'm going to take one look at her beautiful face and lose my fuckin' mind."

"Why don't you write them on your hand like I used to do my vocabulary words?" Easy suggested with a straight face.

Daniel frowned. "I wouldn't be able to read them if I did, my damn palms are sweating."

About that time, the door opened and Benjen and Sam came in. They were all dressed in matching black tuxedos. "God, we look like a quartet of dorky penguins." Sam tugged on the hem of his jacket. "I hope no one from the rodeo circuit sees me dressed like this."

"You look great. We all look good." Benjen preened in front of the mirror, Hope at his side. "The crowd's beginning to gather outside."

Easy checked his pocket watch. "Yea, it's getting about that time. Sara should be here by now."

Daniel groaned, "This is the best day of my life, I should be on top of the world, but I'm as nervous as a bird in a coal mine."

"You're not nervous, you're just excited." Sam tried to reassure him. "What would you have to be nervous about? You're marrying your dream girl."

"I am, aren't I?" Daniel smiled. "I'm just afraid I'll let her down, somehow."

"The only way you'll let her down is if you blow the honeymoon."

Daniel scoffed at Easy, "Making love to my new bride is not what I'm worrying about. I'm quite talented in that area, thank you." He dry-scrubbed his face. "I'm more concerned about being what she needs in other ways. I want her to accomplish her goals, attain her dreams, be and do what she's always wanted…"

"And you're afraid that she'll be so intent on taking care of you that she won't take care of herself," Benjen added, a serious look on his face.

"Exactly." Daniel nodded.

"Look at you, Freud Blackhawk," Sam punched Benjen. "I always knew you were one of those sensitive types."

"He's right." Daniel stood and paced across the floor. "Sara's tendency is to take care of everybody before she takes care of herself."

"If she won't put herself first, I guess you'll have to make it your mission in life to make sure you do."

The new voice caused all four Blackhawk brothers to turn around.

"Jaxson, thanks for coming, man." During the last six months, he'd kept attending the group meetings, finding they helped him put things in perspective. As a bonus, he'd become friends with the big McCoy and his brothers. Despite the differences in their bank accounts, Daniel found they had a lot in common.

"It's a privilege, our whole family is excited about this wedding."

"Your two sisters and two sisters-in-law are standing up with my fiancée and you're standing up with me, we couldn't have done it without you."

"This is going to be a blast." He pointed to the door. "Ryder said it's time for us to line up at the altar. Are you ready?"

"I'm ready." Daniel looked from Jaxson to each one of his brothers. "Let's do this. I don't want to keep Sara waiting."

…Sara was tired of waiting. She was ready to make her dream a reality. "Is my mascara running?"

"No, you look like a princess." Cato patted her on

the shoulder. "Good thing you're getting married at a castle."

"I don't know how to thank you all," Sara said, getting emotional. "You and Molly, Ryder, and Pepper, you've made this day so special for me. The bridal shower, the rehearsal dinner, every bit of it has been absolutely perfect."

"We enjoyed ourselves." Molly handed Sara her wedding bouquet. "Now, there's a handsome brave waiting for you at the altar. I think it's time we got this show on the road."

Sara took a deep breath and nodded. "Yea, I've waited long enough for this moment."

"You don't have to wait any longer, Sara, let's get you married." Ryder helped Sara arrange her dress and Pepper held the door of the summerhouse open, so she could step out into the clear light of day. Sara was dazzled by her surroundings: the stately castle, the ornate gardens, the magical fountain – but nothing equaled the sight of her groom waiting underneath a romantic, Camelot-styled, draped arch. Her heart fluttered in her chest to see his face light up when their eyes met. Standing still and waiting while her bridesmaids preceded her was difficult. The whole thing was incredible – the decorations, the music, the setting, even Hope walking down the aisle to Benjen, with the ring bearer's pillow around her neck was something no one would ever forget.

Sara had foregone anyone giving her away, there was no need, she already belonged to Daniel Blackhawk – body, heart, and soul. So, when her turn came and the music swelled, Sara began the too slow walk to meet the man she loved. Every step she took seemed momentous and when he held out his hand to her, she picked up the front of her dress and ran the rest of the way.

He moved out to meet her, catching her in his arms and lifting her high in the air. "There's my Pet, I thought you'd never get here."

"I wouldn't have missed this for anything," she whispered as Ryder arranged the long bridal train behind her.

The preacher waited patiently, then began the ceremony when everyone was in place. "Dearly Beloved, we are gathered together to join these two in holy matrimony. There is no greater way a man and a woman can affirm their love, than to declare their intent to share their lives before their family, friends, and their God."

As the ceremony progressed, songs were sung, candles were lit, and scriptures were read. When the time came for vows to be exchanged, Daniel elected to go first.

Clearing his throat, he glanced out into the crowd. He was grateful they were here, but they weren't the important ones. Looking into Sara's perfect face, he began to speak. "From the moment I saw you, I began to plan this day. I know it's usually a woman's prerogative to dream about their wedding, but I couldn't help it." He smiled. "Loving you is the most important thing in my life, the foundation of my fondest dream. Without you, I would merely exist. With you, I'll truly live."

Sara felt the tears begin to rise in her eyes. "You're determined to make me cry, aren't you?"

"No, Pet, I just want to make sure you know how much you're loved." He lifted a hand to catch a tear on his finger. "From the moment I first saw you, I wanted you. Your beauty, bravery, and goodness inspires me to be the best person I can be. I promise to love you for eternity, to respect you, honor you, and live each day for you. My love for you is a promise I will keep, a fortune we'll never be able to spend, and a radiance that will never fade. You are my greatest treasure and I will be faithful to you forever. You are…" he smiled at her, repeating the special words he always reserved just for her. "You are my everything, Sara."

Sara picked up his hand and kissed it. "I adore you, Daniel Blackhawk. Because you love me, you have given me faith in myself. My life would not be complete without you. I promise to love you without reservation, to comfort you in times of distress, and encourage you to achieve your goals. I will laugh with you and cry with you. I will be open and honest with you and cherish you for as long as I shall live. I give you my love, in the only way I know how – completely and forever."

After the exchange of rings, the preacher asked them to join hands as he declared them to be husband and wife. When Daniel caught her close, to kiss his bride, he was surprised to hear her speak. "Before you kiss me, I want to tell you a secret."

Daniel cut his eyes to the crowd. "You do realize we're not alone, don't you?"

There were a few snickers from the crowd.

"Yea, I see them." She gave him a brilliant smile. "What if I just whisper in your ear?"

"Okay, my love, tell me your secret." He bent his head to hear what she had to say. If it was about the knife she'd commissioned for him with the topaz in the handle, he'd act surprised, even though he'd found it nestled in her underwear drawer. Yea, he'd been rummaging around, making sure to pack her sexiest lingerie for their surprise honeymoon to Hawaii.

"I'm pregnant. I'm having your baby, Daniel."

Shocked, Daniel almost went to his knees. He wrapped his arms around her and hugged her tight. "A baby? Are you sure?"

He didn't whisper, his voice carried to every person witnessing the ceremony. Sounds of excitement could be heard as everyone reacted to Daniel's exclamation of joy.

"I'm sure. You're going to be a father."

Complete and perfect elation caused his soul to soar to the heavens. "I love you, Sara Riley Blackhawk. I wish I had something equally wonderful to present to you." The honeymoon plans didn't seem adequate now.

"You've given me everything I've ever wanted." Sara gazed at him indulgently, amazed that he didn't understand.

"What do you mean, Pet?" he asked his beautiful wife.

She gave him a radiant smile, one he'd cherish forever. "I have you, Daniel. I have you."

Sign up for Sable Hunter's newsletter

http://eepurl.com/qRvyn

Ryder's Surrender: Hell Yeah!
http://amzn.to/2x5tP8r

Ryder and Pepper McCoy are the pampered sisters of the Highland McCoys – Heath, Philip, Jaxson and Tennessee. The brothers have always been over-protective of the girls, vetting every man who is brave enough to even ask them on a date. Both sisters are spirited, giving their brothers a run for their money – but one is about to give them a heart attack.

Two men are vying for the hand of Ryder McCoy, Samson Duke and his brother Gideon. But this isn't a rivalry, the Duke brothers plan on sharing her. They are determined to lasso, corral, and mark the feisty filly with the DD brand. Resisting one of the Duke boys is difficult, keeping both of them at arm's length may very well prove to be impossible.

But who should she choose? One or both? Could she break one brother's heart to gain the other? Ryder is torn between keeping the relationship with her family intact and following her own desires.

To complicate matters, there's more going on than meets the eye. The Dukes and the McCoys may very well have a common enemy. When Ryder becomes the pawn in a madman's scheme, all of the men who love her will have to work together to save her. Still, entrusting their baby sister to the wild, powerful Dukes is not something the McCoy boys think they can accept.

Will Ryder bend to her family's and society's expectations or will she surrender to what her soul and body craves? She soon finds out that true love doesn't always follow the rules.

Dreamweaver: Hell Yeah!
http://amzn.to/2x6Q3Hd

Was it a dream or just the edge of reality?

For a brief, shining moment, Pepper McCoy belonged to

rock star Judah James. Completely.

The depth of their attraction stunned them both. Every moment they were together, electric heat arced between them like the sweetest fire.

And then everything changed...

For reasons she can't understand, Judah pushed Pepper out of his life. He told her she just imagined their love, that none of it was real. He even brought another woman into the picture to prove to Pepper that their time together was a lie.

And Pepper might believe him, if it wasn't for the adoration in his eyes anytime she finds him watching her unaware.

Even the songs he writes are filled with the words of love he once whispered in her ear.

No... something is wrong.

Something isn't right.

Judah wants her, she can't believe otherwise.

Pepper refuses to give up on love.

And no one should be surprised...

After all, she's a McCoy.

If I Can Dream: Hell Yeah!
myBook.to/IfICanDream

The moment Tennessee McCoy lays eyes on

Molly Reyes sitting astride a horse in the desert sun, love hits him like a bolt of lightning from out of the blue. She is his soulmate, his other half. They speak the same language, they want the same things. Their attraction is complete, the passion they share nearly consumes them. Knowing she is meant to be his, Ten can't wait to make her his bride. The future seems bright until happiness slips through their fingers like grains of sand.

When all seems hopeless, sometimes all we have left is our dreams. Ten can only believe what his eyes can see, what his ears can hear. Molly can't seem to find the words to make him understand that she would rather lose her soul than betray him. Now both Tennessee and Molly must learn to place their faith in one another, to hold fast to love and trust their hearts.

Their journey back to love will be one you'll never forget.

How to Rope a McCoy: Hell Yeah!
http://amzn.to/2x6Uv97

Is Texas big enough for more McCoys? Hell yeah!

Heath McCoy, the oldest cousin of Aron and his brothers spends his days championing his family. He is no stranger to heartbreak, the woman he loved left him at the altar. From that moment on, Heath developed a new attitude - love'em and leave 'em wanting more.

Until he meets Cato.

Cato is determined to experience all life has to offer. She is deaf, yet very adept at listening with her heart. The moment she lays eyes on Heath, she knows he's the one man who will mean the world to her. But Heath doesn't want forever, he wants a fling.

So, Cato decides to give him what he wants and hope he falls in love with her in the process. She takes a gamble on love and the stakes are high.

How do you rope a McCoy? Very carefully.

How do you keep him tied? With love.

Texas Lonestar: Texas Heroes
http://amzn.to/2h7ST7n

Dallas McClain is a Texas Ranger, a loner who lives for his work because he knows no woman will ever forgive his past…until he meets Lennon.

Lennon is under attack. Shots have been fired through her windows, animals have been poached off her land and someone is rustling her cattle. If she doesn't get help, Lennon will lose everything, including her life.

In the heat of the battle, Lennon teaches Dallas the healing power of love. She has the unique talent of convincing those who need her that she needs them even more. At first, Dallas doesn't comprehend how truly beautiful Lennon is until he sees her rising from the waters of a hot spring like Venus from the waves – and then he is lost.

The chemistry between them is combustible. Wild and hot. Together they fight to save one another, her from harm and him from his past. Sometimes love is within our grasp…if we're brave enough to grab it with both hands.

Spanish Eyes: Texas Heat
http://amzn.to/2pJKqhl

When a gorgeous woman asks an unattached man for sex, he'd be a fool to tell her no.

Dr. Drew Haley sees a fool in his mirror every morning.

From the moment Drew gazes into the beautiful Spanish eyes of Angelina Alejandro, he is lost. Her intriguing blend of innocence and sensuality almost brings Drew to his knees.

When she begs for something he can't in good conscience give her, Drew hurts his beautiful angel. He wants nothing more than to help her heal from the torture she endured at the hands of a madman, but in order to do so, she must agree to give him a second chance.

Angelina just wants to forget the humiliation her captors heaped upon her. Her work as a scientist put her in the crosshairs of a power-hungry Sheik who wanted to force her to use the knowledge she'd gathered to harm mankind. When she refused, his unique brand of torture stole Angelina's self-control and her pride. Once she is rescued, Angelina only wants to hide away, to find healing on her own. But Dr. Drew has other ideas. He has a plan to tempt Angelina back into the land of the living and straight into his arms.

Too Sexy For Love
myBook.to/TooSexyForLove

Connor McGregor is one helluva sexy man. He is handsome, smart, and richer than God. Everything he touches turns to gold. Best of all, he's even a nice guy. The man really has no idea how perfect he is. The only flaw in this Prince Charming's character is that he can't see himself with just one woman, he has no intention of settling down. Why should he? His goal is to make as many women happy as possible. And so far, he's succeeding.

Until one day…he accidentally kisses his partner.

His adorable, feisty, snarky little partner.

A kiss that changes everything.

Rey Cassidy is his right hand. The woman behind the man. Whatever he can envision, she can make happen. After the kiss, his focus begins to change. Business is not so important, playing the field is getting old. How did he overlook the amazing woman who was right under his nose?

But identifying her as his soulmate is just half the battle.

Rey knows him better than anyone.

Convincing her to trust him, to give him a chance, just might be impossible.

Godsend (Hell Yeah! Heritage)
myBook.to/Godsend

Godsend is the first novel in the Hell Yeah! Heritage series. If you ever wondered where those

McCoy men came from…these historical novels will take you to their beginnings. Deeply sensual stories of romance and adventure, they will capture your imagination and your heart.

History is definitely worth repeating.

Thrust from his home, Austin McCoy travels west to build a new life for himself in the wilds of Texas. Civilization has not yet arrived to the wilderness where he settles and his nearest neighbor is more than two days' journey through Indian territory alive with bear, cougar and wolves. While difficult, carving out an existence amidst these dangers is not what weighs heavily on his heart. With nothing and no one to share his days, Austin is lost. The answer to his prayers comes from a very unexpected source…

Jolie Dumas has also been torn from the only home she has ever known. The beloved daughter of a plantation owner and his quadroon mistress, she is horrified to be sold into slavery after the death of her parents. Bought and paid for, she is chained and walked from New Orleans to Texas. Before she can be delivered to her master, the slave trader is killed and Jolie escapes. Alone and vulnerable, she seeks a safe place to hide, not knowing the sanctuary she finds may end up being the one place she truly belongs.

When Austin opens his heart and home to the beautiful woman, he has no idea the future she faces. Knowing what awaits her if anyone finds out the truth, Jolie hides her identity from him. Having been betrayed before by those she trusted, she has no idea that in Austin's eyes she could not be more perfect.

She is his Godsend.

A Breath of Heaven
myBook.to/ABreathofHeaven

Cade and Abby have a history. Years ago they were in love. Undeclared and unrequited, Cade waited until Abby was old enough for him to declare his love. Abby wanted nothing more than she wanted Cade.

But something happened.

Abby pushed Cade away and he never knew why. Since then, sparks fly when they're together. Antagonizing one another has become their favorite sport. The only problem is… it's all a front. They bicker because they both want the same thing – each other. A wedding brings them together and Cade is determined to learn Abby's secret. He'll do whatever it takes to win her love.

Meet the King Family of El Camino Real – five brothers, one sister and a legacy as big as Texas.

Unchained Melody: Hill Country Heart
http://amzn.to/2whHPii

Sparks fly when Annalise walks through the door of Ethan Stewart's Bed & Breakfast, turning his life upside down ... again. Six years ago she had simply vanished into thin air after eight short days of earth-shattering passion. Ethan had searched desperately for her, but never found Lise. After being apart for so long can they simply pick up where they left off?

Annalise Ramsey has come to face with the man of her dreams. She has never forgotten what it felt like to be loved by him. Tragedy tore her away from him years before, and now she fears the shadows of that secret will keep them apart forever.

Can Lise overcome the fear of rejection that keeps their love in the dark?

About the Author:

Sable Hunter is a New York Times, USA Today bestselling author of nearly 60 books in 9 series. She writes sexy contemporary stories full of emotion and suspense. Her focus is mainly cowboy and novels set in Louisiana with a hint of the supernatural. Sable writes what she likes to read and enjoys putting her fantasies on paper. Her books are emotional tales where the heroine is faced with challenges. Her aim is to write a story that will make you laugh, cry and swoon. If she can wring those emotions from a reader, she has done her job. Sable resides in Austin, Texas with her two dogs. Passionate about all animals, she has been known to charm creatures from a one ton bull to a family of raccoons. For fun, Sable haunts cemeteries and battlefields armed with night-vision cameras and digital recorders hunting proof that love survives beyond the grave. Welcome to her world of magic, alpha heroes, sexy cowboys and hot, steamy to-die-for sex. Step into the shoes of her heroines and escape to places where right prevails, love conquers all and holding out for a hero is not an impossible dream

Sign up for Sable Hunter's newsletter
http://eepurl.com/qRvyn

Visit Sable:

Website:
http://www.sablehunter.com
Facebook
: https://www.facebook.com/authorsablehunter
Amazon:
http://www.amazon.com/author/sablehunter
Pinterest
https://www.pinterest.com/AuthorSableH/
Twitter
https://twitter.com/huntersable
Bookbub:
https://www.bookbub.com/authors/sable-hunter
Goodreads:
https://www.goodreads.com/author/show/4419823.Sa
ble_Hunter
Instagram
https://www.instagram.com/sable_hunter/
Sign up for Sable Hunter's newsletter
http://eepurl.com/qRvyn

SABLE'S BOOKS
Get hot and bothered!!!

Hell Yeah!
Cowboy Heat
http://a.co/cXA0zgJ

Hot on Her Trail
http://a.co/4kQCuZF

Her Magic Touch
http://a.co/33ePUG4

Brown Eyed Handsome Man
http://a.co/cSxbrRS

Badass
http://a.co/c9PzwDc

Burning Love
http://a.co/1f3Priu

Forget Me Never
 (*With Ryan O'Leary& Jess Hunter*)
http://a.co/3BWO9gU

I'll See You In My Dreams
(*With Ryan O'Leary*)
http://a.co/ilJx6GB

Finding Dandi
http://a.co/emLAK7v

Skye Blue
http://a.co/267fQLh

I'll Remember You
http://a.co/6aCwC0l

True Love's Fire
http://a.co/245EjEJ

Thunderbird
(*With Ryan O'Leary*)
http://a.co/gOzExgv

Welcome To My World
http://a.co/eEyFY7D

How to Rope a McCoy
http://a.co/3a94uzW

One Man's Treasure
 (*With Ryan O'Leary*)
http://a.co/bZvVLYg

You Are Always on My Mind
http://a.co/ecAOk1y

If I Can Dream
http://a.co/hQw3yNY

Head over Spurs
http://a.co/9YdTccp

The Key to Micah's Heart
(*With Ryan O'Leary*)
http://a.co/hoLcMwQ

Love Me, I Dare You!

http://a.co/0arPPSq

Godsend (Hell Yeah! Heritage)
http://a.co/eQH0ARv

Because I Said So
(Crossover HELL YEAH!/Texas Heroes)
http://a.co/fkjuuMM

Ryder's Surrender
http://a.co/iYevm0D

Love Found a Way: Hell Yeah!
http://a.co/dmgj7VP

Toro
http://amzn.to/2xd3t6n

Texas Holdem
http://amzn.to/2x93WES

Dreamweaver
http://amzn.to/2x9wjTq

Lily's Mirage
http://amzn.to/2xcVYMo

Hell Yeah! Sweeter Versions
Cowboy Heat
http://a.co/eA8ESC2

Hot on Her Trail
http://a.co/9mImNrz

Her Magic Touch
http://a.co/eEZCsFs

Brown Eyed Handsome Man
http://a.co/2BdeUtI

Badass
http://a.co/fSnCeQd

Burning Love
http://a.co/5LJ3m6A

Finding Dandi
http://a.co/bOoHVYi

Forget Me Never
http://a.co/g5vUrGF

I'll See You In My Dreams
http://a.co/5JUhOXt

A Guide to the Hell Yeah! World
http://a.co/ginFkNG

Hell Yeah! Heritage
Godsend
http://amzn.to/2mNchb3

Moon Magic Series
A Wishing Moon
http://amzn.to/2ko3pua

Sweet Evangeline
http://amzn.to/2kR57Bj

Hill Country Heart Series
Unchained Melody
http://a.co/cqGZV8l

Scarlet Fever
http://a.co/4zksSmW

Bobby Does Dallas
http://a.co/a6zoxwP

Dixie Dreaming
Come With Me
 http://a.co/eyRIWEP

Pretty Face: A Red Hot Cajun Nights Story
http://a.co/e6SAlvz

Texas Heat Series
T-R-O-U-B-L-E
http://amzn.to/2kR1YkX

My Aliyah
http://a.co/i0CYxhV

Spanish Eyes
http://a.co/aJ86452

El Camino Real Series
A Breath of Heaven
http://a.co/d33xZih

Loving Justice
http://a.co/0clGjvF

Texas Heroes Series
Texas Wildfire
http://a.co/0GvfZkY

Texas CHAOS
http://a.co/eV7om1M

Texas Standoff
http://a.co/9HUqhQ2

Texas Lone Star
http://a.co/ed43s9j

Texas Maverick:
http://a.co/hoOrZ3H

Because I Said So
(Crossover HELL YEAH!/Texas Heroes)
http://a.co/fkjuuMM

The Sons of Dusty Walker
Rogue
http://a.co/bWio2u4

Kit and Rogue
http://a.co/6tiFtS5

Wild West
King's Fancy
http://amzn.to/2xcOitO

Cowboy Craze
She's Everything
https://amzn.to/2xmiYvf

Other Titles from Sable Hunter:

For A Hero
With Jess Hunter
http://a.co/1ESSoDX

Green With Envy (It's Just Sex Book 1)
http://a.co/0pRjmn6

Hell Yeah! Box Set With Bonus Cookbook
http://a.co/3VDlVxW

Love's Magic Spell: A Red Hot Treats Story
http://a.co/geyHzt8

Wolf Call
http://a.co/9Ghzl7k

Be My Love Song
http://a.co/3rT4ti2

A Hot and Spicy Valentine
http://a.co/6UuzEqk

Too Sexy For Love
With Ryan O'Leary
http://a.co/3MsEAqz

Audio
Cowboy Heat - Sweeter Version: Hell Yeah! Sweeter Version
http://a.co/9Zu7lUg

Hot on Her Trail - Sweeter Version: Hell Yeah!
Sweeter Version, Book 2

http://a.co/90q2v5T

Her Magic Touch (Sexy Version)
http://a.co/3M8XDpw

Spanish Edition
Vaquero Ardiente *(*Cowboy Heat)
Amazon US http://amzn.to/1qHMi2G

Su Rastro Caliente (Hot On Her Trail)
Amazon US http://amzn.to/1u2Dd3T

Made in United States
North Haven, CT
04 January 2024

46918498R00202